MW00678291

The Sea Lies Ahead

Intizar Husain

The Sea Lies Ahead

Translated from the Urdu by
Rakhshanda Jalil

NEW YORK • LONDON • TORONTO • SYDNEY • NEW DELHI

First published in India in 2015 by Harper Perennial
An imprint of HarperCollins *Publishers* India

P-ISBN: 978-93-5177-280-4
E-ISBN: 978-93-5177-281-1

2 4 6 8 10 9 7 5 3 1

HarperCollins *Publishers*
A-75, Sector 57, Noida, Uttar Pradesh 201301, India
1 London Bridge Street, London, SE1 9GF, United Kingdom
Hazelton Lanes, 55 Avenue Road, Suite 2900, Toronto, Ontario M5R 3L2
and 1995 Markham Road, Scarborough, Ontario M1B 5M8, Canada
25 Ryde Road, Pymble, Sydney, NSW 2073, Australia
195 Broadway, New York, NY 10007, USA

Typeset in 11/14 Joanna MT by
Jojy Philip, New Delhi 110 015

Printed and bound at
Thomson Press (India) Ltd.

Introduction

'This land is different; its sky is different.'

Azadi vs. Batwara

There has never been a uniform, un-variegated, one-dimensional response to the partition among the Muslim intelligentsia. The Urdu literature of the partition years – which, it must be stressed, was written by both Muslim and non-Muslim writers – reflects a bewildering and often contradictory array of opinions. The Muslim response is equally, if not more, bewildering and contradictory. Taken together, the Urdu literature of the partition years, which comprised the novel and the short story (which flowered rather spectacularly during this period), as well as poetry, reportage, autobiography, diary, journal writing and journalistic writings, presents a broad spectrum of opinion. Reactions vary from nostalgic lament for a lost age to attaching blame and apportioning responsibility for the terrible misfortunes that had befallen all those who had been affected, in some way or the other, by the partition. And indeed, as scholars have noted, such was the impact of the partition that there was hardly any Muslim family that had not lost one member or more, or not been affected by the events spiraling out of 1947 in one way or another.

While there is a general agreement that the murder and mayhem that accompanied the partition was a human tragedy of epic proportions, there is far more ambivalence in the ways of dealing or accepting its consequences. A study of Urdu literature from this period also reveals a wide range of possible reasons why some chose to stay put while others migrated; often economic reasons predominate over religious ones and pragmatism supersedes ideology. While the majority of writers made a conscious effort to hold up the tattered fabric of secularism in the face of communalism, bitter and painful memories also find expression, especially in a range of first-person accounts, diaries, etc. One is unable to discern a commonality of concerns or any coherence and common ground save the obvious assertion that countless innocent lives were lost due to the political decisions of a mere handful.

That there are multiple histories rather than *a* history of the partition is borne out by studying the literature produced on either side of the newly-created border. In contrast to Indian sentiments, a section of Pakistani writers viewed the creation of Pakistan as a logical culmination of a historical process and therefore cause for joy rather than mourning, a reason to look forward rather than over one's shoulder at what once was and had ceased to be. The breaking away of a section of population that was viewed as a tragedy of epic proportions by the 'Congressi' Muslims in India was perceived as a triumph of Islamic nationalism by the votaries of the Muslim League. Moreover, there was always one group (it could be Muslims or Hindus, Indians or Pakistanis though it is often difficult to categorize as one or the other as the writers don't always name the 'other' community) who felt they had been singled out (in comparison to the 'other') for the terrible retributions that accompanied independence and was therefore, more inclined to beat its chest. While many Indian writers refer to the cataclysmic events of the year that was annus horribillis as *batwara* (literally meaning division but commonly referred to as partition or *taqseem* in Urdu), for the Pakistani writers the year marked the beginning of *azadi* (freedom) and the birth of Pakistan as an independent country.

Two worlds – the lost and the emergent – fused and merged after 1947. In the years that followed, pathos, confusion and conflict reigned supreme despite the avowals of joy and celebrations of new beginnings. Delhi and Lucknow, the two great centres of Muslim culture in Upper India – the London and the Paris of their milieu – lay decimated. Across the border, Lahore and Karachi too were bursting at the seams with strangers looking to put down roots in an alien soil that would henceforth be their home. Forces of urban renewal and demographic change were at work everywhere. The inhabitants of these new cities didn't know whether to celebrate their hard-won independence or mourn the passing of an era and a way of life. Should one celebrate the birth of a new nation? Should one rejoice at gaining independence at the end of a fierce and prolonged struggle? Or, should one mourn the loss of an age and the end of pluralism and syncretism? Should one search for new directions? Or, were all routes to regeneration irrevocably closed for this weary generation?[1] These questions, and many others, jostle for answers in the outpourings of partition chroniclers.

To further compound this confusion, one set of writers who had written with joyous abandon on the imminent *azadi* all through the 1940s adopted a taciturn silence. In the polarized arena of the Urdu literature of the late '40s and early '50s, the silence on the partition could also possibly be due to the loquacity of a set of writers called the progressives. The more one group wrote about the horrors of partition, the more the other side lapsed into a silence that seemed to obliterate individual suffering, loss and pain. Quite apart from the distillation of a lived experience that provides valuable clues to the historian and lay reader alike, the literature of this period is of great importance to the literary historian because it shows how

---

[1] Asif Farrukhi has divided writers on partition under two categories: Beginners and Enders. The former see it as the emergence of a new nation-state, the latter 'deplore and lament it as the end of secular South Asia. He also confesses to feeling 'unsettled' by the dichotomy of these two entrenched positions. He goes on to stress the need to have two different discourses on the partition: one being a socio-political analysis, and the other that studies it as a literary phenomenon. See Asif Farrukhi, 'Once Upon a Time: Cultural Legacies, Fictional Worlds of the Partition and Beyond' in Rakhshanda Jalil (ed.), *Qurratulain Hyder and the River of Fire: The Meaning, Scope and Significance of Her Legacy* (New Delhi: Aakar Books, 2011).

political events shaped literary sensibility like never before and the rise of a literary movement called *jadeediyat* (modernism) coincided with the decline of another called *taraqqui-pasandi* or progressivism. But that is not the subject of this introduction! Here I must confine myself to providing as comprehensive a background as I can to Intizar Husain's trilogy on the partition which comprises *Basti*, Aage *Samandar Hai* and *Naya Ghar*.

But I must return, briefly, to the tug-of-war between the progressives and the modernists that dominated the literary scene in the years after the partition: with the creation of Pakistan, several former progressives, who were by now either vehemently opposed to the progressive ideology (most notably M. D. Taseer and Muhammad Hasan Askari) or uncomfortable with some of its jingoism (such as Faiz Ahmad Faiz), adopted defensive postures about an entirely new phenomenon – *Pakistani tehzeeb*. Powerful literary critics and ideologues such as Muhammad Hasan Askari, who mentored upcoming writers such as Intizar Husain through a literary grouping called the *Halqa-e Arbab-e Zauq* ('the circle of men of good taste')[2], expounded the notion of a Pakistani national culture through a slew of columns, op-eds and essays.[3] We get a glimpse of the expectations of the new state from its intellectuals in Qudratullah Shahab's memoir *Shahabnama*, published though it was as late as 1986.[4] Shahab is however not uncritical of the state of

---

[2] For details of the *Halqa*, see my PhD dissertation published as Rakhshanda Jalil, *Liking Progress, Loving Change: A Literary History of the Progressive Writers' Movement in Urdu*, Oxford University Press, New Delhi.

[3] See, for instance, 'Azadi aur Shaoor', 'Pakistan ka Culture', 'Azadi-e-rai aur Pakistan ka Culture', 'Pakistan ka Tehzeebi Mustaqbil', 'Pakistani Adeebon ke Azm ka Jihad', Pakistan ke Adeebon ka Fariza' in Sheema Majeed (ed), *Muqalat Muhammad Hasan Askari*, Lahore: Ilm-o-Irfan Publishers, 2001.

[4] In English, we have several instances of the writer of a Pakistani novel bringing his or her work to a triumphal closure. Varying degrees of introspection followed by an assertion of the 'validity' of the achievement of nationhood is seen in Mumtaz Shahnawaz's *The Heart Divided*, Kamila Shamsie's *Salt and Saffron* and even Bapsi Sidhwa's *Ice Candy Man*.

affairs. In the short story, 'Ya Khuda', he exposes the hypocrisy of those who quote Iqbal yet indulge in hoarding and black-marketing of scarce commodities, making a mockery of the cracks between state and society. As we shall see in the novel that follows, once the rosy idealism of the early years rubbed off, the issues of corruption and moral turpitude became as important as rising Islamism.

The task of the publicists was advanced by a new breed of ideologues who heralded the creation of Pakistan as the dawn of a new era. The works of prose stylists such as Fateh Muhammad Malik opened up a new chapter in Urdu literary criticism called Paksitaniyat, or the study of the sovereign state of Pakistan. Advancing Askari's notion of a writer's commitment to the nation-state, Mumtaz Shirin compiled a collection of short stories on the partition, entitled *Zulmat-e-Neem Roz*; considering the impact of the partition on Urdu literature, it is interesting that this was the first ever anthology on partition in Urdu. New-age Pakistani critics, such as Asif Farrukhi, have admitted to a certain self-censorship on the part of the Pakistani writers, an attempt at what he calls 'to re-write the past.' Farrukhi also points out two important things: one, the fallacy of the Urdu critics – incidentally on both sides of the border – to refer to partition-related literature as *fasadat ka adab*, i.e. literature devoted to communal riots; and two, the 'manipulation' of literature according to a critics' own ideological mooring.

Much of partition literature is personal and cathartic. A compulsive scraping of wounds, a cataloguing of unimaginable horrors and a depiction of a sick, momentarily depraved society is, often, the creative writer's only way of exorcising the evil within. It served the needs of its times in a rough and ready sort of way, but it is patchy, uneven, often incoherent. Much of it falls under what has been termed *waqti adab*, or topical literature. Given the propensity of most writers to focus on violence and communal tensions, the Urdu critics have called these stories *fasadat ke afsane*, or riot literature, again serving to deflect the attention from partition per se and turning the cause-and-effect equation upside down.

Equally worrying is the lack of historical awareness among

the writers themselves. References to political events, resolutions, statements, etc. are vague; the focus is on the 'impact' of partition on the common people rather than *why* the political leaders failed to resolve their disputes over power sharing and ended up carving the country along religious lines. By and large, the Urdu writers have been content to write of consequences rather than reasons, effects rather than causes, of partition. They have even deployed myths, allegories, fables to paint on vast canvases in broad brush strokes. This is evident in the titles of some of the most representative and anthologized of these works: *Jadein* (Ismat Chughtai) or *Udaas Naslein* (Abdullah Hussein). If there are as many ways of interpreting the partition there are no clear answers to why some chose to migrate leaving home and hearth behind in search of a promised land. It remains a mystery why some went while others stayed, often in the same family. Chhote Miyan, a character in *The Sea Lies Ahead*, puts his finger on the nub when he says, 'It was a wave that was sweeping people off their feet. Now, when you think about it, it seems strange that those who went did so thinking what they did, and those who stayed back did so thinking what they did.'

'History alone will decide whether we have acted wisely and correctly in accepting partition,' wrote Maulana Azad in *India Wins Freedom*. As far as the Urdu writer is concerned, the jury is still out. Moreover, a lot depends on the composition of the jury. Is it a Pakistani jury or an Indian one? For on the question of state and nationhood, the Urdu writers on either side of the border seem to have little in common.

The *Muhajir* Experience

A necessary fall-out of partition was migration. The displacement, dislocation, uprootedness and alienation that came in the wake of the transfer of power have been well documented in both autobiographical accounts and works of fiction.[5] While Manto's

[5] This is equally true of works in Urdu, Hindi, Punjabi and English thus exemplifying the notion that the sense of loss cut across community identity.

Toba Tek Singh is the most well known and most anthologized depiction of the trauma caused by such forced removal from one's ancestral land, the literature of this period is replete with examples of how the dearly beloved suddenly, virtually overnight, became forbidden, even alien. Some writers showed pathos or stoic acceptance; others reacted with anger and hostility. Shahid Ahmed Dehlvi's autobiographical, *Dehli ki Bipda* ('The Calamity of Delhi'), written in the centuries-old elegiac *shehr afsos* (literally meaning 'lament of the city') tradition, is a haunting tribute to the vanished glory of Delhi, a glory he likens to other great 'Muslim' cities such as Cordoba and Granada.[6] In lyrical prose, he recounts the irreversible changes wrought to the city's moral, intellectual, cultural and social fabric by the outflow of its Muslim population and influx of refugees. In a similar vein, writers who left East Punjab to find a new home, sometimes barely a few kilometres across the new border, have waxed eloquent on how wonderful everything was in their old home and how new and different everything appears to be on 'this' side of the border. A case in point would be A. Hameed who wrote of Amristar (or Ambarsar as it was pronounced by the locals), the city of his birth: 'For me Amritsar is my lost Jerusalem and I am its wailing wall. I do not remember anything of Jerusalem; he must remember who forgets.'

A commuter train, called the Babu train, ran daily between the twin cities of Amritsar and Lahore, ferrying workers to and fro. Barely 30 kilometres apart, partition cleaved an unimaginable rift between the two cities causing immense sorrow and pain to many. A leading light of a group of Punjabi intellectuals who

---

[6] Spain has been a popular symbol of lost glory for Muslim writers. In the pre-partition generation, poets such as Iqbal invoked memories of Cordoba to sensitize the Muslims to what they once had and what they have now lost. After 1947, it became a symbol for a collective outpouring of loss, suffering and pain, which lies at the heart of the partition experience for many South Asian Muslims. We will see how the leitmotif of the vanished glory of Moorish Spain will recur throughout *The Sea Lies Ahead*.

comprised the 'Amritsari School of Thought', A. Hameed's account entitled 'My First Day in Pakistan' is free of bitterness and blame. It recounts in a matter-of-fact tone the hardships faced by the early lot of refugees: how food was scarce, jobs even more so, how the neighbourhood committee of the Muslim League doled out free flour, but even that stopped after two weeks and how his family faced its first starvation.[7] Even in this dire state, Hameed notes how he heard an announcement in the street one day: 'This is the Pakistan Broadcasting Service. Earlier, we had always heard, All India Radio, Lahore. This is the Pakistan Broadcasting Service. It felt good. We were convinced we were sitting in our own country.' Despite the lingering nostalgia, Hameed's oeuvre shows no regret for the migration across the border. I have chosen to give the example of A. Hameed and his nostalgia – for a city that was a bare 30 kilometres away and Hameed's shared language, dress, cuisine, culture with those on 'this' side of the border – to highlight how those who had come from the 'other' side, from the dusty heartland of Uttar Pradesh, Bihar as well as from towns and villages across the length and breadth of India must have felt in this new land, peopled though it was with fellow Muslims. Imagine how someone like Intizar Husain would have felt for whom everything was new and different! His lament for the neem tree left standing behind in his courtyard in Dibai, his yearning for the taste of Mitthan halwai's sweets in dusty Bulundshahr and his nostalgia for the flavoursome idiomatic *zubaan* of his Phuphi Amma as she regaled him with stories must be seen against this background of all-pervasive loss and dislocation.

Like everything else written during and about this period, migration too has been viewed and interpreted in different ways. As in the depiction of partition-related violence, some writers catalogue the horrors witnessed on the way and the difficulties in finding safe havens on the other side of newly-demarcated borders,

---

[7] Akmal Aleemi, 'A Partitioned Man', *The Friday Times*, Lahore, May 13-19, 2011.

others view it as salutary experiences with the potential to draw lessons from past mistakes. Of all these depictions, Intizar Husain, who migrated in 1947 from Bulundshahr in Uttar Pradesh, has chosen the most unique form; he has depicted the migration as *hijrat*, an experience akin to the Prophet's migration from Mecca to Medina in June 622 AD and therefore an experience that transcends human sufferings.

Compared to the poets who have written sparingly on the partition, the prose writers have given especial importance to it. Their predilection for focusing on the communal violence that spiraled out of it raises some disturbing questions.[8] Did they do so out of the conviction that it was 'bad' or 'wrong' or from any real understanding of the long-term consequences of partition? Or, was it because the only meaningful reality for them was the present, and the present contained violence and degradation and misery in such ample measure? While some modern critics such as Muhammad Hasan Askari believed rioting and violence cannot become the subject of true literature[9], the progressives believed that violence was a natural consequence of the ill-will sown by the Cabinet Mission Plan of 16 February 1946 and the Mountbatten Plan of 3 June 1947.[10] Interestingly, while modernists like Intizar Husain chose to view the partition as *hijrat* or migration in the sense of a recurrent historical event that allowed the writer to explore the past while laying bare the present, for the progressives, the partition was an opportunity to dwell on the present. For, it was in the present, that there was hardly any Muslim family that had not lost one member (if not more) or whose lives had not been affected by the trauma in some way or the other.

---

[8] M. U. Memon, 'Partition Literature: A Study of Intizar Husain', *Modern Asian Studies*, Vol. 14, No. 3 (1980), p. 381.

[9] Quoted by Mumtaz Shirin in '*Pakistani Adab ke Char Saal*', *Mayar* (Lahore: Naya Idara, 1963), p. 171.

[10] M. U. Memon, op. cit., p. 386.

The literature of the early years of Independence reflects a knee-jerk reaction to immediate events. Nothing demonstrates this better than the work of Manto.[11] Writing in a similar vein, Krishan Chander, Ismat Chughtai, Hayatullah Ansari used shock as a strategy to allow their readers to deal with and go beyond the paralyzing effects of what was a tragedy of near-Biblical proportions. It would be several years before some semblance of reflection, introspection and evaluation could emerge. A preoccupation with pain and sorrow, in a sense, blinded the early crop of writers – blinded them, that is, to the moral, political and intellectual contradictions that only a crisis of an unprecedented scale can precipitate. Those who began their literary careers after the horrors had abated somewhat are in a better position to analyse the political and social faultlines revealed by the partition. It was only with the gradual passage of time that the Urdu writer could seize the events of 1947 and view them as catastrophic even apocalyptic events carrying within them the seeds of renewal.

Writers like Intizar Husain, who began their literary careers close on the heels of the great partition chroniclers such as Manto, were better placed to view the partition and its consequences. In story after story, we see him ruing the possibilities that partition presented but were lost or frittered away. He talks of how, suddenly, almost by accident, partition allowed writers like him to 'regain' a great experience – namely *hijrat* that has a unique place in the history of Muslims. Yet, as he has said in an interview, 'And the great expectation we had of making something out of it at a creative level and of exploiting it in developing a new consciousness and sensibility – that bright expectation has now faded and gone.'[12]

---

[11] Several lesser-known writers scored above the better-known ones in writing stories that stood out from the rest. Among these, Hayatullah Ansari's 'Shukr-guzar Aankhein' and Jamila Hashmi's 'Jaage Paak Parwardigar' are worth mentioning.

[12] Interview, *Shabkhun*, Vol. 8, No. 96, p. 19.

Intizar Husain and *Aage Samandar Hai*

There is no denying that Intizar Husain's contribution as a storyteller is enormous, especially in the genre of partition narratives. If Manto laid bare the ugliness of 1947 and its immediate, brutish aftermath with the urgency of a field surgeon, Intizar Husain probes those wounds ever so gingerly, peeling away layers from old memories to reveal wounds that have still not healed and may never heal, at least not in his life time – and certainly not when fresh wounds are repeatedly inflicted on skin that is still sore and tender. *The Sea Lies Ahead* shows us the old wounds and tells us how new ones are being added day by day and year by year while everyone watches helplessly; it talks with searing honesty of the ethnic violence that spiraled out of control in Karachi and how no one made any effort to stem its bloody tide. Asked what would be the sum total of Pakistan's recent history, a character in the novel replies pithily: '*Mushairas* and Kalashnikovs.'

Basti, written in 1979, is set in 1971 when war clouds are gathering, the new country of Pakistan is no longer fresh and pure and hopeful but soiled and weary and entirely without hope, and news from distant East Pakistan is ominous. Its protagonist, Zakir, has already faced one tumult, that of 1947, when he left India and migrated to the Land of the Pure. After the first 'luminous' day spent walking the streets of the new city (Lahore) that was to be his home, savouring the delight of walking about freely without the fear that someone will slip a knife into his ribs, soaking in the new sights, sounds and smells, Zakir stays awake all night, weeping and remembering the city, streets, sounds and people he has left behind. 'That day seemed very pure to him, with its night, with the tears of its night.' But those days of innocence and goodness and large-heartedness of the new people in the new land united not so much by one religion but by a common loss and the feeling of homelessness slip away. 'After that, the days gradually grew soiled and dirty. Perhaps it's always like this.' Gradually the goodness and sincerity leaches out and in its place there is greed, corruption and intolerance. Looking back, Zakir reflects, 'Those were good days, good and sincere. I ought to remember those days, or in fact, I ought to write them down, for fear I should forget them again. And the days afterward? Them too, so I can know how the goodness and sincerity gradually died out from the days, how the days came to be filled with misfortune and nights with ill omen.'

Slowly the vim and vigour of building a new nation begins to sap. *The Sea Lies Ahead* takes up the story from where *Basti* ended, but because all of Intizar sahab's work is cyclical, there are no clearly defined beginnings and ends and even the middles have a great deal of overlap! We must revisit the past, he seems to be saying in story after story, in order to learn from it. And this revisiting does not happen in any particular order. Zakir is replaced by Jawad: burdened with memories of the past when he was Munnan and his closest friend and comrade was his cousin Maimuna – to whom he was betrothed in childhood. A short-lived marriage to a fellow-*muhajir* who dies all too soon, a son who has gone away to make a new life in America, a job as a bank manager that leaves him listless with ennui, Jawad's life 'here' can never be the sum total of its parts because a vital part of his being will forever be 'there'. No wonder, then, that he can never quite fit in.

Early on, in *The Sea Lies Ahead*, a character says, 'All sorts of rogues and upstarts, thieves and robbers and terrorists have a field day; the respectable folk are at their wits' end. Where have we ended up?' And indeed the city they ended up in was unlike any other they had ever seen. For one thing, the sea itself was new and frightening for most of these *muhajirs* who had come from land-locked towns and hamlets. What is more, each *muhajir* brought with him his own Pandora's box of memories, memories that made him name the new enclaves, gardens and housing societies after the ones he had left behind:

> 'Ya Allah, so many cities had collected in this one city as though it was not a city but a sea. And every river, ever stream from across the subcontinent came noisome and rollicking and merged in it.

> But rivers are supposed to mix with the sea and lose themselves. Here every river was shouting and saying, "I am the sea".'

Aqa Hasan, an effete gentleman from Lucknow, who is given to venting his ire about the ways of the new city (Karachi) and its people, also bemoans: 'It is a reign of tyranny and dictatorship. Those who were low born roll in wealth and the *shurfa* go hungry for even one meal. And on top of it all, no one's life or property is safe.' And then addressing his question to Majju Bhai – a blithe spirit and by far the most colourful character in the entire list of dramatis personae in the novel as well as the one who dominates the entire novel by virtue of sheer cockiness – Aqa Hasan goes on to ask:

> 'My dear sir, these are difficult times. Tell me, whom should we go to for justice? What do these people here know about the sorrows we have faced? With such grief we have pulled up our roots and dragged ourselves across these long hard miles? And here ... here we have seen new twists and turns. So, tell me, my dear sir ... that is what I am asking you: what lies ahead?'

To which Majju Bhai blithely replies, 'The sea.'

Majju Bhai's breezy answer refers to an urban legend from Pakistan's hoary past when stabs at democracy and genuine people's representation still seemed possible. In the run-up to the presidential elections to be held in January 1965, a motley group of political parties coming together as Combined Opposition Parties (COP) decide to field Fatima Jinnah, sister of the late M. A. Jinnah and popularly known as 'Mother of the Nation', against the incumbent General Ayub Khan. The COP comes up with an impressive nine-point agenda including restoration of direct elections, adult franchise, democratization of the 1962 Constitution and, among other things, greater representation to the Urdu-speaking *muhajirs* in Sindh. As a warning to the Urdu speakers not to vote for his opponent, Ayub is said to have famously declared '*Aage samandar hai...*'[13] The implicit threat in the seemingly innocuous words was two-fold: one, the *muhajirs* had burnt their boats when they had crossed the border for, clearly, they could not go back; and two, having done so, with their backs to the sea and the combined force of the local ethnic peoples, that is the Sindhis, Punjabis, Pathans and Balochis who constituted the four provinces of Western Pakistan, this fifth entity (*paanchvi qaumiyat*), namely the *muhajirs*, really had no place to go. In other words, if they didn't like it they could lump it!

Not everyone in Pakistan, however, shared Intizar Husain's mournful longing for a syncretic past or yearned for its sights, sounds, smells and seasons. As he himself is perfectly aware, there were many among the Urdu-speaking *muhajir* who were aspirational, upwardly-mobile and keen to shed the baggage of the past. Tausif and Baji Akhtari who, as wagging tongues inform us, were low-caste Kamboh in the past but have successfully refashioned themselves as high-born Saiyads and remodelled their lives by taking part fully in the nation-building project such as it is, are exemplars of a new world order. Tausif – who might have been regarded as a never-do-well in the old world – joins the elite civil services (the coveted CSP) and becomes a card-carrying member of the new aristocracy and his sister, Baji Akhtari, crows over the fact that her baby brother will now 'rule over a district'. It is in their home – at a kabab-paratha party followed by a *mushaira* held during a curfewed night in a neighbourhood that has not fully recovered from ethnic violence (an instance of playing the fiddle while Rome burnt) – that we first encounter the ominous figure of Ghazi sahib who will prove to be the cause of the city's undoing.

Clad in a green robe, a constantly moving rosary between his fingers, Ghazi sahib is the epitome of a monolithic and inflexible Unitarian Islam with his stern gaze and unforgiving relentlessness towards those he considers not true to the tenets of the faith. Guarded by Kalashnikov-toting 'volunteers', he is busy dreaming

[13] Intizar Husain himself told me in the course of an interview that the novel takes its title from General Ayub's alleged remark.

of a nursery of martyrs, young men he will train to lay down their lives for a larger cause:

> 'The passion for jihad has gone cold among Muslims. If you consider the total population of Pakistan, you will note that it is not a small country. The population of Muslims is in crores. Yet I have still not been able to find 313 Muslims. Look around you ... so many people, and all born in the faith but none are Muslims. My passion is calling out for 313 Muslims. But there aren't 313 Muslims to be found on this planet Earth.'

Seamlessly and without the slightest crease or tension in his gently flowing narrative, Intizar sahab is not merely outlining the decay that set in and the apathy and disinterest of his fellow countrymen and women in stemming the rot, he also seems to be suggesting that perhaps decay and decline is inevitable, and that cities are settled simply in order to be laid waste. He gives the example of Dwarka, the city that Lord Krishan created, after leaving his beloved Mathura, knowing full well that this sparkling new city would be destroyed one day. In a manner characteristic of all his writings, Intizar sahab draws upon the stories and incidents in the *Panchtantra*, *Jataka Katha*, *Katha Sarit Sagar*, *Mahabharata* and the *Vedas* as well as the equally ancient traditions in *Alif-Laila* and the *dastaans*. He seems to find a philosophical calm in the words of the Buddha who had said: 'O monks, there is no peace in any birth and no settlement remains settled forever and every homes that is set up is set up to be abandoned.' And what of Cordoba, Granada, Seville and the other great cities of Moorish Spain that have evoked such nostalgia in the collective consciousness of Muslims the world over? What of the pain of losing them, especially Cordoba that has been called the 'bride of Andalusia'? This loss, like the loss of Dwarka, is explained thus:

> '...And among all the mosques was the Grand Mosque that was like an ornament on the forehead of Cordoba. The crowds who thronged it were unmatched compared to all other mosques

> around it. Further away, at the Madina Azahara, the drums would be beaten morning and evening. But when this fragrant city was about to be laid waste, nothing could save it – not the crowds or the drums, not the calls to the faithful to prayer nor the voices of the proclaimers of faith. Only Allah's name remains. There is no Victor except Allah.'

And Maimuna and Munnan, what of them? Would it be fanciful to compare them to the pair of swans – forever meeting only to be separated, birth after birth, life after life – that flit in and out of Intizar sahab's narrative[14]? The swan and its mate meet and separate, meet and separate again and again as though this epic of union and separation, this *dastaan* of eternity and successors[15] is actually the story of the swan and his mate. Struck by this recurring motif, I wonder if this novel is also the story of Maimuna and Munnan, destined to be separated by a fate that is as cruel as it is incomprehensible. Like much else in *The Sea Lies Ahead*, there are no clear answers and Intizar sahab doesn't make it easy for us.

Rakhshanda Jalil

September 2015
New Delhi

---

[14] We have encountered Munnan and Maimuna before – as Zakir and Sabirah – in *Basti*. There, too, Zakir lacked the will (or the courage?) to call Sabirah over and their love remained unspoken and incomplete.

[15] In *Aage Samandar Hai*, the original has the word '*abdali*' referring to the concept of '*abdaal*' or 'the substitutes or lieutenants' or certain righteous persons of whom the world is never destitute, and by whom God rules the earth: The substitutes and successors of the prophets shall always remain. Intizar Husain uses the iconic image of the *hans-hansni*, the swan and his mate, which have been popular in folklore as well as the *qissa*-kahani tradition, to reinforce the idea of an eternal presence of goodness and happiness, which may be threatened by 'storms' and may be separated, but it is destined to be reunited.

The Sea Lies Ahead

One

'Actually, this is about the time when the date palm planted by Abd ar-Rahman I[1] had grown to be a hundred-and-twenty-five years old and many more trees had come up all around it. This beauty from the sands of Arabia had taken root and flourished in Andalusia. The courtyards of Cordoba, Seville, Granada, Toledo were like its own backyard. And the palm tree beside the well in the unpaved courtyard of the elderly Sheikh Abul Hajjaj Yousuf Al-Shabrboli of Seville had grown so tall that the devout who came to draw water for ablutions ...'

'Yaar Jawad,' Majju Bhai looked hard at me and my sentence was left dangling in mid air. 'You are a strange fellow!'

'Why? What happened?'

'Look how far you have come from where we started! You are a master at the art of turning things into circles!'

Where had we started from? I found myself in a dilemma. The fact is that once I get started on the subject of trees, all other subjects get left behind. So, in my opinion, we had started from the trees. But, surely, there must have been some talk before the talk of trees which must have led to the topic of trees? On the other hand, if you look at it like this, no one can ever tell how any talk on any subject began in the first place. Because there is always some talk on some subject before the present subject. So let us say that the talk started with the subject of trees. Isn't it strange where we start and where we end our talk? But does it ever end? That is the problem,

---

[1] Abd ar-Rahman I was the Emir of Cordoba from 756–788 AD.

though. If only it ended somewhere. So, let us say the talk began with trees. The twist came later, just as one topic emerges from another. And it was much later that it became an issue for me. The biggest issue on this earth is the issue of trees. They may appear as dry twigs and bushes and there might seem nothing extraordinary about them. They might appear to be just standing about, but there is no knowing when a tree might become an issue.

Tarawali, the one with the big hips and long, supple thighs, was walking along with her husband when suddenly a storm came upon them. And then what happened was that when the storm abated somewhat, Tarawali saw that her husband was nowhere to be seen and she was all alone in the middle of the forest. 'Where are you, O Master?' she called out again and again. She wept and wailed and wandered far into the forest. But she could not find any trace of her husband. As she wandered hither and thither, she saw a tree and stood stock-still. It was laden with fragrant flowers and bees buzzed about its blossoms. She was entranced by the flowers. And then it so happened that the tree's fragrance swept over her and she too turned into a bee. And buzzing with the other bees, she went and sat upon a flower. Though she had turned into a bee, she could not forget her husband. And as she sat on the flower, she remembered her husband and wept. The tear that dropped from her eye drenched the flower. And in that instant, she saw that her husband was sitting under the shade of that very tree and resting. Like a flower that opens its petals as it blooms, she was so elated that from a bee she turned back into Tarawali. The husband and wife were united and resumed their journey. Then what happened was that a fruit emerged from the flower that had been drenched by Tarawali's tear. And it so happened that just when a *jogi* was passing by the tree, the fruit ripened and fell to the ground and burst open. A beautiful maiden emerged from the fruit: she had full hips, a bud-like bosom, hair as dark as rain clouds, rosy pink cheeks, juicy plump lips, and doe-like eyes. With folded hands, she greeted the *jogi* and touched his feet. The *jogi* was greatly surprised but, in an instant, he recognized her because of his great knowledge and wisdom. 'O maiden, you are the daughter of Tarawali.'

'O Great One, who is Tarawali?'

'Tarawali was the one with the big hips and long supple thighs … the one who had turned into a bee. She had got enamoured of this beautifully mysterious tree. She turned into a bee and sat upon a flower, and from that union, the flower turned into fruit and you were born. So, your name shall be Vanwati, the forest girl. Come and stay with me as my daughter in my hermitage. Your husband, too, will show up soon.'

'Maharaj, I don't have a husband.'

'You have barely opened your eyes; what do you know? But he exists. He is wandering about in this forest. He will show up soon and you will be married to him.'

Hamara tumhara khuda badshah
Kissi mulk mein tha koi badshah
(An emperor who is your God and mine
Such was a king in some kingdom)

Once there was a king … Yes, this was the story told to me by my Phuphi Amma. She remembered many stories. Maimuna and I used to sit, she on one side of Phuphi Amma, I on the other. No, no, Phuphi Amma, first tell us the story about the woodcutter. Yes, yes, I am telling you the story about the woodcutter. Once there was a king and somewhere in his kingdom there was also a woodcutter. The king had one daughter. A pampered little princess she was! But the poor queen … she died and the princess was left motherless. The king married again, and my dear, the moment the new queen set foot in the palace, she heaped such cruelties upon the poor motherless girl that finally, fed up of the daily whiplashes, the princess went away into the forest. The stepmother sent a posse of soldiers after her. What was the poor girl to do? Where could she go? She saw a tree: tall and dense. She went up to it and said, 'O

Tree, hide me.' Lo and behold, the tree's trunk cracked open and the princess dived in. Then the tree closed its trunk and became as before.

And, now, we come to the woodcutter … the woodcutter had a son who had grown to manhood. One day, the father said to the son, 'Son, you have grown up; get down to work.' And so saying, the woodcutter handed his son an axe and a saw and told him to go into the forest and cut a tree. The woodcutter's son set off with the axe and saw. He came upon a copse and saw that one tree was taller and denser than all the others. He hit the tree with his axe. A sweet, muffled sound emerged from it. At first, he was startled; then, slowly and carefully, he began to saw at the trunk. The sweet and soft sound kept coming from the tree trunk. Finally, when the trunk split wide open, lo and behold, out came the princess. Fair as the moon, bright as the sun was she! Fortune smiled at the woodcutter's son.

'Yaar Jawad!' Majju Bhai was getting restless. Finally, he broke out, 'Stop your tree tale and come to the real story.'

'Real story?' I had been cut short; I couldn't think of what to say next.

'Yes, the real story. Don't try to hide it. Tell the real story.'

'Which real story, Majju Bhai?'

'After all, did you only look at trees on this long voyage that you have returned from? Did you undertake this journey for the sake of the trees?'

I had no answer to this question. Why had I undertaken this voyage? Why had I gone there after such a long time? To see the trees? I fell into a dilemma. What was the purpose of this journey? Tree tourism? After all, what is the harm if it were so, I asked myself. Why can't one travel for the sake of the trees? Once again, I began to remember the stories … An old man said to a youth, 'My dear young man, I pity your youth. There is still time; turn back.' The youth answered, 'Whatever will be, will be.' The old man said, 'O young one, listen … there is a dense forest across the seven seas. In the middle of that forest, there is a tall and dense tree. A large serpent lives in its hollow and a birdcage hangs from its tallest branch. A parrot is in the cage and the ogre's life is in the parrot.'

But my mind suddenly leapt and wandered away somewhere ... Abul Hajjaj Yousuf was a strange old man. An age had passed and he had still not reckoned the fact that the tree in his courtyard had grown so tall and become so big that it now posed a problem for the devout.

Actually, this is about the time when the date palm planted by Abd ar-Rahman I had grown to be a hundred-and-twenty-five years old and many trees had come up all around it. This beauty from the sands of Arabia had taken root and flourished in Andalusia. The courtyards of Cordoba, Seville, Granada and Toledo were like its own backyard. And the date tree beside the well in the unpaved courtyard of the elderly Sheikh Abul Hajjaj Yousuf of Seville had grown so tall that it hindered the devout who came to draw water for ablutions. Finally, one day, a pious man said, 'O Sheikh, this date tree has grown so big that it has become difficult for us to draw water from the well for our ablutions.' The old man heard these words with surprise; he opened his white eyelashes wide and looked at the dense date tree standing in front of him. For a long time, he kept looking at the tree in wonderment. Then, he broke his silence and said, 'By the One Almighty God, I have lived my entire life in the midst of these four walls, but I am seeing for the first time that there is a date palm in my courtyard.'

And so saying, the elderly gentleman closed his eyes and began to run his hand over the black hairs on the back of the black cat sitting in his lap. At that very instant, a godly old man, who had travelled all the way from Cordoba, knocked at the door. The cat leapt out of the sheikh's lap and went to the door. Standing on its hind legs, it craned to hug the elderly visitor. At that, the sheikh too got up and hugged the elderly man with the same affection.

Sheikh Yousuf was a strange man. He had such affection for the cat and such disinterest in the date tree that grew in his courtyard! On the other hand, there was Umme Raqiba who lived only for a sight of her tree. Umme Raqiba lived with her date tree in Cordoba, in a small house behind the walls of the palace of Abul Mansur.[2] Now that her parents were gone, the only shade she knew was the shelter of the date tree. How eagerly she waited for the tree to bear fruit and how anxiously she watched the dates turn from green to golden! And her happiness knew no bounds when the fruit was harvested. But one day, just as her dates had begun to ripen, Abul Mansur's men came and made a strange announcement. Umme Raqiba rushed to the magistrate in great distress and put forth her plea: 'O Wise Magistrate of the Holy City of Cordoba, you adjudicate between me and Abu Amir.'

'Adjudicate? Between you and Abul Mansur?' the magistrate asked with great surprise.

'Yes, between me and Abu Amir.'

'But about what?'

Umme Raqiba wept and spoke accusingly, 'Abu Amir's soul is becoming narrow while his compulsion for violence is increasing. May his mother sit in mourning for him … now my courtyard is in his striking range! The royal architect has decreed that the walls of my house should be pulled down so that the palace is kept in good shape and the light of my life, my dear date tree, be removed.'

The magistrate paused, then asked: 'Dear lady, does Abul Mansur have any reservations about paying due compensation for your piece of land?'

Upon hearing this, Umme Raqiba was enraged and exclaimed, 'O adjudicator, that is a strange question to ask! Abu Amir will pay due compensation for the plot of land. But can he set a price for my tree?'

The magistrate heard this and bowed his head. He was speechless.

---

[2] Abu Amir al-Mansur, in Latin and Spanish known as Almanzor (born c. 938 – died Aug. 10, 1002, Spain), was the chief minister and virtual ruler of the Umayyad caliphate of Cordoba for 24 years (978–1002).

But Majju Bhai could not understand. Or, perhaps, he wanted to irritate me. So he said, 'Yaar Jawad, I was asking you something else and you went off on some other tangent. I am asking you now: Did you go there to study the history of Andalusia? And what did you derive from it? One black cat and a date palm!'

Majju Bhai had turned my story into a subject of ridicule. Irritated, I said, 'I wasn't talking about history.'

'What else were you doing, then? In any case, I have no real objection to speaking about history. But if one must speak about history then one must do so the way in which one speaks about history.'

'How does one speak about history? Should I turn into a venerable scholar?' I asked irritably.

'Yaar, you are ready to pick a quarrel. I had made a straightforward point. In any case, everything has a time and occasion. Now, look here ... we were talking about out there and you were not telling the real story. I asked you a simple question. You jumped and reached Andalusia. So be it. But, then, what is this riddle about the date palm?'

'There is no riddle.' I clarified. 'Personally speaking, I have no especial emotional attachment to the date tree. I have never had it. In fact, there are other trees with which I have many memories associated. They are my trees; or you can say they *were* my trees.' As I said this, an entire jungle came up around me in my imagination. Such amazing trees ... how they scared me, and how much they drew me towards them! How tall they were, and how dense! Not like the date tree, which looks as though someone has dug a pole in the ground. Their majesty was such that the taller they were, the more they bowed and bent! As stately as they were humble, their branches with a thousand twists and turns as though laden with layer upon layer of verdure and freshness. And when flocks of birds flew out from their green depths and scattered far into the sky, only then one knew that an entire city was alive within their branches – a brightly coloured city that echoed with their chirping. During the day, those trees – with their dense shade – stood like benevolent old men; at night they looked like ghosts! The peepal that stood on the far side of the dharamshala always looked as though a black ogre was standing there in the night. During the day it seemed as though a rishi were standing there, one who cast a kindly gaze towards the entire city. The tree in the field was no less tall. And how laden it used to be with *kaithoo*, as though it was not the kaithoo fruit but white canvas balls that had been strung from its branches. And the tamarind trees ... yes, they really seemed as though they were speaking to the sky! The greenness of the tallest branches merging with the blueness of the sky and the fruit dangling from the branches! There were only two date trees there ... those two who stood alone, separate from all the other trees. As though they had gone and stood far away, thinking they had nothing to do with the community of trees. Nor did they seem to have anything to do with the birds. I never saw a flock of parrots descend upon them, nor did any bulbul ever make a nest among their leaves. Truly, they looked like exiles. They were not exiles in Andalusia. There, they had struck roots and flourished and could be seen all over the countryside. But here they had competition in the form of one great specimen after another, that too from trees that seemed to have their roots in the netherworld and the tops of whose branches touched the sky. How could these trees let the date flourish here: neem, tamarind, mango, jamun, peepal and especially the banyan tree? The banyan tree appears sometimes like a jungle, and sometimes like an entire city.

But, soon, I sense I am wandering. I tell myself: This is my jungle and if I walk a few more steps into this jungle among these trees, it will become that much more difficult to find my way back. Immediately, I turn back. 'So, Majju Bhai, the fact is that the date tree was an issue for Umme Raqiba, not for me.'

'But you know, yaar, Abd ar-Rahman I did not exactly do a good deed by planting the date tree. He wrecked all the plans of

Tariq bin Ziyad[3] by opening up the routes for return. Every date tree was a tunnel; you could enter one and go back to your desert.'

'Yes, trees have a strong hold.' Saying this, once again I set off to be with my trees. The peepal that stood beside the far wall of the old haveli was so tall. And how many kites dangled from its branches … as though it wasn't a peepal but a tree of kites! A kite that was cut high up in the sky would stay up in a current of air, floating and fluttering in the breeze, staying clear of the tops of tall trees and high buildings, but the moment it came near the peepal, it found it difficult to cross the tree. All the kites that were cut at a height and drifted past this way, ended up entangled in the branches of the peepal tree. With the passage of time, they got so entwined with the leaves and branches of the tree that it began to seem as though the kites too had sprouted and flowered from the same branches. And the kites that flew high in the sky too – whenever they wished to take a respite – swooped down and perched on its branches. And the manner in which they rested, it seemed as though they would never fly off again. And then a dove would come flying from somewhere and it too would sit contentedly on the peepal's branches as though it had found its final resting place. Possibly, the reason for the dove's contentment could also be that no pellet fired from a sling gun could possibly reach the top-most branches of the peepal.

But Majju Bhai had no interest in these anecdotes. He wanted me to spit out something altogether different. But I could spit it only if I had it in me in the first place. He thought I was deliberately hiding something from him. 'Yaar, you are hiding something. After all,

---

[3] Tariq bin Ziyad was a Muslim general who led the Islamic conquest of Hispania in 711–718 AD. Under the orders of the Umayyad Caliph Al-Walid I, he led a large army from the north coast of Morocco, consolidating his troops at a large hill now known as Gibraltar. The name 'Gibraltor' is the Spanish derivation of the Arabic name *Jabal Tariq*, meaning the 'mountain of Tariq', which is named after him. Legend has it that Tariq ordered the ship he crossed over in to be burnt so that he and his men would not suffer from cowardice.

one should know the reality.' And he repeated this sentence so many times that even I fell into doubt as to what the reality was. And, also, whether I was forgetting some of the things. And when I tried to remember what the reality was, so much came tumbling back into my remembrance. Mounds of memories piled up.

Now look what I have come up with! It is of those days when my age was no more than … but who remembers exactly what my age was then. Who thinks of age in one's childhood? And if ever one thinks of age, it is always to wish that one could grow up quickly. Anyhow, what was it that I had remembered? Yes, there was a shop directly in front of our old haveli where, with the coming of winters, an old cotton carder would sit. Not once would he look here or there. Lost in his own world, he would be intent upon his work. His carding paddle worked ceaselessly, the string humming continuously as heaps of freshly carded cotton piled up beside him. In the process, drifts of cotton floated around so much that the entire shop would be covered with snowy white clouds of cotton wool. Even the carder himself would be covered with cotton wool and appear all white as though he were made not of muscle and bone but cotton. I would stand in my doorway and keep looking at him for a long, long time. How surprised I used to be at the sight of him! But now I have become like him. I am a carder of memories. I am surrounded by mounds of memories of distant places and people and I am busy carding them.

'Yaar, you are a sick man,' Majju Bhai pronounced, sounding heartily sick of my preoccupation.

'Majju Bhai, do you remember when we met for the first time and you had asked me where I was from … what was my answer?'

'Everything is not meant to be remembered.'

Majju Bhai had forgotten. But I remembered. Those were my days of self-forgetfulness. Perhaps those were good days. I remembered nothing at all. This was the time when my days were spent in the city's Coffee House and my nights in the shanty. My town, my home, my family – suddenly everything had become my past. What was left behind was the past and so all relations with it had to be cut off. And everything had been left behind. I was wandering around this city with nothing except my body. The entire day, I would walk all over the city and, in the evenings, return to my shanty. Only the fortunate few could claim a shanty. I did not get it just like that. I was living at the railway station, without a roof or a home, when I happened to run into Misbah. Those were strange days. Roaming around the strange city, suddenly one spotted a familiar face.

You? When did you come? How did you reach here? By which 'special'?[4] Were you attacked? A sudden flurry of questions! One felt such surprise, so much happiness every time one met someone like this. There would be some tender-hearted compassion, some lamentations at the loss of all material belongings. It was always so nice to meet another lost soul till this point; after this, when the issues of help or sustenance came up, long-lost friends would display the same alacrity in slipping away. Who would help another? Everyone was looking out for himself. But Misbah turned out to be different. Actually, we had been together in college and then we had joined the same caravan that had boarded the same 'special'. There weren't just the two of us; in fact, there was quite a large group of us on that train. We had made the perilous journey to Lahore together. But when we got down at the Lahore railway station, we scattered to the winds; each one going off where ever he found temporary shelter. And eventually, after much rack and ruin, most landed up in Karachi. But now we were not in touch with each other and unaware of what the other was doing till one day I suddenly met Misbah in the tram. He called out, 'Arre, Jawad!' I turned around and saw it was him. How happy we were to see each other and how many questions we asked each other and how much we told of our lives to each other.

---

[4] Refers to the special trains that ferried passengers to and from the two sides of the border all through the Partition years, i.e. carrying Muslims to Pakistan and bringing Hindus to India.

'So, tell me, what are you doing?' Misbah asked.

'Nothing at present.'

'Where do you live?'

'Nowhere.'

'What?'

'Yes, I don't have a home.'

'I see,' he paused and then said, 'Come and live in my shanty. I am alone; it will be good to have another person with me. Do you have your bedding?'

'Yes, I do.'

'All right, then. That's good.'

And so I began to live with Misbah in the shanty. There were so many shanties all around. And all manner of snobs, gentlemen, dandies, sophisticates, aristocrats and other genteel folk were living in them. How much trouble one had to take to get possession of a shanty, and the fights that broke out over them! Anyone who could claim possession over a shanty felt he had conquered the realm. The shanty was Time and under its canopy a new age was wriggling. Flats, bungalows, plazas – these too were part of this age. Or perhaps they would follow shortly. For, that period was not a long-drawn out one. It was only the most worthless who languished in the shanties. Most of the smart ones aimed for the skies and managed to reach the zenith. And, so, the age of the shanties was a short-lived one. But so much was hidden during this period. So many possibilities quivered within the layers of this age. Some times are short but they seem like an age. So also with the time of the shanties: it seemed short, but it was a seminal age. And if one were to go by Majju Bhai's verdict *that* was the real era of Karachi. 'My dear, the Karachi of today has risen from the yeast of the Karachi of the shanties.'

'*Subhan Allah*,' I laughed out loud.

'It is no laughing matter. I am only saying what is correct. Don't go by all the upstarts who go about calling themselves Karachiwalas. The true Karachiwala is one who has lived in a shanty.'

'Then the old Karachiwalas can't be real Karachiwalas.'

'Yaar Jawad, this is a terrible habit! You stop me just as I am making my point. I am talking about the present lot of inhabitants. They stay in Karachi for four days and, on the fifth day, pretend to become real Karachiwalas.'

'But, Majju Bhai, surely there must be some fault in Karachi too. One can't stay in Lahore for four days and become a true-blue Lahoriya. And the city that was once Delhi … there, people who came from outside lived for generation after generation, yet the Delhiwalas did not accept them as true Delhiwalas. You are tracing a man's roots in a city; whereas a city too must have its own roots.'

'You've gone mad! Does a city beside a sea ever have roots? It always floats on the water.'

Anyhow, there was no way that Majju Bhai could deny my claim to being a Karachiwala. I had lived in a shanty and, had Majju Bhai not incited me, God knows how much longer I would have continued to live there. Misbah departed as soon as his well-to-do relatives arrived in the city. After he left, I became the sole owner of the shanty. At a time when people could not find an inch of space to rest their feet or cover their head, I was the proud owner of an entire shanty. Though I lived in a shanty, my head was in the clouds. I felt as though I was putting down roots in this city. But Majju Bhai uprooted me from there. I had run into him for the first time at the Coffee House.

Dressed in a narrow-legged pajama, black pumps with a bow, a black shervani cut in the typical Aligarh style,[5] a white Rampuri cap[6] worn at a rakish angle, Majju Bhai cut an elegantly effete

---

[5] The uniform of students as well as 'Old Boys' of the Aligarh Muslim University was a fitted black shervani worn over narrow pant-like white pajamas (known to this day as 'Aligarh-cut pajamas'). Even those who had not studied at the venerable University wore the trademark black shervani-over-white-pajamas as a sign of belonging to an educated class.

[6] A velvet version of the Jinnah cap or the Karaquli topi came to be known as the Rampuri topi. It was made popular by Liaqat Ali Khan, the first Prime Minister of Pakistan and was popular among the *muhajirs*, or those who had migrated to Pakistan from India.

figure. He sat surrounded by poets – bearing nom de plums such as Amrohvi, Badauni, Galauthvi, Etawi[7]– and a round of coffee was underway along with a discussion on the ghazal. In a rush of my newly-acquired 'intellectualism', I got into an altercation with him. They were writers of the ghazal; they couldn't sustain an argument. Majju Bhai kept drawing silently on his cigarette and looking at me. He said, 'Let's keep this argument away for another day; recite some of your new poetry for us now.'

'I don't write poetry.'

'You don't write poetry? So you only run on intellectual arguments.'

'Excuse me, I *read* poetry; I don't *write* it.'

'And what do you do?'

'Nothing.'

'Where do you live?'

'Nowhere.'

'When did you arrive in this city?'

'Recently.'

'Have you come alone, or …'

'Alone.'

'Which city have you come from?'

'Whichever the city was, it has been left behind. Now I am in this city.'

'My dear young man, this is the 'City of Neglect', where no one knows or cares.'

'I know.'

'No, you don't know yet; you will one day. Anyhow, surely there must be somewhere you rest your head at night.'

'I live in a shanty.'

'Say that then; so, you are a shanty-man.'

---

[7] Named after the *qasbas* and towns of Uttar Pradesh, it shows how those who migrated from 'there' to 'here' wished to cling to the roots they had left behind. The Urdu poet has traditionally adopted the name of his 'native' place as his pen name or *takhallus* as, for instance, Kaifi Azmi took the 'Azmi' from Azamgarh.

From then on, from Jawad, I became Jawad, the shanty-man. When someone asked 'Which Jawad?' the answer would be: 'Jawad, the shanty-man'. I was helpless. Then, Majju Bhai softened somewhat. 'What is this tag that you have stuck on yourself?'

'Have I given it?' I asked bitterly.

'How long do you plan to stay there? Leave that wretched place and move on.'

'And where should I go? Do I have any other shelter?'

'You know, you should pack your bag and bedding, and come to my place. I am single and so are you. We will get along well.'

I didn't have to be asked twice. In a jiffy, I bid goodbye to life in the shanty.

It was only when I began to live with Majju Bhai that I fully understood what a piece of work he was. There was a lot of spit and polish on the surface. He would sit in the Coffee House with a regal air and pretend to be an aristocrat, but in reality he turned out to be full of hot air.

It was a Sunday. We were both lying in our beds and dawdling when, suddenly, he got up with a start. 'Don't you want to go to the Coffee House? Or, do you plan to spend the entire Sunday yawning in bed?'

'Yes, we should go. It will be quite crowded today.'

'So, do you have an *atthanni* or *chavanni*? We must have at least the bus fare in our pockets.'

I felt my pockets. 'Yes, I can just about manage that, but what about the coffee-cigarette-paan? Shouldn't we a have a paisa or two for those?'

'What a thing to worry about! All we have to do is reach the Coffee House.'

And with that, we got to our feet in an instant.

Majju Bhai was a bachelor and free from any source of livelihood, but God is the greatest provider. Majju Bhai's pocket would be heavy some times and empty at others. But I was the only one who knew about his empty pocket. The crowds who thronged the Coffee House could not have known in their wildest dreams. He wasn't one to pay the bill every day. Every month or two, when he had some money, he would settle old dues. In fact, during the lean days, Deen Mohammad, the waiter at the Coffee House, paid for the paan, cigarettes and taxis. As far as transport went, when his pocket began to lighten, Majju Bhai would abandon the taxis in favour of buses. But when his pocket emptied out totally, he would go back to taxis. His taxi would stop in front of the Coffee House and Deen Mohammad would come out and pay it off. Once, when he had a bit of a windfall, he splurged on a cycle along with his other indulgences. He explained his decision thus, 'Look here, I have devised a way of freeing myself from the bother of finding taxis and buses. I have bought a cycle.'

'Majju Bhai, that's a good idea; now the problem of conveyance will be solved.'

But Majju Bhai couldn't remain true to the cycle for very long. As soon as his lean period started he began his entrapment, 'Jawad, with God's grace you have got a job. But, yaar, it is so difficult to find transport in the morning.'

'Yes, Majju Bhai, that is true. The buses are packed in the mornings; the rush is so great. And I can't afford a taxi every day. In any case, you can't find a taxi very easily during the rush hour.'

'Yes, I know. Yaar, I would recommend that you buy a cycle.'

'Majju Bhai, a cycle is going to cost me an entire month's salary.'

'Yaar, buy a second-hand one. The first month might be a bit tough, but then think of the ease.'

His words made sense. I agreed and looked at several second-hand cycles. But I didn't like any of them. Majju Bhai said, 'Yaar, forget all this. Take my cycle. It wasn't a wise decision for me to buy a cycle in any case; I can't pull it.'

And so Majju Bhai made some money by fobbing his cycle on me. He became rich for a few days. So far, I used to sit on the carrier behind him as we went to the Coffee House; now he began to sit on the carrier behind me as we went to the Coffee House. But this state of affairs could not last for very long. When the days of scarcity set in again, he said to me: 'Yaar, our old place was much better than this. We've had nothing but trouble from this rented house. The landlord is a despicable man; he doesn't let one rest in peace till he has extracted his rent. And I am going through a lean period.'

Indeed, the matter was a troubling one. I said, 'And my state is such that I have exhausted my entire salary and the first of next month is still far away.'

'What shall we do, then?' And Majju Bhai fell into deep thought.

'There is only one thing to do: I should sell my cycle.' The words slipped out of my mouth.

'No, yaar. How will you go to office, then?'

'Like I used to, before.'

'No, yaar,' Majju Bhai said and the matter ended there. But on the second or third day, he threw a new dart. 'Yaar, Jawad, there is this fellow who is badgering me every day; he keeps asking me if I know of a good second-hand cycle. I tell you: this is a good opportunity. Your cycle's tyres are almost gone, in any case. You will get a good price for it. Sell it off and rid yourself of the nuisance.'

At first I demurred, but Majju Bhai made me come around eventually. We sold the cycle and scraped together the month's rent and paid some of Deen Mohammad's outstanding bills. And the two of us went back to being on foot. In any case, the good times rolled back soon enough. They came for all too short a time, but nevertheless while they lasted, Majju Bhai spent four rupees where he could have done with one! The orders for coffees increased as the circle of supplicants became suddenly large. But Majju Bhai had forsaken the idea of having his own conveyance. So the thought of buying a cycle never occurred to him at all. Now, an altogether different issue was troubling him. He said, 'How long will we eat bazaar-bought food? After all, hotel food is hardly worth eating.'

'So, what can be done, Majju Bhai? Yes, the only possibility is that if you were to agree to marry one of these lady poets who hover around you and bring her to grace your home, you might be rid of hotel food.'

Majju Bhai looked at me with distrust. 'Marry? You or me?' After a pause he said, 'Jawad Miyan, they are all smart cookies. Don't even think of it.' And then after another pause, 'I was thinking of something else.'

'What?'

'Yaar, shouldn't we keep a cook?'

Now it was my turn to be surprised.

'Cook? What are you saying, Majju Bhai? Keeping a cook is like tethering an elephant at your door.'

'Yes, Bhai, that is true. But all these fellows who come to the Coffee House in their cars, and whose wives never fail to mention their cooks, on some pretext or the other, are they any better than us? And are we in any way inferior to anyone?'

I agreed. Then, hesitantly, I offered, 'Majju Bhai, you know exactly what my salary is.'

'*Lahoul willah quwwat* ...[8] Do you think I am such a base fellow? Will I ask you to pay for the cook? Now, it is imperative that we keep a cook.'

And, really, within the next few days, a decent cook was engaged in that modest home in which I had come to live with Majju Bhai. A dining table was also bought, and with it new crockery too. For the next few days, there was much festivity. Every day, there would be a new dish on the dining table. And on Sunday afternoons, a veritable feast of dishes! The two of us began to stay at home without fail; one or two of Majju Bhai's cronies would also drop in. In any case, this period did not last very long. Majju Bhai had a hole in his palm; whatever money came his way from some supernatural means, even if it was a large amount, could not stay for very long. And his heavy pocket began to lighten. Soon, Majju Bhai made it known that he was heartily fed up of these

---

[8] A verse from the Quran used variously to express disgust or dissatisfaction; loosely translated it means, 'I turn my face away from Evil'.

rich and heavy meals. 'Yaar, meat every day … that's too much! Good folk need not be such good Muslims.' And he immediately instructed the cook, 'Stop this daily business of chicken … you serve it to us every day.'

'Shall I get mutton?'

'No, no, we have had enough of meat. Make some *daal* or vegetable. Why don't you make some *masoor daal* today? After all, one should eat lentils too.'

And so, we had *masoor daal* for the next seven days. On Sunday, Majju Bhai instructed the cook, 'We are off to roam the city today; we will eat outside. You make something simple for yourself.'

That afternoon, Majju Bhai ordered an omelette and six slices of bread with coffee. That is how we filled our bellies for the day. By now, the cook had figured out our dire straits. In a day or two, he bid farewell to Majju Bhai and took our leave with the promise of coming on the first of the next month to collect his wages. And Majju Bhai drew a long breath of relief. 'Yaar, keeping a cook is a complicated affair. It's no business for single men like us. It is a good thing he has quit.'

Once again, we were back to our old ways. Majju Bhai would make the tea in the morning, toast some bread and call out to me. 'Come, Jawad Miyan, hurry up; it is time for your office.' And when I would come for my breakfast, he would console me thus: 'Yaar, I forgot to buy eggs last night. And the damn butter too is finished. Never mind, make do with what we have.'

'That's all right, Majju Bhai; breakfast should be a simple affair. In any case, I shall pick up some eggs and butter on my way back from office.'

'So, you are being ultra generous, are you? Never mind, so be it.'

And so life continued. Majju Bhai would be a king one day and a pauper the next. While I could understand the pauper bit, I could never quite fathom how he became a king. This mystery was never solved by anyone. Majju Bhai never lifted so much as a leaf by way of work. I had a Khalu Jan several times removed, who did no work whatsoever, was entirely disinterested in work or employment, and had neither lands to manage nor a shop to run. Yet my Khala Amma used to say, 'Bibi, Allah is merciful; we eat meat twice a day and that too mutton. Though, yes, sometimes, your Khalu Jan gets beef just for a change of taste. I get angry and say why should we get beef in our house? He says the butcher had some wonderfully tender beef so I thought why not get some sirloin; it tastes so good with radish. Make *shab-degh* today.' The ladies would hear her and make faces and say, 'The darned ghee has become Rs 2 for a ser and flour is Rs 1 for 16 ser. It is difficult for genteel folk to survive. Khalu Jan does no work; how does Khala Amma eat meat twice a day?' Finally, the riddle was solved. Khalu Jan had recited a miraculous prayer; as a result, his 'clients' came to him at night. When Khalu Jan got up in the morning, he picked up two silver rupees from under his pillow.[9]

Majju Bhai's fame had reached similar heights. The New Age had its own jinns and miraculous prayers. The circle of friends first whispered among themselves: 'After all, Majju Bhai has no discernible source of income, yet he lives well and squanders money. The moment a group of friends comes to his table, he promptly orders coffee … and so it goes on with one group, then the second and the third … and the coffee keeps coming. After all, what's going on?' More whispering would be followed by suspicion-filled questions. And then the pronouncement, 'Surely this is the miracle of supernatural earnings. After all, there must be some reason why Majju Bhai is to be found in the Coffee House at all odd hours.'

'Sometimes I wonder how the news of our conversations in the Coffee House travels from here to there. Surely, it is someone among us who is spreading the news.'

'Yes, it must be one of us.'

A pregnant pause, a hint of a suggestion … someone would say something and leave it half-said and then fall silent. Then another

[9] The clients are jinns who, it is believed, can be made to obey one's commands by special prayers and the practice of chanting certain *wazifas* or special prayers.

would draw a long deep breath and express sorrow at his own condition. 'Yaar, I have remained a frog in a well; I am stuck in this Coffee House.'

'Yaar, sitting in the Coffee House should not mean that we should chop off our hands and legs. There is Majju Bhai too.'

'Yaar, truly, just the other day a friend of mine said, "What is this? You sit in the Coffee House all day long. I will take you along to meet important people." He took me to a dinner hosted by some businessman. There was dinner and an evening of music. All the important personages in the city were gracing the occasion. Senior officers were present along with their wives. And in the midst of them all ... there was Majju Bhai!'

'Really?'

'Yes, really! And he gave me short shrift; he was busy with the officers. For a long time, he was stuck with the Commissioner; they seemed to be speaking about confidential matters.'

'Nice ... our Majju Bhai is quite something!'

Actually, Majju Bhai had created many enemies for himself – some by virtue of his haughtiness and some for no particular reason. One fine day, God knows what got into him and he announced, 'All the poets who attend our meetings must be educated.'

And when people asked him what he meant by education, he said, 'At least a B.A.'

I cautioned him, 'Majju Bhai, that is an odd condition; why is it necessary for a poet to be a graduate?'

'You don't understand, my dear fellow. This is the only way we will be rid of nincompoops.'

And indeed we were rid of them to some extent. But those we got rid of, began to gossip. Once the poets among our circle figured out that Majju Bhai had not put in a word for them among the organisers of *mushairas*, they too began to show their true colours. Majju Bhai was not a poet (though it cannot be ruled out with any certainty), but he was certainly a patron and mentor of poets. Apart from *mushairas*, a word from him went a long way when it came to radio programmes. His devotees were present there, too. And when it came to poetry, it was said that he wrote a great deal, but never ever recited it. In fact, some even said that he never ever let on to anyone that he was indeed a poet.

There seemed little doubt that Majju Bhai's reach went far and wide, nor was it limited to knowing officers alone; his connections extended to all sorts of people. And they were not ordinary connections; he seemed deeply entrenched in their families. As though Lucknow and Delhi were not enough, if some well-to-do family from some far-flung *qasba* of UP migrated to this city, within a week or so, Majju Bhai found out everything about their family history and then proceeded to describe their genealogy with such familiarity as though he had known them for generations. There was not a single well-to-do *muhajir* family which did not have his devotees and disciples. He was feted and lionized in every home. From *khatna* and *aqiqa* to marriages and receptions, he was invited to every occasion and was always present in everyone's sorrows and pains. He was among the chief organisers at every good or bad occasion and advisor at every decisive moment.

This very quality eventually proved to be his undoing. People linked him to all manner of underhand doings. You could say that any bogey that arose in the city, and to whichever secret society that bogey belonged, its source was traced to Majju Bhai. The mystery of supernatural income too was interpreted variously by his so-called friends.

'So, you think this is some sort of Open Sesame?'

'What is it, then?'

'Yaar, this is all about permits and licences.'

'That is hardly a mystery; it is all about buying and selling. This is something else that involves no expenditure of any sort and yet …'

And so the tongues wagged. And I fumed inwardly. When I could take it no more, I took on one of the wags. Matters got out of hand, and the news reached Majju Bhai. He gave me a severe dressing down. 'Are you a loose cannon? If someone is saying something about somebody, what is it to you?'

I was in a temper at the time. I burst out at Majju Bhai, 'Majju Bhai, why are you feeding these serpents? They ask you for all sorts of favours, they take advantage of you, and then they indulge in wild speculation about you.'

'Ustad, you are in a temper right now.' Majju Bhai cooled himself down and tried to pacify me as well. 'But, yaar, why fly into such a rage? Must one die if a colony of crows has set up a dirge? Come on, let us go and drink coffee.'

Anyway, there I was talking about myself when the subject of Majju Bhai came up. Perhaps, it was inevitable. No matter which angle I see my life from, I have always found Majju Bhai to be a part of it, especially during those early days as though I was learning to walk by holding his finger. I had found a roof over my head only because of him. And not just the roof, but even my first job was thanks to him. One day, he suddenly served me with a notice. 'Jawad Miyan, go and meet Mirza sahab tomorrow.'

'Mirza sahab? Which Mirza sahab?'

'Mirza Dilawar Baig. He is one of us. He has a couple of vacancies in his office. You can fit in. Go and meet him tomorrow; your job is as good as fixed. It is a government job; you will do well.'

And so the next day, I went. But I was so surprised when I reached there. I looked and I was astounded. So this is what a government office looks like! Mirza sahab was in charge of the office all right, but the state of his office was such that a large table reposed in the middle of a bare floor, bereft of any ornamentation. A few files lay on one side which, instead of a paperweight, had a washed piece of a brick resting on top. Next to them, a few twigs of a thorny acacia were arranged in a dish. In front lay a few papers, a blue and a yellow pencil – and on a table thus adorned, sat Mirza sahab. Two ancient battered chairs lay in front of him. He met me with great affection, asked my name and then enquired about my education. 'Have you done a B.A.? Which division? What were your subjects?' And then the sudden question, 'Which city do you belong to, my dear?'

'Sir, the sense of belonging is gone; now I roam around like a vagabond in this city.'

Mirza sahab peered at me, from the top of my head till my feet. He was silent; then he said, 'Yes, my dear, you are right. I too seldom mention which desolate place I have come from. When someone insists, all I say is, *Dilli jo ek shehar thaa aalam mein intekhab* ...[10] And then I fall silent.'

And with that, Mirza sahab launched upon an entire essay on the city of Delhi. As it turned out, this was a mere preface. I would be subjected to the essay on some pretext or the other on later occasions too. So, there was Mirza sahab in full flow on the subject of Delhi and I kept mumbling a 'yes' and a 'no' when, suddenly, he paused and said, 'You must have a pen.'

I did not understand and was at a loss for words.

'No ... I mean yes ... yes, I have a pen.'

'All you need is a pen. It would be good if you also had a pencil. Come in the morning tomorrow. I will have your name noted down; the rest of the formalities will be taken care of; that will take some time. Government matters are done like that. Anyhow, you should come tomorrow.'

---

[10] Refers to the verse by Delhi's pre-eminent poet Mir Taqi Mir (1722–1810) who wrote plaintively of the desolation of his beloved city in the terrible years leading up to the great revolt of 1857. Its fragment has, over the years, been used to evoke the image of a desolate or wrecked city, the mockery of the Delhiwallas at the hands of new emerging elites from other cities. The complete verse is as follows:

Dilli jo ek shehar tha aalam mein intekhab
Poocho ho boodo baash kya purab ke sakino
Hamko ghareeb jaan ke hans hans pukar ke
Dilli jo ek shehar tha aalam mein intekhab
Rahte the muntakhib bhi jahan rozgar ke
Jis ko falak ne loot ke barbad kar diya
Hum rahne wale hain ussi ujde dayar ke

In essence, it means: 'Delhi that was once the pre-eminent city in the world/I belong to that desolate place.'

The next day, I reached armed with a pen and pencil. Mirza sahab was pleased to see me. Then some homilies, in the nature of a lecture, followed, 'My dear young man, this is a time of dire straits. Can you imagine the splendour of my office in Raisina[11]? Not one but two *chaprasis* sat outside the door of my office. A visitor had to send a chit and still wait for a long time. Here, in my office, there is neither chit nor *chaprasi*; anyone can walk in. If you ask me, truly, it is still not an office; I am trying to turn it into one. After all, there was no country; how could there be offices? The country has been created thanks to Allah; we too have come here under Allah's care. So, my dear, work here knowing that a building is coming up and we are its builders.'

Mirza sahab proved to be a good builder. Within a matter of months, he built up a monument with much the same splendour that is to be found in most offices. Staff strength went up as well. However, the more staff he got the more he complained about its shortage and aired a commensurate grievance about the neglect of senior officers. The staff was expanding in a strange way. Every other day, a new face would appear and within a week or so new staff would become old staff. Among them, there was also a face that was the most radiant among all the other faces, a face that gradually spread its light within me.

All she did was type all day long. I never ever saw that girl raise her head to look at anyone. If I went to her with a sheaf of papers to be typed, she would take them and keep them on one side as she typed and remain engrossed in her work. I said to myself: This won't do. I handed her the papers one day and said, 'These have to be typed soon ... in the next fifteen minutes.'

'Yes.' And she remained engrossed in her typing.

'Excuse me ... what is your name?'

'Ishrat un-Nisa.'

---

[11] Raisina Hill in New Delhi housed the government offices in colonial India; it continues to be the seat of government in India.

'Ishrat un-Nisa ... That is a nice name! Someone like me can barely get its pronunciation right.'

She paused and looked at me for a moment and then went back to her typing. Her fingers, that had paused briefly, began to move swiftly across the keys once again.

In the monsoon, when the rains come to this alien city, it rains so hard as though the mouths of several thousand *mashaks* have opened suddenly. There is water overflowing everywhere.

That day the rain had lessened somewhat but not stopped, and there was no sign of local transport. It can only be called a miracle when a rain-drenched rickshaw came and stopped right beside me on the footpath.

'Will you go?' I asked.

The man pulling the rickshaw agreed almost immediately.

As I climbed into the rickshaw, I looked towards Ishrat. In an attempt to escape the falling rain, she had shrunk herself into a ball. A wave of sympathy rose within me. 'Ishrat Bibi, there is no certainty about the bus; who knows when it will come or whether you will get a place in it or not. If you like, I can drop you.'

She didn't decline, but she did not show any signs of acceptance either. I looked hesitantly at her and said, 'Arre, there is no reason to worry. How long can you stand here in this weather?'

She bent and said, 'It will be a longer route for you.'

'Yes, it will. But one has to do this in such weather.' And immediately I added, 'Don't delay; come. Who knows when the rain might start again!'

She thought for a minute and then, hesitantly, got into the rickshaw, but she sat shrinking away, hugging the far side of it. I said, 'You will get soaked to the skin. Why don't you sit properly?'

'No, I am all right.'

I could hardly insist. Who knows what she might infer? Throughout the journey, she sat like that and kept getting wet. She would talk quite a bit in the office; now, she was silent and also a little anxious. She answered in monosyllables whenever I tried to make conversation.

She asked the rickshaw-puller to stop at the corner of her alley. 'I will get off here.'

I peered out; there was water and mud everywhere. I said, 'How will you go? There is so much slush.'

'I will manage.'

'You will slip.'

'No, I will manage,' she said and got off.

I too got off. I told the rickshaw-puller, 'I will drop her and come back.' And to Ishrat I said, 'Here, hold my hand.' Perhaps she too realized how slippery the ground was as soon as she got off; and so she immediately held my hand and began to walk carefully. Whenever she felt she might slip, she would clasp her fingers more tightly with mine.

Somehow or the other, we reached her doorway. When she turned to go in after thanking me, I made a jovial remark just to tease her, 'Now you have held my hand.'

And she retorted, 'Don't let go of it.'

And, suddenly, a change came over her. She looked coyly at me and sped inside after waving her thumb at me! I stood transfixed.

With much difficulty, I made my way back and sat down in the rickshaw. And thereafter I did not know if it was still raining or not and whether the rickshaw-puller was taking the right route. This new side of Ishrat that I had just glimpsed had so embedded itself in my imagination that I was completely lost in it. Sleep proved to be elusive that night. All I could visualize was that scene. The next day, I was among the first to reach the office.

A short while later Ishrat too came in. Usually, she would be the first to come in; today, I had reached before her. That was good; the others had not yet arrived. So, we gained a few precious moments of solitude.

'Jawad sahab, thank you for giving me the ride home yesterday. It rained very hard soon after. If you hadn't offered the lift, I don't know how I would have managed. So, thank you once again.'

'I too should thank you.'

'What for?'

'For showing me your thumb.'

She laughed out loud. 'Sorry, Jawad sahab.'

'What is there to be sorry about? I have only one complaint.'

'What?'

'You had only a thumb to show me.'

'Should I have shown you my eyes, then?'

'No, you should have shown me a glimmer of your true self.'[12]

Making a face, she said, 'Hmm, shown my true self!' and then, with great coquetry, she stuck her tongue out at me. Once again, I was wounded. That narrow, red tongue looked so good. I laughed, 'There is no need to show your tongue. I know you have a mother tongue.[13] By the way, where do you come from? Lucknow?'

She looked back sharply at me and retorted, 'Lucknow? Why should I be from Lucknow? I belong to Delhi.'

'Ah, Delhi! Then I am done for,' I said.

'Why? Why are you done for?' she asked curiously.

'Nothing. Just like that. Actually, I was reminded of a warning once issued by a poet.'

'What warning?'

'Mushafi[14] had given the following warning in one of his verses:

> *Ai Mushafi tu unse muhabbat na kijio*
> *Zaalim ghazab ki hoti hain yeh Dilliwalian*
> (Ai Mushafi, do not fall in love with them
> These Delhi girls are terribly cruel)'

---

[12] Intizar sahab uses one word where I have inadequately resorted to five; in the original, he uses the Hindi word *chhab* which also means style.

[13] The play of words in the original is on *zubaan*, which means tongue, and also *ahl-e-zubaan* or 'people of the language', an expression used for those for whom Urdu is the mother tongue. In the newly-established Pakistan, there was a great deal of snobbery. While the newly-arrived *muhajir* were often penniless or destitute, they nevertheless prided themselves on their 'native' command over the Urdu language, especially in comparison to the other communities, such as Punjabis, Sindhis, Bengalis, etc. for whom Urdu was a national language but not their mother tongue.

[14] Ghulam Hamadani Mushafi (1750–1824) was a major poet from Delhi.

'Nonsense! Who was this shameless poet?'

'He liked adolescent boys.'

'No wonder!' And then after a pause, she added, 'You have recited a very vulgar verse. I shall not talk to you anymore.'

I tried to offer my defence, but other staff members had begun to walk in. I immediately got up and came to sit down at my own desk.

And then, it was almost as though a transformation came over our relationship. So far, our relations were confined to the office. We would talk in the office as colleagues do or sit together and drink tea, or once they become a little more comfortable with each other they might indulge in some informal banter. Anyhow, there had never been such informality between us that she or I could exchange casual remarks. But that incident of showing her thumb was a major turning point; it brought about a sea-change in our attitude towards each other. A strange sort of informality crept in between us, and also a hesitation. Suddenly, mid-sentence, it would cross our mind that perhaps one of our colleagues was watching us and may, perchance, get an inkling of what was going on. Immediately, we would fall silent. But what was there to guess? What was there between us? There was nothing.... No ... But doubts and misgivings had begun to raise their head.

One day, as we were talking, I asked, 'Our boss, Mirza sahab, is also from Delhi. Is he related to you?'

'He is my Phupha Jan several times removed.'

'So he is distantly related?'

'Yes.'

'Then, he won't raise any hindrance.'

'Hindrance? In what?' she sounded bemused.

'I mean in yours and my ...' I didn't know what else to say. I fell silent.

'I don't understand,' she was now sounding worried.

'Now, how do I make you understand ...?'

She was quiet. Anyhow, soon she began to understand everything on her own.

Actually, the person who set up obstacles turned out to be Majju Bhai. God knows how he got wind of what was brewing. Perhaps he saw the two of us together at some opportune moment. It so happened that when I bought a scooter, one day I also found a suitable time and place and invited Ishrat, 'Come with me today.'

'Where?'

'You are from Delhi. But there is no Qutub Minar here; where can one go? There is only Clifton.'[15]

She laughed.

I started my scooter. 'Get on.' She hopped on behind me. And when I increased the speed of my scooter, she put her arm around my waist. No doubt, Majju Bhai must have seen us on one such occasion.

One day, he looked closely at me as we were having our breakfast. 'This girl who is being seen with you these days ... she works in your office, doesn't she?'

'Yes.'

'And presumably she belongs to Delhi.'

'Yes, but how do you know?'

'Ustad, I walk about this city with my eyes open. And now you listen very carefully to my words.'

'Yes?'

'There is no harm as long as things are confined to romance, but don't entertain any thoughts of marriage.'

'Why not?'

'My boy, she is from Delhi; you have *had* it!'

'What does that mean?'

'The fact is that those families that have come from Delhi lived with the utmost respectability there. There was a time when their women did not even set foot outside their door. Those girls who set foot outside to go to college did so wearing a *burqa* and getting into a covered *tanga* the moment they came out. They have thrown

[15] Refers to a sea-facing area in uptown Karachi.

their *burqas* away since coming to Karachi. And there is neither *doli* nor *tanga* here for transport. One should be scared of such girls.'

'So, you regret that there are no more curtained *ekkas* and *tangas* and these *muhajir* girls can be seen going about bare-faced to colleges and offices?'

'You misunderstand me. I am not a sympathizer of purdah. But, Jawad Miyan, these girls have not come out of purdah in a normal way; they have torn their burqas asunder and burst out on the crossroads. And that is why I am fearful of them.'

'And it is because of this fear that you have decided to remain a bachelor?'

Majju Bhai let out a hearty laugh. 'I knew you wouldn't be convinced. The most well meaning of friends the world over have never managed to convince a lover. Anyhow, good or bad, my job was to warn you. So, tell me, what do you plan to do?'

I was in no hurry to open up. Or, perhaps, I myself had not made up my mind yet. Nor had Ishrat given any serious thought to the subject of marriage. At present, we were content to flow along without a thought or a decision in mind. This was the only testament to the sincerity of our feelings. But what is the point of remembering such things after such a long time? Arre, the romance ended the day the words of the *nikah* were recited. Actually, the only measure of success in romance is its failure. I have always pitied those men who turn from lovers to husbands. The experience of love gets lost somewhere in married life, and is eventually frittered away. In any case, my married life did not last very long. The business of giving birth made it so very brief; hers was a caesarean case. The mother died; the child remained. Marital life left behind a fruit as it ended … a new nuisance. But then what is the point of remembering those things. That short-lived love and the marital life that was born of its womb left behind its fruit, and disappeared! And with it, I bid farewell to that office, too. It seemed as though I had gone to that office only to savour the taste of that life. I turned one page of life after this experience of working in an office and the romantic interlude, and moved on. There is a time and age for every emotional experience. So the lifespan of this experience and that emotion was over. Whatever traces remained were gradually lost in the worries and anxieties of life. The last remaining trace was lost when I narrated the entire incident to Maimuna; and when she heard me out with sympathy and attention, I was freed of that entire episode. Though, indeed, later I was surprised by her interest in this part of my life.

Anyhow, the old sorrow was gone. There were new incidents and issues, and new sorrows. But I could not understand where to slot that old sorrow that had mingled with these new sorrows: should I put it in the pigeonhole of new sorrows or call it the revival of an old sorrow? It was strange; once where there was a pain, now there was only a scar. And where there was neither pain nor scar, a pain lay buried.

Two

Majju Bhai's curiosity put me in a strange dilemma. He dug and delved into the details of my journey so much that I myself fell into doubt: Was I really trying to hide something? And not just from Majju Bhai but from myself too? But what was it that I was trying to hide? Surely, I should not try to hide anything from myself. After all, I am not a stranger to myself. There are those who treat themselves as aliens. I should not treat my own self as an alien. I should tell myself clearly whatever the matter is. So, I began to scrape away at myself. I did not have to dig too deep. As I went back in time, I soon reached the spot from where this whole story had begun. And I didn't have to go very far back either. It wasn't very long ago when, in my days of hard living, I had asked Majju Bhai a simple and straightforward question. And the entire story began with that. And as a result, I got caught in Majju Bhai's snare and kept getting more and more entangled.

It is about those days when I had freed myself of all my sorrows and was leading a quiet and disinterested life. The tumultuous years of my life were behind me. From the sorrows of love to the sorrows of earning a living – I had known everything. How much I had been through! How much humiliation I had known! How I used to roam around like a vagabond! But now I was free of all my worries. I had been freed of the sorrows of romance after marriage; I had found release from marital life after putting to sleep under mounds of earth the woman I had loved. The jewel of my life had gone off to America, and so I was freed of the anxieties of parenting as well. My working life too had seen some stability. I had been promoted. Now I was quite senior in my bank. I was the manager of a branch. I was content. I had had my fill of parties and socialising. But Majju Bhai had still not had his fill. The Coffee House had closed down a long time ago. But his gregarious spirit had discovered new avenues. Now, he was to be found in the drawing rooms of his wealthy friends and acquaintances. He attended *mushairas* and marriages with great pleasure. I would come straight home after office, whereas Majju Bhai would dress up and go off to a *mushaira* or a wedding reception. We lived under the same roof, but he minded his business and I mine. We seldom met before the weekend. He would come late at night and promptly go off to sleep. In the morning, I would be busy in my own routine: I would bathe, dress, eat breakfast and rush to the car. I had to get to the bank on time. At the time, Majju Bhai would be lazing in his bed. The bed-tea beside him would go cold on most days.

And so we were living our lives in this manner when a disturbance occurred and kept becoming more and more disturbing. I mean in the life of the entire city. The peace and calm disappeared suddenly. Dacoities, kidnappings, murders, bombings ... masked men would appear from somewhere and fire in the middle of crowded bazaars ... one would fall here, another lay trembling there. Warm bodies would turn cold as one watched. A frenzy would course through the bazaar and then there would be silence! And suddenly tyres would be burnt. The burning tyres would catch a bus in their grip and, within minutes, the bus would be burnt to the ground. The shops that were about to open would shut again. And curfew would be clamped. Today one neighbourhood would be under curfew, tomorrow another.

Just as he was about to step out of the house, Majju Bhai stopped at the sound of the phone. He spoke to someone at the other end and postponed his plans, then flopped down in the armchair.

'Majju Bhai, weren't you about to go out for a *mushaira*?' I asked.

'Yes, I had to, but that area is under curfew. Our friends have barred our way.'

Increasingly, Majju Bhai's way would be barred. The curfew would be in one neighbourhood today, and in another tomorrow. And Majju Bhai would mention the curfew with such simplicity as though he was talking of an unexpected bout of rain that can spoil a respectable man's plans for an outing.

'Majju Bhai, things seem to be getting out of hand.'

Whenever I said anything of the sort, I always got the same response from Majju Bhai. 'Why are you losing sleep over the state of the city?'

The practice of robbing banks reached such a pass that armed robbers first caught hold of the guard in the bank in our neighbourhood, then held up the staff at gunpoint and leisurely walked out after robbing the entire vault. They fired at the crowd that had gathered to watch. People ran away and the robbers calmly got into a Pajero car and drove away.

I felt as though the waves that had been pounding the distant shore were now lapping my threshold. That evening I addressed Majju Bhai with utter seriousness, 'Majju Bhai.'

Majju Bhai understood from my tone that the matter was serious. He looked closely at me and asked, 'What is it?'

'Majju Bhai, what is happening in this city?'

'Why, what is happening?' he answered with complete unconcern.

'How surprising that you have no idea what is happening! Do step out of the ambience of the *mushaira* and look at the city; then you will know what is happening. It doesn't seem like the city we knew; it has undergone such a transformation that it is unrecognizable. After all, where are we heading? Aren't we on the way to destruction?' I blurted out everything in one breath. I had been holding it all in for so long.

Majju Bhai heard me out in silence and looked closely at me. Then, he said to me with utter seriousness, 'Miyan Jawad, shall I give you a suggestion?'

'Please do.'

'Stop thinking, or leave this city.'

This was such an unexpected reply that, for some time, I didn't know what to say. Stop thinking, or leave this city. How could I ... From the shanty to this flat where I was now living and that I owned, my entire journey in this city, all my days and nights, flashed across my eyes like lightning. For the first time, I felt that a wave may have brought me and dumped me here, and for a long time, I may have floated about like a broken leaf in a current of air, but now I had put down fairly strong roots. Should I uproot myself again? But why? What was Majju Bhai saying?

'Majju Bhai, are you giving me this suggestion in your right senses?'

'Do you have any doubt?' Majju Bhai laughed. 'I am in my full senses. You are the one who has lost his senses; not me.'

'Stop thinking, or leave this city.' I mumbled angrily. 'That's a good suggestion.'

'All right, you don't have to follow it; there is no compulsion. It isn't the order of some dictator; it is simply the advice of a friend. I have let you in on a secret. This is the only way to live in this city. Stop thinking about what is going on. Whoever thinks has had it!'

In response, I first showed anger then resorted to sarcasm and criticism, and finally tried to laugh it all away. But Majju Bhai did not budge an inch; he stayed true to his position. He heard me out in silence. Then he said, 'Have you had your fill? Will you hear me now?'

'Do you still have anything left to say? All right, say it.'

'Listen carefully. There is no need to get emotional. I will tell you a true story. Jawad Miyan, this city is an extremely quarrelsome one: Sindhi, Punjabi, Balochi, Pathan, *Muhajir* ... our friends have not made a city, they have cooked up a khichri!'

He paused then said, 'And it isn't as though *muhajirs* are all of one type. Some are from the east, some from the west, some from the north, some from the south. Rivers from across the length and breadth of Hindustan came tumbling and gurgling to meet the sea. But they did not merge in the sea. Every river says: "I am the sea." Jawad Miyan, I have swum quite a bit in these rivers.

For instance, there was a time when I moved extensively among the Amrohawalas. It seemed as though Karachi was full of only people from Amroha; as though it wasn't Karachi but had become Amroha itself. These Karachiwalas think Karachi is a second Amroha, as though all *muhajirs* are Amrohvis and all Amrohvis are blissfully content in being an Amrohvi. Jawad Miyan, it is strange that Amroha may have been transformed since the days of Mushafi, but the state of being an Amrohvi is a constant.'

Majju Bhai paused for breath and then started off again, 'And now listen to the tale of the Badaun-walas: Our friend Mirza Hadi Ali Badauni is a dear old man, but he is a Badauni after all. Once he decided it was not possible to rid oneself of all the poets in Karachi, so why not have a small *mushaira* of only poets from Badaun. But, you know, so many poets were found in Liaqatabad[16] itself that they filled up several rows. Then telephone messages began to come from different neighbourhoods: "We too are from Badaun; don't forget us." Poor Mirza Hadi Ali didn't know what to do; so much so that he decided to wrap up the proceedings and swore never to attempt anything of the sort again.'

Majju Bhai paused to draw another breath, and set off almost immediately. 'Jawad Miyan, sometimes I feel that each and every *muhajir* is a Badaunwala. And because he is a Badaunwala, he is in dire straits. Anyhow, so that is Badaun for you ... if not for the sake of Fani Badayuni,[17] at least for its famous *pedas*, you can count the Badaunwalas among respectable folk. But the problem is of those *qasbas* of UP that were entirely unheard of then but whose people are busy blowing their own trumpet since coming

---

[16] Liaqatabad is a densely populated neighbourhood in central Karachi named after Liaqat Ali Khan, the first Prime Minister of Pakistan; though a mixed neighbourhood, *muhajirs* form an overwhelming majority in the ethnic mix.

[17] Fani Badayuni (1879–1961) was a renowned Urdu poet who wrote sweetly lyrical ghazals in the traditional mould, marked by an extreme despondency and richly symbolist melancholy. His hometown, Badaun, a historical city near Bareilly in Uttar Pradesh, has produced many poets and is regarded as a centre of learning and good taste; it is also well known for its pedas.

to Karachi. Now, tell me, had you ever heard of Dibai[18] in your entire life?'

'Dibai? Where is that?'

'Arre, don't ever say that in front of a Dibaiwala or else all hell will break loose. I had met a Dibaiwala once during my Aligarh days. That Dibaivi gentleman was so pleased with me that he loaded me onto an *ekka* and took me to Dibai. It is a tiny *qasba* in Aligarh's backyard … so tiny that it is no larger than the size of a man's palm! There, of course, he was well within his limits. But when I met him here, he was an altogether changed man. He believed that Sir Syed Ahmad Khan chose the wrong place; Aligarh College should have been set up in Dibai. I asked, "But then, yaar, where would the Dibaiwalas have gone? Anyhow, apart from its proximity to Aligarh, what is special about Dibai?" He said, "It has not one but two singular qualities and two special gifts: One, a *chillum* and the other a *gujia*." I said, "The *chillum* is all very well, though its future is not very bright as the *huqqa* is on its way out, but what is so special about this thing called *gujia*." He said, "Ai wah! How can you possibly ask what is special about our *gujia*? If the Badaunwalas were to eat it, they would forget all about their *peda*."'

Majju Bhai was in full spate and I was listening intently. Perhaps my question had served to prod him. He was in full flow and showing no signs of letting up.

'Jawad, the biggest problem is that every *qasba* in our part of the world had cooked up a legend about something or the other. And each one claimed that the rest of India could not match their one single best thing. Once, I had the opportunity to meet an elderly gentleman at a party. He drew a long breath and announced, "I have spent 35 years in Pakistan. In all this while, I have not eaten a *laddu*. Ai sahab, I don't know what's wrong, but there is no taste in the food here, and the *laddus* here are nothing but lumpy

---

[18] This is characteristic of Intizar's Husain's impish sense of humour; he is poking fun at people like himself since he was born in Dibai and educated in Meerut.

mounds of sugar." Later, I was told that the gentleman belonged to Sandila[19]. Well, at least the Sandilawalas can get grace marks on this subject, because their laddus were indeed very good, but I was shocked when I met an elderly man from Shikarpur and heard his tall tales about his city. I could not contain myself. I said, "Hazrat, forgive me, but wasn't Shikarpur famous for its fools." Angrily, he retorted, "Ai, Subhan Allah, aren't you forgetting the *gur dhani*? This mixture of *gur* and *chana* was made so perfectly in our parts that if someone were to taste it even once, they would forget all about the *halwa sohan* of Delhi?"'

I yawned and said, 'Majju Bhai, I want to know why you are telling me all this? It is hardly an answer to my question.'

'What can I do if you don't understand me? Well, never mind … forget about the UPwalas … let us talk about the Biharis. A Bihari friend subjected me to a long lecture on Islam, then pounced on me and asked, "What do you people think of us Biharis? You should know that Mahatma Buddha was also a Bihari." I said, "Yaar, you are very simple. Some humourist wrote that line and you have made off with it. One should never take the words of humourists with any degree of seriousness." He said, "But what's wrong with it?" I said, "There is nothing wrong but, yes, Mahatma Buddha may well have been a Bihari, but he was not a Bihari Musalman." Angrily, he shot back, "How does that matter?" I said, 'Huzoor, of course it matters. Had he been a Bihari Muslim, he would not have gone to Banaras. He would have travelled to Dhaka; and you can well imagine what he would have done there and what might have befallen him."'

The phone rang. I seized the opportunity and interrupted Majju Bhai. 'Majju Bhai, wait a minute; let me get the phone.' I ran to the phone, picked it up. 'Hello … ji … Oh, it is Tausif sahab … How are you?'

'Ask Tausif sahab when he is treating us to *kabab-parathe*?' Majju Bhai called out.

---

[19] A small *qasba* near Lucknow famous for its *laddus*.

'Yes, Majju Bhai is here … he is sitting right here … He is asking when you will be treating us to kabab-parathe … Oh, really? … Yes, please come … No, no … Majju Bhai won't go out at this time … He is talking to me right now … he is in full flow … On which subject? … Come and hear for yourself … All right … Come, we are waiting for you.' I put the phone down and informed Majju Bhai, 'Your Tausif sahab is on his way here.'

'Let him come … Now, let me tell you about the Meerutwalas.'

'Yes, I have been waiting for that,' I interrupted. 'Amroha, Badaun, Sandila, Shikarpur … we have heard about all of them. Why is my Meerut left out?'

'Listen, yaar, this young man Tausif … he is a bit too proud of being a Meeruti. His sister, whom I call Baji Akhtari, was very keen to get a good wife for her brother. I suggested the daughter of Saiyad Aqa Hasan, and she was delighted. Believe me, she drove me mad! She kept insisting that I get Tausif's marriage fixed with her. And so I praised Tausif to the skies before the girl's family. You won't know the lengths I had to go to sing his praises. In fact, the match was nearly fixed. Do you know what Tausif did to undo all my hard work? He sat in front of his prospective father-in-law and launched into a panegyric on the *gur rewri* and *gazak* of Meerut. And that gentleman is an old-fashioned Lucknowi sort who does not refer to a sweet as a sweet but by its correct name, such as *shirini* for a sweet, *qand* for table sugar, *nabad* for crystal sugar, and so on. And, when he wishes to eat cream, he starts by calling it *balai* and not *malai*, then mixes a dollop of *misri* and is perfectly content with one teaspoon. This praise of *gur rewri* and *gazak* could do nothing but annoy a fastidious, impeccably-mannered gentleman of the Old School. The news reached the ladies quarter. Bishho Bhabhi very nearly died of alarm. With tears in her eyes, she wailed: "Ai Majju Bhai, our daughter's fate is ruined. These people have turned out to be village yokels who eat *gur* and *khand*; how will our daughter manage to live with them?" Saiyad sahab added his bit, "My dear sir, we held our peace till the talk was confined to *rewri* and *gazak*; we swallowed the bitter pill and stayed quiet, but then the young gentleman launched into a paean on *til bugga*." When we asked what on earth was a *til bugga*, he replied, "Qibla, it is a concoction of *gur* and *til*. The famed *halwa sohan* of Delhi is dirt compared to it." My dear, I swear by the name of Ali, I was astounded …'

The narrative was in full swing when the doorbell rang. Majju Bhai stopped mid-sentence and said, 'Who has come?' Nemat Khan came out of the kitchen and leapt towards the door and returned almost immediately. 'Rafiq sahab is at the door.'

Rafiq sahab followed close on his heels. Majju Bhai got to his feet and met him with great warmth. 'Yaar, well done … good of you to come!'

'I thought Majju Bhai does not have the time, so let me go and meet him. So, how are you?'

'Don't ask about Majju Bhai right now; he is in fine fettle and going on and on,' I tacked on.

'Going on? But what about?'

'*Muhajirs*.'

'Splendid!' Rafiq sahab laughed loudly.

The talk turned towards Lucknow-walas. Majju Bhai said, 'They have such delicate temper. They won't allow the veritable fly to sit on their nose. You know our Aqqan sahab …'

'Aqqan sahab?' Rafiq sahab could not quite place him.

'Yaar, the same Aqa Hasan … we were talking about him earlier. Actually, his daughter is being married to Tausif. The poor thing is in a quandary.'

'Why?' Rafiq sahab asked. 'What's wrong with Tausif?'

'Is it a small fault that he belongs to a family from Meerut?'

Rafiq sahab laughed uproariously. 'So, the gentleman is in a dilemma, is he?'

Majju Bhai said, 'I told him, "Saiyad sahab, don't you have relatives from Lucknow who have given their daughter to a family from Lahore? I am talking about Rafiq sahab; he is a true blue Lahori." Tell me, Rafiq sahab, how was that?'

'Well said,' Rafiq sahab answered. 'So what did Saiyad sahab say?'

'What could he say? He was at a complete loss for words.'

Rafiq sahab said, 'Now listen to the tales of our relatives. Once, when one of them had to come to Karachi, he decided to bestow us with the pleasure of his company. The first thing he commented on, as soon as he came to our home, was my wife's pronunciation. But what worried him more was why I had chosen to live in this neck of the woods in Karachi. As soon as my wife went out of earshot, he asked in a hushed undertone, "Paaji, you are trapped; you should get out and look for a safer place." I said, "It will make no difference; no matter where I go I will be living in a trap." He asked, "What do you mean?" I said, "My wife is from Lucknow. Unfortunately, all my children are *ahl-e-zubaan*. So I am trapped even inside my home." And I laughed loudly.'

'Well said,' Majju Bhai said approvingly.

'Let me tell you about my younger son. As I was talking to my relative in Punjabi, my son was gaping at me. As soon as the visitor left, he asked, "Papa, what was this language you were speaking?" I said, 'Son, this is the language of your father and his forefathers.' Once again, Rafiq sahab let out a loud laugh.

I asked with utmost surprise, 'Rafiq sahab, you are a native of Lahore and your children do not know Punjabi; how is that possible?'

'Jawad sahab, first you must ask if my children know any Urdu at all?'

'Now that is a new one,' I said in increasing surprise. 'You have reduced Urdu to a language of the domestic realm, and that too not any Urdu but the pure Urdu of Lucknow.'

'Arre, Jawad sahab, don't ask about my state of affairs ... our children do not know any Punjabi because their mother is from Lucknow. And they know no Urdu because their Lucknowi mother studied in IT College.[20] So our children are bereft of both Urdu and Punjabi.'

---

[20] The Isabella Thoburn (IT) College in Lucknow was set up by an American missionary in 1870 to provide quality education to native Christian girls; it was a pioneering effort in the area of women's education in India.

'So which language do your children know?' Majju Bhai asked with some irritation.

Rafiq sahab heaved a long-suffering sigh and said, 'These IT-College types also write novels, you see. Children like ours speak in a pidgin of the IT-brand Urdu of these novels. I grew up reading Aatish and Mushafi; I cannot understand this language. Only they can understand it; them and their mother.' Rafiq sahab let out another loud laugh.

'*Subhan Allah*,' the words broke out of Majju Bhai's lips of their own volition.

'Yaar, Majju Bhai, you must help me in one small matter. You know all sorts of *muhajirs*; only you can help me.'

'Bhai, what do you need? I am at your service.'

'I am researching a special subject ... a truly unusual topic. You will praise me when you hear of it. The subject I have in mind is "Poetry and Hijrat". What do you think?'

'Very nice topic. Carry on.'

'Now I need two *muhajirs* who are *ahl-e-zubaan* but not poets.'

'Have you gone mad?' Majju Bhai asked. 'Are you bent upon proving the impossible?'

'All right, let me relax my conditions ... find me two *muhajirs* who may be poets but not writers of the ghazal.'

'Brother, you have taken up a difficult subject. Jawad, can you think of two such names?'

'It is a difficult question,' I answered softly.

The doorbell rang out. Once again, Nemat Khan came out of the kitchen and ran towards the door. This time when he returned, Tausif sahab was trotting behind him.

'Aaah ... Tausif sahab ...' Rafiq sahab rose to his feet and greeted the visitor.

'Rafiq sahab, it is a good thing we have met here; I have been calling you all morning and no one is picking up the phone.'

'I had left the house in the morning as soon as my wife left for her college; there was no one at home. Is all well?'

'Yes, all is well. I am in a hurry; I won't stay for long. I have come to tell you about the programme.'

'This is no way to show up … you can't come charging on the horse of the wind! Sit down, chat, have some tea,' Majju Bhai called out to Nemat Khan, 'How much longer for the tea?'

He answered from the kitchen, 'Just bringing it.'

'No, Majju Bhai, I am in a hurry; just hear me out. Tonight at 7:30 in the evening, in the kothi of the Nauchandiwalas….'[21]

'In the kothi of the Nauchandiwalas?' Majju Bhai interrupted him. 'Talk straight … you mean in your home … Okay … Carry on …'

'In the kothi of the Nuachandiwalas, that is, my home, tonight at 7:30 pm first, there will be a programme of parathas and seekh kababs and then a *mushaira*.'

'Are seekh kababs and parathas not sufficient unto themselves?'

'That is what I was about to say,' I added my bit.

'You misunderstood,' Majju Bhai said. 'The real programme is the *mushaira*; the seekh kababs and the parathas are the carrot … Think about it, gentlemen.'

'It is difficult,' Rafiq sahab and I spoke in unison.

'No, it isn't difficult at all,' Tausif announced the waiver. 'There is no compulsion to stay for the *mushaira*. You can leave after gracing the kabab-paratha programme with your presence. This special waiver will be applicable only for the two of you gentlemen.'

'But Tausif Miyan,' Majju Bhai said. 'Have some fear of the Lord! Is this the time for kabab-parathas? Terror has been unleashed upon the city and you are thinking of these indulgences!'

'Majju Bhai, poetry and kabab-parathas are entirely free of the snares of this world. '

'But what is the occasion?' Rafiq asked.

---

[21] This is a pretentious way of referring to himself and a sign of the upward mobility that is common among diaspora communities. Tausif is using the word kothi, which sounds grander and more royal, for his own house and calling Meerut by its more archaic name, Nauchandi.

'Curfew has been lifted from our neighbourhood; that's it.'

'But this is a fleeting happiness,' Majju Bhai said. 'Is there any knowing where things are headed? Every day, there is a new mischief, especially in your neighbourhood. Who knows, there might be some uproar tomorrow and curfew may be clamped again.'

'We will see what tomorrow brings; there is no curfew today.'

'Subhan Allah ... what a wonderful philosophy!'

'Majju Bhai,' Tausif said, 'Each one has to carve out one's own philosophy in order to survive. If not this, tell me a better way to stay alive in Karachi?'

Majju Bhai laughed, 'Yaar, you have left me speechless!'

'Majju Bhai,' I said, 'his way is not very different from yours.'

'Yaar, I have already conceded defeat; you too want to extract your pound of flesh right now?'

'All right then,' Tausif got up. 'We will talk again another time; I am in a hurry now. Please reach on time. If you are late, the kabab-parathas will be cold.'

'But, Miyan, how will the *mushaira* reach its real glory. The poets from Liaqatabad will not be able to come; their area is still under curfew.'

Majju Bhai's words stopped Tausif in his tracks.

'Majju Bhai, you are the limit! Can any power in this world stop a poet from coming to a *mushaira*? After all, what is a curfew?' And with these words, Tausif glanced at the watch strapped at his wrist and said. 'It is getting late; I must go.'

And like an arrow, he shot off ...

Three

'Ai Majju Bhai, this wretched city has dealt us a strange blow,' Basho Bhabhi burst out the moment we went and sat beside her. 'This sounds like the preface of a long *shehr ashob*;[22] Majju Bhai has got us in a fine mess,' I said to myself. Actually, we had set out from our home to eat the kabab-parathas of Meerut, and that too with some hesitation on my part. I had told Majju Bhai to go on his own as I wasn't at all keen.

'Arre yaar, how can you say that? It isn't such a bad deal ... you will be treated to kabab-parathas from Meerut.'

'Of course it is a bad deal ... there is the rider of the *mushaira* attached to it. It is all right for the poets ... rather for them it is a two-in-one deal. But for someone like me, who is not at all interested in poetry, of course it is a bad deal.'

'Yaar, you don't have to listen to the *mushaira*; it isn't as though it is mandatory. In any case, Tausif has already exempted you from attendance.'

'You mean I should eat the kabab-parathas and run away without paying their price? That isn't respectable, is it?'

'Then sit in the *mushaira* for some time, make some excuse and leave early.'

---

[22] A form of poetry, literally meaning 'misfortunes of the city', it expressed political and social decline as well as turmoil in the poet's immediate environment. The first proper *shehr ashob* is said to have been written by Mir Jafar Zatalli during the Mughal emperor Farrukhsiyar's reign (1713–1719). In some ways, much of Intizar Husain's work is in the nature of a *shehr ashob*.

'No, Majju Bhai, you go.'

'No, yaar, that can't be ... I can't go and eat the kabab-paratha alone. My conscience will prick me.'

When I saw there was no escaping Majju Bhai today, I decided to go ... whatever will be, will be. And when Majju Bhai got me along, he revealed his true motive.

'Actually, Jawad Miyan, you are becoming somewhat dense. You become agitated in the company of your fellow men. You go to the office and come back ... and that's it. Is that any way to live your life? You should meet people, or else you will become a mental patient.'

'Meet whom? Your kind of people bore me.'

'They seem boring to you because you don't meet them. They are boring, yes, but not as boring as you seem to think. They are as interesting as they are boring. Now I will introduce you to them properly.'

'So, this will be a long programme?'

'Yes, you might well say so. Now that we are stepping out, we will stop by briefly at Saiyad Aqa Hasan's house first. The husband and wife are a very interesting couple, typical Lucknow-walas!'

Majju Bhai has always had the same modus operandi. He has never walked the straight path; he always has these halts along the way. So, this was our first halt. And Basho Bhabhi did not let us pause to draw breath. She got going from the moment we sat down.

'Bhabhi,' Majju Bhai said. 'It isn't just Karachi; this is happening all over the country.'

'Bhai Majidul Husaini, you are correct; this turbulence has engulfed the entire country,' Saiyad Aqa Hasan agreed with Majju Bhai in his ponderous tone. 'This is what I keep trying to tell your sister-in-law that, my dear, why do you fret over Karachi; the entire country is in a mess. It is a reign of tyranny and dictatorship. Those who were low born roll in wealth and the *shurfa* go hungry for even one meal. And on top of it all, no one's life or property is safe.'

'It's all very well to say that the entire country is up in arms,' Basho Bhabhi stressed, 'But my brothers, what is happening in Karachi today has probably never happened anywhere else in the world … no home is safe. Arre, I am saying go and rob the homes of those who have mounds of wealth, but spare the respectable folk. What riches did poor Achchi Bi have in her house? Those black-faced wretches jumped into her home too.'

'Oh,' Majju Bhai said in alarm, 'So there was a theft in Achchi Bi's house?'

'Ai, brother, you didn't know?'

'No, I had no clue.'

'It is a good thing that she escaped with her life at least. Nowadays, one loses one's life along with one's goods. You know how easily I get upset; when I heard about this I nearly fainted. I immediately took a taxi and reached her house somehow or the other. I saw her alive and was hugely relieved.'

'So what were the losses?'

'Brother, forget about losses; after all, Achchi Bi is a Delhiwali. She is not one to suffer fools gladly. She gave them such a tough time that the thieves ran off. But, brother, I am asking you: After all, what is going on in Karachi? Robberies and thefts have been going on since time immemorial; even dacoities are an old practice. My elder uncle used to tell us how once, in his Faizabad,[23] there was such a robbery that the Basant Mahalwalas were nearly swept clean. The thieves had even taken off the chandeliers and walked away with them. My elder uncle used to tell us how the robbers had come armed with pick axes as well as a monitor lizard and ropes. You know how the monitor lizard sticks to walls as though stuck with glue. They tied ropes around it and flung it up the parapets. No wonder they scaled the high walls of Basant Mahal with such ease! But these things happened when we were barely in our senses. Now when we see what is happening before our eyes, it is enough

---

[23] A town in UP beside the historic city of Ayodhya, it was once the capital of Awadh.

to make us lose our senses. Who are these trouble makers? May the curse of Hazrat Abbas fall upon them ... O Sher-e-Khuda,[24] why are you tarrying? Why don't you destroy them?'

'Yes, Sher-e-Khuda can be the only saviour; it is no good expecting anything from these rulers.'

'Arre, I call out to Maula Mushkil Kusha five times a day; I ask him to remove our troubles, rid us of these robbers and thieves. May they be wracked by diarrhoea; they have sown such calamity. They have not the slightest fear of god. The robbers of the past had some fear of Allah and His prophet. Take for instance, Sultana Daku[25] from our part of the world.'

'Sultana Daku?'Aqa Hasan spoke with a gleam in his eyes. 'He was one of his kind; you don't have dacoits like him anymore.'

'The poor thing was needlessly defamed. He was a God-fearing man,' Basho Bhabhi paused, then carried on, 'This wretched world has a strange custom: the bad are good and those who have acquired a bad name are necessarily bad. You can carry on doing the worst misdeeds as long as you have drawn a curtain over them. Those who don't draw a curtain over their actions are the worst culprits. What did poor Sultana do? He robbed the rich and helped the poor. He arranged for the dowries of so many daughters of poor fathers. He only needed to know which home had a young unmarried girl; then, whether he had to rob or pillage, he would arrange for the girl's dowry. And these modern-day robbers? They are stone-hearted.'

'Bhabhi,' Majju Bhai said, 'You are right, but a robber is a robber.'

'Ai Bhaiyya, I am not disputing that; a robber may turn into an angel, but he will remain a robber. All I am saying is these new-

---

[24] Sher-e-Khuda, 'Lion of Allah', was an epithet for Ali. He is also referred to as Mushkil Kusha, the Easer of Difficulties. Abbas was the son of Ali. Given the frequent allusions to Ali and the Battle of Karbala, it is evident Aqa Hasan's family is Shia; as is Intizar Husain.

[25] Sultana Daku was a near-legendary robber in undivided India, a latter-day Robin Hood.

fangled robbers are not even real robbers. They are pickpockets. It is like putting a blade in the hands of a monkey. These robbers have got hold of guns, which they use with great alacrity. They don't see who they are using it on, or which house they are breaking into. May the heavens fall upon them! May the blood of Husain curse them! They broke into the home of our Laddan sahab, pointed a gun at his chest and robbed him of his entire life's savings and still they were not satisfied. One said, "Qibla, you have disappointed us. Maulvis are supposed to have great wealth. I am sorry to trouble you, but give me a talisman." The maulvi asked, "A talisman for what?" The wretch said, "Qibla, what shall I say? I am always troubled; there is no prosperity in this work. No matter how much I gather, everything goes away and I remain as poor as ever. Write a talisman for me so that I may remain in a state of plenty and prosperity." ... Plenty and prosperity indeed,' Basho Bhabhi made a face and muttered, 'Someone should ask that black-faced scoundrel: Has any one heard of plenty and prosperity from ill-gotten gains?'

Saiyad Aqa Hasan began as soon as Basho Bhabhi fell silent. 'Bhai Majidul Husaini, this is nothing but vengeance and calamity. People are being robbed in broad daylight. No one takes any action against the robbers.'

These words served as a prod for Basho Bhabi. She started off again, 'Aji, you are talking of daylight robberies; here healthy young men are being abducted in broad daylight and no one does anything. In our Lucknow, in my entire life, there was only one such incident when on a desolate afternoon, a child was picked up as he was playing in a deserted alley. That caused such uproar in the entire city, even though it was only a child and he was not abducted against his will. Those wretched fellows had a mirror; they would show the mirror to a child and it would follow them blindly. Now things have reached such a pass that a fully grown up man is caught, trussed up and thrown into a car and sped off with.'

Saiyad Aqa Hasan gathered the strands of this conversation and gave them the form of a commonly-asked question, 'Bhai Majidul

Husaini, things have reached a very sorry state. Where will we go from here?'

Majju Bhai was a blithe spirit. Has anyone heard of a leech sticking to a stone? Basho Bhabhi and Saiyad Aqa Hasan had narrated their tales of woe with such heart-felt sorrow and look at the breezy disregard in Majju Bhai's answer. 'Wherever the Lord pleases!'

'Only He knows what He pleases to be, but He has given us some sense too. Surely, you too must be occasionally reflecting on what might happen?'

'Bhai Aqqan, you ask very difficult questions.'

'My dear sir, these are difficult times. Tell me, who should we go to for justice? What do these people here know about the sorrows we have faced? With such grief we have pulled up our roots and dragged ourselves across these long hard miles? And here … here we have seen new twists and turns. So, tell me, my dear sir … that is what I am asking you: what lies ahead?'

'The sea.'

Majju Bhai answered with the same carelessness. Saiyad Aqa Hasan understood partly. He was about to say something when Basho Bhabhi broke in, 'Aji, what is this nonsense you have started? What are you going on about? Let me talk to Majju Bhai. Ai Majju Bhai, tell me who these Meerutwalas were back in the old days?'

And now for the first time in the entire conversation, Majju Bhai looked a bit uncomfortable. 'What were they back then? They were human beings, God's children, well-to-do and respectable.'

'Respectable? I see,' Basho Bhabhi paused and reflected, then said, 'A lady from Meerut had come to our home. She said, these people used to sharpen scissors back then and were Kamboh.[26] I was amazed when I heard this. I lost my sleep from that night.

[26] Also spelt as Kamboj, they are descendants of a Kshatriya tribe that traces its roots to the Iron Age; the Muslim Kambohs, the great majority of whom migrated to Pakistan and settled in Karachi, were agriculturists. More than their occupation, for someone like Basho Bhabhi, marrying a Kamboh is a matter of great shame and dishonour also because they are Sunni Muslims.

Majju Bhai, I swear upon Ali, when we had left Lucknow, never in our wildest dreams had we thought that when we reach Karachi, we will marry our daughter among those who sharpen knives and the tag of Kamboh would be patched onto the *saadat*.'[27]

Majju Bhai had become quite perturbed by now. In an attempt to smoothen things, he said, 'Basho Bhabhi, don't go by idle chatter; you know better than I do that people say all sorts of things when a marriage is being fixed.'

'Majju Bhai, let me talk straight. I was about to say yes because we trust you.'

Saiyad Aqa Hasan picked up his wife's words and said, 'My dear sir, I didn't see any difficulty in this match, but we were a little distressed when we saw the young man's behaviour.'

'Oh,' Majju Bhai asked with some concern. 'Did Tausif sahab do something to upset you?

'No, no, nothing. He seems to be an intelligent and respectful young man, but it seems as though he has grown up too quickly. Let us not talk about his way of speaking or his taste in poetry, for we have seen the state of affairs in this city, where people proffer praise for poetry that is entirely without rhythm or rhyme. And I tell myself that after all this is not Lucknow. This land is different; its sky is different. My complaint about the lack of good taste is out of place. So why should we raise fingers at the lack of good taste in poor Tausif Miyan. It is just that it caused us a twinge of dismay or two.'

Majju Bhai spoke in a consolatory tone, 'Bhai Aqqan, don't get upset over this. I am on my way to their house. I will talk to the young man. And Basho Bhabhi, my sincere request to you is that you don't pay any heed to others and don't be in a hurry to make a decision. You make as many enquiries as you like to satisfy yourself fully.'

'Brother, we have not declined their offer yet; after all, you are the intermediary and it isn't as though we don't trust you. We have

---

[27] Refers to those who are descendants of Prophet Muhammad, Aqa Hasan's family being Saiyad and Shia can claim such a lineage.

to make some enquiries because of the unrest that has been caused by that wretched Meerutwali.'

Majju Bhai thought prudence demanded that we make a hasty exit. So he got to his feet.

'Majju Bhai, you have gotten up; after all, what is the hurry?'

'There is a *mushaira* at the Meerutwalas and also a dinner of Peshawari parathas and kabab … a two-in-one deal. What do you think?'

'Arre Bhai Majidul Hussaini, what can we say? Our ears and our stomach both have something to say. I don't have the patience to listen to these new-fangled *mushairas*, nor the stamina to digest these new kinds of food.'

We came out and breathed a sigh of relief. Ordinarily, we would have left to go towards the Meerutwalas, but Majju Bhai let loose another firecracker on the way. He looked at the watch strapped on his wrist and muttered, 'Yes, there is still time.' And he turned towards me and said, 'Yaar Jawad, what do you say … should we not stop by and look in on Achchi Bi. We should find out how she fared at the hands of the robbers.'

'But you have found out through your Basho Bhabhi,' I said coolly.

'Yaar, didn't you notice her tone? These Lucknow-walas don't let any opportunity to taunt the Delhiwalas pass. The poor lady had a robbery, but still Basho Bhabhi couldn't resist her jibes. We will get to know the real story only from Achchi Bi herself. And, after all, you used to know her husband, Mirza sahab too once upon a time.'

'Yes, I did. In fact, I worked in his office for some time. I meet him sometimes when he comes to the bank. But these official meetings can hardly be called meeting.'

'Well, he remembers you often. Whenever I meet him, he asks after you. He is the constant sort. We too should show some constancy towards him.'

'Yes, we should, but won't your kabab-paratha go cold waiting for you?'

'I have looked at my watch before raising the subject; there is enough time. It isn't as though we have to sit there for very long. We only have to ask about their well-being. After all, it is on the way. And it isn't as though you will use up too much petrol.'

Now there was no way I could say 'No' to Majju Bhai. So, on our way to the Meerutwalas, I turned the direction of my car and ended up knocking at Mirza sahab's door. Mirza sahab was pleased to see us, especially me. 'Arre, where have you been?' and turning towards Majju Bhai, he said, 'Majju Bhai, it is a good thing you have brought Jawad here. I am seeing this dear young man after such a long time. Hope you are well, my dear?'

'Allah be praised.'

'Yes, Allah should be praised, for any time that passes without any mishap is a good time.'

'We had come to ask about you,' Majju Bhai said. 'We are coming from Bhai Aqqan's house and there we found out that the robbers had graced your home too. We are coming straight from there just to ask if all is well.'

At that very moment, Achchi Bi came in. 'Ai, I was wondering who has come ... Who are you talking to?'

'Majju Bhai is here and our dear friend Jawad Miyan, too ... So you have heard about the robbery ... and you want to know whether all is well.'

'Ai Bhaiyya, of course all is well. What was there in our home for them to rob? Our daughter-in-law has swept us clean in any case. What was left for the robbers to take? I told them straight off: "You black-faced wretches, what does a poor woman like me have? Had you come to our home in the Suiwala Mohulla,[28] may Allah forbid me from lying, there we had mounds of riches. We left that house with nothing but the clothes on our back. Whatever we had here, belonged to our daughter-in-law, and she took everything away. Why have you put this gun on my throat? Go and put it on hers; she will spit out all her gold." They asked, "Where is she?" I

[28] A neighbourhood in Shahjahanabad, in what is now Old Delhi

said, "May God's curses be on you; you don't even know that? She has made her own home in Clifton and has walked away with her gold and jewels." Ai Bhaiyya, those fellows could barely believe me. I said, "Okay, my purse is lying in the niche there. My entire life's savings are there. Go and see what is in it. And pass me the *paandan* too while you are at it." The wretches turned my purse upside down; what was there to find in it. They glared at me with hateful eyes as though they would eat me up. My only worry was that they might go off with my *paandan*. My elder uncle had got it especially from Moradabad. It was such a long time ago, but its shine is still intact.'

'Anyhow, so all is well … no harm done.'

'Ai Bhaiyya, there would have been some loss had I gathered my son's wealth. Thanks to our daughter-in-law, we are not in a state to be harmed. Other ladies told me, why did I have to talk about my daughter-in-law's faults in front of the robbers? Earlier, I used to think so too … if you keep a lamp made of dough inside your home, a mouse will eat it and if you keep it outdoors, a crow will make off with it. And so I used to quietly bear it all and never say a word to anyone. But now things have reached such a pass, now whether it is a wayfarer, a stranger, a thief, a robber, a dacoit, I shall hold everyone by the hand and tell them what my daughter-in-law has done to me. Let me see how anyone can stop me?'

'Let it be, Saadat's mother; he will carry the burden of his deeds and we will carry ours.'

'Aji, how can I let it go? I let it go for years; now I will not be silenced. Ai Majju Bhai, this new age of yours has been a calamitous one. The very notion of shame is absent in girls nowadays. Earlier they used to be confined to the house; the only time they crossed the threshold was when they left for their marital home in their *doli*. In our Delhi, old timers used to say that a good wife enters her home in a *doli* and leaves on a bier.'

'Saadat's mother, which world are you talking about? This is a new world. Miyan Majju Bhai, as though this world is not bad enough, on top of that there's this city of yours. I don't feel like staying alive anymore. All sorts of rogues and upstarts, thieves, robbers and terrorists have a field day; the respectable folk are at their wits' end. Where have we ended up?'

'Ai Majju Bhai,' Achchi Bi interrupted, 'By God, we were happily planted like a pillar in the middle of Suiwala Mohulla; we were needlessly caught in the middle of this blasted Hindu-Muslim business.'

'And now we have been caught in the middle of this new business,' Mirza sahab observed softly.

'Aji, now we have no option but to be ruined even more. We are a leaf that was snapped from its branch; those were different days, that time was different. Truly, we were planted like a pillar. *Masha Allah*, we were well regarded After all, we had been there for generations, rich from birth. My dear departed father-in-law was such a renowned hakim that even jinnat used to come to him for treatment! Brother, you may find this hard to believe, but he had treated the king of the jinns. My mother-in-law used to tell us how, once, he disappeared for three days. "People looked for him all over the city. On the third day, he was seen getting off a buggy; two tall labourers carried two sacks filled with gold coins atop their head," she used to say. "I was amazed, and suddenly the buggy too disappeared as did the labourers. Dumbstruck, I looked at your Abba Miyan and then at the sacks filled with gold coins. Your Abba Miyan said, "Don't ask. Just keep them." Later, he told us how the king of jinnat had double pneumonia. "When I reached he was nearly at death's door. Allah is the keeper of honour: he kept my honour and saved him." So, Bhaiyya, that was the sort of hakim my father-in-law was. Till he lived, the king of the jinns would come, offer his gift and go away with a box of *khamira*. It was a special sort of *khamira*. Abba Miyan never told us exactly what its ingredients were.' Then turning towards Mirza sahab, Achchi Bi said, 'Aji, why don't you tell them; after all, you must have witnessed many of his miracles?'

Mirza sahab paused, then said, 'My father, may Allah grant him paradise, was not any old hakim; he was also a man blessed with many great miraculous powers. Along with the medicines, he also believed in prayer; that is why his treatment was more effective. Once, something very strange happened.' Pointing towards Achchi Bi, he said, 'An acquaintance of her grandfather, who had just come back from the hajj, saw my father in her grandfather's sitting room and kept looking at him. When my father left, he asked her grandfather, "Who was that young man?" Her grandfather said, "He was my granddaughter's husband." The gentleman asked, "When did he return from Medina?" Her grandfather asked in astonishment, "You are talking about Medina? He has never set foot outside Delhi." Then that gentleman said, "I have seen him giving a lecture in the Masjid-e-Nabvi[29]."'Mirza sahab fell silent, and then after a pause, heaved a long sigh and said, 'We had witnessed such an age; now we are seeing this one. Truly, one doesn't feel like living, but what can one do? ... One has to live till there is life.'

And with these words, Mirza sahab fell into deep thought. Then, in a sorrowful tone, he said. 'How did this subject arise? I try not to remember those days; it troubles me. There was a time when I remembered it a lot ... that time, that city. Jawad Miyan, you used to work with me in the office then; surely you remember. How I used to suffer like a fish out of water.'

'Yes, I remember. I have heard many a tale about Delhi from you.'

'But can you believe me when I say I do not even mention Delhi anymore? I have accepted my lot. It is only today, when your sister-in-law has raised the subject, I have taken its name.'

'Aji, I have tried my best to forget it too, but that wretched daughter-in-law of mine doesn't let me forget. Out there, could any daughter-in-law have let out even a squeak in front of their mothers-in-law? The mothers-in-law would have pulled out their eyeballs from their sockets. These daughters-in-law go about like tigresses now, and mine is a special case. She is so saccharine sweet on the surface. How

---

[29] The prophet's mosque in Medina is one of the most holy mosques for Muslims.

she goes around pretending to praise me and calling me "Khala". I feel like telling her "Khala's brat, you have turned your khala into a scarecrow and put her away." But then I fall silent thinking she will embellish whatever I say and run with tall tales to my son.'

'Saadat's mother, forgive her; after all, she is your son's wife.'

'I have forgiven her; that is why I say nothing to her. My son should be happy; we two old people are happy if our son is happy.'

'So, Achchi Bi,' Majju Bhai asked, 'should you forgive just because you are relics of the past? These young people don't understand so much that was good in the past.' And with these words, Majju Bhai rose to his feet.

'Ai Bhaiyya, what is this? You just got here, and you are leaving already?'

'Achchi Bi, kabab-parathas are waiting for us at the Meerutwalas.'

And indeed when we reached the Meerutwalas, the round of kabab and parathas was in full swing. A pile of parathas, the size of an elephant's ear, was immediately placed before us. Tausif was working his way around the crowd. How well he played the role of the host; he moved from one table to the next and then raced to the third. At every table, he would ask, 'How are the parathas?' And each time he would say, 'We used to have the Nauchandi mela in our Meerut and that's where we used to get these parathas. They were so delicious that people smacked their lips and waited for the next Nauchandi mela to come around the next year. You may regard this too as our Nauchandiwala paratha and these seekh kababs … the kababi who sat in the Khair Nagar area of our city made such fabulous kababs. These are the Khair Nagar "brand" seekh kababs.'

As he worked the crowd, Tausif came to our table. 'Majju Bhai, shall I get you some more paratha?'

'No, no, this is enough.'

'Majju Bhai, this is the Nauchandiwala paratha. If you find the slightest iota of difference in taste you may beat me on my head with your shoe … Tell me, Jawad Bhai, isn't it exactly like the Nauchandiwala paratha?'

'Hundred per cent Nauchandiwala!'

'Yaar,' Majju Bhai couldn't resist asking, 'If the real Nauchandiwala has come here, the people of Meerut must be cursing us. It isn't good to take someone's curses.'

'His brother is still there.'

'Then it is all right.'

'And the kabab? Yes, do try the kababs … They are fresh off the skewers,' and with these words, he slid a heap of kababs onto our plates. Then he said, 'Tell me, Majju Bhai, are you not reminded of the kababs of Khair Nagar?'

'I told Jawad after tasting the very first morsel, "So, Tausif Miyan has treated us to the kababs of Khair Nagar. Who is the kababi? Must be his son or grandson?"'

'No, actually, there was a young boy those days who used to sit and fan the coal braziers. He was a smart cookie. He made off with the recipe of the spice-mixture and set up business here.'

'Good.'

'Yes, he is better than his ustad. His kababs are even better than those ones.'

'So, Tausif Miyan, tell us how long this business of kabab paratha will continue? When do you plan to start the *mushaira*?'

'Soon. I am just about to wrap up the kabab-parathas.'

Tausif was about to move on when Majju Bhai stopped him, 'Ustad, you look busy. Come and sit with us when you have a moment; I need to talk to you.'

'I will come as soon as I can.'

'And where is Baji Akhtari?'

'She is busy with the ladies.'

'Please send her too.'

'Is it something important?'

'Yes.'

'May god help us,' Tausif guessed from Majju Bhai's tone that it was a serious matter.

'I will come just now,' and with these words, Tausif sped off. Walking among the tables, chit-chatting with the guests, he disappeared from sight.

Soon, Baji Akhtari appeared. 'Arre Majju Bhai, why aren't you eating?'

'We have eaten a lot.'

'Ai wah, how can that be? And, Jawad, you too have stopped … Why, didn't you like the parathas?'

'They were delicious; I ate my fill.'

'And,' Majju Bhai added his bit, 'we ate so much that our bellies are bloated.'

Meanwhile, Tausif too showed up.

'Baji Akhtari,' Majju Bhai broached the subject, 'try and make your brother understand that it isn't good to always jest everywhere.'

'Ai, what happened? Tausif, what is Majju Bhai saying?'

'I don't understand, Majju Bhai.'

'Yes, why would you understand? Miyan, when you went there, could you not find a better subject for conversation … you read a panegyric in praise of the *gur rewri* of Meerut. Those people talk of *qand* and *nabaat*; you want to make them eat the *rewri* of Meerut? Anyhow, that was then … it seems you have been up to some new mischief now.'

'No, no, Majju Bhai, nothing of the sort.'

'Obviously something is wrong. It appears you have subjected them to a lecture on poetry.'

Tausif laughed. 'Oh, I see, Majju Bhai. You see, Saiyad sahab was busy reciting the verses of his oh-so-eloquent poet Hazrat Safi Lucknowi. I thought let me also tell him a thing or two about some poet from Meerut. So I told him a few sparkling verses by Boom Hapuri.[30] His forehead creased at the very mention, even though I had heard the verses of Safi Lucknowi with the utmost attention and patience.'

Majju Bhai struck his forehead. 'The verses of Boom Hapuri, and that too in front of that refined gentleman from Lucknow!

---

[30] Boom means owl; so one can well imagine the level of poetry. Hapur is a small town close to Meerut and part of the belt where Khari Boli is spoken.

Could you think of no other poet from your Meerut? At the very least, you could have read out something by Bayan Yazdani.'

'Bayan Yazdani? What a thing to say, Majju Bhai! I will bring Bayan Yazdani into the battleground when Saiyad sahab recites his Aatish and Mushafi.'

Majju Bhai was trumped by Tausif. Now, he turned imploringly towards Baji Akhtari, 'Baji, make this impetuous youth understand how delicate these marriage-related matters are! It is all very well to talk in this callow manner among friends, but you can't talk like this with your prospective in-laws. The last time he went, he read a panegyric in praise of *til bugga* and *gur rewri*; this time, he recited the verses of Boom Hapuri in front of that elegantly rhetorical and gravely ponderous gentleman.'

'Baji, those people mention their Lucknowi culture with such reverence that I too had to give them a glimpse of our Meeruti culture.'

'Fine glimpse you gave them!' Majju Bhai retorted acidly.

Baji Akhtari heard them out in silence. Then, she said, 'Majju Bhai, you know what a jester he has always been. He is not going to change his ways for them. But, Majju Bhai, I must say these Lucknow-walas have their head in the clouds. And Basho Bhabhi ... she is up there in the skies ... she can't be bothered with lesser mortals. God knows what that arrogance is all about. They may have been big people in Lucknow. Perhaps they had elephants tied at their gate; here, I have seen no sign of their greatness, and it isn't as though there is something extraordinary about their daughter either. Fine, so she is educated. But she is also a bit tart. Doesn't have an ounce of flesh; she is all skin and bone. Arre, that girl from the Hyderabadi family is better; at least, there is some flesh on her body. She is cheerful and what is more, she is extremely domesticated. And those people are all set to fix the marriage. I am stuck here with these Lucknowi people only because I had broached the subject.'

Majju Bhai finally unlocked his tongue. He said, 'Baji Akhtari, that is all right. You seem to like that other girl; why don't you bring her as your brother's bride? But remember that she is from Hyderabad. She will drive Tausif mad by feeding him *khatti daal* and *bhagare baingan!*'[31]

'Ai Bhaiyya, at least she will cook for him. I don't set much store by the Lucknow-wali. These people don't let anybody come close in their arrogance in being Lucknow-walas. Then there is also the girl from the Pilibhitwalas. How friendly they are! And their daughter is a gem! So, there is no shortage of girls for us. Let the Lucknow-walas understand loud and clear ... and let them understand we will not brook any more nonsense. Nor will we wait much longer. We have waited enough. Let them not keep us dangling. Let them give us a final yes or no. We want a clear answer.'

'Majju Bhai,' Tausif added, 'I have had enough of the Lucknow-walas; I want to steer clear of them.'

'What do you mean, Tausif Miyan?' Now Majju Bhai too sounded a bit sharp. 'They are respectable people. You have sent a proposal; you can't run away now. The other side also has their honour.'

'Just think, Majju Bhai. And Jawad Bhai, you are a disinterested party; you serve the cause of justice. I am a Meerutiya, I speak Khari Boli. Can I call *malai balai*? Those people will drive me crazy with their idioms dipped in the waters of the Gomti River.'

Majju Bhai held his head and said, 'Do you see, Jawad Miyan, the state of this fifth community?'[32]

'Ai Majju Bhai, let it be; you know how he has the habit of jesting. He will do exactly as I tell him to.' And she immediately

---

[31] Both are traditional Hyderabadi dishes; the daal is tart and flavoured with tamarind and the dish of aubergines too is extremely spicy and sour. Their flavours are very distinct from Lucknowi cuisine which is more subtle.

[32] The newly-created state of Pakistan (West Pakistan) had four provinces and four principal communities from these provinces, namely Punjabi, Sindhi, Balochi and Pathan. The fifth community comprised the *muhajirs*, referred to as the *panchvi qaumiyat*.

turned towards Tausif and said, 'Arre, exactly what sort of wife do you want? A star from the heavens won't come down for you. I looked for a good girl as far as I could.'

'Good? Why, she is very good,' Majju Bhai took the cue and added the weight of his approval. 'Miyan, she is educated, genteel, comes from a good family. What else do you want?'

'I like her myself. I was hurt when Basho Bhabhi began to find faults with our family. At least, she should have made some enquiries. She believed whatever our enemies told her. So Majju Bhai, please make her see sense. I too will go and meet her. I don't have my nose up in the air, like people from the boy's side usually do. I will give her every possible assurance and they should not have any concern about Tausif not having a job yet. Insha Allah he will get one soon. Their daughter will know no scarcity in our home.'

'I have explained all this to them. The crux of the matter is that some people from your Meerut have gone to them and said all sorts of strange things. But I gave them an appropriate rejoinder. Both Basho Bhabhi and Aqa Hasan are extremely respectable people.'

'Yes, I know that; after all, they are from Lucknow. They are not nobodies from nowhere. And we have no shortage of enemies. That is why I want this business to be concluded soon.'

'I agree; a hundred problems arise when things get stretched out.'

'So, Majju Bhai, get them to agree.' Akhtari Baji had come down from her pedestal and Tausif too put a lock on his tongue. Majju Bhai was in fine fettle. He was counting the many fine qualities of the girl, her parents and her entire family. But my attention had wandered. In any case, I become restless at the mention of engagements and weddings. And this particular conversation had stretched too long … at least for me. My glance wandered to a table and rested on a face. A long beard, a green robe, a green kurta, he looked like a parrot. A rosary clicked away between his fingers. As soon as Baji Akhtari and Tausif took their leave, I asked Majju Bhai, 'Who is that gentleman over there?'

'You don't know him? What a heedless man you are! He is Ghazi sahab.' And then raising his voice he called out, 'Ghazi sahab, adab. Hope you are well. And how far has your movement reached?'

'My movement is an indication of your vigour in your faith and your keenness to save it. I am giving the *azaan* in the wilderness.'

An elderly gentleman, who sat nearby, let out a sigh and said, 'There is no vigour of faith, and no keenness to save it left, now.'

Ghazi sahab came back swiftly, 'Yes, and we are being punished for it. *Fa tabiru ya ullil absar* ...'[33] and with these words, the tone of his voice changed and Ghazi sahab seemed to be delivering a sermon. 'O you who sleep, how long will you be lost in heedlessness? Look how far the world has overtaken you. You prisoners of wrongdoings, you have remained where you were. These people from the West are reaching the skies and we are sinking further in the pit of hellishness. And those devils have done so much ... they have handed our youth their books of science and philosophy and put them on the path of godlessness. And they have created the atom bomb for themselves. People are going on about Musalman-Musalman. I ask you: Who is a Musalman? Where is he? I can't see one for miles all around. If there is a Musalman let him come before me. I will tell him what it means to be one ... *Yeh shahadat gah-e-ulfat mein qadam rakhna hai* ...[34] And my friends, I know a simple truth ... If we were indeed Musalman, we would have created the atom bomb. The others would have gaped at us. May the Lord forgive us our sins! The atom bomb was in our destiny; it was made and ready. Those wretched New Light fellows, who go about as graduates, had they read about the Last Day, they would have known better. But because of our heedlessness and the cleverness of the others, now they have the atom bomb.'

---

[33] A verse from the Quran which means 'See and learn, O you who have sense'.

[34] *Yeh shahadat gah-e ulfat mein qadam rakhna hai*
Log aasaan samajhtey hein Musalman hona
(This martyrdom is akin to setting foot on the path of love
Yet people think it is easy being a Musalman)

This verse is by the Urdu poet Iqbal.

'But my dear Ghazi sahab,' the elderly gentleman sitting nearby asked, 'what is the way out?'

'That is a good question. Those who feel the pain of Islam and the twinge of Belief come to me and ask me the remedy for this decline. Ghazi Ataullah tells them, "There is a remedy, and a very simple one: Compliance and only compliance ... Western science and philosophy will give you nothing, nothing except godlessness. Get out of this valley of thorns. Friends, my passion does not accept these trickeries of the mind. This is nothing but the work of Abu Lahab[35]. I am in search of 313[36] mad men who will come and engage in battle with the Abu Lahabs and Abu Jahls, whose passion will not merely face the mighty mountains of hatred against Islam in the East and the West but also break those mountains into smithereens. Three hundred and thirteen mad men, that is, 313 true Musalmans; the day they get together, that day Ataullah Ghazi will not be seen in the city of Karachi; he will be on the other side of the border. The first namaz will be in the Babri Masjid and the second in the Masjid al-Aqsa.'[37]

---

[35] Abu Lahab was Prophet Muhammad's paternal uncle who steadfastly opposed Islam. He is condemned by name in the Surah Masad in the Quran. Abu Lahab's wife, Umme Jamil used to strew thorns in Muhammad's path and throw garbage on him when he walked past. Abu Jahl, whose real name was Amr ibn Hisham, was one of the pagan leaders of the Quraysh tribe known for their hostility towards Muhammad and the early Muslims in Mecca. Such was his malevolence and relentless enmity, that he acquired the moniker Abu Jahl ('Father of Ignorance') in his lifetime, despite his other gifts of wisdom and courage. The Battle of Badr was the result of his obstinacy and refusal to accept Muhammad as the messenger of a new religion.

[36] In Islamic history, 313 is the number of Muslims who fought in the Battle of Badr and by extension, Islam's, foes. It was a decisive Muslim victory against a force of over 1,000 adversaries: the Muslims lost only 14 men. The battle also took place on March 13, or 3/13, hence the significance of the number.

[37] Masjid al-Aqsa, a mosque in Jerusalem beside the Dome of the Rock, is the third holiest site in Islam after the mosques in Mecca and Medina.

'Ghazi sahab,' Majju Bhai interrupted, 'Isn't it a somewhat long programme?'

Ghazi sahab looked at Majju Bhai with smouldering eyes. 'It is this faintness of faith that has defeated us. Think, you ignorant people, think of what we were and what we have become. We are those who had raced horses in the oceans;[38] why is our resolve broken now? After all, how long is the distance between Babri Masjid and Masjid al-Aqsa? But the feebleness of our faith has made our steps feeble too. I have been shouting for such a long time that I need 313 Muslims for my programme, but it is as though Allah has put locks on their heart and ears.' Ghazi sahab paused and then said in a pain-filled voice. 'Or perhaps, my own faith is limited. If the fire of faith is intense in one's heart, then one's words have heat and passion too. When I think that I will be asked to give my answer on the Day of Judgement: "Ai Ataullah, to what extent did you pay your debt to your faith? Could you not even gather 313 Musalman?", then I break out in goose bumps and find myself overwhelmed.' And with these words, Ghazi sahab became overwhelmed with emotions.

Seeing Ghazi sahab in that state, Baji Akhtari grew alarmed and, in a panicky voice, called out to Tausif. Tausif came running and stood respectfully before Ghazi sahab with a glass of cold water. 'Qibla, have some water.'

---

[38] Referring to a verse by Iqbal in his long poem *Shikwa* (The Complaint): '*Dasht to dasht thhey darya bhi na chhode hamne/Bahr-e-zulmat mein daura diye ghore hamne*' (Forget the deserts, we even raced our horses in the dark regions of the oceans. The Bahr-e-Zulmat is said to be a name for the Atlantic Ocean. The 'we' here is a reference to the Muslims.

Four

'Majju Bhai, what happened to that match you were fixing between Meerut and Lucknow?'

Majju Bhai looked closely at me. He seemed to be amused by my question. 'That's a good question. I am pleased. It means you are in good spirits now.'

I was a bit surprised by that last comment. 'What do you mean?'

'I mean, earlier you were completely cut off from the life of Karachi. You used to taunt me that I am engrossed in the pointless matters of all sorts of useless people. Now, Masha Allah, you seem to be interested in them and in their affairs. It is a good sign.'

'You have misunderstood me. I am not in the least interested in them or in their meaningless lives. If anything, what interests me is that something substantial should emerge from the interest you take in other people's lives.'

Majju Bhai laughed, 'So be it! As long as you have an iota of interest in the life around you! At least you have come here. I am happy; it is a healthy sign.'

Majju Bhai had every reason to be happy. He had succeeded in his mission. Taking me for a mental patient, he had devised a remedy to pull me out of my shell of loneliness. 'He will sit among people and listen to their good and bad things. He will laugh and cry with others and feel better, and perhaps the dryness of his temperament will be removed.' And so, in the early days, he used to drag me to the homes of his acquaintances. The interests of those people, such as *mushairas* for instance, and the sort of conversation they indulged in, used to bore me to tears. Majju Bhai seemed perfectly content in their company; he would talk animatedly with them and laugh while I sat like a statue in their midst. The truth is that so many of their signs and gestures went over my head. The others would laugh approvingly at his jibes and comments, whereas I would gape at him like a fool. The background of those signs and symbols was the life of Karachi, that is, the way of life that these people had forged upon their arrival in this city. I had very little to do with it. I had begun to come and go in some of these homes because of Ishrat, but after she passed away, I slipped back into my old way of life. If anything, I was more cut off from these people than ever before. Now, after an age, Majju Bhai had tried to push me back among them. Because of his insistence, I began to go to those programmes and those homes where he was well known. Initially, as I said, their company bored me, but gradually it so happened that my *boriyat* began to lessen. A strange sort of interest took its place. Now it seemed as though I stood, a little apart from others, watching a tableau, as though whatever I was watching was not a part of a full life but a play.

Majju Bhai was right when he said now our city had become a quarrelsome city. Ya Allah, so many cities had collected in this one Karachi as though it was not a city but a sea. And every river, ever stream from across the subcontinent, came noisome and rollicking and merged in it. But rivers are supposed to mix with the sea and lose themselves. Here every river was shouting and saying, 'I am the sea.' And our Majju Bhai was a part of the noise of every noisome river, part of the fun and festivity of every community. Now he had begun to go everywhere with me in tow. It seemed as though there was a great clamour and I was a part of that clamour, and yet not a part of it. Sometimes happy, sometimes sad, sometimes worried, sometimes content that the seed from which I had grown was breathing among them, sometimes anxiously asking myself: Who are these people? Who am I? What are they doing? What am I doing in their midst?

'Majju Bhai, how are these people of yours?'

'What do you mean, Miyan? How should they have been?'

'It doesn't seem as though they are the same people.'

'Same people? Majju Bhai paused, then said, 'Have you gone mad that you are looking for them? Those people are not here. How could they have stayed the same when they left there? There was the soil of rivers; here, there is the sand of the sea.'

'So one will have to go there to see them,' I laughed and said.

Majju Bhai laughed, 'But my dear, I hope it doesn't happen that when you go there you find those people are not there either.'

'Why?'

'Time, my dear, Time!'

'I see,' I said and I felt sad.

'Yes,' And Majju Bhai issued a notice, 'Let us go.'

'Where?

'Anywhere … there are a thousand shade-giving trees along the way.'

'The mullah can only run till the mosque. We can only knock on the door of the Meerutwalas or the Lucknow-walas.'

Majju Bhai laughed, 'All right, today we won't go to either of those places. Today, I will show you a new specimen.'

'Who are these people?'

'Don't ask; just come along. You will recognize them when you see them.'

'Really?'

'Yes, they are one of a kind.'

Indeed they were one of a kind. His language was different from his wife's.

'Miyan Jawad, this is my friend Saiyad Shabbir Husain Karbalai; he is someone you will enjoy meeting. Qibla, this is my friend Jawad.'

'Miyan, where are you from? Are you a Saiyad? Which family? How many Saiyad families in your basti? And how many Imam Baras?' Such a deluge of questions that I became nervous.

'Miyan, I am from Shikarpur. It was once a famous *basti* of Shias in the Bulandshahr district.'

'A *basti* of Saiyads?' Saiyadani Chachi (this is how Majju Bhai was addressing her) said mockingly. 'There were a bare handful of

Saiyad families there. The others were all Hindus. Ai Bhaiyya, they set up such a din on the day of Holi that I used to go mad. Allah knows why he goes on all the time about "our Shikarpur".'

'Yes, they were Hindu,' said Karbalai sahab, 'But each was a master in his own craft. Majid Miyan, Banwari was a *halwai* par excellence; that fellow had amazing taste in his fingers. It is the truth; after all, we have to show our face to God. I have not eaten the same *besan laddu* since leaving Shikarpur.'

'Now let us hear all about the *halwais*,' Saiyadani Chachi cut his account. 'There was only one alley that had the *halwai* shops. All the *halwais* were Hindu and there was such smoke and such filth that Allah help us! And on top of it, there were the blasted dogs that would barely wait for the cauldrons to cool before they set about licking them. And the sweets? There was layered *gazak* made from *gur*, sweet *sev* fried in sweet oil, and *gur-dhani* ... that was it. I ate far superior sweets when I had once gone to Chhatari[39].'

'Chhatari?' Karbalai sahab asked contemptuously. 'All the place could boast of was the Nawab's moustaches! What else was there? How can you compare Shikarpur with Chhatari?'

'Ai Bhaiyya, talk some sense into him,' Saiyadani Chachi said to Majju Bhai. 'What was there in Shikarpur? Its bazaars had nothing but dust. Broken down *ekkas*, carts pulled by ageing and ill bullocks, shops run by oil merchants and paanwalas. I don't ever tell anyone that we are from Shikarpur. Why should we give others a chance to laugh at us? Thank God, our two children are living the good life in America. They keep writing to us to say, "Amma, leave Karachi; it is no place to live. We have the Green Card for America; you just have to say yes, we will get you a visa, put you on a plane and bring you to America." And, Bhaiyya, I too sometimes think: Is Karachi really a place to live? Bullets are fired night and day. Goons go about abducting young men from its streets. And on top of it all, the dacoits have unleashed such mayhem that Allah help us!'

---

[39] Chhatari, like Shikarpur, is another small town in the district of Bulandshahr in UP.

'Dacoits,' Karbalai sahab muttered. 'I don't consider them dacoits. Majju Miyan, do you know the name of any one of them?'

'If their names were known, would they not have been caught?'

Karbalai sahab laughed. 'What a thing to say, Majju Bhai? The hallmark of a true dacoit is that his name is known and dreaded. Even a child knows his name. And it takes a brave man to catch him. The name of Sultana Daku was known all over India. These are not dacoits, for no one in Karachi knows their name.'

'Arre, you always start your own tales,' Saiyadani Chachi interrupted him yet again. 'I was saying that Karachi is no longer a city worth living. I wouldn't stop here long enough to sip water. One daughter is waiting to be married; the day I am free of this responsibility I, for one, am going to board a plane to America, whether I get a visa or not.'

'What a thing to say, Nazeer's mother! America is not exactly next door; it is a long and arduous journey.'

'The journey to Pakistan was also a long and arduous one. How we offered praises at every step and reached here eventually! The journey to America may be long, but it will be a peaceful one.'

Karbalai sahab drew a long breath. 'Yes, you are right. We left Shikarpur at a strange hour. How fearful we were whether we would be able to reach the station or not. We made that journey by offering thanks for every step we took.'

And then he fell silent and seemed lost in thought. After a while, he said, 'Majid Miyan, just the other night … Yes, the night before last, I had a strange dream … as though I had reached Shikarpur … I was so happy, so happy that I cannot describe it. And also surprised … surprised because Shikarpur had become so beautiful. The tall buildings looked like palaces. Miyan, can you believe it … there was not a *kutcha* house in sight. And the roads … those dust-filled, potholed *kutcha* roads had disappeared. From here till there, there were only *pucca*, metalled roads, glimmering like mirrors, and so many cars! I was surprised … what had happened to the *ekkas*? There were no *ekkas* in sight. I saw a *tanga* with rubber tyres racing along and my alley … how spanking clean it was! There was no one in the alley. But there was a lot of peace and calm. I had just about entered my alley when I woke up.' He paused, then said, 'I was heart-broken. Why did I have to get up at that moment? Why does it always happen like this in my dreams? I am happily going towards my home, thinking that I will soon reach there, but as soon as I set foot in my alley, I wake up … But this was a strange dream.'

'It may have been strange,' Saiyadani Chachi spoke disinterestedly. 'You have been having these strange dreams ever since you came here. All you have done since coming here is have these dreams. Thank god for Nazeer and Basheer … we would have starved if it were not for their incomes. And ever since they have started sending money, he has stopped even trying to work. God knows why he has so many dreams and in every dream he sees Shikarpur. I have never seen it in my dreams … Shikarpur has become beautiful … Of course, it will seem beautiful in your dreams.'

'Well, that's not quite true, Nazeer's mother. I had told you about the dream I had last month. I had seen Shikarpur barren and desolate, as though everyone had left it and gone away. Silence reigned from one end to the other. Just one dog stood barking. I was scared. I wanted to get home quickly. But just as I turned into my alley to go home, and had barely taken a few steps, that I woke up.'

Saiyadani Chachi seemed thoroughly fed up of all this talk about dreams. She changed the subject abruptly, 'Ai Majju Bhai, what happened to that marriage you were fixing for that daughter of the Lucknow-walas?'

'Aji, don't ask, Saiyadani Chachi. These Lucknow-walas of yours are great ones for looking for faults. The match was nearly fixed when they came up with a new one: "These people are such village yokels; how can we give our daughter to them?"'

'I knew all along: I knew they would come up with some fault or the other. It is because of these reasons that their elder daughter is still sitting at home. In any case, she has studied medicine and now, thankfully, she has her own clinic. She is not dependent on anyone. There is so much money in this business that she can feed four others beside herself. But what about their younger one? Parents don't stay around forever. It would have been good if they had married her off; they should think of what will happen to her after they are gone.'

'Well, that is not quite the case; this one too is educated.'

'It isn't enough just to be educated. One should have a skill too. Those with B.A. and M.A. degrees are wandering about; what good is just a degree? Nor is everything to be found in books alone. In any case, this is a man's business; a girl looks good only when she is sewing, stitching, knitting and embroidering. Why does she have to become a know-it-all after reading all these books? Whenever I have been to their home, I have always seen that girl sitting in a corner with her books. One day, I could stand it no more. I said, "My dear, take some interest in cooking too so that you can ease your mother's burden, and you too might learn some good housekeeping. As for the books, had you read even half the books you have, Masha Allah, and read about Hadith and Quran you would have fared better on your Last Day. After all, can these English books match even one *rakaat* of prayer?'

'Saiyadani Chachi, what a thing to say!'

'Ai Bhaiyya, one has to say the truth. Let those who want to take offense, take offense. Let them speak in two tongues who need something from others. I don't need anything from anyone. So, I never refrain from speaking the truth. That is why I am not popular. But I don't care.'

'Chachi, now you have started a new topic. I simply meant that the boy is good enough, comes from a good family, we know everyone, they have no expectations ... the girl would have been happy there.'

'That is all very well. A star won't fall from the firmament for their daughter. Good or bad, this is the stock of boys we have. But these Lucknow-walas have their head in the high heavens. They consider everyone except themselves to be peasants. They go about finding a hundred faults in other people's children and, when it comes to their own daughters, they think they are perfect.'

Karbalai sahab also found his tongue. He said, 'Majju Miyan, I have seen Lucknow. I am not setting it up against Shikarpur. I swear, if you remove the Imam Baras, there is no difference between Shikarpur and Lucknow. If anything, there is a great deal in Shikarpur. Hazrat Bismil Allahabadi has given a fitting response to all the claims of these Lucknow-walas in his verse. He was from Allahabad; see how well he has praised the greatness of his city. He has said:

> *Badha rahe hain bahut Lucknow ki shaan magar*
> *Woh Gomti ko to Ganga bana nahi sakte*
> (They are bent upon exalting the greatness of Lucknow
> But they cannot turn the Gomti into the Ganga)

'Majju Miyan, tell me truly, what do you think?

'Well said.'

'The Lucknow-walas pride themselves on their poetry, but they have not been able to find a fitting rejoinder to this verse.'

'There is no answer to the fact,' and once again Majju Bhai turned towards Saiyadani Chachi, 'that they have turned their being Saiyad into an issue too. In calling the Meerutwalas village yokels, they have raised the question of their not being Saiyads but Kambohs.'

'Hai, is it true?' Saiyadani Chachi nearly jumped out of her chair. 'Are these Meerutwalas not Saiyad?'

'Saiyadani Chachi, I am saying, fine, so let them not be Saiyad; the boy is all right in all respects.'

'Ai Bhaiyya, I will speak the truth; don't take it amiss. Truly, I have no love lost for the Lucknow-walas, but they are right. You can't swallow a fly once you have seen it. You can't marry your daughter off among the non-Saiyads, knowing full well that they are not Saiyad.'

'What's wrong with it, Saiyadani Chachi?'

'Ai hai, is there no harm? What a thing to say? Was this calamity too waiting to strike us in this 14th century[40] that the daughters of Saiyads should go to the homes of the non-Saiyads?'

'And what if one can't find Saiyad boys?'

'That is exactly what I am asking? Why is there such a scarcity of Saiyad boys in this day? The Saiyad boys are running around making a fool of themselves over all sorts of people, while Saiyad girls are sitting at home? On the Day of Judgement, when the women in Paradise[41] will ask them: "O you misbegotten sons, why did you ruin my line?", what answer will they have?'

'These Saiyad boys of today,' Karbalai sahab muttered. 'Look at the state of decline in the *saadat*.' He took a long deep breath and fell silent.

And on that long deep breath, our meeting ended.

---

[40] According to the Islamic calendar, the 14th century AH corresponds with 1883-1980 AD. See footnote 68.

[41] Refers to the ladies from the Prophet's family, such as Fatima; Fatima will be the first among women to enter Paradise.

Five

One evening, Majju Bhai telephoned me and asked, 'Are you at home?' What are you doing?'

'I am home and doing nothing at all. But, huzoor, where are you today?'

'I was getting bored; first I waited for you, then when you didn't show up, I thought perhaps the bank has seized you, then I set out on my own. I thought of meeting Tausif Miyan. When I came here, I met a new trouble.'

'What?'

'There is trouble in this area.'

'Why? What happened?'

'It is being said they were masked men … they came and shot blindly and went away. At that time, everyone was struck dumb. It was only when they went away that the people set up a din. All hell broke loose. The police came immediately and then what usually happens, happened. And now there is curfew. So, Jawad Miyan, I am stuck, and it looks like I will end up spending the night here. Tausif Miyan immediately devised an impromptu night-long *mushaira*.'

'May God give you more such opportunities!'

'What to do? I am stuck … now I am entirely at Tausif Miyan's mercy. There will be no need to go far … this alley is bursting with poets. The *mushaira* will go on all night and there will be *taar-roti*[42] to go with it.'

---

[42] *Taar* is a rich meat gravy, floating with an oily layer on top; its gravy is usually a thin, runny one.

'Where did this *taar-roti* come from?'

'Ama, don't you know, the Rampurwalas live right next door. They have offered the *taar-roti* on their own. So the curfewed night will go well. How are things at your end?'

'There's nothing to worry about.'

'Even so, be careful. Is Nemat Khan around?'

'Yes, where will he go?'

'All right then; as soon as the curfew relaxes for a bit tomorrow, I will leave this place.'

So, thanks to the curfew, Majju Bhai got busy in his interests; I too found something to keep myself occupied. Some time ago, I had found an interesting book in a junk-dealer's shop. I thought of finally reading it today. But the book had got so lost among my books that I could not find it. And so I ended up turning all my books upside down. Strange things happen when one turns one's books upside down; all sorts of old papers are found, some from behind books, some tucked in their pages, others stuck between books, and every such paper revives some long-lost memory, and some forgotten incident comes back to life. In the process of turning the books upside down, several old letters were found. Phuphi Amma's letter? When did this come?

My Dearest Munnan Miyan,

May you live long! Accept thousands of blessings from your poor Phuphi. My dear, are you angry with me? Why do you never write two words to tell us of your well being? At least, let me know what is it about your poor aunt that has distanced you? How much I loved you! Still, if something has hurt you, please forgive me, my son. You have forgotten your Phuphi Amma; but how can your Phuphi Amma forget you? You are the only surviving sign of my long departed brother. How tenderly I looked after you when you were a baby, cleaned your poop. I didn't know the difference between day and night, so engrossed was I in tending you. I slept in the wet to ensure you were warm and dry. So many nights, I slept on one side in fear that if I turned I might disturb your sleep.

You were such a light sleeper; you used to get up at the slightest movement. And once awake, how difficult it was for you to fall asleep again! You used to blink your eyes like a waking-sleeping doll. And I used to put you back to sleep with such difficulty. So, my dear, this is how I raised you. How was I to know that you would grow up and go away so that your poor unfortunate aunt would long for a sight of your face! After all, people used to go abroad in earlier times too. My dear brother, may God rest his soul in peace, had gone and settled abroad, but every week or fortnight, he would send word of his welfare through an electric cable. Such was the love of those days. Now, this is a wretched new age, and Pakistan has been created. How blood relations have changed … whoever goes there does not turn to look this side. May you be happy in your Pakistan; we are not coming there to share your good fortune. We are only hungry for your love. If you were to write a short note every month or two telling us of your safety and well being, we would have been content. Here, we fret over the safety of our children, the stars of our eyes, who have gone so far, far away. May our children remain safe! May they know no grief except the grief for Husain!

And now listen to the tale of woe of your aunt … I was always frail and sickly. Now, you can say, there is only skin on bones. My appetite is gone. My stomach feels bloated if I have even one *phulka*. I long for fresh leafy things. It isn't as though there is any shortage of seasonal fruits and vegetables. Of course, things are not the same as before but, still, there is plenty in the house. Everyone has left; of course, only plenty has remained. Freshly plucked *singhara*, straight from the pond smelling of roses, corncobs that are studded with milky pearls, *sainda, phoot, kharbuz, tarbuz, aam, jamun* … everything still comes in its season. In fact, it comes by the *ser* and there is so much that it rots and goes waste. Still, I long for everything because I can't digest anything. My digestion is ruined … it has become so temperamental. Can you believe that this time during the rains, I could not eat even one *phulki*? And it isn't as though we didn't put the wok on the fire. In any case, there isn't much of the rainy season left. Now the rains have gathered in your aunt's eyes. Still, one has to respect the seasons.

And this time, the rainy spell lasted for so long that we didn't see the sun for fifteen days. So, naturally the wok had to be put on the fire. Chhote Miyan went and bought several seasonal greens from the bazaar. The market was awash with *sainda* – now there aren't enough people to eat it in our home, or *ghewar* too for that matter. Chhote Miyan insisted, "This is a seasonal sweet; and in any case you love *ghewar*." But I swear I did not even look at that platter full of *ghewar*. The wok was on the fire and all sorts of snacks were being fried – *shakar pare, namak pare, purhe, phulkiyan, ghunghuniya*. Their soft moist smell kept tantalizing me and I sat there controlling myself. Yes, when the leaves of the *arbi* plant were being fried, I could no longer contain myself. But how much did I eat? No more than half a leaf or so. Little was I to know ... I had barely eaten half a leaf ... How was I to know it would be my undoing? I fainted and the whole household scurried about. Everyone thought I was at death's door. But I still had life to live, so I lived. After all, it is the string of life that sees us through. The string is a delicate one. Who knows when it will snap?

So, my son, I don't have any strength left; only my breath comes and goes on its own. You will ask: what is the malady? There is no malady except old age. *Yak piri wa sad aib*[43]. Now my only prayer is that the end should come soon. Arre, I am surprised as to why I am still alive. My dear eldest brother is long gone; the younger one has also gone. Why am I left to lug the sacks of misdeeds on the Last Day? Anyhow, the time of my departure is not too far away. Just the day before yesterday, I saw in my dream that an *ekka* had stopped at our front door. My eldest brother and the younger one got off. I was happy, and also surprised, that these two had come. I cannot describe the glow on their faces. And their clothes were snowy white. They got off the *ekka* and said to me, "Sister, we have come to take you. Gather your luggage." And I said, "What luggage can a poor woman like me have to gather? All I have is this bundle, and if I take out this *tiladani*[44], there

---

[43] A Persian proverb meaning 'old age itself is akin to a hundred maladies'.

[44] A small hand-stitched cloth pouch with a strap to cover its mouth; it was used to store sewing material such as needle, thread, thimble and occasionally money.

will be nothing left and, yes, a prayer mat with a *sajdagah*,[45] a string of prayer beads and two books of prayers." So they said. "Why tarry then? Let us go." And suddenly I woke up. In another instant, the cock crowed. And so, my dear, my transport awaits me. My mule for the journey waits. And that is why I have narrated this incident to you. Come and show me your face in my last days. Come and lend your shoulder to the funeral procession of your Phuphi Amma. The sorrow that is gnawing away at me is that when my time has come, the children are scattered to the winds. When my eldest brother had gone, the house was full and the entire clan had wept for him. How loudly everyone had wept! There were so many people about till the fortieth day. And on the fortieth day, relatives had come from near and far and participated in the funeral prayers. When my younger brother passed away, so many from among us had set off for Pakistan; still, so many among the near and dear ones were close by. Now, when it is time for wretched old me to sleep the eternal sleep, all the near and dear ones have flown away like birds. Only Chhote Miyan remains; he is the only one who has decided not to leave the hearth. And as for Pyare Miyan, he has stayed back only so that he can sell off the family estate. And as for the Hindus, they don't even touch our estate. If a deal is fixed today, my dear nephew will board the train tomorrow and leave. My dear son, don't mind it, but the Pakistanwalas have destroyed our home. They could have gone anywhere they chose, but why did they have to destroy our home. Look at Pyare Miyan … he will go to Pakistan and live the good life. And he is doing his best to ensure that the property is sold off at any price and poor Chhote Miyan is left with nothing but a beggar's bowl.

Anyhow, I will spend the rest of my days; my carriage waits. May God give me an early release! I am free of all worries, except who will carry my bier on their shoulder? And, yes, I also worry about Maimuna. Who will support her when I am gone? Had I

---

[45] A small tablet of clay from the sacred soil of Karbala; Shias place it upon their prayer mat at the time of prayers, and when they bow in prostration, they rest their forehead on it.

got her married, I would have gone in peace. Now I will go with her worry weighing on my chest. Anyhow, these are matters of fate. No matter how hard one tries, sometimes it is to no avail. Everything must happen at its ordained time. How I had wanted a match fixed for her, but anyhow ... So, my son, surely you do not have the time to listen to my Ram Kahani.[46] Listen to the long tale hidden in these few words and somehow or the other come and show me your face, even for a few minutes, and take my blessings.

With blessings,

Your,
Phuphi Amma

I turned the letter around to see when it had come, and whether I had even answered it or not. There was no date mentioned on it. I opened the second one to see if it contained any clue.

Munnan,
I don't know quite how to address you. You tell me what is the correct epithet for me to use for you. I don't even know whether I should have written this letter or not. But I can no longer see Amma's condition. When I could stand it no more, I sat down to write this letter to you. What can I tell you about Amma's state? She has been bedridden; she needs help to get up or even sit up. She keeps crying because everyone has gone away to Pakistan; who will lend a shoulder to her bier? And her tears are such that they fall ceaselessly. And more than all the others, she remembers you the most. How longingly she says that if only she could see your face once, then she can die in peace. Jawad, there is nothing left in Amma; she is hanging on to life by a thread. May the devil

---

[46] Ram Kahani can be used for any long tale or epic, though specifically used to describe the story of Ram, his marriage, his exile and eventual triumphant return to rule his kingdom after many travails; the use of this expression is indicative of Intizar Husain's liberal use of Hindi words as well as an indication of how prevalent such expressions were in the spoken Urdu of the common people.

be deaf and may there be ashes in my mouth, but who can tell when this thread might snap.

I have written this letter only to tell you about this; you know best what you must do. You have forgotten us since you went there. I find it so hard to believe. It was only last night when Amma was feeling slightly better that she raised your subject yet again. She spoke about you for so long, sometimes about some mischief during your childhood, sometimes some escapade from your youth. Hai Jawad, how naughty you were in your boyhood! I remember some of your pranks. How you used to tease me? And I too used to get angry at the slightest thing. As Amma often tells me, I was very prickly in my childhood. I would take offense and go off to sulk. It was always you who had to bend and make amends. Anyhow, what is the point of remembering all this? Those days have turned into dreams. You have gone so far away, or as Amma puts it, to God's Own Backyard. When she talks about you, she laughs sometimes, and sometimes she cries.

Actually, I can understand Amma's sorrow. The ties of blood are one thing, but the love that you have for someone you have raised from infancy is greater. As Amma says, she would hold you in her lap even when your mother was alive. You were most attached to her. You wouldn't even sleep till you had heard her lullaby: 'The li'l birdie came hopping and skipping/The li'l birdie brought my mate for my li'l one.' And last night, she hummed this aloud as though she were indeed singing you to sleep. And, then, she covered her face with her dupatta and wept. My eyes brimmed over too …

So, Munnan, come for a visit. Amma's last wish will come true. I too will feel you heeded my call, isn't it? We will all have a grand time, really! So you are coming, aren't you? Till then, may God keep you safe!

Yours,
Maimuna

And along with it, I found the third letter. And this one had a date.

Dear Brother Jawad Miyan,
Accept the blessings of those who are far away and hear this sorrowful news that your dear Phuphi Amma departed from this transient world to the eternal one yesterday, that is, Friday morning on 12th Zill Hajj. After our eldest uncle, her presence in our midst meant everything to us. That presence left us. *Inna lillahe wa innalla he rajaun.*[47] Anyhow, death is a certainty. It is God's will. All one can do is pray for forgiveness for the departed and keep the slab of patience on one's heart.

Our Phuphi Amma went away with one weight on her heart: that she could not see those relatives who had gone to Pakistan. She had even written to you in her last days. Towards the end, she would keep looking towards the doorway. I am sure you had your own compulsions for not coming. Since Mohurram starts from next month, it has been decided that her *chaliswan* will be performed during this month itself and the 27th of Zu-al Hajj has been fixed.

Waiting to hear of your well-being, your well-wisher,

Chhote Miyan

And I remembered that this letter was from those days when my romance with Ishrat was at its peak. I was barely aware of my own body and soul at the time. I was so in the throes of love that I could only think of Ishrat; I did not have a thought to spare for anyone else. These letters came, one by one, during those days. I may have answered them had they made the slightest impact on my heart. Now when I realized the love with which Phuphi Amma had written to me and read Maimuna's words laced with such trust and so much affection urging me to make a trip back, I rebuked myself. How selfish I had become those days, and how stony-hearted too! I began to despise myself. I kept thinking what Phuphi Amma must have felt when there was no answer from me, how hurt she must have been! And Maimuna, how dejected she must have felt! Phuphi

[47] Prayer recited upon hearing of someone's death; it is part of a verse from the Quran which means 'Surely we belong to Allah and to Him shall we return'.

Amma is now lying asleep under mounds of earth. She couldn't care less now whether I am ashamed or not. But Maimuna ... and a wave rose within me that I must immediately plan to get the visa, go there and seek forgiveness from her.

'Sahab, Majju Miyan hasn't come as yet. The food is getting cold,' Nemat Khan said. He had come in so silently, or perhaps I was so lost in my thoughts, that I did not even realize he had entered the room.

'Oh yes, Nemat Khan, I forgot to tell you that Majju Miyan will not be coming tonight. I hope you haven't made the rotis yet?'

'No, I was about to do so. But why won't Majju Miyan come tonight?'

'He had gone to the Meerutwalas. There is some problem there. Curfew was clamped down as soon as he reached; so how can he come back?'

'Sahab-ji, things are really bad.'

'Yes, things are bad.'

'May God have mercy upon us,' Nemat Khan mumbled, then added, 'So will you eat now? I am about to start making the rotis.'

'Wait a while.'

My words did not have a favourable effect upon Nemat Khan. Silently, he went back.

Once again, I was lost in my thoughts. For the first time, I was angry at my love. It was all very well to fall in love, but a person should not become so insane that he should have no feelings for all other relationships. And Phuphi Amma was less of an aunt and more of a mother to me. Maimuna was right: even when my mother was alive, I was always stuck to Phuphi Amma's side. And after my mother passed away, Phuphi Amma became my aunt *and* my mother. What she must have thought about me! And what Maimuna must be thinking of me! Once again, that wave arose within me. I should go there and ... but when I didn't go then, what was the good of going now? My heart sank when I tried to imagine how Maimuna would look at me and the coldness with which Chhote Miyan would meet me, and the desire to go there cooled within me. But the thoughts did not leave me. A fit of shame seized me. The wave that had subsided raised itself yet again. I should go. A shiver ran through my body. Perhaps I might feel invigorated if I go there. But … once again, I was reminded of Maimuna's coolness and Chhote Miyan's poison-filled remarks and my Badi Bhabhi's taunts, and once again my ardour was dampened. Still, I tried to gather my courage, and think …

Six

Those three letters had a strange effect on me. The stony crust that had formed inside me and had gradually grown bigger and bigger, seemed to have melted somewhat, and my memory was coming back. The truth is I remembered nothing. It was as though my memory had been replaced by a niche of forgetfulness[48]. But things were changing. Now, it seemed as though the cavalcade of remembrances had broken out from that niche and was knocking at the doors of my memory. Several times I thought I could now recall everything, but whenever I sat down to remember, some matchless, priceless fragments from those days would rise before me; however, they would always be hazy and blurred. A flood of memories was swelling within me, turning and surging, but it could not, as yet, find a way to break free. My entire being seemed to be in its grip. And then there was the same dilemma: should I go or not? There was that same fear in going: What if I am met with coldness? After all, Phuphi Amma is no longer there who could set aside all her hurts and clasp me heedlessly to her bosom. If I can forget all of them, why is it necessary for them to remember me? And Maimuna … she may very well not have forgotten me,

---

[48] Intizar Husain uses the Persian expression *taaq-e-nisiyan*, which refers to that place where forgotten memories go, sometimes never to be retrieved. In Urdu, the creative writer has long used this expression to evoke a sense of wonder and the capability of the human mind to seek refuge from its own hurts. In contrast, the concept of 'memory hole' propounded by George Orwell is a sinister, organized, ideology-driven mechanism to willfully hide memory and subvert history.

but how could she forgive me? In fact, it was Maimuna's coldness – more than anything else – that was stopping me from going there, and also troubling me the most. Once, the thought crossed my mind that possibly she might not even be there anymore. How could it be that she would still be living there with our Badi Bhabhi? In other words, a hundred different doubts assailed me. At the same time, the thought of going there was becoming increasingly undeniable. A desire had suddenly woken up; and it seemed difficult to put it back to sleep. The memories that were coming back were providing nourishment to that desire. And suddenly, I was struck by a new thought. What if this is because of my advancing years? The thought saddened me very much.

'Yaar, these days you seem to be more lost than usual,' Majju Bhai said. He was quick to spot what lay hidden in my heart. I tried to throw him off the scent, but the truth is that by now I could barely suppress my own feelings.

'Majju Bhai,' Finally, I unlocked my lips and broached the subject, 'I have been thinking …'

'What?' Majju Bhai looked closely at me with questioning eyes. 'What are you thinking?'

'I have been thinking that I have indeed grown old.'

Majju Bhai let out a hearty laugh, 'And how did this knowledge dawn upon you?'

'Long lost memories are coming back to me … days of long ago, people of long ago.'

'Really? Since when?'

'That night when you had stayed back at Tausif's house … do you know what happened to me that day?'

'What happened?'

'While the *mushaira* and curfew held you in their thrall there, I thought now that I have some spare time, let me read that book I have been meaning to. I was turning my books and papers around to look for it when I found some letters. I had no memory of those letters. When did they come? Had I answered them, or not?'

'Letters? Really? Whose letters?'

'One was from my Phuphi Amma. It was possibly written during her last days. The letter after that was to tell me about her illness. The third contained the news of her death.'

'When had these letters come?'

'That's what I can't remember now. And the strange thing is that the first two letters do not carry a date.'

'My dear fellow, you have no recollection of when your Phuphi Amma passed away?'

'It is precisely this realization that is eating away at me.' I was quiet and lost in my thoughts. Then I said, 'Ever since then, there has been a virtual deluge of memories. I am reminded of all sorts of things from long ago. But then I can remember nothing in its entirety. It is almost as though my memory is fighting shy of gathering all those reminiscences. You can say that I am hanging between remembering and forgetfulness. It is a very painful state to be in.'

'There is only one cure for it.'

'What?'

'Get married.'

'Majju Bhai, I have described my anguish to you. And you can think of nothing but your usual levity. At least, sometimes you must listen to others with some degree of seriousness.'

'I am perfectly serious and I know exactly what you are experiencing. That is why I have said such a thing. My dear, get married.'

'Do you not see my age?'

'Why? What's wrong with your age? My dear nitwit, this is the right age to marry. The age in which you got married was not the right age for marriage. I told you not to get married, didn't I?'

'Yes, you did.'

'You did not pay heed to my words then, and later you regretted it. Miyan, loneliness does not pinch during one's youth. It begins to gnaw as the years go past. And this is only the beginning. Wait and see how it gets worse. So, listen to me; you will do well.'

'And what do you think about yourself?'

'Me?' Majju Bhai let out a thunderous peal of laughter. 'Ustad, I had rid myself of the thought early on in life. I never could abide the thought of this nuisance. And that is why I am doing well; loneliness can do me no harm. And you can see my habits and pursuits. But if someone has tasted the pleasures of married life once and, as luck would have it, is also the father of a child, he is troubled by loneliness. My dear fellow, you should at least have kept your son with you. You could have got him married by now. He would have had children. You would have forgotten your loneliness in the midst of your grandsons and granddaughters. By the way, how is Arshad? Has he written any letter recently? Does he plan to return, or not?'

'Under these circumstances, what will he do if he returns? I never ask him to come back.'

'And marriage? What does he say about that?'

'At present neither he has any views on the subject, nor do I.'

Majju Bhai laughed. 'Today, neither of you has any views, but tomorrow it can pose problems. What will you do if he marries a *mem*? And if he has to stay there, then I can find a Green Card holder for him. There are plenty of such women available in Karachi. In fact, I have a couple in mind; if you want, I can set the ball rolling.'

'We'll see; there is no hurry.'

Nemat Khan brought us tea. I made a cup for Majju Bhai, and then poured for myself. One sip transported me far, far away. Meanwhile, Majju Bhai also lit up his cigarette.

'Majju Bhai,' I was struck by the strangest thought as I was sipping my tea. 'These friends of yours … thanks to you, I have started meeting them too. I don't even know why. Earlier, I had not the slightest desire to meet them, and you too did not make any especial effort for me to meet them. There must be some wisdom in it because you take me along when you go to meet them. Anyhow, as I was saying, these people …' And I didn't know how to say it.

'You will say that these people don't appear to be like that. Yaar, you must stop repeating things. It gives the impression that you are indeed getting old.'

'Yes, perhaps I am repeating myself. Yaar, I sometimes feel as though something has gone missing in them.'

Majju Bhai laughed, 'Something? Why, they have gone entirely missing. In fact, they are transformed. Now they have become true-blue Karachiwalas.'

'And what about all that talk of "our Delhi" and "our Lucknow" that they used to go on about?'

'It is all a big fraud. Anyhow, you should forgive them; this fraud was their compulsion.'

'How was it a compulsion?'

'Because if one has to survive in Karachi, one has to engage in some fraud or the other.'

'That is tough; what is one to do if one wants to escape from them?

'How is it difficult for you? You have always shunned human company and lived in a world of your own. Now you have come up with a new one,' Majju Bhai paused, then said, 'Miyan Jawad, sometimes when I see you I am amazed: you are something else! Now you have burdened yourself with this new nuisance of memories. Why, for heaven's sake?'

I laughed. 'Majju Bhai, I have my own compulsions. I too needed a fraud in order to live in Karachi.'

Majju Bhai laughed uproariously. 'Yaar, you have rendered me speechless today. Truly, you have!'

'But there is one big difficulty.'

'What is it?'

'At first, I thought I remembered a great deal. But when I sit down to reminisce, it seems as though my memories are sliding out of my recall. Or perhaps I am imagining that I can remember,' and I became sorrowful as I said these words. 'The truth is I don't remember anything anymore ... I am empty ... completely empty.'

'Yaar, you were a hundred per cent true to begin with, but then you came back to your usual nonsense. Come on, get up; let me take you out for some great tea somewhere.'

'Great tea? Where will you take me?'

'That depends on which brand of tea you wish to drink. The Lucknow brand, the Delhi brand, or the Meerut brand? Each has its own distinctive flavour.'

'None of these are acceptable to me. If we must go, let us go to the Shikarpurwalas.'

'All right, all right,' Majju Bhai laughed. 'Look where you have met your match! Remember they are from Shikarpur! Anyhow, I knew from the first instant that Chacha Karbalai had made an impact on you.'

'Majju Bhai, Chacha Karbalai may be from Shikarpur, but he is any day better than your crowd from Lucknow, Delhi, Meerut and Amroha. There is a still a spark of truth in him.'

'Let a few more years pass; you will turn into another Chacha Karbalai. You are going in the right direction.'

'Maybe.'

'Well, never mind. I am happy in whatever makes you happy.'

And as soon as we reached, the first thing Majju Bhai said was, 'Chacha, my friend Jawad has become a great admirer of yours. And so I said to him, "Let me take you there to meet him."'

Karbalai sahab was pleased. He said, 'Miyan, what good will it do anyone to meet me? I am just sitting here with a few broken-down memories. I am the lamp that will be snuffed out at dawn; I will flicker on till the Angel of Death does not think of coming for me. And the day he remembers, this lamp will be snuffed out.' And then his tone changed as he asked, 'So you are Jawad Hasan?'

'Yes.'

'The other day you had mentioned that you are from Meerut.'

'Yes, I once had some ties with Meerut.'

'It is the same thing, Miyan. I have seen Meerut. That's the benefit of a government job; one keeps getting transfers and gets to see many different cities. So, I was transferred to the Government High School in Meerut. I taught there for three years. Did you see that theatre show called the *Murder of Tameezan*?'

'I had heard about it, but I hadn't seen it.'

'Then obviously you wouldn't have seen Tameezan either?'

'No.'

'Then what did you see in Meerut? What a fine looking woman she was! You know, she was a real firecracker! She got murdered in the end, but drove so many to their death with her killer looks. I have seen with my own eyes that *kotha* where she was murdered. I didn't go up, though.'

'There is no harm if you had gone up.'

'No, no. I have never let anything come in the way of my faith. While passing by, a friend had pointed out the *kotha* where Tameezan used to stay. Though I must say I had often seen Boom Hapuri. He would stand at the Lorry Station and sell his verses in such a loud voice and with such relish! Boom's new verses in four annas! *Chamarinama*[49] in two annas! If nothing else, at least the good man wrote the *Chamarinama*. After all, if the *tehsildar* had lost his heart to the *chamar* girl, what is it to you? These things go on. A woman is a woman, whether she is a *chamar* or a *mem*. Be that as it may, Jawad Miyan, there was certainly no match for the Nauchandi fair of your Meerut.'

'Yes, there was a lot of excitement during the Nauchandi fair.'

'Yes, there was such splendour. People talk of the *numaish*[50] at Aligarh, but it was actually Nauchandi that was more splendid. In fact, a poet from Aligarh had come up with a verse … what was it … Yes, I remember …

> *Sajawat mein, banawat mein, lagawat mein, dikhawat mein*
> *Aligarh ki numaish Hind bhar mein sab se behtar hai*
>
> In ornamentation, constitution, appeal and show
> The *numaish* of Aligarh is better than all others in India

---

[49] Literally meaning 'The Chronicle of the Chamar Woman', it may have been a spoof on the verses of Nazir Akbarabadi, the 18th century people's poet who began the genre of 'bazaar poetry' and wrote long poems on common people and gave them titles such as 'Aadmi Nama' or 'Banjara Nama'

[50] The *mela* or fair at Nauchandi travelled to different towns in western UP. In Aligarh, it was known as the *numaish*, literally meaning 'exhibition'. It was, and continues to be, a high point in the social calendar of the Aligarhwalas for the food, fun and shopping it offers.

'Wrong, all wrong! You didn't get anything there except Peshawari kabab-parathe and black burqas. And in Bulandshahr you didn't even get that! But the Nauchandi fair ... it had everything! Subhan Allah! One round of the fair was enough to fill your eyes with light and suffuse your heart with intoxication.' Chacha Karbalai was mumbling as though he was indeed strolling in the Nauchandi fair. He paused, then said, 'Miyan Jawad Hasan, there was no dearth of splendour in our Shikarpur. There would be an animal fair that drew hordes from all the villages in the neighbourhood. And during Muharram, there was an altogether different kind of splendour. Miyan, don't think I am lying, but when the Imam's procession was taken out ... I would stay there for the entire ten days. That reminds me ... Last night I had a dream where ...'

'So you have had another dream,' Saiyadani Chachi stopped him mid-sentence. She had finished her chores and come and sat with us during this conversation. She had opened her *paandan*. She stopped Karbalai sahab's narration and said angrily, 'Again, that wretched Shikarpur must have appeared in your dreams! Ai Majju Bhai, talk some sense into him. How long will he go on invoking that city of ill fortune?'

A river that was in full spate stopped. Chacha Karbalai looked at his wife with the utmost innocence and helplessness, and became silent. Now, it was Saiyadani Chachi's turn to start talking. She had her own interests. Right away, she fired the first salvo. 'Ai Majju Bhai, whatever happened to that doomed match you were trying to fix? Have the Lucknow-walas given their answer or are the talks still on?'

'It is dangling mid-air. I have tried to make both parties see sense. It is not so much both as the Lucknow-walas who have flown off the handle; they are the ones who have to be brought back to the discussion. I have tried my best to make them see reason. I have told them that they will not find such a good match, and those who have tried to misguide them are waiting for things to be called off so that they can jump in and grab the groom for their own daughter.'

'Ai, really? Is that the truth?'

'Yes, that is the real truth. You know how it is when a match is proposed and someone or the other cuts in because of their own interest.'

'What can one say about people these days ... they just have to hear the faintest whiff of a rumour and they start to keep tabs! They root about in the past and do everything they can to break up a prospective match.'

'That is exactly what I tried to make them understand. I asked them who are these people who are going around spreading the rumour about them not being Saiyad? After all, I am here, I know them. And as for the genealogical tree[51] ... We should not forget the circumstances in which we left our homes. At that time, who had the time to keep the genealogical tree? We escaped with our lives; was that not enough of a miracle?'

'What did she say then?'

'At that time, she was in her senses. She understood things. Now, I am trying my best to ensure that the *nikah* is performed at the earliest.'

'Yes, that is what I am trying to say too; there should be no further delay. The moment you give the slightest slack, all sorts of things begin to come out. I have decided that the day I get a good match for my daughter, I will have the simplest possible *nikah* and send her away.'

'What happened to that match that was being set up among the Sarsiwalas?'[52]

'Ai Bhaiyya, that turned to be a real can of worms: six sisters, three brothers and a gaggle of their offspring. And on top of it all, the job of a professor with no extra income. The boy's mother told us he wrote books. I said a marriage doesn't run on books. These days, people with the smallest jobs earn so much that they have lakhs of rupees.'

---

[51] Most Saiyad families maintain a genealogical tree called the *shajra-e ansab* that traces their family's roots to the family of the Prophet.

[52] Sarsi is near Pratapgarh in UP.

'Yes, the avenues for earning money have really opened up.'

'Bhaiyya, I am sick and tired of people telling me that their boy is an M.A.! Arre, what good is an M.A. or a B.A.? The boy should also know how to earn. Now, may God keep him well, there is my niece's husband. He had just cleared his Entrance when his parents had him admitted in the police as a constable. He is a smart boy; he served his seniors so well that they promoted him to a thanedar. The house he has had built for himself looks like a palace. Two cars stand in the driveway. Apart from that, he has a plot of land too. I want that sort of boy for my daughter. Don't you know someone like that?'

'Chachi, what can I say ... Unfortunately, all the accursed young men I have in mind are educated. What is more, they keep on getting more and more educated and are showing no signs of stopping. Wherever you turn, you see someone madly engrossed in some research or the other. I told that son of the Lucknow-walas, "My dear, if all young men were to become Plato, how would Pakistan go about its business?" He said, "There is no need for educated people in Pakistan, in any case. I am studying for my own interest."'

'Now, Majju Bhaiyya, you tell me: Can one give one's daughters to such mad men? One can't knowingly push one's own offspring into hell.'

How restless I was becoming. I could barely control myself though my dearest wish was that somehow Saiyadani Chachi could be silenced and Chacha Karbalai could start again, and that too from the point that he had been interrupted. He had been interrupted just as he was about to describe his dream. Who knows what the dream was all about? Saiyadani Chachi was in full flow. My curiosity about the dream was growing. So, when Saiyadani Chachi stopped to draw breath and turned her attention towards her *paandan*, I thought it best to make use of this interval. I threw the ball in Chacha Karbalai's court. 'Qibla, what are your views about this?'

'Yes, Chacha, you should also say something.' Perhaps Majju Bhai too was fed up of Saiyadani Chachi's views and wanted a change. 'You are not saying anything.'

'Arre bhai, what should I say?' And he lapsed into silence as though he could not understand what to say after he was cut short just as he was preparing to describe his dream. Whereas I was sitting there hoping that Chacha Karbalai would seize the opportunity and describe his dream. Saiyadani Chachi too sensed the possibility that he might do just that. She immediately sensed the danger and averted it, 'Yes, what will he say? That is our problem; he has nothing to say about whatever is happening in our home. Had he the slightest interest in this home, he would think of something to say. Everything circles back to the description of his dreams and in every dream there is nothing but the narration of that ill-fated Shikarpur.'

'Chacha, I also want to ask you something,' Majju Bhai interjected. 'Why does the landscape of your dreams never change? Fine, let it not be Karachi but you have been to Karbala. By landscape I mean how come you don't ever see Karbala in your dreams?'

'Miyan, that will be my last dream.' And with these words, Chacha Karbalai turned towards me. 'Miyan Jawad Hasan, have you been to Karbala?'

'No, sir, I have not had the pleasure so far.'

'Oh, I see; that is unfortunate. One must go to Karbala at least once in one's lifetime. That one journey ends all one's suffering.' He stopped and then after some thought, said, 'Miyan, I made a mistake; I regret it now. It was a big mistake.'

'Mistake? What mistake did you commit?'

'Don't ask, Majju Miyan. Now, as you know, only the fortunate few can go to Karbala. Only those whom Ali remembers can go there. So, I was called and I went. But why did I come back? I am wracked by regret. It was a huge mistake.' He sighed. 'I was destined to face these travails in life. Somehow or the other, we reached here. And now we are languishing in Karachi. Our children are in America and we are in Karachi and my heart is in Shikarpur and my spirit is in Shikarpur. I am in a dilemma, Majju Miyan.'

'Yes.'

'Truly, I am in a dilemma. I am hanging between Shikarpur and Karbala. My soil tugs me in one direction and my faith in the other.

My spirit tells me what is there in that desolate soil; a window into heaven is open for you here. I am in such a difficult spot.' Karbalai sahab fell silent and remained quiet while Saiyadani Chachi kept prattling on. Lost in his own thoughts, who can tell which journey he had set out upon? Had he embarked on a journey to Karbala or to Shikarpur?

That night, as we talked, I finally told Majju Bhai what lay in my heart. 'Majju Bhai, I have been thinking of going there.'

'Oh?' Majju Bhai looked askance at me. 'You have thought of going there after such a long time? So Karbalai sahab's influence has rubbed off on you?'

'It isn't Karbalai sahab's influence. Actually, it is those letters that have created a sense of guilt in me. I am thinking that …'

I couldn't say anymore. And Majju Bhai did not give me enough time to complete my sentence. He said, 'Yaar, why do you sound so apologetic? What is wrong if you want to go? You have relatives there. Of course, you must go.' And after a pause, he muttered, 'Land is the most God-awful thing. One is better off till one is not reminded of it. There are some people who live their entire lives and don't let the thought of their land come anywhere near them. But the moment one thinks of it, the thought seizes you.'

'Have you never thought of going there? Some relative, friend, someone … anyone …'

'Some beloved? That is what you want to say, isn't it? No, there isn't.'

'You are a lucky man.'

'You can say that. Anyhow, my view is that once one has left that place and the humiliating manner in which one left it, one should never go back.[53] No, never.'

---

[53] The wording of the original Urdu carries echoes of Ghalib's verse:

Nikalna khuld se Adam ka sunte aaye thhe lekin
Bade be-abru ho kar tere kooche se hum nikle
(We had heard of Adam leaving Paradise
But we too left your home in great disarray)

'You have enormous self-respect,' I laughed.

'That is the way I think. But that does not mean I am stopping you. This is the only cure for that sense of guilt you have so needlessly built up inside yourself.'

'I am only thinking about it; it isn't so easy to go there.'

'What is the difficulty?'

'The first difficulty is the visa.'

'Leave that to me; what next?'

I was left speechless. And at that time, it seemed to me as though there were no more obstacles in my journey. Even if I didn't wish to go, Majju Bhai would push me there.

Seven

Suddenly I noticed a change in the tempo of the train and I could sense an impulsiveness in the sound of its whistle. It was running at a fast pace, but there seemed to be no evidence of haste in its speed. It was moving along swiftly and, every now and then, it would blow its whistle loudly which would tear through the silence and travel far into the night. Now it seemed as the train too was rushing along impetuously and in a hurry to reach its destination. I was trying to understand my own condition when a fellow traveller woke up with a start. He got to his feet, looked at his watch and said, 'Vyaspur is coming.' This brief statement had a most startling effect on the other passengers who had been sleeping and snoring all this while. All of them woke up in a hurry. 'Vyaspur has come?'

'Yes, it is about to come.'

Those who had not woken up yet were awakened by their neighbours. 'Get up; Vyaspur has come.'

'Vyaspur has come?' And those who had just woken up hurriedly began to roll up their beddings.

There was a bustle in the entire train compartment. Vyaspur has come, Vyaspur has come. These people were all strangers for me. All night long, I had sat disinterestedly away from them. Now I was suddenly experiencing a suspense-filled relationship with them. So, all of us were travelling to Vyapsur. I now looked at the faces of my fellow travellers with a new attachment. Someone had switched on the light and now the compartment was brightly lit. In any case, the darkness outside too had lessened somewhat. I peered out of the window. Dawn was breaking. The sky was brightening. The trees across the track that had been running backwards and had looked like ghosts till a short while ago, were lightening up too. Everything around me was awakening as though the entire earth and the sky above had come to know that Vyaspur was coming.

The train was making a new kind of noise. The rumbling of the wheels had acquired a new rhythm, as though they were turning with an impetuous haste. More than the rumbling wheels, it was the sound of the whistle that was carrying tales of the train's restlessness. The scene around me was changing swiftly and becoming brighter by the minute. Everyone seemed to be in a hurry to reach Vyaspur. The swiftly passing trees seemed familiar to me. It seemed as though I had recognized each one of them and they had recognized me. Happiness was gushing out from deep within me and was impatient to reach out to the trees. Perhaps a stream of happiness was gushing out from them too, and was impatient to reach me. Suddenly I was struck by a new thought; I immediately removed my gaze from the scene right across my window and looked into the distance. Earlier, one could see Dilkusha[54] from a moving train. Now I could not see it. I was still pondering on this when I realized that there was a change in the tempo of the noisome wheels. The train had slowed down somewhat. And there was a change in the speed of the trees and sights running in the opposite direction. Heedless of the scene inside the compartment, I was completely engrossed in what was unfolding outside. But the clamour inside the compartment forced me to turn my attention to the scene inside. Several passengers were standing with their luggage. 'Vyaspur has come.' And, with a rumble, the train entered the station. I looked outside the window. A train was parked at the far side of the railing, packed with passengers; its engine was emitting clouds of black smoke. It presented a stark contrast with the clean, fresh air as it billowed and surged.

---

[54] Literally meaning, 'that which pleases the heart' but used in the sense of 'charming' or 'attractive'.

The train was now chugging along the platform. The mass of people standing on the platform were rapidly sliding past in the opposite direction. I caught hold of one of the coolies who had jumped on the moving train, handed him my luggage and got off the train in a rush. But my impetuosity lasted only so long. Once out of the train, I drew a long contented sigh. I stood and looked about me – till as far as my eye could see. I took in every minute detail of the platform. Then my gaze travelled to the tall tin-roofed awning; the wild pigeons sitting on its beam looked down on the crowd with a disinterested calm. I looked at those pigeons for a long time. Then I said to myself with a huge sense of relief: 'Everything looks as it was.'

A person was tearing through the crowd and rapidly coming in my direction. I recognized him as he came closer. I went eagerly towards him. 'Arre, Shankar, it is you?'[55] And the two of us hugged each other.

'Yaar, Jawad, you have changed so much.'

'And you?'

'Yes, I have too. One had to change. After all, it has been such a long time. I could not believe that you would actually come.' And with a change of tone, 'So where is he?' he looked around for the coolie and said, 'Come on.'

'Wait, yaar.'

'Why? What is it?'

'Let me see.' And once again, I examined the scene at the station. From the tracks running off into the distance to the tin-roofed awning, I closely examined every single detail. Then I turned to look at the pigeons sitting among the beams overhead. 'Yaar, Shankar, nothing has changed.'

'Well, let us get out of here ... then you will know how much has changed. Everything has changed.'

---

[55] In the original, Jawad and Shankar address each other as 'tu'; the casual form of address used by children. Unfortunately, the English 'you' does not convey the affection, informality, ease and equality of 'tu'.

Shankar was walking swiftly with the coolie whereas I was dawdling, looking here and there and lagging behind. As I emerged from the station, I stood on top of the stairs and looked at the *tangas*, wagons and rickshaws lined up on the road. Surprised, I asked, 'Yaar, Shankar, so rickshaws also run here?'

'Yes,' Shankar answered carelessly and walked swiftly in the direction of his car. The driver got out and opened the dickey and stowed away my luggage. I watched closely. Then, when I could no longer restrain myself, I asked as I sat down in the car, 'You used to have a *tanga*.' And with these words, a gaily decorated *tanga* pulled by a tall and handsome horse swam before my eyes.

'Yaar, my father put an end to the hassle of maintaining a *tanga* after Ramu died.'

'Ramu died?'

'Yes, yaar.'

I was so sad to hear this. This was the first news of death that I had heard since setting foot in Vyaspur. For some time, I stayed absolutely quiet. But the sound of the peacock, which came from somewhere close by and was hastily despatched to echo far in the air, immediately nullified the sense of sorrow. Actually, at that point, the car was passing the garden of Lala Hardayal. I asked the driver to slow down and turned expectantly to look towards the garden. My eyes went past several stunted trees to the well around which I could spot several *dhoti*-clad men cleaning their teeth with twigs. The well, the trees that stood around it, the roses in the flower beds, the kewra bush – I recognized them all with perfect ease. I could not recognize the men cleaning their teeth with the twigs.

The garden soon passed by, and so did the large houses nearby that stood surrounded by trees. Soon, the market began. The Amrit Dhara Building and a few steps ahead the Daal Mandi. The market was closed. Where mounds of wheat, cotton, gur usually lay in large numbers, at that time there was nothing. A few grains lay scattered and flocks of wild pigeons had descended to do justice. A few mynahs too could be seen who had come to pick their share.

People had vanished, only birds remained. Occasionally, a few sweepers could be spotted sweeping the streets. There was calm in the air. I drew a deep and contented sigh. In my heart, I said, 'Nothing has changed. Everything is as it was.'

❦

We continued talking even as we sat down at the dining table, as though we had no heed of what we were eating or even whether we were eating or not. Talking, talking, talking … Incidents of such long-ago stories of here and there.

I stopped as I was talking. I stayed quiet for some time, then I said, 'Shankar, yaar, I have to go to my house too.'

'House?' Shankar looked at me with surprise. 'Does someone live there still?'

'I don't know who is there and who isn't. In any case, Chhote Miyan must certainly be there. Don't you know anything about them?'

'No. The last time I had gone was when your elder uncle had passed away. I couldn't go again. Then I heard someone say that Dilkusha is being sold. I thought that they had finally decided to go to Pakistan … Do they know you are coming?'

'No. I thought since I haven't written a letter for so long, why write about my coming. I will just go there and meet them.'

'All right, then. We will go there tomorrow at our leisure.'

'Earlier, I had thought so too. But now, I am getting restless, yaar. To come here and not go home feels strange. I must go there now.' Quickly I finished my meal and got to my feet. 'Come on, then; let us go.'

❦

In the morning, there had been no living thing present, except pigeons and mynahs in the Daal Mandi; now all of God's creation had descended upon it. A sea of heads could be seen in the bazaar and, caught in it, cars that moved at the speed of an ant. And the dust that flew about! And as one crossed the lane of the sweet-makers, smoke mixed with the dust, and also the flies. How serene Vyaspur had appeared in the morning! And how bright! Now one could see how soiled it was. Somehow or the other, our car came out of the bazaar and I felt immediately better. My heart beat fast as we turned into the road that led to Dilkusha. But then I was so surprised. From here till there, there were only shops and people. In my imagination, this had been a quiet street with tall trees and fields on one side and, on the other, a red brick wall that stretched from one end to the other. I could never quite tell what lay behind it. All one could see was a large pillar made of the same red bricks which on some days, stood still as death, and on other days, constantly spluttered and spewed clouds of smoke. Actually this was a cotton-carding mill and as soon as its boundary ended, we walked a few more steps and entered Dilkusha. But now, a row of shops had come up along that massive wall and stretched from here till there. And the tall trees and fields on the other side … where had they gone and how had so many people come on the street? The sight of so many people was horrifying.

I got out of the car and walked a few steps, only to be confounded. 'Where is Dilkusha,' the words escaped from my lips instinctively. How far the *tanga* used to go on that narrow *kutcha* path that led from the gate! On the left and right, there were so many trees and more trees behind them, some tall and dense and some bushy. How good it felt to sit in a *tanga* as one drove past twin rows of mango, guava, jamun followed by pomegranate, apricot, plums and bananas. What happened to all the trees? And the building that was Dilkusha? I ran my gaze over the dust-filled grounds. I could see a pile of bricks in the far distance: it was a tumbled-down building. I went close and peered at it in an attempt to recognize it. In that pile of broken masonry, I spotted a staircase that I recognized instantly. It was strange. In that fallen down building, there was only a staircase that had, somehow or the other, managed to hold onto its form.

I sat down on a clean slab of the stairs and tried to collect myself. I too seemed to be turning into rubble. How long I sat there, quiet and lost. Shankar, too, did not think it necessary to speak. Though after some time, as he looked around and inspected the ruins, he mumbled, 'There is no one to be seen here; who is one to ask?'

I heard these words and looked up and inspected my surroundings closely. In the far corner, I spied some signs of life. A neem tree, a string cot under its shade, a horse tethered close by and an unyoked *tanga*. And facing it a mud wall and on its door a tattered old rag for a curtain. I suddenly remembered: Bhupat used to stay here. I got up and swiftly walked in its direction, and knocked on the door.

A large fat man, wearing a filthy vest and *dhoti*, appeared. He looked closely at me as though he was trying to recognize me. And then, in a flash, he blurted out, 'Munnan Miyan, it is you?'

And I was amazed: who could he be? 'I am sorry but I am not able to recognize you.'

'I am Bholu, Bhupat's son.'

'Oh, oh, I see, Bhupat's son.' Now I could remember. 'And where is Bhupat?'

'He is dead.'

'Oh … when did it happen?'

'Oh,' Bholu sighed and said, 'when the house and gardens were parcelled off, he was heartbroken. He collapsed and was gone within a few days.'

I didn't know what to say next. Hesitantly, I asked, 'Where is everyone?'

'Everyone? Who is everyone? There is only Chhote Miyan left. He has gone to the old house.'

'Old house … I see …'

Bholu wanted to add to my meagre knowledge. Once again he raised the subject of the old house and was about to tell me something more when my glance fell on the building in front of us. 'What is that?' I asked with a start.

'This … this is the *dharamshala*.'

'*Dharamshala*?' I was astounded. 'Surely this must be some new *dharamshala*. That one was different.' And the *dharamshala* and its environs rose in my imagination, along with every tiny detail. The long boundary wall made of small bricks and the small gate in it gave the impression from outside that that was all there was to it and nothing inside except peepal trees. And all around, there was such immense silence as though it was situated in the middle of a wasteland. And the air was so mysterious that even if a leaf stirred, it created a sense of terror and surprise.

'Munnan, O Munnan … monkey.'

'Monkey?…. Where?'

'On the peepal in the *dharamshala*.'

I was Munnan then. I became Jawad gradually. And standing here, a small boy, who had been scampering and prancing among the trees, suddenly came and stood before me – as though his was a being distinct from mine, one that had got lost in times past. I looked at him as though he wasn't me but someone else. Suddenly he disappeared; must be glued to Maimuna's side. The two of them were always off wandering here and there.

'Oh I see, on the peepal in the *dharamshala*?'

'Yes, that's where I'd just seen him.'

Munna inspected the tall and dense trees in the distance from where he stood. 'But there is nothing there.'

'It was there.'

'Then where did it disappear?'

And then the two of them set off in search of the monkey. They reached a large thicket of reeds. The spot marked their final limit beyond which lay a desolate territory, a land where it was dreadful to even set foot. In any case, what lay beyond the reeds? From here till as far as the eye could see, there were only clumps of weeds standing about. After the sandy stretch stood the *dharamshala* and beyond the *dharamshala* there was nothing.

One would have known what lay beyond had one ever gone that far. All one could see from a distance were a few reeds and a few tall trees: that was all. The two walked till the cluster of reeds and came to a stop.

'Where was the monkey?'

'There ... on that peepal,' Maimuna pointed towards the tallest peepal in the *dharamshala*.

Munna inspected every branch of the tall trees from where he stood in the distance. 'There is nothing there.'

Suddenly, Bholu too showed up in search of them. 'Munnan Miyan, what are you looking for?

'Monkey.'

'Monkey?' Bholu asked with great surprise.

'Yes there was a monkey on that tall peepal. Maimuna saw it. God knows where it has gone.'

'It couldn't have been a monkey.'

'Why not?'

'All the monkeys have fled from the town. The king of langurs has shown up; and so all the monkeys have disappeared.'

'But I just saw one; it had a tail as long as a coil of rope. Its body was all brown and its face was red.'

Bholu laughed. 'Then it was a langur.'

'Langur?' And with a shiver he said, 'Come let's go and see.'

'Munnan Miyan, be very careful when you go there.'

'Who lives in the *dharamshala*?' Maimuna asked curiously.

'Yes, who lives there?' And he fell into confusion.

'I know,' Bholu answered confidently.

'How do you know?'

'Once, I gathered all my courage, and went inside the *dharamshala*. And there I saw, sitting under the peepal tree an ascetic with long hair and moustaches, his body covered in ash. His eyes were closed and a smile played upon his lips. A pot was boiling away in front of him. In the light of a flickering lamp, I saw a woman sitting in front of him, and smiling. She wore rings in her ears and a hoop in her nose ... I ran for dear life from there.'

Munnan and Maimuna looked at him with terror and surprise. Munnan shivered and then said, 'Lies!'

Maimuna agreed, 'Liar!'

'Fine, don't believe me.'

'Let's go and see,' Munnan announced suddenly.

'No,' Maimuna sounded scared.

'Maimuna Bibi,' Bhola tried to bolster her courage, 'Don't be scared; I will walk ahead.'

And indeed Bholu stepped forward with confidence and began to walk ahead. And the two of them followed. The *dharamshala* had seemed so close, but it seemed to be slipping further and further away. As they walked on the sandy porous stretch, it seemed as though they were walking in some desert wasteland.

Suddenly, he stopped and, in a voice filled with fear, he whispered, 'Serpent.'

The two of them stopped, too. A long serpent was slithering just a short distance away from them. Maimuna clutched Munnan's fingers in her hand with terror. The serpent completed its serene, swaying journey to the clump of bushes that grew beside the wall of the *dharamshala*, and disappeared from sight.

'Let's go back,' Munnan announced. And immediately the three of them turned back. They walked slowly for some time; suddenly, they began to run. Bholu was in front and Maimuna was at the back.

They stopped to draw breath only when they reached the Persian wheel where the camel was going round and round at its steady pace and drawing water at a steady pace that was flowing through a channel and reaching the fields. Bhupat sat nearby, smoking from his chillum. He looked at the three of them as he drew on his chillum and saw that they were panting for breath.

'Where have you been running around in this heat?'

'There is a serpent, Bapu,' Bholu informed his father. 'It was near the *dharamshala*; it was soo long.'

'Was it jet black?'

'Yes.'

Bhupat became thoughtful. He took a long draw on his chillum. Then, he said, 'It is extremely poisonous. I was about to kill it but an ascetic came out of the *dharamshala* and stopped me. He said, "You fool, are you about to cause pain to the son of the Serpent God?" And I broke out in a cold sweat and my staff lay where it fell.'

The three of them were transfixed. Maimuna wiped the sweat from her face and neck with the end of her shirt. How terror-stricken she looked! It was only at night when she lay beside Phuphi Amma and narrated the afternoon's adventures that her fear dissipated somewhat.

'Amma, do you know what happened this afternoon. You know those bushes near the *dharamshala*, those clumps of sugarcane …'

'Near the *dharamshala?*' Phuphi Amma interrupted him. 'My dear, what had you gone to do there?'

'I wasn't going. Munnan got after me that we go to the *dharamshala* to see who lived there.'

'Lies,' Munnan, who was lying on the other side of Phuphi Amma, immediately shot back. 'It was this wretched girl Maimuna who told me that there was a langur on the peepal tree in the *dharamshala* and I said let us go and see it.'

'No, my darling, you should not go there and in any case it is very desolate in the afternoon. Those ascetics are busy doing their sorceries out there. And all sorts of ghosts and spirits haunt the place.'

'Phuphi Amma, I am not at all scared of ghosts.'

'Not scared at all,' Maimuna mimicked his voice and said, 'He began to shiver with fright at the sight of a serpent. Amma, we saw such a long, such a thick serpent today. It swayed right past us.'

'Hai Allah, you unfortunate creatures, why do you run around here and there?'

'Phuphi Amma, if only I had my catapult; I would have taken such a perfect aim that it would have died of pain.'

'My darling, don't ever do such a thing even by mistake. May God keep us safe from such a poisonous creature! It brings misfortune whether it dies, or survives. A wounded serpent is very dangerous. But if it dies, its mate goes around hissing and biting in revenge.'

'Amma,' Maimuna raised a question, 'How will the mate know who killed the serpent?'

'Ai, how will it not know? It comes running when the serpent dies and peers into the dead serpent's eyes. The serpent looks at whoever has killed it in such a way that a picture of the killer forms in its eyes – almost as though someone has taken a photograph. And the mate immediately sets out in search of the killer to take her revenge. And if the serpent survives, then it does not rest until it has taken revenge on whoever tried to kill it. And if can't take revenge from the person who tried to kill it, then it goes after that person's son, if not the son, then the grandson. That is what happened to King Parikshit.'[56]

'King Parikshit? What happened to him?' Munnan and Maimuna asked in unison.

'It so happened that King Parikshit's grandfather was a great warrior. Once, armed with a bow and arrow, he entered a forest full of serpents. He killed the serpents by piercing them with his arrows, one after the other. But Arjuna's arrow lanced past one of the serpents and it escaped. But even though it escaped, it was enraged and it vowed to take its revenge against the brave Arjuna. However, it could not touch Arjuna and even his son remained unharmed. However, when the grandson ascended the throne, the poisonous serpent said, "The grandfather and father have managed to get away, but I will not leave the grandson." Parikshit came to know that a certain serpent was after his life. Don't think I am lying, but he got such a palace made for himself where even a bird could not enter from above and an insect could not crawl in from below. But this poisonous serpent was made of sterner stuff. One day, he saw that a basket of fruits was going in for the King. Immediately, he turned himself into a worm and entered a guava. And now here is what happened inside the palace … Of all the fruits before him, it was the guava that caught the King's eye. He was about to cut the guava and eat it when he saw a worm wriggle out of it. He laughed and said, "So this is the creature that is supposed to bite me to death." Barely had the words left his lips

---

[56] Parikshit was the grandson of Arjuna, and the son of Abhimanyu from his wife Uttara. He succeeded his uncle, Yudhishtira, to the throne of Hastinapura, but he died of a serpent's bite.

when the worm shuddered and turned into a huge serpent. With a hiss, he bit the King in his neck. And while people ran around here and there, the serpent slithered away. And within the blink of an eye, the King died.'

'Munnan Miyan, you had seen this place. You remember what was here before ... four broken walls that were crumbling down, one door and the peepal trees.'

'Hmm,' I drew a long sigh. The scenes from my imagination scattered.

'And that sandy stretch too has gone.'

'And this spot where I am standing?' I said to myself. It felt strange to see that the place that was green and verdant yesterday had turned into a wilderness and in contrast that piece of land that once held nothing but a mysterious-looking desolation had become so populous that the air of mystery around it had entirely gone. 'Yaar, Shankar, this place is ruined; let us go.' And I began to turn away with leaden steps.

'Munnan Miyan, are you going to the haveli?' Bholu asked.

'Hmm.'

'I will come with you.' Swiftly, he flicked the ragged curtain aside, went in, and within the blink of an eye, came out, with a kurta over his vest, and began to follow us.

We went back to the road that had once had trees and fields from one end to the other on one side and a long red-brick wall on the other with arches in which pigeons had made their nests. Now, there were two rows of shops; of these, a few had proper roofs, the rest were tent-like structures that sold a variety of items ranging from bangles and combs to assorted hair accessories to kohl-boxes, pipes and trumpets, spinning toys and tops. There were also several shops that sold kites and had all sorts of strings and bobbles draped over the shop front. But the excitement that had built up inside me while coming here was absent now. I was angry at the narrowness of the street and the large numbers of people present all around.

'Yaar, Shankar, why has this mass of humanity descended upon Vyaspur?' And with it, these words escaped from my lips, 'Vyaspur has changed so much.'

And after this, whichever bazaar or street I passed, I was amazed. The same sense everywhere: how much Vyaspur had changed! Time, Miyan, Time! I was reminded of Majju Bhai's blasé remark made with such blithe unconcern, and a sudden sadness enveloped me. Time, Miyan, Time!

'Look, here is our alley ...'

I looked around. Yes, it is the same alley, I thought. But suddenly I was overcome by surprise. How did this alley become so narrow? It used to be fairly wide once. How spacious it used to look! And there aren't any new shops here either. There are the same old shops: some selling milk and *rabri*, others selling kites and hair braids, and in the end a shop selling *itar*. I looked especially closely at the *itar* shop because I wanted to see if the old man who used to sit there with his back bent as he pounded some herbs in his pestle or folded them carefully between a square of paper. But I saw a stranger sitting in his place. My enthusiasm dampened. Immediately after the *itar* shop came the gate of the haveli. I was astounded. I was happy to see it but also surprised. How high this gate used to be, and how wide too! Now it appeared so small. I now began to realize that it wasn't just the roads that had become narrow in Vyaspur, but even those houses that once seemed so large and spacious now seemed small and weary as though they had shrivelled and shrunk. The old haveli too looked shrivelled. How high and mighty it used to look! And a spate of images swelled in my eye. My Dada Miyan in his trimmed white beard and white kurta-pajama would stand amidst the assembled mourners and say in a loud voice: 'Ya Hussain!' And suddenly the dirge-like crying and beating of breasts would stop. He would raise the index finger of his right hand[57] and start speaking, '*Ya*

---

[57] The index finger of the right hand is raised as mark of bearing witness during prayer.

Assalam alaika ya abd Allah, Ya Assalam alaika ya Ibn-e Ali, Ya Assalam alaika ya Ibn-e Husain …'

Actually, the rest of the household had been shifted from the old haveli to Dilkusha. Only the Azakhana had not been shifted. The *alam* are strange objects. Once they are put in a place it is almost as though they take root there. And then such a growth comes up around them, that to shift them is like uprooting a lush green tree. My Dada Miyan had agreed to accommodate his son to the extent that the family moved from the narrow congested lane to a large house in a spacious place. And so a *kothi* was built in the middle of the family orchard. But my grandfather insisted that once a year the entire family – with all their attending paraphernalia – move to the old *haveli* for ten days and camp there. These ten days were ten counting days, but actually they encapsulated an entire age. So much happened during that time and how agile and energetic Dada Miyan seemed during those days. He had handed over the family estate to his dearest son, along with all the responsibilities regarding family issues and matrimonial alliances. He had kept his own engagement limited to Muharrum. All day long, he would run about getting things done; the only time he sat down was at the time of the *majlis*. Sitting in the front, right next to the pulpit, he would sway to the words of the person reciting the *marsiya*, shower praises on particularly evocative verses, invoke blessings upon the Prophet and his family at appropriate intervals and intersperse the proceedings with loud cries of lamentation. With his sonorous cries, he was the life and soul of the assembly. In fact, the assembly would break into sobs only after his pathos-laden shout of anguish rang out. And the mourners would take their cue not from the speaker but from that heart-rending shout. And they too would begin to cry loudly and, yes … Suddenly, another picture rose before my eyes. Once again, my lost existence came and stood before me in the form of Munnan, an existence that had entirely vanished for me. Adjusting the little cap studded with star-shaped spangles on his head, he would enter the *Imam Bara* hesitantly and run to sit beside his grandfather. 'Dada Miyan, I will also recite.'

'Certainly, my child.'

And when he would sit on the pulpit, Dada Miyan would say, 'Recite the *rubai* by Dillu Ram Kausari.[58]' And he would launch forth almost immediately:

Kya pahuncha masiha jo falak pe pahuncha
Maqsood ko apne na Sikandar pahuncha
Allah ghani Kausari aisa chaalak
Ganga se jo phisla lab-e kausar pahuncha
(Look where the messiah has reached the high heavens
Where even Alexander could not reach his destination
O Allah, this prosperous Kausari is so clever that
He slipped from the Ganges and reached the rim of the paradisal fount)[59]

And suddenly the Imam Bara disappeared and another image of Dada Miyan appeared before my eyes. This time, he is seated in the old *haveli*. Bande Ali is sitting with him. A huqqa is placed between them. A lament on the decline of the Muslims is presented by Bande Ali, after a thorough perusal of the *Zamindar* newspaper, followed by a requiem, rendered with the utmost strenuousness by Dada Miyan.

'Saiyad sahab, I can not understand one thing. The Muslims are an ancient people. Allah has promised them salvation on the day of resurrection. Why are they then being disgraced and dishonoured today?'

'Bhai Bande Ali, every individual must pay the price of his misdeeds. See the state of the Muslims' conduct. Why go far? Let us look at the Turks. Turning away from the word of god in Allah's own tongue, they have ruined their namaz. So when Muslims do not remain Muslims, naturally the wrath of God will smite them.'

'You speak the truth, Saiyad sahab. All this is the result of a

---

[58] Dillu Ram was a Hindu poet who wrote quatrains in praise of the Prophet Muhammad; he lived in Delhi.

[59] There is a play upon words in the best tradition of Urdu poetry here. Kausari is the poet's pen name; Kausar refers to a spring or fountain in paradise.

disinclination towards religion.' How quickly Bande Ali seized the nub of the argument.

'Bhai Bande Ali, you must read *Jawab-e Shikwa* by Dr Sir Muhammad Iqbal. You will understand the true reasons for the downfall of the Muslims.'

Bande Ali drew on the huqqa and said, 'I have heard that Dr Sir Iqbal has written a poem in which he has written about the ruin of the people of Andalusia in an extremely powerful way. My nephew Yaqub-ul Hasan studies at the Aligarh College. He had come a few days ago and he was telling me that the poem is being much talked about in Aligarh. And Dr Sahab's poetry is such that it is leagues ahead of the likes of Maulana Altaf Husain Hali.'

'Really? If that is so please ask your nephew to get us a copy of that poem.' He sighed deeply then continued. 'Bhai Bande Ali, the history of Andalusia is in itself a cautionary tale. How the Muslims reached a zenith and how they fell into the abyss of humiliation that they became extinct from the pages of existence. And there is only one reason for this: because they turned back from their faith. Till the day they remained true to their faith, they made such progress that all of Europe watched in awe. And so many enlightened men were produced during this period. Bhai Bande Ali, have you ever heard of a conqueror, or emperor or ruler who had conquered Koh Qaaf?[60]'

'Koh Qaaf.' Bande Ali fell in thought. Then he said, 'Saiyad sahab, Koh Qaaf is the abode of fairies and spirits. How can a human survive there?'

Dada Miyan smiled, 'Yes, you are right, but Sheikh Moosa Abu Imran al-Sadrrani offered the namaz on top of the Koh Qaaf. And not one among the meanest of spirits had the temerity to hinder his namaz.'

'Really?' And Bande Ali's mouth flew open with surprise. 'This is the first time I am hearing of it. Who was this elderly man?'

---

[60] Legendary mountain said to be in the Caucasian region, it is evoked as a metaphor for a fairyland.

'He was from Andalusia and he was a leading light of his time! One day he decided that he would go to Koh Qaaf and offer namaz at the top of the mountain. He only had to say the words in his head and lo and behold, he found himself on Koh Qaaf! He offered the *zuhr namaz* on the mountaintop and the *asr namaz* at the foothill. A devotee asked him, "O Sheikh, how high is Koh Qaaf?" He answered, "It is equivalent to a journey of three hundred years."'

'Subhan Allah, Subhan Allah,' and for a long time, Bande Ali kept saying 'Subhan Allah, Subhan Allah' over and over again.

'Bhai Bande Ali, do you know what is around Koh Qaaf? There is a python that protects the mountain. Hazrat Sheikh Abu Madeen had told Sheikh Moosa, "I can see that one day you will go to Koh Qaaf. When you go there, don't forget to offer your salutation to the one that protects it." The Sheikh was reminded of these words as he climbed the mountain. Immediately, in a loud voice, he proclaimed, "O Protector of Koh Qaaf, may my *Salaam* reach you!" The python replied, "Walekum Assalam!" And then it asked, "How is Abu Madeen?" The Sheikh asked, "O you who live on the ground, you who are the protector of Koh Qaaf, how do you know Abu Madeen?" The python laughed and said, "O simple soul, is there anyone on this earth who does not know Abu Madeen?"'

Dada Miyan fell silent and brought the nozzle of the huqqa to his lips. He sat gurgling away at his huqqa as Bande Ali kept sitting beside him, lost in his own thoughts. Finally, he said, 'Allah be praised, I can sacrifice my life for His creation!'

'Bhai Bande Ali, these things are divine secrets; you and I cannot fully comprehend them. And the coming and going of sultanates is also part of the divine secrets. Think how large this sultanate once was and how many children of Allah were born during this era. I have already told you the incident of Abul Hallaj Sheikh Yusuf. But you know what happened later: the unfortunate Muslims became neglectful of their faith. They got into squabbles over colour and creed. They fell into the pleasures of a luxurious life. Poetry, dance, music, wine, food, dancers, promiscuous entertainers, and those who talked of the beloved's lips and cheeks and the curls of her hair ... naturally the sultanate had to go. And with the sultanate, they too were lost.'

After a moment's hesitation, Bande Ali said, 'But Saiyad sahib, surely this must have been already written by the Inscriber of Fate. I have read a certain Hadith regarding this. It is ascribed to Hazrat Ibne Abbas Razi Allah. He says: "Once I had gone to meet the Prophet – may peace be upon Him. I saw that he was crying. I watched for a long time, then I said to Him, "O Prophet of Allah, I have seen that you have been crying so hard that you are drenched in tears. After all, what is the reason for this?" The Prophet answered, "O Ibn-e Abbas, I have seen far from the peninsula of Arabia, there is a land called Andalusia where Islam is flourishing. But suddenly there is a decline. The Muslims are thrown out of Andalusia and all trace of Islam vanishes from that soil."'

Dada Miyan listened to the narration of this Hadith very attentively and then said, 'But we also find a prophecy in the Holy Book where it says that on that very soil the sound of the *azaan* will be heard once again. Three victors will march upon that land from three different directions and a day will come when all three will sit down at the same table and break bread together.'

'When will that happen?'

'When Hazrat Imam Mahdi appears,' Dada Miyan said and bowed to offer his *Salaam* to Imam Mahdi who is here but hidden from this visible world.[61]

This picture too disappeared from my eyes. A third picture emerged, this time of Dada Miyan in Dilkusha where he was never ever seen sitting and talking to Bande Ali in quite the same manner.

---

[61] According to Islamic eschatology, there is a Guided One, a prophesied Last Prophet who is concealed at present but will appear to rule over the world for seven, nine or nineteen years (according to different interpretations) before the Day of Judgement. Differences exist in the concept of the Mahdi between Shia and Sunni Muslims. For Sunnis, the Mahdi is Muhammad's successor who is yet to come. For Shias, the Mahdi was born but disappeared and will remain hidden from humanity until he reappears to bring justice to the world and rid it of all evil.

It was almost as though he had been uprooted from his spot. He was lying in bed, enfeebled and debilitated. He opened his eyes and looked at Phuphi Amma who was sitting beside his bed, reading from the Surah Yaseen for the past several days. His entire family was gathered around him. Those relatives who had gone away too had come to be close to him in these last moments. Those days Death used to give the dying person ample time to say what one wanted to, to see whom one wanted to. Dada Miyan had gone into a stupor, but he opened his eyes now and said softly, 'The Amir has come.' And with these words, he closed his eyes for ever and Phuphi Amma began to cry loudly. Everyone was crying ...

'Let me go and tell Chhote Miyan,' and Bholu went past the gate like an arrow and, at the same speed, I too returned from the thoroughfares of days gone by. And a strange sense of surprise came over me. Rows upon rows of girls with satchels full of books on their shoulders were coming out of the gate. Has a school opened here? I asked myself; after all, who else could I ask? Bholu had already gone in. He came back at the same speed that he had gone in. 'See, Chhote Miyan is coming out himself.' And I saw an elderly gentleman, tall, slimly built, fair, with a slight white beard, dressed in a white mulmul kurta and a narrow-legged white pajama, a black Rampuri cap on his head – in short, a complete picture of my departed father – was coming towards me with a walking stick in hand. I was amazed. Chhote Miyan had grown so old! How quickly I had forgotten so many years had passed by. I stepped forward and offered my *Salaam*. How affectionately he embraced me! Badi Bhabhi embraced me with the same affection when she welcomed me at the entrance to the women's quarter. 'Ai Bhai, where did this Eid moon[62] come out from? How can anyone come so suddenly? Arre, you should have

[62] The proverbial Eid moon is a rare sighting because it is a mere sliver and visible for only a short while. Its sighting heralds that the next day will be Eid-ul Fitr.

at least informed us on a two-paisa postcard and we would have come to the station to get you.'

'Shankar had reached with his car.'

'Yes, yes, he is your sole relative. We are outsiders. How did you come here? You should have stayed there with him ... in the *kothi* of Seth Mahinder. After all, they have servants, cars, everything ... the comforts you will get there you won't find here.'

'These complaints and grievances, these taunts and excuses can happen later. Let him at least draw his breath.'

'I have let him draw enough breath! Now I will trouble him all I want. He has tasted the easy life in Pakistan; let me deal with him my way. Arre Miyan, tell me: is there a shortage of post offices in Pakistan? After all, what is the price of a postcard? Would it have lessened your wealth if, every six months or so, you had written a few words about your wellbeing on a postcard and sent it to us?'

'He would have written had he considered us his own,' Chhote Miyan added.

'Bhaiyya, I want to know what is mixed in the water of Pakistan that whoever goes there loses all interest in blood relations.'

'Badi Bhabhi, let me ask something too. I cannot understand how you all came to live in the old *haveli* again. And Dilkusha ...'

'Bhaiyya, don't ask,' Bhabhi said in a heart-wrenching tone. 'Why do you sprinkle salt on our wounds? We have been ruined by those who went away to Pakistan.'

I was abashed. All I could say was, 'And now we are ruining ourselves there.'

'It isn't good to cause distress to others. I had told Pyare Miyan, "You are ruining us by going there. If Allah wills, you too will not rest content." And that is exacty what happened. He had come last year. He said, 'Badi Bhabhi, you gave me such a curse that I am still without a roof over my head." I said, "Bhaiyya, I did not curse you; your land did. It isn't good to turn inhabited land into a deserted wasteland. Pyare Miyan, the land also curses. You should not have ruined us in your desire to go and live in Pakistan, and made a mockery of your family."'

'I did not know anything. I went straight to Dilkusha. There is nothing there now. It is a good thing I met Bholu who brought me here. So we can thank Pyare Miyan for this turn of events?'

'There were others who agreed with Pyare Miyan. And chief among them was your Chhote Miyan.'

'That deceitful fellow,' Chhote Miyan burst out in tones of extreme distaste, 'inveigled his younger brother in his schemes.'

'Don't think Achche Miyan was any less clever. In fact, it was he who put the idea in Pyare Miyan's head. It was he who first came up with the plan of moving to Pakistan. They changed colours as soon as Miyan Jaan passed away. First they set up a clamour for going to Pakistan. Then they let loose the firecracker about dividing the property. And your Chhote Miyan ... he agreed to their plans. You know what is the worth of the property of the Muslims these days? They sold it for a song, took their share and went away to Pakistan.'

'It is a good thing they left. What would they have done here had they stayed?' Chhote Miyan asked, lending the stamp of legitimacy to their decision to leave.

'Yes, it is good they went. Of course, they should have gone. But they should not have ruined us. They were about to sell the *haveli* too. It was I who stood barring their way with my shoe in hand. I said to them, "You scoundrels, you will go to Pakistan and live the good life, where will we poor homeless souls go?" And when he tried to throw his weight around, I told him clearly, "This *haveli* is family property. The children of Deputy Dil Husain are not the sole owners of this *haveli*. Munnan, sitting in Karachi, has a share too; ask him. Go to Aurangabad and persuade your younger Phupho. And then there is Maimuna – the only heir of Phuphi Amma; get her signature too." That was enough to fob them off.'

She entered: tall, slim, wheatish complexion, a lock of hair that had turned completely silver, dressed in a white sari. I gaped at her.

'Ai hai, why have you stopped? It isn't some outsider who has come into the house. It is Munnan. Didn't you recognize him?'

And then Badi Bhabhi turned towards me. 'Bhaiyya, you didn't recognize her either? It is Maimuna.'

All I could find to say was, 'Oh, you have become so big.'

'So, could she have stayed that little! Who could have known then that she would become so tall.'

'Yes, she was tiny then,' Badi Bhabhi laughed at my words. Maimuna showed no reaction whatsoever.

'Is the school over?' And then after a pause, Badi Bhabhi said, 'Now look after the kitchen. Munnan Miyan is here, too. I don't feel like getting up.'

Maimuna quietly turned towards the kitchen.

'Those two have been in Karachi from the start; don't you meet them?'

'I am hearing for the first time from you that they are in Karachi.'

'I have heard that this is what happens to people when they go to Pakistan,' Badi Bhabhi started off again. 'People leave together from here. But as soon as they reach there, they scatter to the winds and have no knowledge of each others' joys and sorrows; they join in neither each others' good times nor bad. I have heard that even their marriages are now with outsiders.'

'That is what happens when people are uprooted from their place,' Chhote Miyan interjected once again.

'By the way, what are they doing there? If I get their address, I can try and meet them.'

'You know what Pyare Miyan is like,' Badi Bhabhi said. 'What has that God's own child done in his entire life? He had his father and grandfather's wealth, which he was used to spending lavishly. He always spent money like water. He did the same there. And he possibly found someone who hastened the ruin. And so he was spent. There was no ancestral property there to shore up his downfall. He was completely ruined. Thankfully, God has given him a son. I have heard that he has become an engineer. The boy is his sole support in his old age. That leaves Achche Miyan; you know he was always the clever one. He has heaps of money, but his state is such that even if he spots a coin in a puddle of filth, he will pick it up with his teeth. Bhaiyya, obviously I haven't seen any of this with my own eyes; I am only telling you what I have heard. Achche Miyan apparently is a great one for keeping the officers in good humour. And that is how he gets his tenders.'

'Why blame him? It is the way things are done in Pakistan.'

'Arre, who am I to blame anyone? A person makes himself blameworthy with his own actions. I am saying, no one should walk around with his head held high under this wretched sky. Achche Miyan had come recently with his wife. And, Bhaiyya, she wouldn't set foot on the ground. I said, "May the good Lord keep you as white as pearls and as bright as gold, I am your elder sister-in-law. Whatever I say will be for your own good. Your husband was born as a result of many prayers and entreaties. On the night of eighth of Muharram, he would be dressed as the the cup-bearer of the martyrs who died of thirst in Karbala.[63] My mother-in-law, may Allah grant her a place in paradise, had made a vow that when her child grows up and begins to earn, the offering to Chhote Hazrat on the evening of the eighth of Muharram would be made from his side. And now, by the grace of God, Chhote Miyan is earning. You send a money order each year and we will do what has to be done here; and as far as the giving of water is concerned, for that Chhote Miyan can go to the Shah-e Khurasan and offer water on the night of the eighth of Muharram."[64] Ai Bhaiyya, she turned livid. She turned on me and said tartly, "We live in Pakistan; why should we make our offering here? Maula Ali is here as much as he is there. The offering can be made there too." I was left feeling foolish for opening my mouth. After that, I didn't say another word.'

---

[63] As one who was born after a *mannat* or vow, the child would offer water in memory of the martyrs who died of thirst in the Battle of Karbala. The child would be dressed in a green kurta and carry a small *mashaq* filled with water; he would either go to people's homes to offer water or stand by the road and offer water to wayfarers. The child is called Bibi ka Saqqa, he who gives water to Bibi Sakina, daughter of Husain. The Chhote Hazrat is a reference to Abbas, son of Ali, bother of Husain and paternal uncle of Sakina.

[64] A mosque and Imam Bara in Karachi.

Bholu knocked at the door. 'Bibi-ji, shall I go? Does Munnan Miyan want to go somewhere?'

'Ai hai, let Munnan Miyan draw a breath! And you, where have you been all this while, you accursed creature? We are seeing your face after ages. And, after all, why not? You have also seen that there is nothing but dust here? And what good is that to anyone?'

'No, Bibi-ji, it isn't so at all.'

'Of course ... what else is it? If Bhupat had been alive, he would have been here with us whereas you are an ungrateful wretch. Your new masters must have promised you the sun and the moon. Naturally, you will do nothing but praise them.'

'Bibi, one praises the masters only if they have any praiseworthy qualities. I am myself so fed up of them that I am looking for a way to get away. But what to do ... I am holding on to a piece of land there.'

'I have heard that the Seth has had all the trees cut down,' Chhote Miyan asked.

'He has ruined everything. That Seth has turned out to be a damnable fellow.'

'What does he plan to do?'

'He wants to set up a mill.'

'What do we want with the Seth? What do you do?' Badi Bhabhi asked.

'I drive a *tanga*. The *tanga* that used to belong to Bade Sarkar ... that is with me, you know.'

'The *tanga* had been bought with such joy! How grand it looked! But how many days did he live to sit in it?' Badi Bhabhi sighed.

'It still gleams like new. I have taken very good care of it.'

'Come with the *tanga* tomorrow. We will go and meet some friends and relatives. In any case, there are hardly any friends or relatives left. Dulhan Khala, Nanhi Chachi, Murad Ali Taya ... and that is it. That is the sum total of our relatives. How large the family used to be once! It has scattered now like seeds.' And Badhi Bhabhi sighed once again.

'All right, then, I will come early in the morning.' Bholu went away.

'Let me go and see what is happening in the kitchen. Poor Maimuna is managing all by herself. That wretched girl, Gulshan is of no use; she does nothing till you stand on her head and get things done. And she can do no cooking at all whatsoever.'

'So Maimuna lives with you?' For how long the question had been bubbling inside me. Finally, though still hesitantly, I managed to ask it.

'Who else would she live with? Does she have any brothers or nephews sitting around here? The ones she had have all flown the coop.' And after a pause she said, 'Perhaps you are trying to ask why she has not married. Bhai, you should first look at your own conscience, and then ask this question.'

'He asked a simple question. You love to go off on a tangent, don't you?' Chhote Miyan interrupted her.

'Aji, I have also given a simple straightforward answer. In any case, I remember Phuphi Amma almost all the time. What did she have left in her life to live for? She had nobody left except her daughter. How dearly she wanted her daughter to get married! And her dearest wish came to nothing. How she used to chatter and chirrup earlier! But she became so quiet after Munnan went away. And then her decline set in. And Miyan Khan too fretted and fumed at her state. His sorrow was doubled. After all, the nephew that he loved more than any father would love his own child went away and left him to fend for himself in his old age. He used to say, "What will the world say? That his nephew was such a burden on him that he pushed him away to Pakistan! And look how tightly he has held on to his own children!" And I would say to him, "Miyan Khan, if that were so, why did you not rebuke him when he first raised the subject of going to Pakistan? Would he have had the temerity to set foot outside the house?" And he sighed and said to me, "He was my brother's child; after all, he wasn't mine."'

'Why are you raking these old stories?' Chhote Miyan interrupted her. 'Why pick on Jawad Miyan? It was a wave that was sweeping people off their feet. Now, when you think about it, it seems strange that those who went did so thinking what they did, and those who stayed back did so thinking what they did.'

'Ai hai, the poor girl,' and once again Badi Bhabhi was reminded of the kitchen. 'She is bent over the stove all alone. She comes back exhausted from the school and once here, she sets to work on the skillet and the fire.'

'School.' Now I understood why rows upon rows of girls were coming out of the *haveli*.

'Yes, my dear, we have started a school in the *haveli*,' Badi Bhabhi clarified. 'It has killed two birds with one stone. For one, such a large *haveli* would not have stayed in our possession otherwise. Would the wretched god-forsaken government have let us keep it? Opening the school has allowed us to keep this *haveli*, thank the Lord, and it has also given a hobby to Maimuna. Now she is neither a burden on herself nor on us. And Munnan Miyan, what shall I tell you, how efficiently she is running the school!'

'Badi Bhabhi, the food is ready.' Maimuna came and announced, and went back immediately. Badi Bhabhi's description was left incomplete. Everyone stood up to eat.

Eight

Now I was in my own surroundings. It felt as though all my scattered parts had come and joined me, including Munnan. And now I was together and whole. The feeling suffused me with tranquillity. This sea change had come over me in one night. I cannot say what had changed within me while I slept or who had whispered which magical chant over me, but when I opened my eyes in the morning, I was whole and alive. It was difficult to say when I woke up. For a long time, I kept trying to understand if the sound that was coming from afar was that of a koel. Was this a dream? I kept lying there, with my eyes closed, motionless, lying on my side, fearful that if I were to turn the sound of the koel would be lost. And my dream would break into smithereens. It was as though a koel sitting on a twig of some distant tree had sensed it. She fell silent. Then I opened my eyes and then I came to know that I was awake. I looked up as I lay on the bed. A sky filled with serenity and pleasure was above me. I had slept under the open sky after such a long time. As I lay, I gathered as much of the sky as I could in my eyes. How fresh the sky looked, and how familiar! I was seeing the sky of Vyaspur after ages.

A clamour arose from the middle of the neem tree that stood in one corner of the compound. I got up and went close to the neem. The clamour stilled suddenly. Then suddenly, whorls upon whorls of birds erupted from its branches and, within the blink of an eye, disappeared from sight. A stream of joy coursed through me.

I came back and sat down on a reed *mondha*. I took out a cigarette from the packet kept beside the Thermos flask on the table in front of me. I was about to light it when my eyes fell on the parapet of the roof in front of me where a monkey was sitting quietly. I kept looking at the monkey for a long time. It too seemed to have come to rest as it sat with its back against the parapet.

Suddenly I spotted a dark-skinned, slovenly boy, dressed in a filthy tattered vest and an equally grubby pair of shorts, holding a long stick, climbing the stairs with great preparedness. 'Hey, boy, come here.'

The boy seemed impressed by my imperious tone. He came close and stood in front of me.

'Where are you going with this stick?'

'I was going to hit the monkey.'

'Go back. Don't do anything to the monkey.'

The boy looked surprised by these instructions. Could anyone stop from hitting a monkey, that is, anyone except a Hindu? He went towards the verandah and called out, 'Bibi-ji, he is stopping me from hitting the monkey.'

'Who is stopping you?' Maimuna's voice came from the kitchen.

'He ... who has come from Pakistan.'

By now Maimuna had come out on the verandah. She looked out and ran her gaze all over, then came and stood in the lawn. Softly, she asked, 'Is this monkey very dear to you?'

'Whether it is dear to me or not, tell me what harm has it done to you? It is sitting on the roof; how is it troubling you?'

'So you think that this monkey is innocent; do you know what it did yesterday?' She looked again at the monkey sitting on the roof. 'Yes, it was the same rascal. My dupatta was left lying outside yesterday. Even my angels did not come to know when this villain took off with it. I came to know only when Dina told me. How I tempted him, tried to scare and threaten him, but he did not let go off it. Not till he had torn the dupatta to shreds!'

'And what offering has been kept for him today?'

Maimuna could think of no answer. She was silent for a bit, then she said, 'Why don't you take a bath and freshen up, I am about to lay the breakfast.'

'So early?

'I have to go to school, too.'

'Oh?'

'Yes, hurry up.'

I got up obediently and went towards the bathroom. In my heart of hearts, I was happy that Maimuna was loosening up a little.

I was so happy when I came and sat down at the table after washing and bathing, as though the scum that had collected years upon years had been washed away. How much lighter I felt!

'Arre, Dilbar Hasan's son has come ... where is he?' Nanhi Tai, with her bent back and white head, called out the moment she entered the doorway.

'Nanhi Tai has come,' Badi Bhabhi forewarned me as she stood up and went forward to welcome her. 'Nanhi Tai, why did you take the trouble? Munnan was planning to go to your home to meet you. We just got a bit delayed with the breakfast and that wretched Bholu has also not turned up yet with his *tanga*.'

'Ari, my heart turned over when I heard. Where is he?' I came out of the dining room into the verandah where Nanhi Tai had by now occupied her seat on the *takht*. I bent low and offered my *Salaam*. Nanhi Tai patted me on my head from her place on the *takht*, showered me with good wishes and cracked her knuckles against her head, as though taking all my misfortunes upon herself. 'May you live long, may you stay happy.' Then, after leisurely examining me from my head till my toes, she said, 'My child, what have you done to yourself? You have salt and pepper in your hair whereas you used to have such thick black hair.'

'Nanhi Tai, which world are you talking about. What was my age then, and what is it now?'

'Ai hai, it is hardly as though you have become very old. Why, it is only yesterday that you, may God keep you well, passed in your B.A. exam and your Taya had distributed laddoos in the entire family.'

'Ari Dulhan, which of your brothers-in law has come?'

First came the sound, then Dulhan Khala came into view. Badi

Bhabhi got up to welcome her and brought her close beside me. 'Munnan is here.'

'Munnan?' Dulhan Khala looked confused.

'Ai Dulhan Khala, what is wrong with you? It is Munnan … Dilbar Chacha's son.'

'I see, I see … Dilbar's son Munnan. Arre, what can I tell you? I have become 70 or 72 years old. My brain has turned into a rock. Arre, I had washed his bum when he was little. Ai, my dearest, how are you?'

'I am well with the grace of God.'

'And the greatest grace of God is that you felt like coming to see lowly beings like us. You have shown your face after years. But at least one is thankful that the thought occurred to you – better late than never.'

'Yes, Bibi, one must be thankful for that,' Nanhi Tai said. 'Take my wretched grandson, for example. I had said to him when he was leaving, "My precious one, hurry back and return to us with the same speed with which you are turning your back on us. Come back soon." And he had said, "Grandma, I will come back very soon. And I will return with everyone." And he has not shown his face till this day."

'Ai Bua,' Dulhan Khala said, 'It wasn't just your grandson; all those who went said the same thing. I wrote to my daughter-in-law, "May you live long and prosper in Pakistan. We are only greedy for a sight of you. We won't snatch the gems off your tiara." But it didn't have the slightest effect on her. In any case, how can I complain about her when my own offspring has become stone-hearted; she is, after all, not related to me by blood.'

Anwari too sniffed my presence and showed up at our door. 'Badi Bhabhi, I have heard that Munnan is here. Many congratulations to you!'

'Come, sit down. And congratulations to you too.'

'Arre, Bhaiye, how are you?' And then after a pause, 'Have you come alone?'

'Yes.'

'I see,' she said in a meaningful way and became quiet.

And then she proceeded to narrate a thousand different things. Listening to her, Nanhi Tai and Dulhan Khala grew acutely aware of their own ignorance and how little they knew about the goings on in the extended family.

'Saliman Chachi's grandson is also here these days.'

'Really? But hadn't he gone away to Pakistan too?'

'Pakistan can't stop someone from coming if they truly want to come. He had gone eight years ago. With the grace of God, he is earning well. The mother wrote to say she had fixed his engagement, and he should come and get married. No sooner had the mother written that he took leave and came here.'

'It shows what an obedient son he is,' Nanhi Tai said.

'Nanhi Tai,' Anwari said, 'You can well imagine his obedience from the fact that he lived in Pakistan for eight years, and that too in a city like Karachi, which is famous for its women who are such hussies, and yet that God's own child did not so much as lift his eyes to look at any one of them.'

When everyone had gone, Badi Bhabhi angrily recalled each one of the things Anwari had said and called her by a hundred bad names. 'Did you see the way she was talking? No matter who she was talking about, her darts were pointed towards Munnan. His marriage was long ago; why rake it up now? I controlled myself somehow otherwise I would have ticked her off so sharply she would have remembered it all her life. In any case, I ask you: why be ashamed of something that is permitted in the *sharia*? After all, a *nikah* was performed. And who is she to object?'

'Shabrati has come,' Dina called from outside.

'What does he want?' Badi Bhabhi asked, putting the brakes on her tirade.

'He has come to offer his *Salaam* to the Miyan-ji who has come from Pakistan.'

'These people don't give us a moment's respite. Yesterday, after you went off to sleep, there was such a rush of people wanting to meet you that I cannot tell you! I can't even begin to tell you how your poor Chhote Miyan coped! All the shopkeepers from down the road lined up to meet you. In fact, even those from a street away began to come as the news spread. And your Chhote Miyan turned them all away by saying, you had come after a long journey, you were tired and resting. And now this wretched Shabrati has shown up!'

'All right, I am coming,' I called out to Dina and got up.

A *tehmad* tied around his waist, a grubby vest covering his torso, a talisman hanging from his neck and a leaf-plate covered by a piece of paper in his hand – this was the appearance of the man who stood in front of me. He saw me and burst into a smile, 'Salaam ji, Munnan Miyan.'

'Salaam,' I spoke as I tried to recognize him.

'It looks like Munnan Miyan has not recognized me,' Shabrati addressed Chhote Miyan who sat on a cane *mondha* nearby as he puffed away on his huqqah. His favourite pastime was to sit on the *mondha* kept in the patio and smoke his huqqah while exchanging pleasantries with all those who passed by. He removed the pipe of the huqqah from his lips and said, 'This is Shabrati, the son of Maula, the sweet-maker; he has a shop selling milk and curd just down the street.'

'How quickly you have forgotten, Munnan Miyan; I used to be your friend. Once you had used your sling in the alley of the sweet-makers; the shot had hit a mynah and the bird was thrashing about in pain. Rakhu, the sweet-maker, had spotted you and set up a din saying, "A *Musla* has taken the life of an innocent creature!" And I ran and scooped up the wounded bird, grabbed you and ran towards the alley of the tinsmiths. And the sweet-makers were left high and dry.'

I listened to him in surprise; for the life of me, I could not recall when such a thing had happened.

'Look here, I have brought *rabrhi* for you,' and Shabrati extended the leaf platter towards me.

'*Rabrhi*? What sort of *rabrhi* is it?'

'Now listen to this … Munnan Miyan is asking what sort of

rabrhi it is! The *rabrhi* from our shop is so famous that people come from far and wide to taste it.'

'Come on, take it,' Chhote Miyan said as he gurgled away at his huqqah.

I took the leaf platter and made some small talk with Shabrati. Fortunately, he soon took his leave saying, 'The shop lies unattended; I will come again another time.'

I went back inside the house holding the leaf platter, still covered with a piece of paper. By now, Maimuna had finished her work at the school and returned; in fact, she had even laid out the food on the table.

'The food is ready,' her glance fell on the leaf platter in my hands as she made this announcement. 'What is that?'

'*Rabrhi*. Shabrati came just now with it.'

'*Rabrhi*,' Maimuna spoke with relish, as though her mouth was watering. 'We will eat it after our meal; it will be wonderful.'

I spoke as we ate, 'He brought this *rabrhi* as a token of friendship. He said he used to be an old friend of mine. He was telling me all sorts of yarns from long ago. I couldn't recall even one of them.'

'He remembers. You don't. How strange is that,' Maimuna laughed as she spoke.

'Yes, I don't remember anything anymore.'

She grew suddenly serious and stopped laughing. 'You don't remember anything?'

'No,' and then as though it was necessary for me to present a justification, 'After all, it has been such a long time.'

'Really?' she said as though she had received a jolt. Then, softly, she said, 'Yes, it has been a long time.'

And then she didn't say another word till the meal ended.

'Maimuna, you didn't have the *rabrhi*,' Badi Bhabhi said. 'You like *rabrhi* so much.'

'I am full, Badi Bhabhi; I will eat it another time.'

The floor of the men's quarter was so cool despite the hot weather. Dina had sprinkled so much water on it that all the heat that had accumulated here during the day had all but died away by now. When I came to lie down on the bed that had been made for me here for the night, I felt a strange happiness. The cool floor, the scent of damp earth rising from it, the gurgling sound of Chhote Miyan's huqqah, and a sky filled with stars – I felt as though soon I would fall asleep and sleep more soundly than I had the previous night. My eyes began to droop as I gazed up at the stars. I was fast slipping into a state of somnolence and, in that half-asleep state, I was reminded of Shabrati's words. And the entire scene swam before my eyes. I saw the mynahs setting up a din in the peepal tree as I crossed the alley of the sweet-makers and, instinctively, my hand went to my sling. I fished out a pellet from my pocket, fitted it in the strap of my sling and shot at the mynahs; while most of them flew off, one mynah fell from the branch and began to writhe with pain on the ground below. And suddenly a roar emerged from the rows of shops on either side. I panicked. Shabrati showed great agility. He scooped up the writhing mynah in one hand, held my hand with the other and said, 'Run, Munnan Miyan!' How long we ran – from one alley to the next, then the third and then the one after. It seemed as though we were stuck in a web of alleys. I can't remember how we got out of that snare. One memory led to another, the second to a third and so on. And once again I was lost in a web of alleys. Memories are like alleys. Sleep had fled from my eyes. I was wandering about among the alleys.

I came and sat down at the breakfast table – feeling fresh and lively, like the day before. But while I ate, as I remembered last night, I felt a momentary pang of surprise. 'How strange it is!'

'Why? What happened?' Maimuna asked.

'I couldn't sleep last night.'

'It was very hot last night.'

'Hot? No, it wasn't so hot; in fact, there was a nip in the air.'

'Then you might as well admit that this place is a new place for you. It is usually difficult to fall asleep in a new place. After all, you will spend one or two sleepless nights here.'

'No, it isn't that. The night before last was my first here and I fell asleep as soon as I lay down. And when I woke up the next day, I felt as though I had slept so soundly after a long, long time.'

'Then what happened last night?'

'I was about to fall asleep when I got distracted …'

'And?'

'And I was reminded of Shabrati's words and after that so many lost memories came tumbling back.'

'But you keep saying that you don't remember anything of the past. What brought about this revolution?'

'It's always like that with me; at first it seems that I remember nothing, but then sometimes the memories come surging back with such force that I am swept away.'

'Fine habit you have,' she smiled. There was such contentment in her smile.

'Do you know what has happened to me since I have come here?'

'What?'

'I went straight to Dilkusha – as I used to in the past. But there is nothing left there, nothing except the rubble of a solitary building. One look at it and my mind turned into a barren wilderness. I tried my hardest to imagine Dilkusha along with its inhabitants, its trees and birds. But my imagination failed me. Clumsily, I wandered about. It was only when I saw the new building of the *dharamshala*, that I was roused from my stupor. And, in a flash, the old building of the *dharamshala* – that used to seem like a mere boundary wall to us all those years ago – swam before my eyes. And then I remembered everything in such minute detail. Do you remember, Maimuna, once you had spotted a langur on the tall peepal that grew there and how eagerly the two of us had gone off to see it. And on the way, we had spotted a snake … Do you remember?'

'No.'

'No? You don't remember? I am so surprised.'

Maimuna seemed lost in her thoughts. But she pulled herself together with a start and said, 'Yes, I remember.' She was silent for a while. Then she said softly, 'It is strange; I never saw the langur there again.'

'Just that one memory brought to life so many memories associated with Dilkusha. All of a sudden, I have remembered so much!'

'Munnan,' Maimuna seemed stuck in that same memory still.

'Yes?' I looked at Maimuna with some surprise because she had addressed me by my nick name for the first time since I had come back, and that too with such friendship and familiarity.

'What a long snake that was! I nearly died at the sight of it. What if it had bitten us?'

'What if it had ... we would have died,' I smiled as I answerd simply.

She said as though she hadn't heard me, 'Munnan.' And there was so much surprise and such fear steeped in her voice.

'Hmm.'

'What was inside that *dharamshala*? No one was ever seen going inside, or coming out. All we could see from outside were the peepal trees.'

'Or the langur?' I smiled, as I added my bit.

She laughed and said, 'And that too was spotted just once.'

Nine

The clouds had been gathering since the morning. Badi Bhabhi cast a fleeting glance at the sky and announced her verdict, 'The clouds are fit to burst; the rain will come down in a torrent.' And then, as she ate her breakfast, she added, 'It's a perfect day to put a wok on the fire. God knows if there is any chick-pea flour in the house?'

'Chick-pea flour?' Maimuna said, 'No, there isn't any in the house. I had made some *khandoi* last Friday with what we had left.'

'Then we will have to send for some.'

Maimuna finished her breakfast in a hurry and went off to her school. But she came back soon enough.

'Arre, you are back!' How happy I was to see her.

'I thought of taking a holiday today.'

'Why? What's the occasion?'

'The rains have come! I thought I will fry some pakori for you with my own hands. And, yes, we have some *arbi* leaves too. You will remember the feast!'

'Thank you,' I smiled.

The truth is that by now we had both become quite at ease with each other. We had become so comfortable with each other that I had told her every detail of the joys and sorrows of my years in Pakistan and the story of my life. She had scraped out every bit of information from me: how did I get married? How was my wife? What was her illness? How did she die? No one had asked me these things ever before. And I had never told them to anyone either. And if someone were to ask, I would have told them the bare facts. But Maimuna asked me with such familiarity that I narrated every detail of every incident in the most heartfelt manner possible.

'There is only one son?'

'Yes.'

'And you have sent him to America. Why didn't you keep him with you?'

'The thing is, Maimuna, in Pakistan the sons are doing exactly what the fathers had done to *their* fathers. They had turned their faces away from their fathers and taken the road to Pakistan; now their sons are leaving them to their fate and running off to America.'

Bit by bit, I told her every detail of the entire story of my life, and she heard me out with the utmost attention and sympathy. And, later I felt so much lighter. The burden that had been weighing down my heart for years – and getting heavier by the year – was miraculously removed. I had never met anyone who would listen to my tale with such empathy. Badi Bhabhi and Chhote Miyan had shown only a cursory interest in my departed wife and son, and had been satisfied by my perfunctory answers. Only Maimuna's behaviour had shown the true meaning of asking questions and listening to answers.

So, now, I was lightened. And if there was some disquiet in Maimuna's heart, that too had been subconsciously removed. How close we had come to each other! With the utmost absorption, she was wrapping the *arbi* leaves in the spicy chick-pea batter and frying them in hot oil, and I was eating them with great relish. After such a long time, my taste buds had reawakened. I was eating them myself and urging Bhabhi to eat them, too.

'Arre, Bhaiyya, what can I tell you … we have changed and so have the rains!' Badi Bhabhi was less interested in eating and far more engrossed in narrating tales of the rainy seasons of long ago. 'The wok would be brought out in the month of *sawan* and stay in use till *bhadon*. And the rains used to come down in buckets. And heaps of *pakwan* would be fried; after all, there were so many of us. And every day there would be new requests for new delicacies.' Badi Bhabhi suddenly fell silent. She drew a long sigh and when she spoke, the sadness had thickened in her voice. 'Those times are long gone. Now, when it rains, I sit and gaze at the cold hearth. I don't know how Maimuna thought of putting the wok on the fire.' She paused and then said, 'Even the wretched rains have changed. How they used to last and how an entire week would go past without the sun showing its face! And once it rained so hard that an entire fortnight passed and the water would not stop coming down. Sometimes a trickle, sometimes pitter-patter, and sometimes a deluge! Till finally, Phuphi Amma went and hung a rosary on the tree and, as the day slipped past, a rainbow could be seen arcing across the sky shaped like a perfect bow.'

'Maimuna, do you remember,' I said as I too recalled one rainy season from long ago. 'Once when, in the middle of a blisteringly hot day, we were wandering about in that sandy stretch catching will o' the wisps. Suddenly, the clouds rolled up and it rained so hard that the sandy basin turned into a mini lake. And Bhupat had pulled us out with such difficulty.'

'And, Munnan, do you remember,' Maimuna also remembered another rainy season from another time, 'when lightning had struck the old neem tree in the garden at Dilkusha? It had seemed as though the sky had burst open. And the tree had smashed into smithereens. Bhupat had told us that at that very moment a snake had appeared from under the tree, and the lightning had actually fallen on it.'

And then a train of memories of monsoons of long ago followed. Badi Bhabhi perhaps felt that these were our common memories in which she had no share. She must have felt like a spare wheel, and so she quietly got up and left us.

One monsoon, second monsoon, third monsoon ... we suddenly remembered so many monsoons together, like the surging of dark, swollen clouds. The rush of memories is a cruel surge. We turned into children again. Maimuna and Munnan, holding each other's fingers, wandered far and wide. That day it had rained so hard that a river ran through the middle of the courtyard. The two sat in the verandah counting the bubbles as they formed and burst ceaselessly. A bubble would form suddenly amidst the falling raindrops and get swept away by the rushing waters. 'Look, look, that one there is as round as a sahab's hat!' they would shout gleefully. But at that very moment, the bubble would burst, and another bubble would form, and then a third! Then they made their paper boats and put them in the rushing water. How their paper boats sped along. Filled with joy, Maimuna clapped her hands. 'Look, my boat is going faster than yours.' Munnan was beginning to feel peeved when Maimuna's boat capsized suddenly. A large brick was lying in the middle of the courtyard and Maimuna's boat collided with it, stopped and, as it began to get drenched, also began to come apart. Now it was Munnan's turn to clap his hands with glee. His boat was swimming along marvellously. Maimuna was close to tears. Munnan's boat came to a halt when its bow struck a tub full of mangoes that was lying in the middle of the courtyard, and began to disintegrate almost at once. Both the boats had capsized, but Munnan had already found something else to occupy his attention. He took out his top and twirled it really fast between his fingers and slid it down to the floor where it kept whirling and spinning away till as far as the twine would let it go; with one expert tug of his hand, he would pull it back and scoop up the still spinning top in his palm. Maimuna kept watching this. Then, as though in response, she took out her yellow and red toy windmill and began to twirl it about. Maimuna always had to do something rightaway in response to anything Munnan might do. That day when Munnan had bought a nice *Tesu* from the bazaar, Maimuna had wanted one too, but Phuphi Amma scolded her, 'Tesu is not for girls; girls go out with a *Jhanji*.'

And so a clay *Jhanji* was brought for Maimuna; it had eye-shaped slits and on the slits were colourful bits of red and green kite paper. A small earthern lamp was lit and placed inside. Soon, people began to toss a few coins beside the *Jhanji*. 'That's a good one … Look at you, collecting money for free! Shouldn't you be singing the *Jhanji* song to collect money?' But how could she? She didn't remember the words. So, instead she promptly sang the *Tesu* song:

Mere Tesu yahan arha
Khaye ko mange dahi bada
Dahi bade mein panni
Dhar de mai atthanni
(Here stands my Tesu
Asking for curd dumplings
There's tinsel in the curd dumplings
Give me eight annas, O mother)

'Phuphi Amma, what's all this about *Tesu* and *Jhanji*,' I think it was Badi Bhabhi who had asked this question. And Phuphi Amma launched, almost immediately, into an explanation, 'Arre, that wretched fellow, that son of Gandhari, was not letting the Pandavas get on. Kanhaiya-ji created *Jhanji* and got her married to him just so his attention would get diverted.'

'Hai Allah!'

'These are Hindu beliefs. Who can tell how much truth there is in it, and how much lies? The good and bad will rest with the Hindus; I am telling you what I have heard. People say that *Jhanji* was actually Tesu's wife.'

'Tell us the truth, Phuphi Amma.'

'Ai Bibi, how would I know? I am telling you what the Hindus say. Though I must say, who would give their daughter to this black-faced Tesu? Kanhaiya-ji did him a favour by creating a doll and giving it to him and saying, "Here, play with her."'

And Maimuna broke into a song:

Gaajar ki paindi, gulkhiro ka phool
Lo miya gudde tumhe gudiya qubool
(A belly made of carrot, a flower of hollyhock
Here, my dear, is a bride for you)

'It is raining harder.'

'What?' I was startled.

Maimuna had looked at the swiftly falling rain and made a casual remark. But it served to scatter the clouds of my memories.

The rain had indeed started to fall faster. At first, it was coming down in straight lines, then it became slanted, and after a phase of pouring down in sheets, it had settled down to a steady downpour. Its pace had slackened, so had its noise. But such was its steadiness that it seemed as though it had been falling for ages and would continue to fall for ages to come. For so long, and with such absorption, the two of us sat and watched the falling rain that we did not realize that the rainfall had changed direction and was now drenching us.

With a start, she said, 'The drizzle is making us wet.' And pushing her *mondha* backwards, she admonished me, 'Munnan, you are getting wet; get your *mondha* out of the rain.'

'No.'

'No?' Maimuna looked at me with surprise. 'The drizzle is quite strong; your clothes will get soaked.'

'Indeed they will,' I answered carelessly. But then I elaborated, 'Don't you remember, Maimuna, how much I used to enjoy getting wet in the rain?'

'So your childhood is not quite over yet?'

Her comment made me sad. 'If only I could have saved my childhood.' With these words, my eyes fell upon the neem tree standing in the courtyard and getting wet. I was transfixed as though I was seeing the tree for the first time since I had come back. How contendedly it stood there, getting wet. As though that contentment had burst out of it and steeped into the very air around it. There had been a restlessness in the rain when it had first started falling down, which had caused an unrest in the atmosphere. But now there was a steadiness about it. It was coming down at the same measured pace. Trees, plants, walls, parapets – everything was soaked in the water as though they had all quenched their thirst and were now sated. And the neem tree seemed to be in a state of surrender, yes almost a state of surrender. A scene from another age swam before my eyes. The neem used to shake from top to bottom when a storm raged, its branches trembling with the tumult. Thunder, lightning followed by a burst of torrential rain, and then the storm would abate somewhat. Its flailing branches would quieten and become still as they got drenched in the steadily falling rain. And then the neem would come into a state of surrender; first the neem, and then everything around it.

'Maimuna, do you see the neem?'

'Yes, I do … what about it?'

'I hadn't quite seen it till now … it is the same as it always was.' And I was greatly surprised as I spoke these words. It had been just the same even then. There used to be two ancients around here: my Dada Miyan and the neem. It was as though they were the same age. But my Dada Miyan's back kept getting bent with age. His hair had already turned snow. One day, his eyes too closed forever. That day the neem had appeared so sorrowful; it had been left all alone, after all. But once again it became glad and cheerful. The two of us used to run around it all day long, as though we were a part of it, as though Maimuna had emerged from its trunk – bit by bit – and I was one of its branches. But then I saw that the other branches were green and intact – as they had always been. At first I was saddened, but then an amazement overtook me. The tree was exactly the same. It was a miracle. We change, but trees do not. Our tree was still the same, though now … And then, so many different scenes, from so long ago, rose in my imagination.

A swing would dangle from its sturdy branch. Maimuna used to take such long swings on it that her head, with her hair coming undone, used to nearly touch the topmost branches. But Maimuna could only sit in the swing and take those long, long swipes. She could not climb the neem; though actually even I could not climb too high. I could barely reach its lowest branch. It used to be such fun to sit on that branch, as though I had risen from the ground and become a part of the neem, a branch among its many branches. How Maimuna used to burn with envy! But I was hardly to be blamed; it wasn't as though I stopped her from climbing the tree. If anything, I always offered her support to help her climb up. I used to like doing it. I used to feel a strange relish. The mere touch and the attempt to do so ... so many such occasions suddenly rose in my memory. And some times, while I would be supporting her, she would slip in such a way that ... The memory made me blush. I wondered if Maimuna also remembered those things. Surely, she would.

'Maimuna,' I finally found the courage to say, 'this neem has not changed one bit ... I mean from the time when we ...' Embarassed, I spluttered to a halt. I don't know if Maimuna remembered anything at all, for she said, 'Hmm,' and then fell silent.

And then I was reminded of something else, 'Maimuna, you used to have that hobby.'

'Which hobby?'

'Sitting on the swing and singing *sawani*.'

This time Maimuna looked really sad. Though all she said was 'Yes' and then she remained quiet.

'The wok was put on the fire, but the swing was not tied on the tree. The celebration of the rains has remained incomplete.'

'These are the pastimes of young girls; do you see any girl in this house?'

'What happened to your interest?'

'Can you not see my age?'

'I can see it; what's wrong with your age?'

Confused, she became quiet. Then she got to her feet and went inside the house. The rain kept falling at a steady pace, in the same slanting way. And I was indeed soaked to the skin. But I felt good. And in front of me, a river ran down the middle of the courtyard. Raindrops were falling like dumplings in boiling oil. Some drops would fall in such a way that they would blow into a bubble; the bubble would flow some distance and then burst. One bubble, two bubbles, three bubbles ... I was watching the bubbles form and burst. The rain kept falling and I kept getting wet. Actually, it was raining inside me too. And the accumulated dust was getting washed away and a clean new self was coming out. Or perhaps the old self had emerged and was gleaming. In any case, I was feeling lighter and glowing, as though I had been washed inside out.

She came back and said, 'Munnan, you are completely drenched. I have kept a *pajama* with a drawstring in place and a *kurta* in the bathroom. Go take a bath and change your clothes.'

I got up feeling sage and mature, and went towards the bathroom. I took a bath, wore clean fresh clothes and came out. The rain had stopped by now and Maimuna was sitting on the *mondha* and watching, with utter absorption, the water fall from the drainpipe like falling pearls. I nudged my *mondha* close to hers and sat down. At first the water fell from the drainpipe in a rush. Gradually, its speed slackened and the swollen stream became slender. And when this stream fell in the gutter, it looked as though molten silver was scattering.

Suddenly, a mynah descended upon the parapet in front of us. Its body quivered, its wings trembled and, almost abruptly, it broke into a loud cry. Within seconds, another mynah flew down and almost immediately, it too began to cry loudly. The two set up a loud din and, just as abruptly, flew away.'

'Maimuna, did you hear what they said to each other and why they flew away?'

'You would have heard; no doubt you would know.'

'The first mynah was a male. It called out and said, "My darling, the rain has stopped. Come on, let us go out for a bit." The other heard this and came out of her hiding. Pleased, she said, "The weather is so nice; it will be such fun to go out." And both went off for an outing.'

Maimuna burst out laughing.

But by now my eyes had slipped from the parapet and were examining the entire wall in front of us. That moss-encrusted wall had been swept clean and was sparkling brightly.

'Maimuna, do you see the wall in front of us; how dark it had become and how the green moss was breaking out in patches all over it?'

'Yes, really,' and she began to look at the wall as though she was seeing it for the first time.

'Looking at the wall, one can tell how many monsoons this house has seen. The monsoons must have come before us too, which our elders must have seen. But we too saw many seasons of rain in the time I lived here. It seems as though we have lived an entire age, an entire century of rains … yes, a whole century … those who come after us will see the next lot of rains.'

'Those who come after us,' Maimuna looked sharply at me. A slight bitterness crept into her tone. 'Who will come after us? Everyone has gone.'

I became quiet, like the culprit falls silent when reminded of his crime. For a long time, I sat quietly. I did not have the courage to meet Maimuna's eyes, or even to talk to her. A few drops of rain began to fall once again. Then they began to come down harder, and I kept thinking that this house was witnessing its last rainy season.

Ten

That day Badi Bhabhi's betel-chopper, and her tongue, were both showing exceptionally good speed. She was recounting old incidents from long ago with such flair, as though every door and window of her memory had been flung wide open. In any case, she had told me so much over the past few days that by now I was intimately aware of every incident that had befallen our family since the day I had gone away – down to the smallest possible detail. I was in any case unaware of what had happened after I had left but now, listening to her, I realized I was far less informed than I had ever imagined about my family history even when I had lived here. I was at the crossroads between being informed and being uninformed when I had left. The history of a family is never revealed in its entirety to any of its members. As one travels from unawareness to awareness and from mindfulness to a full understanding, or as one listens to the words of one's elders, and quite without realizing it or even meaning to, the history of one's family seeps into one's consciousness. I now realized there were so many things that I knew nothing about. For instance, I had seen Phuphi Amma living with us in our house from the time I had opened my eyes. She enjoyed immense authority and respect; her stature, if not more than Tai Amma, was certainly no less. After all, she was the sister of two well-to-do gentlemen of some means. One brother doted upon her as an elder brother should; and upon the younger one, she exercised firm control as only an elder sister can. At Dilkusha, the young and old alike held her in the greatest possible awe. Her word was law in the kitchen. And I never knew, nor bothered to find out, why Phuphi Amma lorded over Dilkusha when her own husband was not only alive and well but a gentleman of independent means living in a neighbouring *qasba*. It isn't as though she and her husband were estranged, for had they quarrelled and separated, why would boxes upon boxes of mangoes arrive from his orchard monsoon after monsoon, and bundles of sugarcane and clay-pots filled with sugarcane juice come with unfailing regularity every winter? It is true, however, that he himself never came. I remember seeing him only once when he had come for the wedding of Pyare Miyan; he was accompanied by a barber who, according to him, could match any cook from Delhi when it came to making *qorma* and *biryani*. And all through the wedding, whenever I saw him, it was always in the kitchen. He would sit with a huqqa and puff away as he chatted with the cooks and their helpers about all sorts of things. If the maid came from the women's quarter, he would chat with her and then go back to gossiping with the cooks. 'Yes, so what were we saying, Miyan Bulaqi?'

'We were talking about Qadir.'

'Yes, Qadir ... He turned out to be a strong lad. Do you remember his wrestling bout with Jani Pehelwan?'

'Yes, sir, of course we remember.'

'The Hindus had brought Jani all the way from Meerut with great fanfare. He was a much-renowned wrestler. When he entered the pit and rubbed the earth on his body, he looked like a bull elephant about to go on a rampage. Compared to him, Qadir looked like a gnat, but the fellow knew a mean shoulder throw. Qadir hoisted that giant of a man over his shoulder like a washerman throwing a bundle of dirty clothes and left him spread-eagled on the ground.'

'But, Agha Miyan, that singing woman was the end of poor Qadir.'

'What can I say, Miyan Bulaqi? I tried my best to tell Qadir to stay away from these wretched women. I told him he would be finished. But words did not penetrate his thick skull.'

'Agha Miyan, once I had thought of grabbing that woman by her hair, giving her one tight slap and saying, "You harlot, go look for some other home if you must ply your trade. Leave our wrestler friend alone." But what to do, you know, I kept quiet.' He drew a long sigh and then continued, 'The strength of our ring was confined to Qadir. After him, there will be nothing. All these lads who come along, rule for a few days and think they are going to be the next legendary wrestler Gama Pehelwan. And then, with stars in their eyes and dreams of becoming a hero, they dash off to Bombay.'[65]

'You are right, Miyan Bulaqi. Take the case of that faithless Shaddan. I poured canisters upon canisters of ghee into him. What a good looking youth he turned out to be! Such a wide chest he had! And then what happened? The wretched fellow went and saw the film called *The Cat of Bombay* and was floored by Sulochana.[66] After that, all he wanted to do was to go to Bombay. I tried my best to reason with him. I told him she was a Jewess; she would eat him up and not even spit out the bones. But he didn't listen to me. I said, "Fine. Go, go and die there." He went. And then what happened was that he could not even reach Sulochana's doorstep. He roamed about like a vagrant in the bazaars of Bombay. And when he returned, believe me, Miyan Bulaqi, he had turned into a mouse.' And after a long puff of the huqqah, he continued, 'Miyan Bulaqi, woman is an evil spirit. He who is caught in her snare is as good as dead.'

And so, this was the Phupha Agha who arrived at the time of a wedding or birth or death in the family, but in such a manner that he would spend his time sitting with cooks and helpers, among

---

[65] The reference here could well be to Dara Singh, an undisputed master of the Indian free style wrestling by the late 1940s, who also found fame in the Bombay film industry.

[66] A silent movie star of the Indian film industry, her real name was Ruby Myers and she was of Jewish descent. The correct name of the film referred to here was *The Wildcat of Bombay*; it was made in 1927.

whom he scattered the pearls of his wisdom, and then disappeared till the next such occasion. Phupha Jaani was his exact opposite. A Turkish cap on his head, a *shervani* cut in the Hyderabadi style on his body paired with Aligarh-cut *pajamas* and laceless pumps with little bows on his feet, he looked magnificent. Really, he looked like a Phupha should! He was employed in Hyderabad. When he arrived, it was always with great pomp and ceremony and he would sit in the men's quarter and have elegant conversations with special guests. His usual topic of conversation would be anecdotes about the nobility of the Asif Jahi dynasty. Our local worthies would be greatly impressed by him and listen with the utmost amazement to his stories. Chhoti Phupho, on the other hand, seemed a bit subdued. She was so overshadowed by the splendid personality of her elder sister that she seldom found the courage to open her mouth in Phuphi Amma's presence. And it wasn't just Chhoti Phupho, most people did not have the temerity to speak when Phuphi Amma was around. In fact, even Phupha Agha turned into a pussycat when he appeared before her no matter how much he threw his weight around in front of the cooks in the kitchen. He left all his airs behind the moment he set foot in the women's quarter. In any case, he hardly ever entered the women's quarter, and when he did, he seemed distant. What is more, I don't remember ever seeing him talking to Phuphi Amma. It appeared as though they were separated by a distance of many miles.

It is only now that I have fully understood the situation thanks to Badi Bhabhi and her stories. The root of all the trouble between them was Mushtari Bai.[67] Phupha Agha's nights were spent in the dancing hall of Mushtari Bai; how long was Phuphi Amma expected to tolerate this? One day she came back to her parent's home in a huff and never went back. The attachment she had for

---

[67] Mushtari Bai was the mother of Akhtari Bai Faizabadi, later known as Begum Akhtar. She was a famous *tawaif* (courtesan who sang and danced) of her time. The reference here could be to her but could also be a generic name. For instance, there is a *tawaif* called Mushtari Bai in Ahmed Ali's *Twilight in Delhi*.

her brother's well-lived well-kept house never let her feel lonely. And Phupha Agha's attitude was 'I don't give a damn for your anger'. He was safe from the taunt of celibacy and at the same time free of the perils of married life, and a daughter was enough to lend credence to the fact that their marriage was not entirely fruitless.

Perhaps Phuphi Amma's influence rubbed off on my Papa Jani as well because he too ran away in mortal dread. For as long as he lived, he remained abroad. He would visit us once a year laden with all manner of gifts, enough to fill the house. He would meet friends and relatives and then go back. He was content with his firstborn. On one trip, he saw his young niece chattering away and was so entranced by her that he asked for her hand for his only son. Perhaps that was the reason why he had come that time. After that, he never came himself; only his dead body reached us. A clamour was let loose both inside and outside the house. There was no one who did not have tears in his eyes. But the one person who was most affected by this death was my Ammi Jan. As it is, she had been slowly suffering the pangs of separation; now she was reduced to skin and bones, and within a year she passed away. But the reason behind that untimely death was revealed only now. 'Chacha Jani was so happy on that last visit, and when Phuphi Amma gave her consent for Maimuna, his happiness knew no bounds. He felt as though his sister had gifted all the wealth in the world to him. But, soon, she would lose everything and so would he. Some wicked person advised the king against him. The king was easily influenced. Where once he had trusted Chacha Jani implicitly and had entrusted him with all the important work of his kingdom, he now turned his face away. Heartbroken, Chacha Jani swallowed a diamond and ended his life.'

Having taken me on a whirlwind tour of countless bright and dark moments from the past, Badi Bhabhi finally came to the real issue. 'Bhaiyya, I must say something to you if you will listen to me.'

'Yes?' I could not guess what Badi Bhabhi was trying to say.

'Bhaiyya, I am not your enemy. Whatever I say will be for your own good. You married outside the family; how much happiness did it bring you? You are as alone now as you ever were. It is still not too late. Marry Maimuna.'

I was flustered. All I could say was, 'Now?'

'Ai Bhaiyya, it isn't as though I have said something wrong. It is for your own good, and what your father had thought for you was also for your own good. May Allah grant him the choicest place in paradise, but when Phuphi Amma gave her consent, his happiness knew no bounds. And to be fair, even Phuphi Amma doted on you. When you went away, believe me, it was almost as though a silence descended upon her. The sorrow of your departure weighed her down. Maimuna, poor child, was left all alone. And after Miyan Jan's death, she became lonelier than ever. Who does she have now in the whole wide world? The poor, poor girl!' She was silent for a moment; then she addressed Chhote Miyan who had quietly come and sat down near us and was puffing away at his huqqah. 'Arre, why don't you say something? Surely, you must have some opinion too?'

'My sister is very nice, very virtuous,' Chhote Miyan answered briefly.

'Well, if she weren't virtuous, would she have spent her life like this? There was no shortage of proposals for her. There were several, each better than the other, but the poor girl had her heart so broken that she never agreed to any of them.'

'She is a very good girl. She has never made us feel the lack of a daughter. Now she is like a sister to me, and a daughter. She has filled two gaps in my life.'

'What do you think, then?' Badi Bhabhi shot a straight question at me. I remained quiet, hesitated and then said, 'It is very late.'

'Ai Bhaiyya, come on! How is it late? It seems like yesterday when you had gone happily from here. God knows what misfortune befell you there that half your hair turned white. In any case, I have seen people get married in their old age.' Once again she addressed Chhote Miyan, 'Aji, what do you think? Do people not get married at this age? And Maimuna, with the grace of god, looks exactly as she did then. The sorrows of her life have pulled her down a little, that's all.'

Chhote Miyan took a long pull of his huqqah and said, 'Let Jawad decide for himself. He does not have to give an answer rightaway.'

'Yes, yes, Bhaiyya, think about it. Don't turn around tomorrow and say, Chhote Miyan and Badi Bhabhi trapped me.'

How grateful I was to Chhote Miyan! If Badi Bhabhi had her way, she would have put a knife at my throat and got me to say 'Yes'.

How terrible that night was! I tossed and turned all night long. It seemed like I had been split in two halves: one part said 'Yes', the other said 'No'. Who should I listen to? Who should I ignore? A desire from long ago, that had got buried somewhere along the way, reappeared. Its influence was growing within me. But a voice of dissent was welling up from deep inside me too. The decision was reached by my memories, for every memory that rose up provided nourishment to the yearnings that surged inside me, and the voices of opposition seemed to subside.

By the time morning came, I began to feel as though I was at peace now. Perhaps a decision had been reached inside without my knowledge. And I was feeling hesitant about accepting that decision, or perhaps announcing that decision. I thought it might be better to postpone it for another day. But Badi Bhabhi had conceded me one night's respite with the greatest trouble; there seemed no possibility of any further reprieve. Suddenly, I remembered that I also had to meet Khairul Bhai. And so I announced even before I had reached the breakfast table, 'I am going to Meerut today.'

'Really? Badi Bhabhi said.

'To meet Khairul Bhai.'

'Khairul Bhai?' Chhote Miyan looked a bit perplexed. 'That madcap? You are going to meet him?'

'You are calling Khairul Bhai mad whereas our entire generation considered him a genius.'

'Genius,' Chhote Miyan said in a tone laced with dersion. 'Are geniuses like that? Good-for-nothing fellow, he has done nothing in life. Anyway, who can stop you? Go, by all means, go and meet him.'

I was amazed: Ya Allah, is this Khairul Bhai? This can't be him. What happened to that perky, wilful, happy-with-himself Khairul Bhai? Perhaps Chhote Miyan was right when he gave him the moniker of 'madcap'. But when did he become like this? He was always a bit eccentric. When I was leaving, God knows what got into him and he unpacked his luggage. Our group had resolved to go to Pakistan only because of his support. We had always believed him to be at the forefront of the Pakistan Movement; in fact, he was supposed to have access to all the top leaders. If he were with us we need fear nothing. And truly, had he been with me would I have had to live in a shanty? But at the last moment, he served us a notice, 'Yaar, you carry on; I won't go.'

We were perplexed, 'But why?'

'I will stay here.'

'But … and we …'

'You go; I am telling you: I will stay here. After all, someone must stay here, too.'

No one could make him budge once he made up his mind. And now when I had returned after a lifetime away, I was surprised and shocked to see how much Khairul Bhai had changed. And everything around him had changed too. I mean everything except that alley in the Kotla Mohalla where Khairul Bhai lived. The old hustle and bustle had gone from that alley and also from that house that used to look large and full back then; now it looked so empty and deserted that, except Khairul Bhai, all I could see was a cat. The alley was deserted too, though its appearance was the same, with not a whit of change. I mean to say it looked the same except that it wasn't as inhabited as before. In fact, except the alley, the entire city seemed to have changed. All those things with which I associated this city seemed to have been rubbed off. New things seemed to have taken their place. Buildings, shops, street corners – everything had changed. And the crowds! God save me from the crowds! As I walked along, several times I felt as though this was not that city. Perhaps I had come to some other city by mistake. Perhaps the problem with all cities is that only the most stubborn of signs remain from the past; everything else changes. It is a good thing our Vyaspur is not a big city because at first glance, I had thought that nothing had changed. You can say that it was the rubble of Dilkusha that opened my eyes because till then, everything had seemed to be the same.

'Khairul Bhai, your Meerut has changed a lot,' I said because I couldn't find the courage to say, 'Khairul Bhai, you have changed a lot.'

Khairul Bhai heard the news of Meerut having changed with great surprise. Then, when I began to list those changes according to what I had observed, his astonishment grew. He heard me out with the greatest amazement.

'Really?'

When he repeated these words again and again, I had to eventually intervene. 'Khairul Bhai, your amazement surprises me. You live in this city. Have you not realized how much has changed here since then?'

Khairul Bhai said, 'Miyan, till I was in Meerut College, I used to pass through these bazaars and I never noticed any change.'

'Khairul Bhai, surely you are talking about those early days, for you bid farewell to the College long ago. When I heard about it there, I was surprised that you chose to give up a perfectly good teaching post.'

Khairul Bhai was quiet. Then he said, 'Miyan Jawad, the thing is that I never realized this when I was studying in Meerut College. But I began to experience a strange disquiet when I became a lecturer. "Arre," I said, "There are too many Hindus here." And that was that; I left.'

'But in that case, you should have felt at home in Aligarh.'

'Yes, I should have,' Khairul Bhai spoke pensively. 'After all, I had studied at Aligarh too. But the strange thing is that those days I never realized it. But when I went to teach I saw that there were too many Muslims there. Wherever you turned, you saw Muslims. Miyan Jawad, believe me when I tell you, I began to feel suffocated. And so I left.'

'And you came and settled down in Meerut,' the words came out of my mouth instinctively.

'Yes, on my roost. But now you are telling me that Meerut has changed. So then it is a good thing that once I came home to roost I never set foot outside.' As he spoke, he spotted Rahimuddin Baba coming towards us. 'Look, Rahimuddin Baba got wind of your coming. See how quickly he has made tea for you.'

I could recognize Rahimuddin Baba with some difficulty. He was hardly a young man when I had last seen him, but now his back was truly bent over. 'Hope you are well, Rahimuddin Baba.'

'Allah is merciful.'

As he put the tea down and began to go away, Khairul Bhai stopped him. 'Rahimuddin Baba, it seems you haven't recognized him. This is Jawad Miyan; he has come from Pakistan.'

Rahimuddin stopped and peered closely at me. He was pleased and blessed me. And as he was going back, he turned around and came near me. 'Miyan, my Karmu is also in Pakistan. Did you ever see him?'

'No. Which city does he live in?'

'I would know if that wretch had ever bothered to send a letter. He is somewhere there in Pakistan. Miyan, have pity on my old age and find him. And if you find him, beat him with a shoe on my behalf and tell him, "You miserable creature, go and show your face to your old father. And if nothing else, at least write him a letter to tell him you are well."'

'All right, Baba, I will if I ever find him.'

When he went away, Khairul Bhai laughed and said, 'Rahimuddin Baba tells me that I should have an advertisement placed in the Pakistani newspapers announcing that he is worried about and waiting to hear of his son's welfare. I tell him that if we get such an advertisement taken out, there will be many such notices with the same sort of appeal. To this, he said that I should get a visa for him to go there: To see his son's face and to see Pakistan.' Khairul Bhai paused and then said, 'It is strange, but everyone here gets this worm inside their brain at some point or the other. The worm wriggles out and says that they should make at least one trip to Pakistan.'

'But Khairul Bhai,' I seized the opportunity and finally asked him, 'Did you never want to visit Pakistan even once?'

'Me?' he stared hard at me and said, 'No.'

'But Khairul Bhai, it isn't as though you were cut off from Pakistan. After all, you were at the forefront of the Movement.'

Khairul Bhai was quiet. Then he said, 'Yes, that is true. But at that time, it was not a country; it was a dream.' And then he added softly, 'A dream contains the promise of a morning till it remains a dream, but …' And at that very moment his cat, which he had turned away because of me, jumped in. Khairul Bhai cuddled the cat, and he became so engrossed in tickling it that he did not feel the need to complete his statement.

My meeting with Khairul Bhai remained unsated, yet it had the strangest effect upon me. The perplexity inside me had gone away. I was so content by the time I left him, and so happy from inside. I returned home late at night and so did not encounter Badi Bhabhi. But now I was mentally prepared to face her. The next morning, I went and sat at the breakfast table. But soon I noticed that Maimuna was a bit subdued. I guessed that something must have taken place in my absence the day before. I glanced at her several times, and a couple of times even tried to speak to her. But she answered in monosyllables and stayed quiet. And then I noticed that she seemed restless, as though she was trying to say something.

'Maimuna, what is it? You are very quiet today.'

'Nothing.'

'Then why do you look so worried?' I was speaking with great confidence. 'I think you want to say something.'

After a pause, she said, 'I don't have to say anything; I want to ask something.'

'What?'

'All I wanted to ask was,' and suddenly her tone became rapid, 'when are you leaving?'

I was at a loss for words. What an unexpected question it was! There I was expecting all sorts of things and she ended up asking me this! 'Perhaps you don't like my staying here ...' But before I could complete my sentence, she called out, 'Badi Bhabhi, the breakfast is getting cold. Please come.'

'I am coming,' Badi Bhabhi's voice came from the verandah, and with it, the sound of her footsteps. I left my sentence dangling in mid-air. But I also wanted to say something before Badi Bhabhi reached us.

'Soon,' I said softly.

Badi Bhabhi heard me. 'Ai hai, what is the hurry for? Tell me too.' And she cast a maternal gaze, first at me, and then at Maimuna. Then she was quiet and began to eat in silence.

Maimuna finished her breakfast in a great hurry and got to her feet. 'I am getting late for school.'

'Late? It's hardly late at all,' Badi Bhabhi said.

'I have to reach early,' and she was gone.

And at that very moment, Chhote Miyan also showed up. But by now, I had figured out what I had to say and what I must do.

'I have been thinking that I might as well make a quick trip to Aurangabad while I am here.'

'Yes, yes, you must go there,' Badi Bhabhi said. 'But what is the hurry? You can go later.'

'Badi Bhabhi, the days are slipping past. After all, I have to go back too.'

'Yes, that is true. You might as well get that done at the earliest,' Chhote Miyan summed up the discussion.

'Fine, you might as well,' Badi Bhabhi too finally agreed. 'Chhoti Phupho will be so pleased to see you. Poor Chhoti Phupho ... I can't bear to see her so unhappy.'

'Why? What happened?'

'Well, what is left to happen? After all, things aren't what they were in the good old Hyderabad days.'

'No one has those good old days anymore,' Chhote Miyan said.

'Phupha Jan too has changed a great deal.'

'Why don't you say he's "gone off"?'

'You know, your problem is that anyone who takes the name of Allah and his Prophet, you say he has "gone off".'

'Well, Jawad Miyan shall see for himself.'

Eleven

The *ekka* took a tortuous route to enter that narrow alley in Aurangabad that was thin as a finger; open sewers carrying muddy waters ran on either side of the alley, which had unkempt, halfbroken and half-built houses with sack cloth curtains covering their doorways. The mouth of one alley led to another, the second to a third. And I was amazed … so *this* is Aurangabad? And the scene had been so different before I had entered that maze of alleys; the very air had been different. The city had looked so beautiful. What happened to Aurangabad as soon as I entered the grid of alleys?

The *ekka* hobbled along and finally stopped at a door with a piece of sack cloth hanging over it.

'There you are … this is the house.'

'Is this the house?' I looked worriedly at the door of the ramshackle house. 'It can't be; you must have brought me to the wrong place. It doesn't seem to be the right house.'

'I have brought you to the address you gave.'

I was in a quandary. I could not believe that that my Phupha Jan, the same person who wore a Turkish cap, shervani cut in the Hyderabadi style and pumps with little bows, would live in this house in this lane. But the *ekka* driver showed great alacrity; he jumped off his *ekka* and reached the door. With a smart rap on the door with his whip, he called out, 'Syed sahab, your guest is here … from Pakistan.' The door opened instantly and an elderly man with a long white beard appeared before us. I was amazed at the sight of him, but then I thought he might know my Phupha Jan and he might send me to the correct address. I was about to say something when he peered at me and recognized me instantly. 'Arre, you are Jawad; come, come.' He pulled me inside and called out, 'Shakur's mother, where are are you … Look, who has come!'

Chhoti Phupho, dried up like old leather, her back bent double as a bow, her hair white as snow – I was amazed at the sight of her. She looked closely at me as though she was trying to recognize me. 'Ai hai, this is Munnan!' she exclaimed as she hugged me, and burst into tears. 'My son, you went to Pakistan and forgot all about us!' And then she went on in the same vein, 'Little did we know then that our precious ones would go away like this and we would long even for a sight of them. I want to know what is mixed in the water of Pakistan that the blood of those who go there turns white? But what are we to do about our heart? The fourteenth century[68] has dawned in Pakistan; whereas we unfortunate people are still where we were.'

When she had finished crying over those who had gone away, Chhoti Phupho launched into an account of all that had befallen her, 'The fall of Hyderabad ruined us, my son. And your Phupha Jan … his mind was so badly affected by it. He lost all interest in worldly matters. He only ever talks of Allah and His Prophet. How is the house to run like this? And this Shakur … if only he were to get a decent education, then there might be some hope of improving our lot. But that boy is showing no such signs.'

'I had told you in the beginning,' Phupha Jan finally opened his mouth, 'not to send him to college. There is nothing but

---

[68] According to H.A.R. Gibb's, J.H. Kramer's, *Shorter Encyclopaedia of Islam*, E.J. Brill, Leiden 1953, p.24., the Promised Messiah is an article of Islamic faith whose 'coming early in the 14th century of the Hidjra was predicted by Muhammad.' 'Early in the 14th century of the Hidjra' would be approx. the 1930s and 40s, and by this reckoning, the formation of Pakistan is seen by some as the fulfilment of a destiny. In common usage, especially among working-class people or those with little knowledge about Islamic history, 'the coming of the 14th century' is used in the sense of an apocalyptic coming.

Hindugardi[69] there. He will also become like them; and that is exactly what happened. Do you know what happened last week? When the Pakistani team won last week, the street urchins got after our neighbour, Mirza Izzat Baig. He had to stuff their face with a *laddu* each to get them to quieten down and he offered one to our son, do you know what he said? He said, "Mirza sahab, go to Pakistan and give this *laddu* to them; why are you giving it to us?" And when Mirza sahab complained to me, believe me Jawad Miyan, I had to hang my head in shame.'

'Bhai Jan, tell me: did I do anything wrong? The team of a rival people has won; why should I celebrate?'

'Arre, you wretched boy,' Chhoti Phupho said, 'This brother of yours who is sitting here, is he also a rival? The two of you are from the same family.'

'That makes no difference; we are, after all, from two rival nations.'

'Are you listening to him, Jawad Miyan?' Annoyed, Phupha Jan appealed to me. 'Now you respond to the reasoning of this crazy boy.'

What answer could I give? Shakur had left me puzzled. I had never looked at things from such a perspective.

'Jawad Miyan, let me not get started about the state of affairs here. The world around us has changed so much that even our children have taken to speaking to us like this. Sons think that whatever their fathers thought or did was all wrong, and whatever they do or think is right.' And then turning towards Chhoti Phupho, he said, 'Shakur's mother, you might as well resign yourself as far as your son is concerned. Now that he has cut himself off from his

---

[69] It was tempting to retain the original word here – laden with communal intent though it is and anxious though we are to be politically correct in these perilous times. Hindugardi is a commonly-used word; it refers to a blatant or pronounced practice of Hinduism and a conscious use of images associated with a right-wing ideology. It would be used by an Urdu speaker in much the same way as 'Islamization' would be used in English.

religion, he has slipped out of our hands. He has become a *kafir* … a *kafir*!

'Hah!' Chhoti Phupho spoke with sadness, 'I have become resigned about both my husband *and* son. One has been left without religion; the other has gone so far into religion that he is lost to us.'

Chhoti Phupho said this and fell silent. Then, when she spoke again, it was on an altogether different subject. She now wanted to ask about me and my state of affairs. Then she said, 'I got a letter from your Badi Bhabhi. She told me all about you; she also wrote about her suggestion. My son, whatever she is trying to suggest to you is correct. How long will you remain rootless? Just think … old age is almost here – both for you, and for her. And if this moment too passes, there will be nothing but regret. So, get down to living a settled life; life is all too short.'

And so Chhoti Phupho went on in this vein, and I kept listening to her. This was the chief topic of her conversation. And Phupha Jan's topic of conversation remained what we had started with. 'Jawad Miyan, the empire had to go. A *faqir* had blessed Asif Jah I only till the end of his life and the empire ended with Huzoor Nizam. But had we not turned away from our faith we would not have come to such a sorry pass. Miyan, I am going to give you a pamphlet; make sure you get everyone in Pakistan to read it. I have written clearly in this: whenever Muslims have denied their faith, their decline has been certain.'

I heard all of Phupha Jan's declarations, which were like a sermon in parts, in respectful silence. Disappointed in his son, he had made me the centre of his attention. And in these few days, he had begun to have such trust in me. The trust shattered on the last day. I had already fixed the programme with Shakur. I had told Phuphi Jan that morning; it was my last day with them.

'I am thinking of going to Ellora for a quick trip.'

'Ellora?' Phupha Jan was shocked. 'Had you come to meet your Phuphi, or see these idols?'

'I thought since I have come here I might as well see Ellora too.'

Phupha Jan was silent for a while. Then he said, 'By the Grace of God, there is a temple in your Pakistan, too; I have heard that right next to Islamabad there is a Kufristan[70]. There is a place called Taxila where there is supposed to be some ancient temple. And the idols remain arranged in their places as they were before the creation of Pakistan. Phupha Jan drew a long suffering breath. It is precisely because of these deeds of the people of Pakistan that they are being punished today.'

Phupha Jan was disappointed to note that his sermon had not the slightest effect upon me. The penny dropped when he saw Shakur was ready to go with me. 'Oh, I see, so it is my son who has led you astray. The wretch has gone completely off the track himself and incites others to stray too.'

And as I took my leave, he said. 'You are our guest. You have come after such a long time. What can we say to you? If you are bent upon seeing those idols, go by all means and may Allah forgive you this great sin.[71] Anyhow, now that you are going, remember to stop by at the dargah of Hazrat Alamgir Rahmatullah Auliya, which is on the way. If Allah grants you divine guidance, stop and offer a prayer.'

---

[70] A coinage meaning 'A place of Kufr', 'kufr' meaning idolatry, paganism, heathenism, disbelief.

[71] There is a list of great sins (*gunah-e kabira*), which render void other good things a person may have done.

Twelve

I remained in a state of trance for several days after my return. I felt as if I was still there. It happens sometimes, doesn't it, that you wake up suddenly in the middle of a dream. And while you may be awake, your mind is still wandering in the landscape of that dream. And so you lie still, with your eyes shut and you think you are still in the dream. I was in a similar state. I was walking about in that spell and in that state, I ended up spilling a great deal in front of Majju Bhai. Later I realized that this was irritability on my part. But what could I do? In such situations, one usually loses one's capability. I had to come clean in front of Majju Bhai. In any case, he had guessed something was going on. He could see I was lost in my own thoughts and had no interest in my surroundings. He had to nudge me only the slightest and I began to unravel effortlessly. I don't know what all I told him. I came to my senses only when he looked sharply at me and said, 'And then you ran away.'

He said it in such a way, in a tone that was half accusatory and half sarcastic, that I was left abashed. 'Yes, then I left.'

'That is, when it was time for you to stay put, you pulled out.'

This sentence made me even more nervous. 'I don't know what happened to me at that time. In any case, the situation became so complicated that it was difficult to stay any longer in that house. There I was, thinking how well I had got settled into that way of life all over again, when suddenly this new development changed everything. I had to go to Aurangabad in any case, so I seized that excuse and left immediately.'

'My dear, you should have gone back and stayed there for a few days before returning to Pakistan.'

'I couldn't find the courage to do that.'

Majju Bhai was quiet, then he spoke thoughtfully, 'Yaar, it wasn't a nice thing to do.'

'What?'

'You should have stayed there. It was good you went away for a bit. You should have gone back after Aurangabad.'

'Majju Bhai, you are not trying to understand my position. What could I have done by staying? She had ended the matter.'

'My dear, the matter began from there.'

'What are you saying, Majju Bhai?'

'You can't comprehend this fully right now. But in later years, you will realize what you have done – to yourself and to her. And then this realization will trouble you a great deal.'

Majju Bhai's reproach made me restless. I did my best to dismiss his words and reject everything he had to say, but deep inside me the thought was gaining strength: perhaps Majju Bhai was right. The thought made me restless. I could not bear to continue this conversation any further.

'Never mind, let it be,' I spoke irritably. 'Let us talk of something else.'

'Of Andalusia, for instance,' Majju Bhai spoke sarcastically and then, after a pause, 'I have noticed that you have become quite an expert in history ever since you have returned from there. Did you come across a tome on history while you were there? Now things have reached such a pass that I ask you a simple question and you get started on here and there. Sometimes it is about Granada, sometimes Cordoba. That's a fine strategy you have evolved of dodging the issue.'

'Majju Bhai, have some fear of God! I wasn't talking about history; I was only telling you about the trees out there. I don't know how the date palm appeared in the middle of all this. And from there, I don't know how ...'

'What do you mean you don't know … You are a past master of the High Jump!'

Perhaps Majju Bhai was right here, too. I was telling him so much without being fully conscious of it. Majju Bhai would delve deep and pull out some nugget and draw some inference and I would be left gaping with astonishment. Ever since my return, I myself didn't realize how I had begun to get swept away and in which direction. In fact, I was beginning to get quite concerned about myself. These were not good signs. I needed to watch over myself. Or else, I would end up becoming neurotic. I began to believe that one way of getting past my neurosis was the one which Majju Bhai had shown me long ago. It included all those people he had introduced me to over the years and with whom I had begun to socialize. I hadn't met any of them since my return, nor even wanted to. But now, it seemed to me, as though it was essential that I meet them.

'Majju Bhai, how long will you cross-examine this culprit? Don't you want to go somewhere?'

'Sure; tell me where.'

'What about Karbalai sahab; shall we go to his place?'

'Karbalai sahab,' Majju Bhai laughed loudly, 'has departed.'

'Departed?' I was worried.

'No, no, he is hale and hearty. I meant he has departed from this country.'

'You had me worried there. So, where has he gone? Karbala? Or Shikarpur?'

'Neither Karbala nor Shikarpur … he has gone straight to America.'

'America!' I was taken aback.

And now I began to realize how much had happened while I had been away. And when I glanced around me, my amazement kept growing. So, all this had happened while I was gone. On the face of it, everything seemed the same, but the deterioration had become more evident. One has seen the decline of cities, but deterioration usually happens slowly. And it is only after a long time that one realizes how much has happened. The speed with which the decline had set in here terrified me. It wasn't as though I was gone for a long time. So much had happened in so few days? Anyhow, to get back to the strange case of Karbalai sahab …

'Majju Bhai, what are you saying? Karbala or Shikarpur? That was his dilemma.'

'No matter what his dilemma, the decision was taken by Saiyadani Chachi and his son. What could Karbalai Chacha do before the united front of mother and son? The son came. He got the visas ready for the father, mother and sister and he herded them away.'

'Poor Karbalai sahab,' I was saddened.

'My dear, these are the twists and turns of life.'

'And there is such a distance between our dreams and their realization!'

'God works in mysterious ways … He sends those who dream of going to America to Shikarpur and to those who yearn for Shikapur, He gives a taste of America!' Majju Bhai laughed and then, changing the topic, said, 'Anyhow, these things happen. I suddenly remembered: there was a phone call from Aqa Hasan. He will think I am avoiding him. Let us go over to his place.'

'Oh yes, so what's the progress? Have Lucknow and Meerut found a meeting ground?'

'No, no, it has hit an obstacle.'

'What happened?'

'You see, what happened was that Tausif had taken the test for the CSP[72] in jest. And he managed to clear it successfully.'

'Well, that is good.'

'It would have been good, except that this success meant the end of a perfectly good alliance. Now you will ask how? There was a time when Aqa Hasan and his wife were becoming as stiff

---

[72] CSP or Civil Service of Pakistan, derived from the colonial legacy of the Indian Civil Service (ICS), this was the bureaucratic machinery of Pakistan. It was subsequently renamed CSS or Central Superior Services.

and unyielding as dough made from *maash* daal; but they melted like wax when they heard this news. The question of whether the boy was a Saiyad or not was put away on the upper-most shelf, the match was agreed to with alacrity and great insistence was shown that the *nikah* be performed immediately. On the other side, your friends from Meerut have begun to reach for the skies. Now even the nobility from Lucknow seem lowly and beneath them. And so they are now trying to break off the match. And now, Jawad Miyan, spare a thought for my position ... I am being ground between the wheels of Lucknow and Meerut.'

'This had to happen to you one day, Majju Bhai. You had to pay the price for getting into these traps of fixing marriages and engagements.'

'Aqa Hasan's wife has caught me by the throat; you cannot imagine my state.'

Poor Majju Bhai was in serious trouble. No matter how much he went on and on about his dear 'Bhabhi', the lady from Lucknow was in no mood to let him off the hook.

'My dear brother, I want to know what these Meerut people have taken us to be? First, they came to our door asking for our daughter, saying they were content even with the dust from our doorway. And, then, when we – out of sheer human consideration – finally said "Yes", they were struck dumb! Mind you, we had agreed only out of sheer humanity, for it isn't as though there was anything special about their boy. You know we would not even show our backs to someone who is not from a Saiyad family. What is more, they were rustic folk. But we thought: So what if they are not Saiyad, at least they are from the same religion, and they are from our side across there. And then, we are no longer in Lucknow that we will find rows upon rows of good Saiyad boys from the noblest of families. This is the best one can find in Karachi. Keeping all this in mind, we had agreed to the match.'

'Brother Majidul Hasan,' Aqa Hasan interjected, 'Your sister-in-law is right. We were not exactly very satisfied with the match, but then keeping the changing times in mind, we kept aside our

Lucknowi ways and decided to make our peace with the new world. And so we had agreed to the match. But now we feel their attitude has changed, and not for the better. They seem to be avoiding us.'

'But Majju Bhai, they have given their solemn word. And then, after all, you are also in the picture. And if truth be told, we had agreed to the match because it came from you.'

'Brother, please have some patience – considering you have waited so long and have made them wait for a long time. I shall go and ask them today itself what their intention is.'

'What a thing to say, Majju Bhai! We hardly made them wait! In fact, we would have made them wait had we been in Lucknow. Your friend is sitting here; he will tell you that when his proposal had come to my parent's home, my dear mother showed no sign for two whole years – she said neither "Yes" nor "No". It was only in the third year when people from the extended family began to urge her and also give full guarantees about the boy's family that she finally gave in.'

'Well, those times have gone with those people,' Aqa Hasan again interjected, 'These days, people want instant results. They send a proposal today, and they want an answer tomorrow. We had to take some time to consider the proposal, after all. And I think we did not take too long. Now, why are they delaying?'

'Brother, please tell them that they have sent a proposal for the daughter of a genteel family, and they have given their word. We shall not let them wriggle away,' Basho Bhabhi served us a clear notice.

The other party was looking for an excuse to back out. Or, rather, had already found an excuse. Tausif's sister was flying high, so high that she was not setting foot on the ground.

'Majju Bhai, you know well enough how many times those Lucknow-walas made us run around. "Yes, we will think." "Our daughter is still studying; let her exams get over, we will think afterwards." The studies became as unending as the devil's entrails. Now let them educate their daughter to their heart's content. We don't want a daughter-in-law who is as wise as Plato. My brother has to get his house in order – not start a library! And God save us from the airs of these Lucknow-walas. "We are high born." Well, we are also not exactly low born. Now they should keep their high-bred daughter to themselves.'

'Well, you are right actually,' Majju Bhai said in an attempt to pacify her. 'These Lucknow-walas are victims of tradition. They always take very long to respond to a proposal. Anyhow, now they have agreed to the match.'

'Majju Bhai, be fair. After all, we also matter to you, don't we? Tell me, when did they agree to the match? At first, they wouldn't even give us the time of day. In fact, the lady even went so far as to announce to all and sundry that we were actually from a family of knife-sharpeners from Meerut! It was only when they saw that the boy had cleared the competitive examination and would shortly be appointed a high official and, also, when they heard about the Pilibhit-walas making the rounds of our home that they said "Yes" in a jiffy.'

'Be that as it may, they have said "Yes".'

'Let them say "Yes". It is too late now. Are we expected to wither away waiting for them to say "Yes"? There is no shortage of girls for my brother. With God's grace, he will now rule over an entire district; his writ will be law in all the police stations of his area. And you are well aware of his habits and temperament. My brother is a real diamond. You won't find such boys in this day and age. And if you dismiss such a boy, then only a star that has come down from high heavens can be good enough for your daughter. And then there are the Pilibhit-walas; they speak with such humility. It isn't as though they are nobodies; they have known wealth for several generations. And their daughter is so well brought up. The mother doesn't even set foot in the kitchen; the girl does all the cooking and cleaning. With the grace of God, the girl runs the entire house on her own. And then there is the daughter of these Lucknow-walas; she cannot even make rotis. One day they asked me to stay over for lunch. I was horrified to see the roti made by the girl. She had put raw bits of dough in front of us.'

'So, Baji, in other words, you have fixed the match with the Pilibhit-walas?'

'No, no, I have not fixed anything. I am still trying to gauge them. I will investigate thoroughly. We are in no hurry. It's not as though our boy will no longer be of marriageable age. After all, he is still so young. It was only the year before last that I had had a feast when his moustache sprouted. So I will bring home a bride after I am fully satisfied. And you wait and see, the bride I bring will light up my brother's home. And one who will listen to her husband and stay under my control. After all I am tired too; I want to lie in bed with my *paandan* beside me, and I want someone to press my feet and serve me food.'

'Yes, it is a perfectly reasonable desire,' Majju Bhai said, 'but I was simply pointing out that the Lucknow girl is educated and sensible.'

'Hai Majju Bhai, God save us from these educated girls! They have been known to split up families. That is what they have learnt from their colleges. The moment they step out of their palanquins and enter their husband's home, they set up a din for a separate house. The very sight of their mother-in-law or sister-in-law is anathema for them. My eldest uncle, may Allah grant him paradise, used to say that if a daughter-in-law has never experienced cruelty at the hands of her mother-in-law then you may as well assume that she is wanton.'

Majju Bhai smiled, 'That's a nice axiom.'

'Ai Majju Bhai, he was not exactly wrong. And our eldest uncle was no ordinary father-in-law. He was as stern as our eldest aunt was easy-going. Our aunt was terribly sweet; she loved my mother like a daughter. When my mother got married and came to their house, our eldest aunt handed over the keys to the house as well as the running of the kitchen to her. But our eldest uncle ... he never ever ate a morsel cooked by my mother. He always used to say that a daughter-in-law can never be trusted; she can poison her father- and mother-in-law anytime. The most ordinary incident happened one day: my father said to my mother that he hadn't eaten parathas for a long time. And so my mother, in all innocence, cooked parathas for him. Our eldest uncle got wind of it and he roared with anger that she had made parathas for her husband and given him roti with a bit of ghee. And he swore never to eat anything cooked by her. My father offered to keep a separate cook just for our eldest uncle … Anyhow, these are tales of long ago. Let someone try and do something like this with our new-age daughters-in-law. The news will be splashed all over the newspapers the very next day. Majju Bhai, bad times are here to stay.'

'Yes,' Majju Bhai said in a half-hearted assent, 'the old days are gone. It is a new age, with new ways.'

'New age! Call it the fourteenth century! The wretches are such hussies, I tell you: they can get anything they want. And the boys are such fools that they can be driven off in whichever direction their wives lead them. And this Tausif, he has all the potential to run to do his wife's bidding.'

'Baji, do I have the permission to say something?'

'Yes, yes, say whatever you have in your heart. I know you are head over heels in love with her.'

'Me? Head over heels in love with her! Never!'

'Don't pull the wool over my eyes. What do you take me for? I can count the feathers of a bird in flight. And I know you far too well; I have washed your dirty diapers. Majju Bhai, believe me, our mother only gave birth to him; I am the one who tended him ever since he was an infant. My arms would tire from holding him when he was a baby. And as he grew up, I was the one who went to pray for him at the grave of every saint, I was the one who got all sorts of talisman from all sorts of holy men, I read all manner of special prayers for his well-being, I was the one who spread my hem and prayed that by the blessings of our Prophet and His family, may he clear his examination with top marks and rule over a district. And now all that has come to pass. So now, what does he need a sister for? Now he will sing the praise of that impure creature.'

'Which impure creature?'

'Go on ... don't force me to speak up. And listen well ... if you dare to marry against my wishes, I will throw such a spanner in the works that the entire city will come to know. Not that I wish ill for the one who will come to our home. May Allah make her as white as pearls and as yellow as gold, but may she also be someone who can make us hold our head high among our people! In any case, there is no shortage of good girls. If I have my way, I will bring a bride who will, God willing, light up this house. Let me make one thing amply clear: I will not be reduced to a scarecrow in my own house. Make her the queen of your home by all means. Let her get what she is entitled to as your wife, and let the sister get hers.'

And so she was in full spate while Majju Bhai was at a loss as to the way forward. All his hard work had come to nought. The honour of being a bridge between Lucknow and Meerut, an honour he had sought to earn with great dedication and hard work, was slipping away from him. For the first time, I saw the signs of weariness on his face. For, he was always delighted to be in the thick of such action, and always known to be unabashedly successful in such battles. By the grace of God, it so happened that Ghazi sahab showed up at the very moment that Baji Akhtari got steadily angrier and her temper reached its zenith.

As always, Ghazi sahab wore a green turban on his head, a kurta that reached below his knees, a shalwar that ended just above his ankles, and a constantly moving rosary in his hands. I had seen him for the first time in this very house at a dinner of kabab and parathas. And perhaps he too had set foot in this house for the very first time that day. At that time, Baji Akhtari had been merely impressed by his appearance; she became a devotee only after she heard the news of Tausif clearing the CSP. That was when she realized that it was made possible only because of Ghazi sahab having set his blessed feet in their home. Now she had become a believer and was forever on the lookout to find new disciples. God knows how she spotted the signs of a believer in me for one day she accosted me and said, 'Ai Bhaiyya Jawad, why don't you contact Ghazi sahab?'

I looked at her with complete puzzlement and asked, 'Regarding what?'

'You look very worried to me. Ghazi sahab does not believe in talismans and amulets, but he is a firm believer in prayer. He can blow such a prayer on water that all your troubles go away after you have drunk it. The truth is that all our misfortunes have gone away only because of Ghazi sahab. Tausif's example is before your eyes. Who could have imagined that he would clear the entrance examination? The truth is that Ghazi sahab prayed for him. You also ask him to pray for you.'

'But I do not have any worries.'

'Ai hai, what is there to hide? Everyone has worries.'

'You may think so.'

'All right then, so you are right and I am wrong. Don't doubt me. I have never wished ill for anyone; I have only ever wanted good for others. If people don't agree that is another matter. And in this case, too, I tell everyone that there is great power in Ghazi sahab's prayer. I have given the water that has been blessed by him to so many people. And whoever I have given it to has become a believer in him. And so, I said it for your own good.'

Anyhow, this little matter being in the nature of a digression, as I was saying Ghazi sahab appeared at that very moment looking like an angel of mercy. Baji Akhtari, who was like a river in full spate, became still. Majju Bhai too got a moment's respite; he addressed Ghazi sahab, 'Qibla Ghazi sahab, so where has your movement reached?'

Ghazi sahab drew a long sigh and said, 'My dear, don't ask. The passion for jihad has gone cold among Muslims. If you consider the total population of Pakistan, you will note that it is not a small country. The population of Muslims is in crores. Yet I have still not been able to find 313 Muslims. Look around you ... so many people, and all born in the faith, but none are Muslims. My passion is calling out for 313 Muslims. But there aren't 313 Muslims to be found on this planet earth.'

'Yes, it is very sad indeed, 'Majju Bhai said. 'But this huge population that is to be found in Pakistan and the crowds that sweep into Karachi are all Muslims. It is a different matter that they are not drawn towards your movement.'

'My dear, do you call them Muslims? I do not see any Muslims among them. Forget their character; they do not even *look* like Muslims in their appearance. Their beard and moutaches are gone, the clothes ordained by Sharia are missing, and instead they are wearing the Christian dress of tie-coat-pant. I sometimes wonder – and grieve – how will these people be identified on the Day of Reckoning? And let us, for the sake of argument, suppose that they are somehow identified, the question of namaz still remains. Just think how many among them would be those who had prayed regularly all five times a day, for

> *Tujhe namaz ki fursat nahi taajub hai*
> It is strange that you do not find the time for namaz

'And even among those who pray, how many whose namaz is truly a namaz? My friend, be fair and tell me honestly.'

'You are absolutely correct.'

'I know just one simple fact: if these people were true Muslims then the Atom Bomb would have been with them, and not the others.' And then, after a pause, he continued, 'From the banks of the Nile till the dust of Kashgar,[73] there are people who have read the *kalma*. But their breasts are empty of the inner pain, their hearts free of softness, their spirits desolate – what shall become of these people? Tell me, my friend, am I wrong?'

'No, no, you are absolutely right,' Majju Bhai shook his head in agreement.

'Anyhow, all the young men who have become associated with my movement are, by the grace of God, people of faith and their hearts are warmed by true emotions. I have taught them only one lesson: "O Children of Islam and Sons of Unitarianism, just believe that this life that you have been given is actually not yours. It is simply

---

[73] The oasis city in western China, located along the border of Kyrghistan and Tajikistan.

given to you in trust; and any breach of trust is not permissible. It must be returned to its rightful owner at the earliest. So, be forever ready for martyrdom." And my dear Majju Bhai, believe me they *are* ready. They go about with a shroud tied around their heads. The passion for jihad is bursting out of them. Alas, it is wasted upon these heedless Muslims. I am running my movement somehow while they are sitting in their cocoons, deaf to my calls. But I am wrong in calling them Muslims; they are not Muslims. If someone claims to be a Muslim let him come before me. I will tell him what it means to be a Muslim. My dear Majju Bhai, my volunteers ask me impatiently: "If these people are *kafirs* then who has given them permission to be amongst us? And what right do they have to remain alive?" And I counsel them saying: "O Youth of Islam, be patient! The time shall come when we shall enquire of them." And the young men writhe with haste. But my dear Majju Bhai, how long can I overlook their wish? After all, I too have to answer on the Day of Reckoning when this disobedient sinner will be asked: "O Ataullah, you saw these Muslims turn away from the Righteous Path and you remained silent. Now you burn in the eternal fire of hell." When I imagine the fire of hell, my body breaks out in a rash. I break down in tears.' And indeed Ghazi sahab broke down in front of us.

When Baji Akhtari saw Ghazi sahab weeping inconsolably, she too broke down in tears and covered her face with one end of her dupatta. Tausif got up with a start and rushed to get a glass of water for Ghazi sahab, 'Qibla, drink some water.'

I looked at Majju Bhai with harassed eyes. He seemed to be waiting for a signal from me, and immediately sprang to his feet. His words of apology were heard with inattention by Tausif and Baji Akhtari, and neither made the slightest effort to detain us.

We came out and saw a Pajero parked at the gate. Inside sat Kalashnikov-toting volunteers who glared at us with suspicious, angry eyes.

'Majju Bhai,' I spoke softly, 'what is going on?'

'Quiet,' Majju Bhai answered equally softly, 'this is Ghazi sahab's security posse.'

'Security?' I was perplexed. Why did Ghazi sahab need security? But Majju Bhai was in no mood to answer any of my questions.

We had barely set foot in our house when Rafiq sahab landed up. 'Arre Jawad sahab, you are back?' he seemed surprised to see me. 'I thought you were going to be away for a long time.'

'Do you hear that, Jawad Miyan? Are you listening to Rafiq sahab? He is saying exactly what I have been saying.' And Majju Bhai turned towards Rafiq sahab, 'Rafiq sahab, we will accept it if you say so though I personally feel that Jawad Miyan has not really come back.'

Rafiq sahab let out a hearty guffaw. 'But Majju Bhai, why single out Jawad sahab? I have noticed this among all my Karachi friends. They come back, but then you find out that actually they have not really come back.'

I tried to avoid answering them, but suddenly a shiver ran through me and I said, 'Perhaps the two of you are right when you say I have not yet come back. But my own experience is different. I *have* come back, but I feel that the city I have come back to is not the city I had left; this is some other city.'

'If only it were some other city,' Rafiq sahab quipped.

'I don't know,' I said, 'But I feel as though I have come back to some other city ... some city from some fable.'

'And as though you are Hatim Tai,'[74] Majju Bhai tacked on as Rafiq sahab let out another peal of laughter.

I felt as though I had been roasted over live embers. I answered sharply, 'I am certainly no Hatim Tai; how can I be? This age is not worthy of such characters – although this city has indeed become the City of Summons.'

Rafiq sahab's laughter stilled and he became serious. 'Jawad sahab, you are absolutely correct.' He became quiet and then, after

---

[74] Hatim Tai was an iconic figure in Arabian history who lived sometime in the 6th century AD and is still remembered for his generosity and large-heartedness as well as his many adventures. In one of the episodic adventures, Hatim has to bring back an account of the *Koh-e Nida* (Mount of Summons, where the summon of death is issued from. In calling Karachi the City of Summons, the reference is to the summon of death that can come at any moment and the uncertainty that prevails in the city.)

a moment's reflection, said, 'We are all awaiting our turn; who knows when the summon will come from the Mount of Summons.'

Majju Bhai looked hard at Rafiq sahab and said, 'So you are caught in Jawad's trap too. He has caught you in his snare of *dastaans* and is trying to kill me with history.'

'Then you are done for, Majju Bhai. The *dastaan* allows several exits for escape, but history does not let a man get away.'

'History is correct in its place; the question is: what do you draw from it?'

'What has Jawad sahab drawn from it?' Rafiq sahab smiled.

'Only a date palm has been found so far.'

Rafiq sahab laughed out loud once again. 'Majju Bhai, whatever is in your history will be drawn from it. Jawad sahab cannot add anything from his own side to it.' And then after a pause, 'Majju Bhai, you know, I have been wondering what would be found if someone were to sift through the history of Pakistan.'

'My dear, first let the history of Pakistan get formed! It has been such a short while ... what can you expect to find in it?'

'That isn't true, Majju Bhai; surely in this brief period of time two things can be found quite easily.'

'And what are those?'

'*Mushairas* and Kalashnikovs.'

Both Majju Bhai and Rafiq sahab laughed to their heart's content when they heard this.

'So will you give me some tea, or shall I leave?'

'Of course, we will give you tea,' and Majju Bhai instantly called out to the cook. 'Yaar, Nemat Khan!'

Nemat Khan appeared in an instant. 'Yes?'

'Yaar, make some tea. Don't you see, Rafiq sahab has been sitting here for some time?'

Thirteen

This incident is from that day when our Society had set a new record of burning tyres. The entire neighbourhood was clouded with thick fumes … fumes and the noise of loud slogans. The day, however, had dawned ordinarily enough, in fact, absolutely according to the daily routine. I woke when I heard the alarm clock kept beside the bed go off. Almost instantly, I heard a cock crow somewhere in the distance and with it came the sweet medley of birdsong. As is my practice, I kept lying in the bed for a long time, tossing and turning from side to side. I nodded off and woke up several times after waking up. Then, with a sudden resolve, I got out of bed and went straight into the bathroom.

And then the everyday ritual of newspaper, shave, bath, breakfast. What was new or special in the newspaper that would keep me engrossed for very long? There were the same routine stories: robberies, murders, abductions, gangrapes. A motor theft in one neighbourhood; a hold-up at a bank by Kalashnikov-wielding robbers who shot dead a resisting watchman and decamped with forty lakh rupees while a notice was issued to find the robbers within twenty-four hours; a senator abducted from a certain highway and a ransom demand for fifty lakh rupees. And so on and so forth.

And the breakfast too was nothing out of the ordinary. There were just the two of us: Majju Bhai and me. And there was minimal conversation at the breakfast table, that too less with each other and more with Nemat Khan who would rush in and out with fresh toast or hot tea. He would hurry from the kitchen, deposit a fresh pot of tea and hurry out. After breakfast, a round of cigarettes would commence, and with it, one more look at the pages of the newspaper – though that day the cigarette-and-newspaper routine had stretched a bit longer than usual. And Majju Bhai had commented on it, too.

'Yaar, you are sitting about as though you have all the time in the world. The car from your bank has not come yet. Aren't you planning to go to the office today?'

'I will go, but a bit later.'

'How much later?'

'Oh Majju Bhai, you are grilling me! Why are you so interested in my office?'

'I am not interested in your office; I am thinking of myself. I was thinking of setting out with you.'

'That's a good idea, but you don't have to go for a duty; does it matter if we are a bit late?'

'But you have to go for duty.'

'It is such a bore! I am fed up of this daily hustle. Majju Bhai, you are so lucky! You have no daily grind, no restrictions. Nothing but peace and quiet for you! I am so envious. Yours is an ideal life.'

'My dear, one has to pay the price for this life.'

'There is a price for everything, Majju Bhai. Look at me ... whirling around like a top all day. A banker's job! ... Don't even ask how tough it is! I am sucked dry by the end of the day.'

'Oh come on, don't exaggerate. Anyhow, come to the point ... when is the car coming for you?'

'Actually, I got very tired yesterday. So I thought I would rest a bit and go late. So, I had told my office to send the car later than usual ... by 10.30 or 11.'

'My dear, you don't work, you rule over an empire.'

'Majju Bhai, I am about to leave this job.'

'Why?'

'They make one work very hard.'

'And the next job won't make you work as hard?'

'It will be a change. I am sick of the routine. I am a human being, not a dumb plodder.'

'Jawad Miyan,' Majju Bhai took a long pull on his cigarette, 'There is an age for changing wives and jobs. You have passed that age. At this age, it has been seen, that no matter what sort of wife one might have or what kind of employment one might have, one is expected to make do.'

'The first one doesn't apply to yours truly; and about the second one ... I never really thought about it. Allah granted me release without my asking. And as far as your philosophy regarding employment is concerned, I have a few reservations about it.'

I had not yet completed my sentence when a loud noise accompanied by sloganeering came from outside. Majju Bhai rushed to the window and peered out; then he turned around and, just as quickly, came away. There was nothing new. Majju Bhai perked up his ears when so much as a leaf fluttered in the neighbourhood. When someone suffered so much as a nosebleed, it would be a major incident as far as Majju Bhai was concerned. So I paid no heed to him or to the noises, taking them to be the usual slogan-mongering we heard everyday. I went back to my newspaper, but I could not remain immersed in it for long. Majju Bhai returned, looking extremely worried.

'So, there ... they have started again.'

'How?' I had not yet derived any absolute inference from Majju Bhai's worried demeanor, but when he made his announcement with such seriousness, I had to ask.

'A young man from the neighbourhood has become the target of the masked men. His name was Sharif ... though of course you wouldn't have seen him. He was a nice young man. He had done a lot of patrol duty during the last curfew. The poor thing was shot. He has been taken to the hospital; let's see what happens.'

Majju Bhai was right. Who was Sharif? What was he like? I wouldn't know whereas Majju Bhai knew everything about everybody. Every child in the neighbourhood knew him, and he knew every child in it. I, on the other hand, lived there like a stranger. The couple of people who knew me in the neighbourhood did so because of Majju Bhai. Was it possible for one to stay in one place for years upon years and yet remain a stranger? But I was such a person. If someone is bent upon remaining aloof from the lives and times of one's neighbours, then who would know him? Such a man will remain a stranger. Now look at it like this ... Majju Bhai heard the commotion and instantly got immersed in it with all his emotions and feelings. And there was me ... I was not in the least affected. Majju Bhai had narrated the incident of the youth being shot with such intensity. And it had had not the least effect on me. 'Oh,' I said with the utmost unconcern and became quiet.

'People have gathered at the Abbasi Shaheed Hospital and passions are running high. The crowd is dangerously out of control. If the young man dies, things will get out of hand.'

I let out a long 'Hmmm' by way of answer and got back to my newspaper. I remained engrossed in it for a long time. Majju Bhai saw my evident disinterest and went out of the room. I was startled in the middle of my perusal of the newspaper; suddenly, I looked at the watch strapped on my wrist. Immediately, I put down the newspaper and got up. 'It is time; the car should have come by now. Where is that fellow?' Then I remembered, 'Jamaluddin is habitually late. He has never come on time. He will come up with some lame excuse yet again.'

Nemat Khan tottered in, laden with bags of groceries. He looked frightened. 'The shops are all shut; I somehow managed to buy these things.'

'Really?' Majju Bhai asked in a voice laden with anxiety. 'What's the news about Sharif?'

'He has passed away.'

'May God have mercy upon us,' Majju Bhai's anxiety increased manifold. He was about to say something when the telephone rang.

I picked up the phone, 'Hello. Jamaluddin, where are you? I am waiting for you ... Really? ... If the tyres are burning, let them. You find a way to get through ... I see ... So there is no way of getting here ... Hmmm ... Hmmm ... Hmmm ... All right then, you go back. I will call up the office and talk to them.'

I put the phone down. 'So, the car can't come now. The main road is blocked.'

'What was Jamaluddin saying?'

'He said tyres are burning on the main road and the window panes of passing cars are being broken. A bus has been set on fire.'

'That means it has started,' Majju Bhai turned towards Nemat Khan almost as soon as these words had left his mouth. 'Is there enough milk in the house?'

'Yes, I have got it. And I have also bought some vegetables and enough meat for the next several days.'

'Meat and vegetables are not my concern; I can pass the days on even daal. At times like this, when one has to be imprisoned in the house, what one needs are enough quantities of decent tea and a sufficient supply of cigarettes. Then whatever has to happen can happen in the world outside.' With these words, Majju Bhai got to his feet and said, 'Let me go out and inspect the state of affairs.'

'Will it make any difference to the state of affairs if you go out?'

'It won't make any difference, but surely a man must remain abreast of his surroundings. At least, one should not die in a state of ignorance.' Majju Bhai answered with great patience. My sarcasm had had not the slightest effect on him. He paused, then spoke thoughtfully, 'Though there are enough cigarettes, I will go and see if any shops are open so I can stock up some more. One never knows how long this state will last.' And with these words, he quickly went down the stairs.

Nemat Khan stood rooted to the spot, looking as worried as ever. After some time, he went into the kitchen. I could hear a commotion outside. Loud, angry voices were coming from a loudspeaker, saying all sorts of things that I couldn't understand. I went and stood beside the window. I had thought I would look out to see what was happening and who or what was passing by. But what was the point? A wave of futility washed over me. I shut the window without looking out, turned back and returned to sit on the chair.

The window was shut, but the noise could still be heard. At an emotional level, I was completely unconcerned by that noise. Yet I could not remain unaffected by it. For a long time, I sat anxiously for I had nothing to do. Till I had been reading the newspaper, I had not noticed the noise coming from outside. I took up the magazine I had been reading the night before and tried to read the remaining articles, but gave up soon enough. I could not concentrate. So what was I to do? There was no office to go to. So I thought of cleaning up my room. My room had been upside down for days and the books … Dear Lord! They were coated with dust! At that moment, I was momentarily reminded of Ishrat. She had brought order in my home. Till she was alive, heaven forbid that something should move from its rightful place. The house used to look neat and clean. After she passed away, the house invariably looked unkempt. Everything was in disarray and the house looked deserted. With Majju Bhai being here, at least I was spared a sense of loneliness. But his presence could not guarantee cleanliness and order in the household.

'Sahab-ji.'

Busy wiping the dust from the books, I was startled. 'Yes? What is it?'

'I want to find out when they will be taking away the dead body for burial.'

'All right, but come back quickly.'

'Yes, I will come back right away. I just want to know so that I can prepare lunch before going. I want to lend my shoulder to the corpse.'

'All right.'

Nemat Khan went away and I went back to dusting and wiping the books. I don't know how long I remained absorbed in my task, for I lost all sense of time. I came to with a start only when Majju Bhai returned and set up a din.

'Nemat Khan! Nemat Khan … Where are you? I am dying of hunger.'

'So, you are back?'

'There is clamour all round. Things are likely to get worse … But where is Nemat Khan?'

'He left shortly after you did.'

'And pray why did he do that?'

'For the same reason you did … he said he wanted to find out when the corpse would be taken away.'

'Why does he need to know when the corpse will be taken away?'

'He will lend his shoulder … that is, he will lend his shoulder to the corpse of a martyr so that some of the reward will rub off on him too.'

'In that case, we might end up lending a shoulder to *his* bier.'

Majju Bhai's fear turned out to be right. Things took a turn for the worse and curfew was imposed by evening. Now Majju Bhai posed a new dilemma.

'Tonight shall be a difficult night.'

'Why?'

'There is danger.'

'Of what?'

'Of an attack.'

'Attack? Whose attack?'

'Yaar, don't argue. You have no idea about anything. I have smelt something; that's why I am saying it.'

'All right, so what can we do?'

'We should not sleep at night. My sense is that the entire neighbourhood will be awake. There is a great danger.'

'All right, in that case we shall stay up too.'

'Yes, yaar, we shall stay up all night. As long as we keep getting tea, it isn't difficult to stay awake.' And then he called out to Nemat Khan. 'Nemat Khan!'

He came running. 'Yes?'

'We have to be on guard all night; you do know that a curfew has been clamped, don't you? Things are very bad.'

'Yes.'

'Do you have everything you need for tea?'

'Yes, I do.'

Interestingly, after broaching the subject of an all-night vigil, Majju Bhai promptly pulled the sheet over his ears and went to sleep. After his announcement, the burden of keeping the vigil fell on my shoulders. In any case, I was not in the least sleepy; sleep was miles away from my eyes under these circumstances. But how long could I read my book? Eventually, I kept it aside. I yawned and went to stand in the balcony. A strange sight greeted my eyes. The street that stayed alive all night long, with small shops doing brisk business selling tea and cigarettes and *paan*, was silent and deserted. Such silence after such clamour all day long! I was surprised, and also scared. Although the silence of the night is not, in itself, a novel experience for me. I had known it long before I began to live in this city. In fact, that experience is a part of my childhood. I was born in an age when electricity was unknown; I mean to say that electricity had not reached the small settlement where I lived as a child. Night used to start so early there and how long and how dark it used to be. The silence of a dark night is more impenetrable. The sound of jackals coming from the other side of the *dharamshala* would not break that silence; it would, instead, deepen it.

And the silence I experienced after that was the silence of 1947 and thereabout. I had become a city dweller by then. I had to come and live in the city due to my education. The cities used to be different back then. There would be a hustle and a bustle. The shops would be open. There would crowds of shoppers. The merrymakers would be laughing and joking. The hawkers would be calling out their wares. And suddenly a rumour would course through one end of the market to the other with the speed of lightning. The shops would begin to close down at the same speed. Shutters would be pulled down and doors slammed shut. Shopkeepers would close shops and buyers would gather their wares and run for dear life. Within a matter of minutes, the market would close, the streets would empty out and the very air would become desolate as though it was not a rumour that had rippled down the street but a call from the Mount of Summons.

There was the same silence now, but with an added terror. Every age brings its own silence, its own fear and, yes, its own violence. Darkness lends another colour to silence. But here the lamp posts were standing in their places with their lights intact. The street was filled with light. But there was no trace of life for miles around. Ya Allah, how did the crowds disappear so suddenly? A rush, a stampede, cries and screams and then, all gone without a trace! Not a slogan, not a shout, no sound of shutters coming down or doors being slammed shut – only an empty and silent street bathed in the light of the electric lamps. And scattered here and there were pieces of half-burnt tyres, bricks, stones and the bus that had been burnt to a cinder. The only sign of life was the Kalashnikov-toting policeman who stood in the middle of the flood-lit crossroad, still as a statue. For a long time, I stood looking at him with great surprise. Was he a flesh-and-blood living human being or a statue fashioned like a human being and installed in the middle of the road?

… And then he began to drown in a sea of surprise. Terror engulfed him. Suddenly, an elderly man could be seen coming from up ahead. He leapt to come closer and this is what he said, 'Please, sir, can you tell me what is going on? Is it a trick or is this a place of calamities? When I had set foot in this settlement, there was much hustle and bustle and there were crowds everywhere. Its streets and alleys were lively and all around there was light and happiness. The quarters of the courtesans were brightly lit. Moon-faced maidens were aplenty. Music wafted in the air. The ogglers jostled on the streets looking up at the brightly-lit quarters and making eyes at the ladies of the night. And now what do I see? The bustle is gone, there is only noise, and in all four directions there is nothing but terror. And there is desolation everywhere. I cannot understand what has happened here. I am in a dilemaa; I don't know where to go.'

The elderly man heard this and looked at him from head to toe in such a way that one of his eyes cried and the other laughed. Then, with infinite sadness, he said, 'Young man, I pity your youth. You poor wretched man, this city is now the City of Calamities. Which tyrant showed you the way to this place? You have been misled to your doom. Listen to me … Leave this place as soon as you can.' He heard the elderly man, wept a bit and said, 'Fate has brought me here. The heavens have conspired to bring me here. How can I now take the high road to freedom, for such a course of action defies my sense of honour and yours truly is bound by honour.'

'Yaar, have you gone mad? Are you bent upon killing yourself? The bullet doesn't ask if it should come and hit you. Come inside.'

Majju Bhai was awake and was calling out to me from his bed. I tiptoed out of the balcony and returned to the room. In any case, what was the good of staying on outside? Majju Bhai's loud voice had shattered the spell of the silence.

'What were you doing outside?'

'Nothing … I was just looking out.'

'Looking out? What is there to look at, at this time? The curfew is on. You can't even see a tiny birdling at this time.'

'I was looking at the silence.'

'Nice,' Majju Bhai spoke with bitterness. 'You think this silence is a spectacle. That's because you are sitting inside your house. Ask me, I will tell you the state of the city. Thank your stars that I was able to save myself and get back safely home, or else you would have been scouring the city searching for my corpse … Yaar Nemat Khan, you are awake, aren't you?'

'Yes.'

'Then let's have a round of tea. A curfewed night can only be passed with the help of several rounds of tea.'

'All right.'

After Nemat Khan went away, the two of us remained quiet for some time. Perhaps Majju Bhai hadn't fully come out of his sleep. Only a good cup of tea could do that. And I too hadn't entirely come out of my own drift. So, when I spoke, I was still on the same track. 'Majju Bhai, what is happening in this city?'

'What is happening?' Majju Bhai spoke carelessly.

'Do I really need to tell you what is happening?'

It was almost as though Majju Bhai had finally emerged from his sleepiness. He looked hard at me and said, 'Whatever is happening is not new.' And then after a pause, 'Yaar, I had said something to you; you did not think it appropriate to pay any heed.'

'And what was it that you said?'

'That if you must live in this city, you must stop thinking; or else, leave this city. I ask you: Can we stop whatever it is that is happening? Then what is the use of thinking and fretting?'

'That is all very well. But I am wondering: What am I doing in this city.'

Majju Bhai laughed, 'What am I doing in this city?' he repeated my words in his sardonic tone. Then he said, 'Even if you had lived somewhere else, what would you have done? What did you do when you went where you did and where you had the opportunity to do something?'

'Yes, that's true, but ...' I don't know what I was trying to say.

Irritably, Majju Bhai cut me short before I could complete my sentence, 'No buts ... All our ifs and buts are of no consequence. So, don't say anything. Just watch. Therein lies safety.'

'So, there is some hope of safety? You are saying as though we are sitting in some safe spot, as though whatever is happening will keep happening somewhere far removed from us. And that we will remain safe as long as we sit in our little nests.'

'As far as safety is concerned, my dear Jawad Miyan, only those who are fortunate will remain safe. No one will be safe because he was more vigilant or more careful. Those who are dying are dying in a muddled way. Whoever lives shall live because Allah has so willed. In any case, there is no logic to life or death. And you and I are, in any case, living a meaningless life.'

'If that is so, pray tell me why you have been instructing me to be more careful?'

'Well, we should all be more careful even though whatever will be, will be. Neither you nor I can stop what must happen from happening.'

Meanwhile, Nemat Khan brought the tea and kept it before us. Majju Bhai felt instantly better. He took his first sip and sighed deeply, 'Aqa Hasan is even more anxious than you. He looks worried all the time. He's becoming thinner by the day worrying over the state of affairs in the city. He asked me once, "Brother Majidul Hussaini, what do you see ahead?" I said, "The sea." And he gaped at me as though I was joking. Then he said, "Brother Majidul Hussaini, I had asked you this question in all seriousness." And I said, 'Qibla Aqqan sahab, I too had replied with utter seriousness." And then he was quiet.'

Now even I was quiet. What could I say? Majju Bhai had cut me short in such a way that I did not know what to say anymore.

'Majju Bhai,' I finally unlocked my tongue, 'I keep remembering something my Badi Bhabhi had said to me.'

'And what was that?'

'I have a cousin; his name is Pyare Miyan. When my grandfather died, he sold off all our ancestral lands and property – in fact everything except an old haveli – for a pittance. He took his share – or rather more than his fair share – and came away to Pakistan. Once here, he spent all the money he had made from the sale and could never quite settle down here. When he returned to India, he described his plight and said, "Badi Bhabhi, your curse has ruined me." Badi Bhabhi replied, "Bhaiyya, I have never cursed you. But whether I wished you ill or not does not really matter. You ruined your land; of course, the land will call down curses upon you. Those who have been cursed by the land can never be happy ..."'

'Yes, that's a thought,' Majju Bhai actually looked serious.

'Majju Bhai, I feel this is not applicable to Pyare Miyan alone ... and whether it applies to anyone else or not, it certainly applies to me.'

'What had I said to you?'

'What had you said to me?'

'You should have remembered. I had said to you that either one should not travel; or if one must travel, then one should not leave midway. You undertook the hardships of travel and yet you did not bring it to its logical culmination. You left your journey incomplete. This incomplete journey will trouble you. And, my dear, my sense is that it has already begun to trouble you.'

'Perhaps.'

'Not perhaps but certainly! My dear, you are reminded of what your Badi Bhabhi had said. Soon, you will remember other things said by other people,' Majju Bhai said and yawned. 'Yaar, I am sleepy.'

'You are feeling sleepy even after the tea?'

'Yes, that's really strange, isn't it? Usually I can be up all night as long as I have enough tea. I don't know what is wrong today; in any case, you are awake, aren't you?'

'Sleep seems to have fled from my eyes.'

'Fine, so stay awake then; I am going to sleep,' and with these words, Majju Bhai – who had woken up just a short while ago – lay down on his bed again. And strangely enough, began to snore almost immediately.

There was no trace of sleep in my eyes. There was a clamour in my mind. There was a mixture of surprise and anxiety: So is this really the same city? Has it changed so much? Do cities change like this as though a sea change has come over them? Alive, bustling, teeming, and then as though the entire city underwent a transformation. I was reminded of what I had said to Majju Bhai the other day. And suddenly a doubt arose within me. It seemed as though the Mount of Summons was somewhere close beside me. It had been hiding somewhere all this while; now it had suddenly revealed itself.

* * *

… And it so happened that when a month passed and the date came again, then everything happened in the same way all over again. And he was surprised at the voice and where it came from. Why were people so terrified? Why were their faces pale and why were their eyes wide open with terror? And why had he forgotten everything in his haste to get back home? He was thinking of this when suddenly he saw a young man coming towards him, almost falling in his haste. And behind him ran an old woman, crying and shouting, 'My son, my son ...' He tried to reach out and catch the young man and chide him as to why he was troubling his old mother, but the young man freed himself from his grasp, wriggled away like a fish and ran in the direction of the mountain. And he too followed him in hot pursuit. But within the flash of an eye, he reached the mountain and disappeared from sight. Saddened and disappointed, he turned back. He thought he would console the old woman, but he found that she too had disappeared. And all traces of that terror had gone. Once again there were the same crowds and gaity, the gatherings big and small as well as the buying and selling. Jewellers, bankers, money lenders, sellers of perfumes and flowers – they were all in business once again, getting the best prices from their customers. The hustle was back. The alley was once again as fragrant as a perfumer's tray. Seeing this, he was even more surprised and terror mounted within him. Ya Ali, what was going on? What was that? And what is this? The sight that his eyes had seen – and were now seeing – was it reality, or was it nothing but a place of illusions?

Fourteen

'… either one should not travel; or if one must travel, then one should not leave it midway … This incomplete journey will trouble you. And, my dear, my sense is that …' And once again, I became restless. There was no tranquillity for me after what Majju Bhai had said – though he had said the same sort of thing using different words several times before. Sometimes something has no effect on you and yet the same thing is said again in such a manner and at such a time that it penetrates deep within you and touches some chord in such a manner that it creates a commotion inside you. God knows at which moment of that silent night – perhaps it was the middle of the night or past midnight – when Majju Bhai made those remarks. I could not sleep not only that night but also for a long time thereafter, I could not rid my mind of those remarks. A strange restlessness came over me. And indeed that journey began to trouble me. I began to remember all sorts of things – from here and there, sometimes a half-finished sentence and sometimes a mere sign. And my restlessness began to increase. Majju Bhai had been so right when he had said, 'My dear, you are reminded of what your Badi Bhabhi had said. Soon, you will remember other things said by other people.' That time had come and I was in the net.

Actually, one should not let one's self flow like that; for, one can drift away. And so I made an attempt to control myself. I began an academic assessment of my travel as though I hadn't gone on a journey but written a poem and I was now reviewing it to see what flaws remained and why it had not become a successful poem or had fallen short of being a successful poem. Though it is also true that the thought of going on this journey had come to me all of a sudden – like the subject for a poem occurs to a poet and makes him restless and, till he has succeeded in giving it some poetic form, he knows no peace. Similarly, the idea of the journey occurred to me suddenly and, day in and day out, all I could think was that I must go there one day. I could no longer deny that I wanted to and the thought that I might not be able to go gave me palpitations and a feeling of near-hysteria. At that time, Majju Bhai did me the greatest kindness by lending me his support. He helped me get the visa and made all the arrangements for my travel – just like a child is held by the hand and brought to a road where he is pointed in the right direction and told to keep walking straight ahead. And now it was his sharp and acerbic criticism that was forcing me to make this assessment as to where the sickness lay. And I realized that what had happened to me was exactly what happens to that incompetent practitioner who launches into a prayer but at the penultimate stage – just when the prayer reaches its crescendo – he stumbles. 'My dear, the journey began to acquire real meaning only from the point when you ran away'.

In a poem, a story or a journey, a turn always comes when that turn becomes a challenge for the traveller, or you can say for the person undergoing that experience. If one accepts the challenge, if one resolves to face it, then the experience manifests itself in some form or the other. And if one runs away then the entire exercise gets washed away in the blink of an eye. Majju Bhai was right when he said, where you thought the matter had ended and when you ran away, *that* was the starting point. The snake had long since emerged from its burrow; I was sitting there and going over its tracks and wondering where I had fallen short and this journey – upon which I had embarked with such excitement – what was its net result? Now all I could see in this journey were potholes and quagmires. It began to appear as though the entire journey was wasted due to my haste and impatience, or you may say my stupidity and clumsiness. To mistake an instant reaction for a final or last word was hardly an intelligent way to react. And then to run away like that thinking there was no point in staying back! 'Arre wah, Subhan Allah, as though you are doing anything very important after coming back,' as Majju Bhai rightly pointed out. Truly, what had I done since my return? In any case, what was there for me to do here, considering I did not know how to use the Kalashnikov?

So now I was beginning to realize that my entire journey had come to naught. My haste had ruined everything. I had been able to go back to that place after an age. How could that land reveal itself fully to me in such a short time? The curtain of separation had fallen between us and it would take some time for it to recognize me again. And then sometimes, it is known to get angry too. Once the land gets angry, it takes a long time to cajole it. The wretch becomes as hard as rock and it does not melt easily. And it had only just begun to get to know me when an obstacle came up. I could now remember who had first recognized me: it was the trees. Actually, it is always the trees that are the first to recognize you, then the birds, then the four walls. Human beings recognize you much later; perhaps they are the last to recognize you. When I talk of the trees, I don't mean the banyan for the banyan has a distinct place; the banyan stands removed from the others, apart and aloof from the world. It pays no heed to who comes and who goes. A person has to undergo strenuous preparation to forge a relationship with the banyan. The fruit-bearing trees possibly recognize a person sooner than others; they are also among the first to get angry, and are equally quick to be pleased. In the barter of fruits, several good and bad things happen and sometimes there is good behaviour, and sometimes bad behaviour. In the process, a relationship is forged. And I had, after all, spent an age here, that too an age when a hundred different issues besieged the trees. Of course, the usual way to tease the tree was to pluck a half-ripe fruit; or else trample all over it to reach a bird's nest nestled among its branches. And if one had a slingshot in one hand and one wished to take aim at a bird sitting on a branch, of course the poor tree too would get hit along with the bird. I had already played all these cruel tricks upon them. And so the bond I had formed with them in the good old days was by no means a weak one. Time had not been able to harm that bond. They had recognized me rightaway when I was still in the train. They caught a fleeting glimpse of me in the moving train and recognized me. No, they began to run heedlessly alongside the train.

So, the trees are an altogether different matter. But others too were gradually beginning to recognize me. Maimuna's eyes had held such unfamiliarity in the early days. And gradually she began to show such familiarity. That morning when the dark clouds had surged, how sportingly she had put the wok on the fire. When she saw the massed clouds ready to burst with rain, she had taken leave from her school, quickly made the chickpea batter to fry the savouries. Hot oil bubbled in the wok and she got down to frying the spicy snacks. For whom was she taking this trouble? The curtain of otherness was lifting bit by bit. In any case, it hadn't been very long; I had barely set foot on that land and drawn my first few breaths. And a wondrous sight of happiness and surprise was unfurling before me: I could recognize some faces, and not recognize others. And when I recognized someone without any prodding, I would feel such surprise, and so much happiness. And there were so many things that I could recognize only partly. Some were known, others unknown. So there I was ... just beginning to know everyone – those who had been separated and I in their midst. Badi Bhabhi had shown undue haste.

Actually, she was the one in a hurry, not me. Be that as it may, my journey was left incomplete. I had seen many things and met many known and unknown people. And the things I had seen, I hadn't yet seen them properly. My eyes were barely beginning to open. And the people I had met, I had barely had the time to meet them properly. My biggest regret was regarding Khairul Bhai. My meeting with him had remained strangely incomplete. In fact, all my meetings remained incomplete. After all, my journey was all too brief. Rather, I had cut it short and made it brief. But strangely enough, it was expanding now. The more I remembered it, the longer it became. The truth is that I still have not gone into its details. The small details were only just coming back to me. Every detail that I touched turned from a drop into an ocean at the merest touch – just like the fish of Manu[75] which was, to begin with, the size of the smallest finger till it grew and grew and could not be contained even in the mighty river Ganga. A memory has no end. One memory is found hidden inside another memory, and yet another memory comes out of that one. And so, a chain of memories is formed, and it keeps becoming longer and longer. Yet, we would like to believe that we retain so little and forget so much of what has happened to us. Memory has its own deficiencies. It has its own niche of forgetfulness; and a great deal becomes a victim of this niche. What remains is no more than a few drops from the ocean or let us say, the few droplets of rain that remain on a leaf after a torrential downpour. And these few drops are sufficient to drench the soul of any human being. But I was troubled by a strange malady: all I could remember were tiny droplets of incidents. Now these droplets were turning into rivers in spate. Some other memory lurked behind a small memory; and hidden behind that small memory lay coiled yet another memory. And in this way, wisps of memories would swell into banks of clouds and heave and pitch across my imagination. And, yes, there was yet another difficulty. Narrow tracks would emerge from these memories and any one of these tracks would widen suddenly and turn into a long and circuitous road. There was no knowing which dense and dark jungle it would enter. Ages and lands would get entangled in it, and yet I would feel as though I had forgotten something that lay in between. When I had set foot in the ruins that was Dilkusha, I had felt the same thing. I

[75] In Hindu mythology, Manu is the first man and law-giver. In the story of a great flood, reminiscent of the Biblical story of Noah who preserved life from extinction, Manu is warned by a fish of a coming deluge that will wipe out humanity. Manu ties his boat to the fish and is steered to safety.

had remembered so much the moment I reached there, and I had thought that I had remembered everything. It was only later that I realized, and was troubled by the realization, that I had forgotten something that lay in between. And now that I was remembering that journey, once again I found myself in that same situation. I could clearly remember so many details, and yet I was troubled by the consciousness that there was much that I was forgetting, there was something that had slipped from my mind. Or perhaps it was the way that Majju Bhai was prodding me for details that put the doubt in my head.

'Ustad, you are hiding something from me.'

'No, Majju Bhai, I have told you everything that happened to me.'

'My dear, I have seen something of this world. Moreover, from what you yourself have described, I can tell that some other things have also happened in the middle. You are skipping over those.'

'I haven't tried to hide anything, though I can't say if something has been left out unknowingly.'

'It may well be unknowingly, but your narration tells me that something else too happened in between. My interest lies solely in that.'

'Now that's a problem; if there is indeed something left out in the middle, then I truly do not remember it.'

'Try … you will remember it. One should know the whole thing.'

Look at my simplicity – or call it my blind trust in Majju Bhai – that I began to believe that if he has felt it to be so, then it must necessarily be so. And I began to make strenuous efforts in real earnest … efforts, that is, to remember what it was that I was forgetting from the middle. In the process, I ended up repeating the entire journey in my mind. And what happened as a result? What happened was what usually happens when you set out to look for a lost object in a room full of things: you don't find that object, but in the process, you end up finding so many other things that you had never even imagined you had in your possession.

By now I had realized that this journey was a journey of another kind altogether. It was far bigger than what I had taken it to be. Strangely enough, I hadn't been aware of it till now. In a cursory sort of way, I had thought that my journey was incomplete, and that I should have stayed there longer so that I wouldn't have the sense of longing I was experiencing now, and I might have met those people that I hadn't met fully, and Maimuna ... Yes, I must try and and understand this business of Maimuna by going over it once again. So now when I repeated that journey in my imagination, it had transformed into something else: a journey within a journey, as though it wasn't a single journey and every journey seemed as though it was without end. It seemed as though I had set out on these journeys and after crossing some stages, I had returned – sometimes due to fatigue, sometimes out of fear, and sometimes because I had faltered. Now I was troubled by even greater regret that my journey had remained incomplete. If only I had completed my journey! And I was suddenly reminded of that incomplete practitioner who had resolved to recite the magical prayer, but had faltered at a crucial juncture.

'Yaar Jawad, you are a real nitwit! You ran away at the first sign of trouble. You should have waited a bit. After all, what are a few more days when you have waited so long? You should have waited to see what appears from beyond the Invisible Curtain.[76] Why were you in such a tearing hurry? One has to be patient in order to ...'

'Majju Bhai,' I cut him short impatiently, 'What are you saying? It's hardly my age to exercise this sort of patience.'

'There you go ... being a nitwit again! How does age come into this?'

'Majju Bhai, age is a cruel thing. No man can escape it; it has to come into everything.'

---

[76] *Parda-e-Ghaib* or the curtain that demarcates the visible and seen world from the invisible and unseen, referring to the mysterious forces or the hand of destiny that has unknown things in store for mere mortals.

'Hmm … Naturally, you will look for some sculpture to embellish.'[77]

Yes, perhaps this was an attempt to sculpt a dream. Those who get left behind end up becoming Aazars sculpting their statues. But what good is served by such an attempt? Though no good was served by Majju Bhai's darts and arrows either; his sarcasm only served to reiterate the obvious. The truth is that my real sorrow lay in the fact that I had embarked upon this journey with such excitement and it had ended up being so sour. I had gone back after an age to a place where every nook and cranny, every tree and stone, its birds and its very air had been calling out to me for such a long time. No, they were urging me from deep inside me, they were pushing me there. But when I went there, I lost my head. Every meeting remained incomplete, every outing unfulfilled and what of Shankar in whose house I had gone to stay? What must Shankar be thinking? On the one hand, I had announced my arrival with such gusto and promised to stay with him as his guest, and then I had upped and left with not one backward glance. Anyway, he is a friend. I can always write to him to apologize and mollify him. And Maimuna … anyhow, let's not talk about her. She was the one who made me run. So if that meeting remained incomplete, it was because of … Anyhow, let us talk of Khairul Bhai … my meeting with him left me wanting more. He didn't open up at all. Perhaps if I had met him two or three times, he may have opened up somewhat. In any case, Khairul Bhai is a man who stays up all night long. One should meet him only at night, whereas this time I could not meet him for even one night when we could have stayed up all night long, when I could have told him about myself and heard his stories. Khairul Bhai always opened up during the night-long vigils. As the night got steeped with dew and endless cups of tea were consumed … one cup followed by the second,

---

[77] The reference is to the dream of Aazar, the master sculptor who sculpted a perfect female form and promptly fell in love with it. English readers would be familiar with the story of Pygmalion.

then the third … how much tea Khairul Bhai used to drink! He would announce at the beginning itself: 'Friends, this first pot is a communal one; we shall all drink from it. Cover the second pot with a tea-cosy and set it aside for me.' And the real conversation began when that second pot of tea would be poured. As the night waned and the bitter brew from the second pot of tea slid down our throats, Khairul Bhai scaled new peaks as though he had now truly come into his own and began to show his true colours.

At that time, when Khairul Bhai was living the life of a senior student, he was the lodestar for young men like us. For me, he was my ideal. And not just mine. Countless students and educated young men had made him their ideal. Dressed in khadi and extremely individualistic in his dress and demeanour, he would be found holding forth among a gaggle of friends and admirers. If it weren't for Sandali, his cat, he would have been all alone, for his other brothers and sisters as well as nephews and nieces had all gone away to Pakistan. And there they lived a life of comfort and enjoyed good jobs and good positions, whereas he stayed on in this narrow lane in Meerut, in this large rambling house where he lived in the men's quarter, and his widowed sister was the sole occupant in the women's quarter. And his only friend and companion was the cat. Life can show you many strange sights. Sometimes there is such a crowd of people milling about you that it seems as though they will always remain with you. And then, suddenly, the world changes: the crowds disperse, the gaggle of friends and admirers scatter to the winds, and the comings and goings end. And there is silence all around and one is left sitting all alone on one's perch. And it is much later that you realize that that is the only truth. That day, as I was about to leave, Sandali – who had God alone knows when reappeared and snuggled up to Khairul Bhai – got to her feet suddenly as a shiver rippled through her. To me it seemed as though she would stand on her hind feet and become so tall that she would start … Now, re-imagining that sight, a ripple coursed through me like lightning. So, it was that cat! How did she appear here? The cat had been in Seville. Abul Hajjaj Sheikh

Yousuf Al-Shabarboli was quite a strange old gentleman. There he was sitting in meditation, far away from the rest of the world. He had spent an age in the confines of those four walls and boundaries, so much so that even his eyelashes had turned white. He did not even spare a glance to notice the tall date tree that had come up beside the well in his courtyard. And yet he had such affection for his cat … Oh, but his cat was black … Such was his affection that he held the cat in his lap all the time. And Abul Hajjaj's cat was a fine specimen too; it wouldn't let anyone come close. She would lie in the Sheikh's lap and purr contentedly, or she would be fast asleep. She recognized saints and mystics. She would growl and snap if a commoner approached. But if an evolved person arrived, she would stand on her hind feet and embrace them. When Sheikh Abu Jafar Aryani came to their abode, the cat jumped out of Sheikh Abul Hajjaj's lap, went to the chamber next door, sniffed the air and came running back. She looked at the glowing visage of Sheikh Aryani, stood on her two hind feet and embraced the Sheikh. Abul Hajjaj was wont to say. 'I don't know the newcomers; it is my cat who tells me who is good and who is bad.' So now I understood what he meant, and I was surprised too. And, yes, there was a tinge of sorrow too. The very thought was enough to make a shiver run through me. And when the cat ran indoors, I drew a sigh of relief. At the same time, a sense of deprivation came over me as though I had lost the great good fortune of being embraced by the cat of Sheikh Shabarboli, a chance that I had missed by a whisker. And then I promptly forgot all about Khairul Bhai. His cat snuggled deeper and deeper into my imagination, and took me from here to there. She herself seemed to be an evolved soul. The truth is not all cats are alike. And every cat is not merely a cat. Back then I could not comprehend this simple fact. The very sight of a cat used to make my palms itch. I used to pick a piece of a brick, take aim and hit. And immediately I would be scolded by Phuphi Amma, 'Son, how many times have I told you not to hit the cat? It makes me superstitious, but no matter what I say, it has not the slightest effect on you.'

'Phuphi Amma, why do you feel superstitious?'

'My dear, you never can tell with these cats … you don't know which cat is what, especially black cats. You should never raise your hand to hit a black cat.'

'Phuphi Amma, what happens to a black cat?'

'I don't know what is the great mystery associated with a black cat; I have always heard it from my elders. All I know is that, on one occasion, a wretched black cat put its mouth in a pitcher of milk. I threw a stick at it in anger and it disappeared from sight within the blink of an eye. But for the next three days, she kept appearing in my dreams. Then I read the *qul* three times and blew it all around me before going to bed. Only then did that black cat leave me alone.'

But Khairul Bhai's cat was a sandy brown, the colour of sandalwood. Yet I fell into doubt as soon as I saw it. While I knew Khairul Bhai well enough, his cat was different; an air of mystery surrounded her. But for him, she seemed to be a better deal in exchange for all his friends and relatives and all past and present companies. How grandly and how contentedly he sat in his place, having bid adieu to everyone. At the time, I hadn't understood anything; I was simply too confused. And now, suddenly, I understood so much. That dark and narrow desolate lane in Meerut was no longer merely a dark and narrow lane. It had travelled and led to such a strange place. And that evolved cat had taken me from here to there …

And when Ibn-e Habib finished eating the fresh-from-the-oven *naan*, he took a bowl from Abdullah the naan-seller and poured himself some water from the clay pot and drank it. Then, he thanked the merciful God and wept a little as he was reminded of something. For far too long he had been wandering, alone and desolate, in this strange territory amidst a crowd of pain and poverty. He would eat whatever little he could find and lie quietly. After several days, today he had found himself in a place where he had a roof over his head and a fire lit in an oven close beside him. The heat from the fire warmed him and the scent of freshly-baked *naan* drenched him with its redolence. And Abdullah the *naan*-seller – who had guessed his troubled state from one glance at his dishevelled appearance – placed a bowl of *saalan* and a freshly-baked *naan* in front of him, and – with great affection – invited him to eat. And when Ibn-e Habib had eaten his fill, he remembered those who had been separated from him, whom he had so far not been able to remember due to his troubled state, and he wept.

In an attempt to console him, Abdullah the *naan*-seller said, 'O stranger, your troubled state and your helplessness is amply evident from your appearance. I was silent. But when you cried, you stabbed my heart. Now it is imperative that I ask about your circumstance. My dear, the heart feels lighter if you talk about your troubles and the listener too gets a chance to share the other's sorrows if he is good hearted. So tell me which country do you come from?'

Then Ibn-e Habib took a grip of himself and after a moment's pause spoke thus, 'My dear consoler, this unfortunate wanderer who is roaming about in this dark desolate place without a roof over his head is from Maalaqa in Syria. But the truth is this desolation is not new to this unfortunate soul. For generations, it has been the misfortune of our tribe to be lost and wandering. Let it be known that this wretched person is from that land of desolation known as Seville. The skies would not have known a land such as that. Its fame was known from Rome till the Levant. Enthroned in this land of learning and wisdom were names greater than Aristotle and Galen, whose learning and wisdom was revered even in Baghdad. In this land of plenty, our ancestor Sheikh Abul Hajjaj Yousuf Al-Shabarboli occupied an exalted position in much the same way as a gem sits in a ring; the realm rang with stories of his miracles. Our ancestor lived till the ripe old age of a hundred years. But his cat had a longer life, for when Seville was being emptied, she was present at the scene of devastation. What happened to it thereafter and when she bid farewell to this transitory world, God alone knows better.

'So let us then talk a little about this cat. Let it be known that even though it was black in colour, it had the greatest love for the brightest of consciences. It growled at worldly folk and embraced the pious with enormous affection. She was a favourite of our glorious ancestor. She lay snuggled in his lap all the time. When the hour of our ancestor's death approached, he pronounced his last will and testament: his children must do whatever the cat bids them after his death. And with these words, he passed from this mortal world to the eternal one. And soon thereafter, that pure and virtuous cat sat down resolutely beside the corpse. She would growl at whoever ventured close and not let anyone come near the dead body. The news reached Sheikh Aryani; reciting many a holy verse, he reached the spot. At the sight of him, that cat with the brightly-lit heart and black body, that was by now a picture of learning, stood up on its hind legs. She embraced the Sheikh and wept, and immediately stepped aside. The Sheikh bathed our glorious ancestor with his own hands and buried him in the largest graveyard in Seville. The black cat adopted the grave as its abode and took to spending its days and nights beside it.

'I heard this from my grandfather and my grandfather heard it from his grandfather, who was a descendant of Abul Hajjaj Sheikh Yousuf. And finally a day came, when the cat got up from the grave with an air of restlessness and went to the house where the Sheikh had once lived and where his son now lived with his entire family, and there she wept. Thereafter, all night long, she would weep and keep watch over the house. No one knew what the mystery was. The secret was revealed only when the Christians attacked the city. The attack proved to be severe for Seville. Al-Mu'tamid[78] had already departed from the city, taking

[78] Muhammad ibn Abbad al-Mu'tamid (1040–1095) reigned c. 1069–1091, was the third and last ruler of the *taifa* of Seville in Al-Andalus. He was a member of the Abbadid dynasty. Not only was he a great ruler but also a fine poet. In 1091, Al-Mu'tamid was taken into captivity by the Almoravids and exiled to Aghmat, Morocco where he died in 1095. His grave is located on the outskirts of Aghmat.

with him his many unfulfilled desires and yearnings as well as his poetry and his sword. And filled with the pain of captivity, his spirit had completed its designated imprisonment and flown out of its mortal cage. Now it was the turn of the other sons of Seville, whose swords had rusted. It was a perilous moment. Seville was drawing its last breaths. Every swordsman worthy of his name had been defeated. My grandfather's father too fell in this battle. The harassed population left their homes and scattered in different directions. My dear friend, I heard from my grandfather and my grandfather heard from his that in the midst of this great commotion, that black cat rose from the shrine of our exalted ancestor and embraced my grandfather's grandfather, weeping copiously all the while. My ancestor understood this to be a signal from the spirit of our venerable sheikh to depart from the city. And so he gathered his entire clan without further delay and set out from his home. The black cat accompanied them till the outskirts of the city and then stopped abruptly. Once again, she embraced my grandfather's grandfather. And then, crying all the while, she returned to the shrine. Contemporary accounts tell us that soon thereafter, Seville emptied of all its people. For three days, that lone black cat, weeping and roaming its streets, was the sole occupant of the city.

'Those who had left had not merely left Seville; they wanted to leave Andalusia too. But my grandfather's grandfather's wish was to look for shelter somewhere within Andalusia itself. A wise man saw his intent and rebuked him thus, 'O imprudent son of a prudent father, what is this foolish thought you seem to be harbouring? Do you not see that Cordoba is already gone? Now Seville too is lost. Now which city in Andalusia has the strength to resist; they are no more than bubbles with foundations as fragile as water. Now there is no safe haven for us anywhere in Andalusia. Be sensible; come with us for we have decided to leave this place and find shelter in Fez.'

Hearing this, my grandfather's grandfather wept and said, 'We held fast to the staff of patience when we left Seville for that was the signal we received from our revered ancestor, but must I forsake Andalusia and leave forever? I swear by the Purest of Pure who holds fast to my life, I shall not be able to betray Andalusia thus. So, O Wise Elder, I shall henceforth part ways from the people of Seville.'

Saying this, my grandfather's grandfather took his own path and, pulling the burden of his sorrows, enduring all manner of hardships along the way, reached the settlement of Malaqah.[79] The soil of this ancient city held fast to his feet and he settled down there. Soon, he built himself a house of some sort. In its courtyard, he planted a date palm. In the shade of the palm, he put a wooden bed and, all day and all night long, he sat on it and wept. And he would remember the date palm in that long lost courtyard which, according to the best of his knowledge, was a veritable princess among date palms, and he would cry. On the morning of his last day, he called my grandfather to his side and smiled; my grandfather would say, that was the first time he saw a glimmer of happiness on his father's face since the day they had left Seville. And he said to my grandfather, "Son, this is the morning of union. I had a dream at the break of dawn that I have gone to Seville and I am sitting in the shade of the date palm planted in the courtyard of my home and the black cat has come and embraced me." Saying this, my grandfather smiled and said, "Dreams of early morning usually come true." With these words, he hiccuped and handed over his life to the Creator.'

And Ibn-e Habib fell silent. And then with a great effort, he spoke in a tone of immense sorrow, 'My dear, I too have left my village like my forefathers before me, and I have come to your city and I am more ill-fated than my forefathers. They had one sorrow. My grandfather's grandfather had entered Malaqah carrying in his breast the pain of separation from his beloved Seville. My breast is burdened with two sorrows: the separation from Seville which was my ancestors' sorrow and the separation from Malaqah which

[79] The historic ancient city of Malaga in Spain, along the Costa del Sol.

is my own sorrow. The graves of my ancestors are in Seville and my own umbilical cord is buried in Malaqah. And so my comforter and friend, I am wandering around in your city with two aches in my heart and these tear-filled eyes of mine, these are two sources of the worst torment for me. One is forever shedding tears for Seville, and the other cries for Malaqah.'

And saying this, Ibn-e Habib wept. Abdullah, the *naan*-seller, too became moist-eyed. He wiped his tears and said, 'O you who belong to the sacred soil of Seville and have come from the city of Malaqah, you have refreshed my pain, a pain that I had buried in oblivion for long years. Though I am a son of Granada, for my umbilical cord is buried here, I belong to the soil of Cordoba. My ancestors' ancestor left Cordoba and, after great travails, reached here. To be fair, Granada gave him much encouragement. Like a mother who lavishes great affection upon a son who has returned from foreign lands, so did Granada embrace those who had come from Cordoba. But all the love of this city could not find a cure for my ancestor's sorrow. The sorrow of separation from his beloved Cordoba kept eating away at him like a weevil that worries away. I heard from my grandfather's grandfather that my ancestor had a recurring dream: he has gone back to Cordoba and he can see the Grand Mosque of Cordoba in the distance. Impatiently, he rushes towards the Grand Mosque and he is almost there when he wakes up. Every morning, he would gather his sons and narrate his dream and weep and say, "O my sons, pray for your ill-fated father ... pray that at least once he may reach the steps of the Grand Mosque in his dream."'

As he finished his narration, Abdullah the *naan*-seller's eyes filled with tears. He fell silent. And for a long time, both men stayed silent.

After a long time, Abdullah the *naan*-seller spoke up, 'O you who carry two burdens on your breast, you and I have a common sorrow. So understand this: you are no longer alone in this city. Consider this roof, under which you are sitting, as your own. Sit beside this oven and refresh the memories of your village. Perhaps in this way, I too might refresh my memories of that fragrant city to which I belong.'

Ibn-e Habib heard these words and broke down with a surfeit of emotions. He said, 'Today I have received confirmation of all those stories of the fabled hospitality of Granada.'

Upon this, Abdullah the *naan*-seller said, 'My dear, Granada is a strange city and stranger still is the fact that there has been a deluge of those who have been uprooted. From distant corners of Andalusia, caravans upon caravans of those who have been uprooted and forced to flee their homes have been arriving to camp in Granada. Things have reached such a pass that there are fewer people from Granada in Granada and far more migrants and homeless people from outside.'

Ibn-e Habib swallowed a bitter draught and said, 'Including myself.'

❦

'Yaar Jawad, I think you too are one of them,' I was startled. Whose voice was this ... so startlingly different as it was? Like a jute patch in velvet! My entire train of thoughts scattered and broke; rather, it disappeared all together. Now I was reminded of Majju Bhai.

'Yaar, I do feel you too had set off with them. Your first stop was Granada; perhaps you are still camping out there. Enough is enough, Yaar; come away.' Majju Bhai laughed.

I truly fell in deep thought. Was it true? I tried to remember. Was it this that I had forgotten? I kept thinking, and remembering without paying heed to Majju Bhai's tone of voice when he made this pronouncement. Anyhow, I tried my best to remember. But I could not remember anything. I laughed at my own foolishness. 'Majju Bhai is known for his tall tales; you are a strange one to take him seriously.' Yet my seriousness did not go away. When I could not remember anything, I became even more sorrowful for I was not one of them. 'No, Majju Bhai, no. I am sorry to say that I am not one of them; I am one of your multitudes. I came with their throng to this useless city and set up camp here.'

'Don't say that, my dear. It has become a useless city now. Had it been a useless city then, you would still have been rotting away in a shanty.'

What a memory Majju Bhai had revived! He was an ace marksman. I was reminded of my days in the shanty. What a catastrophic downpour had devastated the shanties! The rain came a bit late; I had shifted to Majju Bhai's flat by then. Or else my cot too would have been seen floating down that river of cots and beddings. Those were sobering days of great reckoning for, right in front of one's eyes, one saw the owners of mansions and palaces turn into shanty-dwellers. But now I felt that the Golden Age of Pakistan, or at least of Karachi, was that era of the shanties. You can get an idea of those times by virtue of the fact that you saw neither masked men nor wielders of Kalashnikovs, and cars were not hijacked in broad daylight. In any case, who had cars those days? People had neither money nor worldly possessions, nor pennants and banners or carriages! What could the world take from you even if it turned against you? What was there for thieves and robbers to snatch? The only wealth was one's memories. Actually, I was trying to see that age from this angle, for everyone had a lot of memories those days; if anything, people had a surfeit of memories. Though they lived on memories, they were actually living in a world of imagination, high up in the clouds. They talked of the Lal Quila though they were living in Lalu Khet.[80] But this age passed all too soon. The shanty-dwellers became house-owners and began to be counted among affluent folk. A wealth of memories was bestowed upon me. And with it came my share of taunts – taunts, sarcasm, jibes and ridicule.

---

[80] Lalu Khet is a neighbourhood in the densely-populated Liaqatabad area of Karachi; the reference here is to the *muhajirs* who spoke fondly of the Lal Quila or Red Fort they had left behind in Delhi when they had crossed over to find a new home in this migrant-dominated neighborhood. Lalu Khet was once an agricultural farmland; the Government procured it to build a rehabilitation colony for the *muhajirs*.

'Excuse me, Jawad Bhai, but why had you gone to Meerut?'

'What?' I looked askance at Tausif. It seemed as though his tone and tenor had changed since he had become a part of the bureaucracy, or as Akhtari Baji would have it 'the ruler of a district'. And his world view along with it.

'See, Jawad Bhai, the other day we organized a feast of Nauchandi parathas for you as well as kababs from Khair Nagar.[81] And then well-wishers like us are always here for you. What is left there?'

'Only Khairul Bhai and his cat,' Majju Bhai added as a riposte.

Tausif let out a feeble laugh. Then he said, 'I had once gone to Meerut. Baji used to talk a great deal about Kotla[82] once upon a time; but it was deserted when I saw it. I saw a few wizened old men who looked as though they belonged to the previous century. Khairul Bhai was sitting in his living room all by himself looking rather the worse for wear. I felt sorry for him. Had he come to Pakistan, surely something or the other could have been arranged for him.'

'How could he come?' Akhtari Baji spoke up. 'His brain was addled. We were distantly related, but the bonds of neighbourliness were stronger. How much my mother had tried to make him see reason, "Son, what is left for you here? Will you stay back to do menial jobs like a cobbler stitching old shoes? Come to Pakistan." But his brain was addled; he wouldn't listen. He ruined his life. His parents had suffered such hardships to give him a fine education; it all went waste.'

'Majju Bhai, I got bored out there in just two days! For one thing, I was heartily sick of the bathrooms in the homes of my elderly relatives. It is so strange ... they are still using the old-fashioned open-air lavatories.'

'I feel such pity for those people,' Akhtari Baji said, adding her bit to Tausif's account. 'What is left there? The truth is that the

[81] An old neighbourhood in Meerut.

[82] A busy neighbourhood in Meerut; its full name at present is Kotla Bazaar Chauraha.

real excitement was because of us. Who is left there now? Only the no-good inconsequential types remain … Those who belong to the low castes such as *teli, tamboli, bhatiyare, ghasiyare,* or idlers like Khairul Bhai. The only reason I went back was out of love for my poor Khala Amma when her husband died. I nearly went mad in the first four days. I somehow managed to stay on till the fortieth day ceremony and then fled for dear life.'

And Majju Bhai was happily agreeing with every word she was saying.

'Majju Bhai,' Basho Bhabhi was saying, 'I am not one to talk big, but one must speak the truth, after all. Our family was the pride of Lucknow; there is nothing but dust left there since we came away.'

'My dear sir,' Syed Aqa Hasan spoke up, 'I don't even feel like remembering that lost land. Our home, believe me, was a palace. A tumble-down ruin stands in its place today. Now you decide for us: why should we remember that desolate ruin?'

I was suddenly reminded of Dilkusha. There, in the place of Dilkusha, lay a heap of rubble. All that remained of the building was one staircase – that too dilapidated and falling to pieces. It was odd; an earthquake can certainly wreck an entire building, but it does nothing to a staircase. That is why it is said that one should take shelter under a staircase during an earthquake; one will be safe there. So, all that remained of Dilkusha was a decrepit and dilapidated staircase. And this decrepit and dilapidated staircase brought back to life the memories of the Dilkusha of days long gone. Now I am going about with this staircase inside me. Yes, and that tumble-down moss-encrusted old wall of the *haveli*. Who is to know all that lies hidden in a moss-encrusted wall? Surely, there is a magical quality in a wall that is so moss-encrusted that it has become black as a griddle. It draws a person so; it seems as though it isn't a wall but an entire era standing there in front of you. The wall of my *haveli* had cast just such a spell on me on that rainy evening. I was caught in the magic of that wall. How long I had stood there, gazing at that rain-drenched, stained dark, high wall. I had tried to include Maimuna in my wonder. 'Maimuna, do you see how black the wall of this *haveli* has become? It tells us how many rainy seasons it has seen.'

Maimuna became a part of my wonderment. She said, 'Really,' as though she had seen the wall for the first time.

As I was recounting the many rainy seasons I had enjoyed along with the wall, somehow I let slip the following sentence, 'Now, those who come after us shall see the coming rains.'

Maimuna heard this sentence and looked at me in anger, an anger which contained a sadness too and said, 'Who shall come after us? Who will stay here?'

I fell so silent that for a long time not a word escaped my lips, nor did I find the courage to meet her eye. She too became quiet after that one sentence. For a long, long time, the two of us kept sitting silently and still – like two islands of silence, miles apart from each other.

That *haveli* was like a dream for me now. In fact, that entire age had turned into a world of dreams and imagination. But from that day onwards, that black wall got after me. And that unbroken staircase from Dilkusha. I began to feel as though I was stuck between the wall and the staircase. Those magical powers had me in their thrall. Together, time and rain can transform a wall. A simple, straightforward wall can become a wall of wonder. If an entire building collapses but one staircase remains standing upright, stairs begin to emerge from within stairs. Now those stairs were inside me, and were going higher and higher. And I ... I was finally beginning to understand why the *dharamshala* with its moss-eaten wall and its tall peepal tree had seemed such a riddle to us. The wall and the peepal were not part of the *dharamshala*, but the two entities that together constituted the *dharamshala* and made it an enigma. The wall and the peepal ... Arre ... Suddenly, I was reminded of our neem. Look at me, I had forgotten all about it! True, the staircase and the wall had their rightful place, but the greatest magical force was that ancient neem tree that stood in the courtyard of our *haveli* whose dense branches had bent to drape the top of the black wall. If there is a tall and dense neem tree and a moss-encrusted black wall with an equally black and moss-encrusted parapet and if the branches have bent over it, then a veritable mountain of magic stands before you. It is strange that I went there after such a long time. I was looking at every nook and cranny of the *haveli*, and every object in it with wonder and amazement, yet I had overlooked the neem tree. As though it wasn't there! I was taken by surprise in that rain-washed moment, as though the neem had caught me. I felt as though I was seeing it for the very first time, even though I had spent some of the finest moments of my life under its shade – along with Maimuna – hidden among its boughs, like two birds, chirping and cheeping on its branches. But in those days, the neem held no great mystery for us. Why would it be a mystery when it was one of us? Rather, we were a part of it. Among its densely-foliaged boughs were two tender green branches. The mystery began now. The bark of its trunk was transformed. It seemed as though it was opening up and somewhere deep from within it, from somewhere far away, a voice could be heard. Slowly-slowly, softly-softly, as though Maimuna was not sitting next to me but had appeared from within it. Dear Lord, how do things turn into mysteries? Or they are mysteries but are revealed to us only in a certain special moment? What is all this, after all? What is this thing called a cloud?[83] What is the wind when it is swaying the branches? And what is the neem? How do those little berries appear on its branches? And what of the moss-encrusted wall and parapet? If I had the slightest spark of a Sufi in me, that day, at that instant, I would have entered the realm of wonder incarnate, and then all life long, I would have spent it just so: that is, sitting still and gazing at the neem. And also at the moss-encrusted wall. The walls of our *dharamshala* too had endured many rains and turned black with moss. How startled Maimuna used to

[83] Reference to a verse by Mirza Ghalib: *Sabza-o-gul kahan se aayein hain/Abr kya cheez hai, hawa kya hai*, meaning 'Where does the flower and greenery come from/ What is the cloud, what is the wind?'

get whenever she spotted a monkey on its parapet, even though it wasn't unusual to see monkeys roaming around our house. But the monkey sitting on top of that parapet was not merely a monkey; it turned into something else! In any case, a monkey and a cat are two animals that can suddenly transform into something else. That is, a cat is not merely a cat and a monkey does not remain merely a monkey. Among the many mysteries of nature, the cat and the monkey are two mysteries.

Shankar stopped mid-stride and said, 'Jawad, this is an ancient temple. There is a story about it among the local people. I will tell you about it later; first, come and see it.'

Indeed, its moss-encrusted walls and parapets were indicating that it was a very old temple. Eagerly, I stepped forward. But I paused as I was about to enter. 'No, yaar, I have seen it.'

'Yaar, see it from inside. No one will say anything. In any case, you hardly look like a Muslim.'

'It isn't that.'

Somehow or the other, I got out of it, and we moved on. Do you know what the matter was, really? There was a monkey sitting on the parapet of the temple. A lone monkey sitting silently atop a blackened moss-encrusted wall of the old temple … a fear came over me. I felt as though it would come down from the parapet at any instant, stand on its two hind feet and embrace me. Or, perhaps I thought it may not embrace me but – sitting right there – its tail would get longer and longer and it would appear before me in such a way that I would neither step forward nor move back. And who was to know if he would remain a monkey, or not. That is to say, who could tell if he might become something other than a monkey? You can never trust a monkey and a cat, for who knows what they might turn into at any instant? But my Phuphi Amma used to say something else altogether; she used to say that monkeys were not monkeys to begin with.

'Really?' I was amazed, so was Maimuna. 'Phuphi Amma, what were they then?'

'They were God's own children, just like you and me. But the wretched things had stopped offering namaz. Such a calamity befell them that they turned into monkeys.'

I was scared, and so was Maimuna. We began to offer namaz five times a day. Soon, a fresh doubt began to torment me. 'Phuphi Amma, are these monkeys actually monkeys?'

Phuphi Amma paused to consider. Then she said, 'They are monkeys, but some of those wretched monkeys are actually not monkeys.'

'Not monkeys?' I was astounded. 'What are they, then?'

'Son,' Phuphi Amma cautioned, 'don't ask too many questions. The world is a riddle. And Allah Miyan has kept many answers with Himself. He alone knows the answers to His riddles.'

'Amma,' Maimuna spoke up suddenly, 'Why did Jan-e Alam turn into a monkey?'[84] Phuphi Amma had told us the story of Jan-e Alam; much later we also read it in a book. Yes, I remember now … A monkey got aboard a ship. That story too had been told to us by Phuphi Amma. Or perhaps we had read it in *Alif-Laila*.[85] Anyhow, the monkey boarded the ship like all the other passengers. But the ship that was ready to sail, stopped still. There was nothing wrong with the ship, but it just wouldn't move. The ship's captain became suspicious. He announced, 'Gentlemen, something is the matter for the ship is not moving. Pen and paper has been placed before you. Each one of you should write your name so that we know who is who. Everyone wrote down their name. When it was the monkey's turn, he too held the pen in his hand and wrote his name on the paper. Commotion rippled through the ship: the monkey was a calligrapher! How beautifully he had written his name, each letter as perfectly formed as a pearl. An elderly man looked knowingly at the monkey, and then warned his fellow-passengers: 'My dear

---

[84] Intizar Husain has written an entire story on Jan-e-Alam called *Mahaban ke Bandaron ka Qissa* ('The Story of the Monkeys of the Big Forest'); see my translation of this story in my collection entitled *The Death of Sheherzad* (Harper Perennial, 2014).

[85] Refers to the stories contained in the Arabic work of fiction, better known as *The Arabian Nights*.

gentlemen, get a hold of yourselves. Is it necessary that this monkey is a monkey? Obviously, it is an unsoundness of your intellect if you don't follow what I mean.'

'Shankar, do you remember that man with the monkey?'

'Which man with the monkey?'

'Arrė, have you forgotten? There was only one man who used to come with unfailing regularity to the *chowk* and play his little drum as all the children gathered around him.'

'Yes, I remember now. He had turned into a monkey because he spent all his time with his monkey. Do you remember his face? He looked vile.'

'And that monkey,' I said. 'He looked as though he wasn't the monkey, but its owner.'

At least there is no such fear in the case of a cat. The cat is made of an altogether different sort of clay. No matter how much man may come to love a cat and no matter how much a cat may become attached to a man, both remain fixed to their own appearances. And cats have their own inclinations. Sheikh Abu Yousuf's cat was wont to be pleased at the sight of saints and would stand on its hind legs to embrace them. Khairul Bhai's Sandali was forever morose. She would get bored if a guest dropped by. She would get up indolently, yawn mightily and then go inside the house. Yes, I remember another cat. I had read about her somewhere. She was a new age cat; she stood on a bus stop with an eight-anna coin in her mouth. When the bus came, she too got on the bus with the other passengers. When the conductor approached her as he gave the tickets to the other passengers, she rose on her two hind legs and placed the eight-anna coin on his palm, took the ticket and held it between her teeth. She got off when the bus stopped at the next stop. When she got off, the conductor realized that she too had bought a ticket. He was surprised: what sort of cat was she and who was she? But the bus had moved on and the cat too had gone far away by then. But in Phuphi Amma's stories, all the birds and animals, all the creatures that crawled and swam, seemed full of mystery – as though every animal was a riddle and every bird carried the grain of a mystery in its beak. 'And so my dear, it so happened that that day, too, the fisherman went to the river with his fishing-net. But he only managed to catch one fish in his net and then he set off for the market with that one solitary fish. And my dear when he reached the market, the fish began to laugh. All the buyers were surprised to see the laughing fish.'

'Phuphi Amma, the fish was laughing?'

'Yes, my dear.'

'Why was it laughing?'

'Be patient, my son. There was a mystery even in this; it will be revealed later. So there was the fish laughing away and the people in the market who were surprised out of their wits and worried by this strange sight.'

The world seemed full of mystery in stories. But it wasn't just limited to the stories; the world around me, too, seemed full of mysteries. Temples, monkeys, banyan trees, peepal, the roller bird sitting on the highest branch of the peepal, the snake slithering and swaying on the ground – everything was a mystery and there was no knowing who was what, who was in its own form and who had changed form and become something else. As though all guises were false and everyone had adopted more than one guise. And on top of it all, there was the business of rebirth. What were once the swan and its mate were now the king and queen! And who was now the princess would later become …

After an age, as I sat with Maimuna that evening, taking in the antiquity of that *haveli*, I don't know how my mind wandered in that direction. 'Maimuna, do you remember that *sadhu* who used to say he remembered his last birth?'

'Which *sadhu*?' she said and became pensive. Then she said, 'Yes, I do, but how did you remember him suddenly?'

'That is what is surprising me too … it is strange. I am reminded of all sorts of things from long, long ago as though … as though I too remember my last birth.'

Maimuna looked closely at me. I don't know what was there in her glance because I could not complete my sentence. My comment dangled mid-sentence as I fell silent. And then for a long time, she was quiet, and so was I. But that *sadhu* was roaming around in my imagination. People were gathered around him – old and young, men and women. In the middle of them all, he stood with his white matted locks, his eyes closed, hands folded, mumbling something incoherently. He spoke in strange tongues, asking all sorts of questions.

'Maharaj, when was this?'

'My children, this was centuries ago. I used to live in Dwarka then. It was a good time. Blessings rained down upon the place. Every morning, at day break, the Lord himself appeared, his chariot looking like the clouds, as though it had just descended from the skies. The two milk-white horses pulling his chariot looked like two white clouds and, when they neighed, the entire firmament echoed with the sound. Nymphs accompanied his chariot, in the front and back, and a primordial sound rose from the ground till the skies. And the music of love …

Tring-tring-tring … the grating sound of the telephone struck a discordant note. There I was, and suddenly here … It was as though someone were scaling the heights engrossed in his thoughts and suddenly his foot slipped and he came tumbling all the way down. How hateful was that sound at that instant! Not that I had ever liked its sound. It was just another discordant sound in the many discordant sounds of the modern age. Whoever has kept a telephone in his bedroom, has arranged to ruin his life. But there was no getting away from it either. How I had hated that sound at the time! Yet I had to attend to the telephone. The wave that I had been riding had quite subsided by now. I was back in my present dissipated times, holding the receiver close to my ear and listening to a worried voice.

'I had called in the morning itself and informed you that I am not well and wouldn't be coming in today.'

'But, Sir, there is a crisis here; it is very important that you come.'

'Crisis? Why?'

'Sir, there has been a robbery in the bank next door. Four masked men came. They killed the gunman at the entrance, came in and tied up the manager with ropes, brandished their guns and silenced the others, looted all the cash from the cashier at gunpoint, and fled.'

'Really? ... That is terrible news.'

'So, Sir, as a result there is a crisis in our office.'

'But surely this concerns their bank. Why is it a crisis in our office?'

'The staff has decided to go on strike.'

'Well ... But there is no car here at this time.'

'Sir, Jamaluddin has left for your home; he must be about to reach you.'

And indeed the sound of the horn could be heard after a few minutes. Jamaluddin had reached. I pulled on some clothes in a hurry and set off.

Indeed there was a full-blown crisis in my office. The entire staff was in a tizzy. From the peon till the cashier – everyone who ordinarily sought permission to enter my room and spoke ingratiatingly to me – were speaking to me in the most threatening tones. 'The bank makes us work hard, but what has it done to ensure our security?'

'What can a gunman do in this day and age? They finished him off in the beginning itself; the field was clear for them thereafter.'

'So, how many gunmen should we have to ensure our safety?' I asked.

No one had a clear answer to this question.

'My dear brother,' I said, 'It isn't exactly great foresight to have far too many gunmen. Too many gunmen can themselves pose a danger.'

But logic doesn't work in such a charged atmosphere. A union was formed, several demands were placed and many slogans were raised. And then someone announced, 'Sir, the bank will be closed tomorrow.'

'The bank will be closed? Why?'

'The corpse of the slain gunman will be taken away tomorrow. The union has decided to strike work in the bank tomorrow. We must take part in the funeral procession.'

It was no use making them see reason, or offer arguments. Who listens in such times, and who comes round to good sense? A crowd had gathered outside and slogans were being raised. The smoke from burning tyres and the noise from raised voices were seeping indoors.

Fifteen

'Miyan, I want to die.'

'Arre Mirza sahab, what a thing to say!'

'Ai Majju Bhaiyya, make him see sense,' Achchi Bi said. 'This is the only thing he goes on about these days … I want to die, I want to die … I tell him that he should not speak such words of ill omen, but he doesn't understand. He has lost it … it is always the same thing … I want to die!'

'Yes, Miyan, I have lived long enough, After all, I don't have to be around to lug the sacks of my misdeeds on the Day of Reckoning.'

'But why, Qibla?'

'Miyan, the thing is it is best if I were to move on now. If I am not around, I shan't see …' He paused and then said, 'Majju Miyan, you are younger than me. Perhaps you may not remember that time so well, but I remember each and everything about it. When I came here and took charge of my office, there was a state of utter chaos. My staff complained that there was neither pen nor pencil nor paper; how was one to even start work. I urged them to show some patience; everything would be arranged. The very next day I bought some stationery from my own pocket, and so the office got going. Today, that office is located in a sky-scraper. If one were to tell someone of those days, who would believe me? But Miyan, you were there; you have witnessed it.'

'You are absolutely right; it was just so. That's the way things were in the beginning.'

'So, Majju Miyan, I have seen this city become what it is.' And after a pause, he continued, 'Our Delhi too was once a vibrant city.'

'Ai Majju Bhaiyya, I too can bear witness to that. I can barely describe its hustle and bustle.'

'Miyan, just the steps of the Jama Masjid were such that if you went around them once, you didn't need to see anything more in the world. And beyond that lay Chawri; the row of tall houses had moon-faced maidens from one end till the other. But Chawri was ruined by the time we came of age.'

'Bhaiyya, everything changed so suddenly. We received such a jolt, such a jolt, that houses full of people became desolate overnight. And what had I said? That no matter what happens, yours truly would not forsake the city of twenty-two sufis[86]. Ask him how I refused to budge from that soil.'

'Yes, indeed you held on to that soil, but that soil did not hold on to you,' her husband said and then turned to address Majju Bhai. 'The soil has its own compulsions. When it allows you to leave, it can do so within a matter of a few minutes. And if it refuses to give permission, you may beg and plead all you like, but it will remain unmoved. I read in the *Malfuzat* of some saint – I can't recall his name (my memory isn't what it was, you see) – who said he was sitting beside a tank. And close beside the saint sat a man muttering to himself, who did not seem to be in full possession of his senses. The man would sigh deeply and say, "When I had set foot in this city, I was like gold; now I have turned to silver. If I stay here any longer, who knows what I will turn to?" The saint asked the man, "My dear, do you live in this city of your own free will?" He said, "No." The saint asked, "Why don't you leave this city if you are unhappy here?" The troubled man drew yet another long sigh and said, "I went to my spiritual master and complained about my unhappiness with the city. My master asked me if I stayed in the ammunition depot. I said I did. My master told me that there

---

[86] Delhi was called *Bais Khwaja ki Chaukhat* or the 'Threshold of 22 Sufi masters' because of the number of sufi shrines and hospices here.

was no peace in the city, nor would there be any in the future. But I shall remain here, my master said. If you can leave, you must do so. Happily, I returned to my room, gathered my belongings, tied them up in a bundle and set out to leave the city. But as soon as I tried to set foot outside the city limits, the earth caught hold of my feet. I said, 'What are you doing? I have taken permission from my master to leave this city.' She said, 'I haven't received the order yet; how can I let you leave?' The next day again I set off from my room, with my bundle under my arm, but again the same thing happened: the earth caught hold of my feet and said that she hadn't received the orders yet, so how could she let me go? My dear sir, this has been happening for the past twenty-five years. Every day I leave my room with my bundle under my arm, I walk till the outskirts of the city, but the earth catches hold of my feet and says she hasn't received the orders yet so how can she give me permission to leave." The troubled man narrated his story and drew yet another long and deep sigh. Then he said, "God knows when the order will come and when the earth will give me permission to leave the city. When I had set foot in this city, I was like gold; now I have turned to silver. If I stay here any longer, who knows what I will turn to?"'

Mirza sahab narrated this account and fell silent. Then, he spoke in a sorrowful tone, 'Who can tell who was more unfortunate: he who was not given permission to leave by the earth or those who were given permission in such a way that, in the blink of an eye, they became homeless and shelterless?'

'Ai Bhaiyya, now listen to my tale,' Achchi Bi said. 'We were settled in the Suiwala Mohalla, like a staff planted deep in the ground, but suddenly we were uprooted and had neither home nor roof.'

Mirza sahab sighed and said, 'Yes, it was almost as though the earth had suddenly become narrow. I am now reminded of my dear father who said, "Son, when you see the earth becoming narrow, shake yourself free and leave. Understand that the waters of this land are no longer for you." So while the land of Delhi gave us much joy and nurtured generations of our family, now its gaze had turned. So we bid farewell to it and said, "Wise men have come and camped here, but now you dislike our company so we will pull up our tents and leave." And we set off for this land.'

'Arre Bhaiyya, we had thought that if our own people hurt us, they will at least let us lie in the shade. Who could have known that our own people would turn strangers? Once we came here, even our own family turned away in case someone asked for help. Just think ... why would we need help from anyone? We were the sort of people who fed four others before we put a morsel in our own mouth. May God forgive me if I am wrong but here too we have given, not taken anything from anybody! But the people here have become ungrateful. And why complain about others? Our own daughter-in-law has become a stranger to us.'

'There you go again ... talking about your daughter-in-law! Let her be.'

'How can I let her be? Ever since my boy has been taken from me, I haven't known a minute's rest. Ai Majju Bhaiyya and Jawad Bhaiyya, tell me truly: that witch has cast such a spell on my boy that he has left us here to face a shower of bullets and gone off with her to live in Clifton.'

'My dear, he did tell us: "Leave this neighbourhood; this is a never-ending calamity. Come and live with us in Clifton." We are the ones who wanted to be excused. We said, "Son, you are a family man now. Live comfortably on your own. Let us stay where we are."'

'I know well enough how he said it. Ai Bhaiyya, my daughter-in-law is a clever woman; she clips away at the roots in such a way that one doesn't even come to know. She seems so sweet on the surface whereas she is a poisonous pill in reality.'

'Mirza sahab, there is one clear advantage of staying in this neighbourhood; there is no shortage of *mushairas*. I hope you are coming for the one this evening.'

"No, Miyan.'

'Why, Qibla?'

'There was an excitement in the *mushairas* till there were poets like Ustad Sahail Dehelvi and Ustad Bekhud Dehelvi; what is left in these gatherings now that they are gone? I can't understand the new-fangled nonsense that your modern poets recite.'

Majju Bhai had deliberately broached the subject of the *mushaira*. After all, we needed an excuse to make our getaway. We left them and went to meet Rafiq sahab. Actually, Mirza sahab's home was on our way and Majju Bhai – who was never one to tread the straight path – decided to peep in for a bit. Though his real plan was to first meet Rafiq sahab catch up on gossip and then take him along to the *mushaira*. Rafiq sahab saw us and beamed with delight.

'Yaar, so you are both alive?' How happy he was to see us! 'We've been getting extremely worrying news from your neighbourhood. We had heard about the gunfire.'

'Yes, there was was some gunfire but mostly tyres were burnt,' Majju Bhai said. 'But no matter how much gunfire we may have had, it was far less compared to yours.'

'You can never compare yourselves with us; we have set a new record.'

'So if *you* can survive your shower of bullets, why can't we?' Majju Bhai replied.

'It is an everyday affair for us; we have learnt the art of living in the midst of all this. So don't talk about us. But tell me: how did these blessings come this way today?'

'What shall I say?' Majju Bhai spoke with great ennui. 'I have bid adieu to the Coffee House days, but those days won't leave me alone. There used to be some lads who used to write some excruciatingly bad poetry. At the time, I thought there was no harm in uttering a few words of encouragement. But the times have changed and now they are regarded as respectable poets in the city. Today some of their cronies and fans have organized a *mushaira* here; they insisited so much that we thought of popping by for a bit. We thought we will meet you, too. What is more, I had Jawad's car with me.'

Rafiq sahab let out a mighty laugh. 'So the *mushaira* has pulled you here.' And then after a pause, he said, 'You and I have our compulsions. These people are your friends and disciples from long ago. And I have to show good neighbourliness, so I must go. But what crime has poor Jawad sahab committed? What are you punishing him for?' And immediately he turned around to address me, 'Jawad sahab, what is this? Are you going to attend a *mushaira*?'

'It is not necessary,' I said. 'The intention was to ensure Majju Bhai reaches his destination; and then I was hoping to meet you, too.'

'Nice ... so you have killed two birds with one stone.'

'Yaar Rafiq sahab,' Majju Bhai said, 'Talk some sense into Jawad.'

'Why? What happened?'

'This man has driven me round the bend. Every now and then he asks me the same question: Majju Bhai, what is happening in this city?'

Rafiq sahab let out a peal of laughter. 'Great! But I should love to know what answer you gave.'

'I have only one answer: Dearie, stop thinking. Or else, leave this city.'

Rafiq sahab let out another peal of laughter. Then he said, 'There is no need to leave the city. You just need some panache to live in this city. If you have acquired the art, then here is no hardship for you.'

'Tell us the trick too, yaar,' Majju Bhai said.

'I have told my wife ... As you know, when my wife and I set out, she drives the car ... So I have told my wife that when a Kalashnikov-wielding person asks us to stop the car, she must do so immediately and, before he can say anything, hand over the car keys to him. And for my part, I remain mentally prepared to hand over my wallet as soon as the car keys have been given to him.'

Majju Bhai laughed. 'Subhan Allah! What a wonderful technique you have devised to stay alive!'

'It isn't a laughing matter, Majju Bhai; tell me, will he be able to say anything after this? In any case, it is tried and tested.'

'Really?'

'Yes, really; it was just last month. Two masked men appeared from nowhere and my wife was terror-stricken. I said, never mind, just hand over the keys. We gave them the keys and immediately I took my wallet out of my pocket, and gave them that too. They took the wallet, but one of them, who appeared to be the leader of the gang, asked if we had enough money to pay the taxi fare. I said, "Dear Brother, don't worry, we shall go on foot." He said, "No, how can you go on foot?" Then he instructed the man who had taken the wallet, "Deduct Rs 50 from this." And the youth took out a fifty-rupee note and swiftly handed it to me. Then they got into our car and disappeared from sight.' I showed them courtesy; they extended the same to me. They even gave us fifty rupees so we may be spared the trouble of walking. And from that fifty, we even saved ten!'

'Well done!' Majju Bhai said.

'And look at my wife ... she asked me who those people were? She wanted us to file a report with the police. I said, "Begum, let it be. What good will it do? And don't ask who they were. They looked like lads from Lucknow." That was enough to enrage her. We seemed to have an ethnic riot in our home; I immediately withdrew my statement.'

Majju Bhai spoke with the utmost seriousness, 'Rafiq sahab, I fully agree with you. After all, what else can we do in these circumstances? Good sense demands that we learn to bend our stiff necks, hand over whatever we have without the slightest demur, and do our bit. The rest is up to them. If indeed your name is written on a bullet, then there is no getting away from it. Do you understand, Jawad Miyan? This is the way to survive in this city.'

'Yes, I am beginning to understand,' I answered with great distaste.

'No, Jawad sahab, you don't understand,' Rafiq sahab's tone became suddenly serious. 'My wife thinks like you do. I have been trying to make her understand, but she doesn't. Exasperated, finally one day I told her clearly, "My dear, this is not your Lucknow. This is Karachi ... You understand ... Karachi." She was irritated and said, "Yes, it is Karachi and so what should I do?" I said, "Do what your slang asks you to do: When in Rome, do as Romans do."'

Rafiq sahab was in full flow when his wife appeared looking worried. She said, 'You are sitting here and talking; do you have any idea what is happening outside? Gunfire has started again.'

'Is that news? It is a daily occurrence. I thought some new calamity has befallen us.'

'Yes, it is not new for us anymore. We live in hell. This is written in our fate. But what about these two respectable gentlemen who have come as our guests? I am worried about them.'

'Begum, do you think they have come from heaven? They too have walked over from hell. The only difference is that they have come from their hell to set foot in ours.'

'That is all very well but what if these poor things get stuck here?'

'That's nothing to worry about; all you have to do is serve them tea; the organizers of the *mushaira* have arranged the dinner.'

'*Mushaira?*' Begum Rafiq asked with part amazement and part anger. 'Who are these wretched people? Will they hold a *mushaira* in this hail of bullets?'

Rafiq sahab was pretending as though he was least concerned by the turn of events and therefore his guests too had no real need to get worried. But I could not hide my anxiety. Actually, I had left the house thinking I would drop off Majju Bhai here, chat with Rafiq sahab for a bit and slip away before the *mushaira*. Now I was beginning to feel cornered. Rafiq sahab sensed my unease. He said, 'Arre Jawad sahab, you are getting needlessly worried; this is perfectly routine here. The youth of this neighbourhood have only two pastimes: firing and *mushairas*. And today they don't have the patience for lengthy firing. After all, they have to go to the *mushaira* too.'

'You are quite incredible, Rafiq sahab!' Majju Bhai said. 'You are living so contentedly between two raging fires.'

Rafiq sahab laughed and said, 'Well, actually, this second fire, that is, the poets, is actually far more cruel. Believe me, Majju Bhai, they don't let you live in peace. Even if you were to give the *mushaira* a miss, they catch hold of you as you go about your business. My life is a torment. Whenever a new ghazal is revealed to any one of them, calamity rains down upon me. And look at my helplessness; I have to perforce applaud every verse of every ghazal.'

'Truly my friend, you are caught in a net,' Majju Bhai said with a show of sympathy.

Rafiq sahab laughed uproariously. 'Majju Bhai, you are telling me that I am in a net according to your estimation. One of our Lahori relatives said to me, "Pa-ji, you are in a net; get out of this place." My wife says the same thing in her own way. I said to her, "Begum sahiba, you are from Lucknow; what harm can these verses of the flower and the nightingale do to you? Ask me how I suffer? Where am I to go?" She said, "The city is big enough. If we must stay in a rented house, we can go and live anywhere. And your friend was helping us get a perfectly good flat in Gulshan."[87] I said, "But what is the guarantee that there won't be more poets where we go to live than there are here, and that we shall not have to offer praise to worse ghazals?"'

'You are right,' Majju Bhai said. 'No one can give such a guarantee about any neighbourhood in this city.'

'Majju Bhai, I am truly caught in a net. Do you know how many poets live in this very alley? Believe me when I say that every shopkeeper on this road, and every buyer in every shop, is a poet. And such is the flow, that a ghazal is completed at every transaction. I try and sneak out of my alley, yet by the time I have made my way out, I have drunk the bitter draught of at least ten or twelve ghazals. The moment one sets foot outside one's house, one gets pounced upon by a poet. You escape from the clutches of one only to fall prey to the next. It is almost as though they are sitting in ambush.'

'But is it necessary to go out? It is not as though you must go out to work.'

---

[87] A large residential and commercial neighbourhood in Karachi, its full name is Gulshan-e-Iqbal.

'I have tried that too. They land up at home then. "Rafiq Bhai, I haven't seen you for several days. I hope you are not unwell." And immediately thereafter, they launch into their new ghazal. Majju Bhai, soon enough a queue forms. Someone is a Naginvi, another is a Pilibhiti, one is a Kasmandvi and yet another is a Khurjvi. Poets from every town and hamlet have gathered in this city. One has to listen to every one of them; after all, it is a matter of good neighbourliness.'

'Well, that is the price you must pay for living among your brothers.'

'By the way, I had found a locality that had very few of our brothers. The house was a fine one, too. Everyone around me was a true-blue Lahori. But there was another sort of problem with them. Every Lahori in that neighbourhood thought he was a Meeraji.[88] I would have ended up from the frying pan into the fire. I thought it better to stay among the pupils of Dagh rather than live among the disciples of Meeraji; at least I could savour the taste of the language. And at least I know what they are talking about.'

'The fact is my dear,' Majju Bhai said, 'The sheep will be sheared no matter where it goes. You are a decent bloke; so, my friend, hold on to your patience.'

'Arre sahab, I have been patient. People keep making me acutely aware of it. Listen to what one kind soul had to say. He said, "Rafiq sahab, I have heard that there is a torture chamber behind your house." I stayed quiet. He persisted, "You have not replied." I said, "What can I say? Arre sahab, if not a torture chamber, I would have had a whorehouse, and if not a whorehouse then a police station. In any case, there would have been something or the other." He said, "But it is very dangerous to have a torture chamber in one's neighbourhood, and very painful too. Don't the screams of anguish trouble you?" I said, "My brother, nothing is more painful than the din of political sloganeering. When we have learnt to tolerate

---

[88] Meeraji (1912–1949) was a poet from Lahore; he is considered a pioneer of modernist-symbolist poetry in Urdu.

that noise, what meaning can the cries coming from the torture chamber have?"'

I was getting restless; Rafiq sahab was not saying anything clearly. He was brushing aside the truth in jest. Finally I asked him, 'Is there really a torture chamber behind your house?'

Rafiq sahab sighed. 'Jawad sahab, you and I are living in a gigantic torture chamber. So if there is some small torture chamber in the neighbourhood, what possible significance can it have? So, let it go.'

Meanwhile, a boy appeared with the tea trolley. Rafiq sahab pulled the trolley close to himself and said to the boy as he poured the tea, 'Dina, has the firing stopped yet, or not?'

'I don't know,' and then as he was about to leave, the boy asked, 'Shall I go and check?'

'Yes, go out and see and come and tell me.'

A wave of energy coursed through Dina. He rushed to the door and swiftly went out.

I drank my tea and unlocked my tongue once again. 'Rafiq sahab, shall I ask you something?"

'Yes.'

'It is a very personal question.'

'Feel free.'

'Majju Bhai and I are helpless before this cruel city. But you have an ancestral home in Lahore. So what is your compulsion in staying here?'

'My compulsion is my Lucknowi wife,' he said and laughed.

'Well said,' Majju Bhai added. 'Can there be a greater compulsion anywhere in the world than a wife?'

How beautifully Rafiq sahab side-stepped the question and began to drink his tea with great contentment.

Dina returned after some time.

'So what is the news?'

'It's over now, though it went on for a long time – rounds after rounds.'

'How many dead?'

'Five.'

'Oh, only five? But there was so much firing? These people waste far too many bullets. Anyhow, Majju Bhai, let me tell you the horizon is clear.'

'Tell Jawad. Jawad, are you listening: the horizon is clear now.'

'But for how long?' I blurted.

Rafiq sahab laughed. 'Well said.'

Majju Bhai said. 'Why don't you also find out when the *mushaira* is likely to start?'

The subject of the *mushaira* made me restless. I finally spoke up, 'Look here, the two of you are constrained to attend the *mushaira*. For Rafiq sahab it is a question of good neighbourliness. Regardless of whether there is a shower of bullets or bombs going off, he must go for the *mushaira* in any case. And as for Majju Bhai, well he acquired the taste for poetry during his Coffee House days. He can leave the blanket, but the blanket won't leave him. But I don't have any such compulsion.'

'Miyan, you have a compulsion too,' Majju Bhai said. 'And that is that you cannot get out of this area unscathed. Bullet or ghazal? You choose.'

'It would be infinitely better to get a bullet than to have to listen to a ghazal in a *mushaira*.'

'Think again.'

'I am in God's care.'

'But how will you get back?'

'Don't worry about that; one of my Coffee House crowd will have to perform this duty. After all, we are going to offer praise; then surely we must extract the price.'

As I got to my feet, Rafiq sahab too got up to bid me adieu. He said, 'Jawad sahab, Majju Bhai is right. Don't dwell too much on these things. You see, what difference will it make if we worry or think about it? What is in our control?'

Meanwhile, Begum Rafiq appeared. She looked at me in surprise. 'Arre, are you leaving?'

'Yes.'

'Have some fear of God! Why are you bent upon killing yourself?'

'The firing has stopped.'

'There is no knowing with these wretched people.'

'One can trust no one these days. But the business of life cannot be suspended for this reason.'

'Is it imperative for you to go?'

'Yes, you could say so.'

'All right, but be alert. And remember to telephone us as soon as you reach home safely.'

'Yes,' Rafiq sahab spoke in a confirmatory tone. 'Remember to telephone us. Though, God willing, everything will be all right.'

Rafiq sahab and Majju Bhai came to see me off till the door; the car stood right in front with Jamaluddin sitting all bundled up inside. He saw me and straightened up with a shiver. But as soon as I set foot outside the door, I became aware of a frightening silence. The alley did not look like the bustling crowded alley that we had seen when we had come. It was full of life then. The noise of trundling vehicles, the laughter of groups of people sitting on the shop fronts, voices and sounds of people passing by, the haggling and bargaining between the buyers and the sellers – there was nothing now. The shops were closed, the pedestrians had disappeared, and it looked as though it was well past midnight. In the distance, I could see one open shop. I was alarmed; surely something was wrong. But then I had got up with the intention of leaving and it seemed insulting to let the fear inside me show. In any case, there was no need for me to say anything. Rafiq sahab and Majju Bhai saw the same scene.

'Yaar,' Majju Bhai spoke in a troubled tone, 'has your alley gone to sleep so early today?'

'Yes, I can see that. It seems that the shopkeepers have shut their shops due to all the commotion over the firing. And once people have shut the shops and gone home for the night, why would they come back?'

'My dear, the signs are not good,' and almost immediately Majju Bhai addressed me, 'Jawad, I think you should stay back. We will go back together after the *mushaira*. There will be others too; it isn't wise to go alone at this time.'

'Come on, Majju Bhai. You are stopping me from going alone as though I am a child,' I said in an attempt to show courage.

'In any case, Jawad sahab,' Rafiq sahab added, 'what is the harm if one were to occasionally get a taste of a *mushaira*? A *mushaira* has its own utility, especially in the sort of times that we are going through.'

'Really? And what is that utility? Kindly do explain.'

'If we have a cure for the kind of times that we are passing through, it is a *mushaira*. The point that the friends of Damascus could not grasp, the people of Karachi have understood.'[89]

'Subhan Allah,' the words escaped me inadvertently.

'Rafiq sahab, why are you wasting your time,' Majju Bhai said. 'Our friend here runs away at the mention of poetry itself, forget *mushaira*, like a cow runs at the sight of a butcher.'

'He must be one of his kind among the *muhajir*,' Rafiq sahab said and let out a loud peal of laughter.

'Weren't you looking for two such *muhajirs*? Look we have found one for you.'

'But where shall I find the other?'

'You will find the other too – a searcher or a believer.'

I hurriedly sat down in the car and said, 'Fine, so I am off.'

'All right then, but do telephone us once you reach home,' Rafiq sahab said and turned to address Jamaluddin. 'Be careful when you cross this area. And yes, keep your windows rolled up.'

'Don't worry,' Jamaluddin said and started the car and swiftly left the alley.

But it wasn't just one alley; there was a web of alleys. For the first time I realized where we were; I had always imagined Rafiq sahab's house to be off the main road. Next to the petrol station, one turned right, and then left after skipping one turn, then again

---

[89] Referring to the political decline of Damascus after the Byzantine period.

left and after some time right – and there you are! At Rafiq sahab's door! But at that time, it didn't seem like a few alleys but a veritable web of alleys and our car seemed stuck in that web and we were moving from one alley to the next and then the third and then another. Some shops were open and the area around them seemed better lit than others and a few people could be seen near the open shops. But those few people seemed scared. They spoke in lowered voices as they bought their wares.

'Jamaluddin, there is no need to be worried; drive carefully.' The high speed of the car gave me the excuse to speak. At that time, the only way to conquer my fear seemed to be to speak up.

'No, sir, what is there to be worried about?' He stopped then said, 'I have to cross such areas every day. I wouldn't be able to do my job if I got scared of this.'

'Of course, you have to come for your duty, no matter what the circumstances. You must also have to traverse those areas where firing is going on. Even a chauffeur's job has become dangerous these days.'

'Life and death are decided by the Almighty. Why should man worry?' And Jamaluddin accelerated the car.

Sixteen

I reached the office quite late the next day. Rafiq sahab had reached long ago. I was surprised: why had he come here early in the morning? I soon realized he must have some work in the bank. He saw me and laughed out loud. 'So you are alive? Thank God! You are the sort who always comes to office on time; so when I came here and found you hadn't yet arrived, I was seriously alarmed.'

'Yes, I got a bit late leaving home. Have you been waiting for long? I do apologise.'

'No, I haven't been here for very long. I was only worried where you might be. Anyhow, thank God.'

'One should always thank God in every circumstance. But I can't quite understand why you are giving thanks at this moment.'

'I am happy to see you alive and thanking God for it,' Rafiq sahab laughed loudly again.

'So you had made up your mind that I had passed on? But one must have some excuse to pass on. I had none.'

'Brother, if someone comes to our locality and returns with his life intact, he is considered a fortunate man; so you are a fortunate man.'

.Good.'

'Now call for some sweets. Well never mind, send for some tea instead.'

I immediately sent for my peon and asked for some tea. And then with the intention of changing the subject, I asked, 'Rafiq sahab, you are not one to leave the house early in the morning. And why should you; you don't have to go to the office. Why have you set out so early today? Though of course I am happy that you have come to see me ...'

'Arre Bhai, I have come to enquire about your well being.'

'Really?'

'So you don't trust my good intentions?' And then his tone changed and he spoke with utter seriousness, 'Jawad sahab, truly I am so embarrassed. I have come to apologise.'

'Apologise for what?' I looked at him in surprise.

'The thing is that after you left my wife scolded me. She said I am a strange fellow and a bad friend because I let you go alone despite the danger. I tried telling her that I had done my best to stop you and that you considered the *mushaira* a far greater danger and what could I do if you chose not to stay. But my argument could not convince my wife. Her berating made me realize that perhaps I had erred. I should have made you stay, somehow or the other. First thing in the morning, my wife told me to call you and find out if you were all right. I said, No, I shall go to the bank and find out and also apologise for my mistake.'

'Arre Rafiq sahab, why are you talking like this? What is there to apologise? And it isn't as though there was any great danger out there. I had no problem in coming back. The only thing is that it was a bit quiet; otherwise there was nothing out of the ordinary.'

'It seems as though there is nothing out of the ordinary. A man may think nothing is wrong and yet a lot may happen.' Rafiq sahab paused, then said, 'Jawad sahab, you mustn't think from either my tone or Majju Bhai's that we are unaware of the danger; perhaps we may be even more aware of it than you. I, for one, am extremely scared. My wife is always terrified; if she were to know that I am scared too, she will simply collapse.'

'You are right.'

'Remember that day I was talking about the torture chamber?'

'Yes, what about it?'

'This piece of gossip that has been swirling in our neighbourhood reached her ears one day. I tried my best to evade the subject by telling her that hundreds of different kinds of stories were doing the rounds and that it would be difficult to survive if we begin to lend our ears to every bit of gossip. But one night, she woke up with a start. "Aji, are you sleeping? Can't you hear?" I got up. "Why? What is it?" She said, "I can hear someone screaming." I strained my ears for a long time; there was no sound. "Begum, you are imagining things." "Imagining things? I clearly heard a scream." Then another night, she got up from deep sleep. Again she said, "Can you hear?" I said, 'What happened?" She said, "A cat is crying somewhere." I said, "So what?" "Does it mean nothing to you?" she asked. "It isn't a good thing if a cat cries." I tried my best to persuade her that actually the cat was calling out to the tomcat, but would she listen? In any case, those of you who have come from there have come with bundles of superstitions.'

I laughed, 'Meaning therefore that people here were innocent of superstitions?'

'There were superstitions here, too, but not so many that an epic can be written on the trembling of a leaf. One statement that I hear on a daily basis is, "May Gold help us, my right eyelid has been quivering since the morning." And for the life of me I can't understand, Jawad sahab, why it is always my wife's eyelid that must quiver? Sometimes my eyelid should also quiver. Nature seems to give all these signs only to my wife; she doesn't find me suitable enough.'

What could I say? I just laughed.

'Yaar, you are laughing. We are going through a very difficult phase. Moreover, the area where we live ...'

'Yes, indeed you need to be brave to live in that neighbourhood. I am surprised how you have managed to stay there.'

'Don't ask; it is a daily test of endurance. We have had to be extremely careful or else we would have been done in by now.'

'Yes, it would appear so.'

'Death is routine; in fact, staying alive is a miracle.' And then after a pause, he said, 'Miracle or not, one still has to be careful. In fact, miracles are pledges of entreaty. Now Jawad sahab, this bank of yours is also a dangerous place. Those who are sitting in the bank are the worst affected. You have one gunman sitting at your gate; but what can he do? You must have a proper security arrangement.'

'What are you saying, Rafiq sahab? How much can we arrange? Even if we have two more guards, what difference will it make? The way those people come armed and the way in which they attack, what can our security arrangements do?'

'That is all very well but surely one must do what one can. The rest is whatever Allah wishes.'

I was encouraged by Rafiq sahab's mood and asked him the question that Majju Bhai never considered worth answering. Majju Bhai's stock response to my question has always been: 'Stop thinking, or leave Karachi.'

Rafiq sahab let out a tremendous peal of laughter, and with it his normal tone of voice too returned. 'Why Karachi? Then you will have to leave Pakistan.' He paused, then said in the same laughing tone, 'Do you think I am lying? Majju Bhai thinks only Karachi is an unsuitable place for a thinking person. Subhan Allah! The other day you were asking why is Karachi my compulsion when my ancestral place is Lahore, and you were saying it in such a way as though Lahore is not in Pakistan but outside it …'

At that moment, Mirza sahab appeared out of the blue, dressed in a *shervani* and holding a walking strick. 'Oh, so Rafiq sahab is also here! Two for the price of one!'

Rafiq sahab stood up and embraced Mirza sahab exuberantly. 'How are you, Mirza sahab?'

'My dear, don't ask how I am. I have this wretched shackle on my feet and I can see no way of cutting it loose.'

'What shackle, Mirza sahab?'

'The shackle of life … what else? Miyan, I want to die.'

'What a thing to say Mirza sahab! We won't let you die.'

'That is the problem,' Mirza sahab sighed. 'I don't have the permission to die. I don't know what the Writer of Fate has written for me. At present, I am neither among the living nor the dead. Just the other day, I was complaining about this to Jawad Miyan and saying how once upon a time good believers used to resolve to die. It has been written about Hazrat Abul Badar Quddus Sirah that once when a murder took place in the city, he cried and said that crime had increased in the city and it was time for him to die. He immediately sent word to Sheikh Jaleel al-Haqqui to take a bath. The sheikh replied that he was clean and did not require a bath. Once again, he sent a message asking the sheikh to take a bath; once again, the sheikh sent the same reply. Then he sent another message saying the sheikh must do as he bids so that he may fulfil his duty. Only then did the sheikh follow the instruction and took the bath. He had barely completed his bath when a messenger came to inform him that Hazrat Abul Badar had passed away. With great surprise and sorrow he asked how it came to be. He was told that the Hazrat had prayed for it to be so, but before he passed away, he had asked for Sheikh Jaleel to give his dead body the ritual bath before the burial. And soon thereafter, the Hazrat closed his eyes forever, hiccupped once and gave his life over to the Creator. Sheikh Jaleel al-Haqqui has recorded that when he was about to bathe the dead body of the Hazrat, he opened his eyes and looked at him, smiled and closed his eyes again. And so my dear, when the good believers of Allah take leave from this world, they themselves hand over their lives to the Creator. But for sinners like us, it is a case of "When I go drown myself I find the river shallow". There are all these bullets being fired all over the city and I am sitting here praying for death, but no bullet ever comes my way.'

'Well then, Mirza sahab, understand this to be a sign from the universe that it isn't yet time for you to leave us,' Rafiq sahab smiled and asked, 'Qibla, who was this gentleman called Abul Badar?"

'Hai, hai, Rafiq sahab you don't know him? He was only attached to birds in the whole wide world. But when the birds troubled him too much, he would gather them all up in his fist and swallow them up in one gulp. But soon he would become sad to find the birds missing around him and begin to spit them out. No sooner did each bird come out of his throat that it would fly away. And soon they would be hovering around him and setting up a din.'

'Subhan Allah,' Rafiq sahab said spontaneously and got to his feet.

'Miyan, are you off? So soon?'

'I have been sitting here for some time. Jawad sahab is a busy man; I have already taken so much of his time.'

'Arre Rafiq sahab, what a thing to say! In any case, I am not as busy as you seem to think. Why don't you stay?'

'No, no, I must go now.'

'My dear, this meeting was all too brief. We have met after such a long time and for such a short while.'

'I shall come to your home one day soon and then we shall talk at length.'

'Yes, yes, certainly; you must come. Believe me when I say I am flickering; my wick is nearly burnt out, the oil is almost finished. I shall be snuffed out any moment. So come and meet me before I am gone.'

'I will come soon,' Rafiq sahab said, shook hands with Mirza sahab and me and off he went.

'Rafiq sahab is a good man. It is difficult to find a decent person these days,' and with these words, Mirza sahab took out a cheque from his pocket and slid it towards me. 'Please have this taken care of.'

Mirza sahab had an account in this bank for years. He found it especially convenient since I was here. His provident fund, gratuity and cheque for monthly pension – everything was in this bank. And it was in this account that he deposited his cheque and withdrew the money for his monthly expenses. Earlier, his son used to perform the chore but now that he had moved to Clifton, the task of depositing the cheque and withdrawing the cash had fallen on him. And so he came here every now and then.

'Miyan, I have come with great difficulty. The taxi driver was very hesitant about coming here.'

'But this area is quite peaceful; possibly there may be some tension in the areas you would have had to cross.'

'He said the same thing; all roads are dangerous now. No area is safe. May Allah have mercy on us!' And after a pause, he said, 'I won't stay for long today; I will leave as soon as I can.'

'Don't worry, Mirza sahab; I will take you home.'

'Miyan, will you do your bank work, or take me home?'

'I have the driver in any case; but today is a half day. I too have to leave early.'

So I had Mirza sahab's cheque encashed and left the office soon after.

'Jamaluddin, is there any tension along the way?'

'There is no such news yet; everything seems all right so far.'

'We have to go to Mirza sahab's house first.'

'Yes, sir.'

We reached his home and found a worried Achchi Bi standing at the door, peering out at every passing taxi and rickshaw. She saw the car stop at her door and was surprised at first, then on spotting Mirza sahab getting out of the car, a wave of relief and happiness spread over her countenance.

'What took you so long? I have been running around like a mad woman – from the courtyard to the door and back.'

'Saadat's mother, I had told you I was going to the bank and that it might take long there.'

'But why so long?'

'It didn't take very long; Jawad Miyan had my cheque encashed right away and then he immediately got up to bring me home in his car. He is here; won't you get him something?'

'No, Achchi Bi, please don't trouble yourself; I have to go.'

'No, my son; I can't let you go like this. Surely you can't be in such a hurry? Stop a while. I will make some tea. What can I tell you of my troubles? We used to have that lameduck servant; he too has run away and the wretch didn't even tell us. He just disappeared one fine day. How I fed and clothed that wretched fellow, but servants these days don't know the meaning of loyalty. But then if one's own don't show loyalty, how can we complain about servants; they are not our own, after all.'

'It is hard to find servants these days,' I tried to make a general observation. But Achchi Bi found a topic suited to her taste in it.

'Even if you find one, they don't stay on. And it isn't just servants, everyone – insiders and outsiders – are like that. And how can we complain about outsiders when our own daughter-in-law has shown such disloyalty towards us. Now you tell me: is it my age to be running around managing a household? I have spent my entire life working in the house. My back is bent. I have reached an age when I should be lolling about on my bed while my daughter-in-law manages the household. But she uprooted her husband by insisting they live separately. And there she is – living separately.'

'Let it be, Saadat's mother; stop talking about your daughter-in-law. Talk of something else. Jawad Miyan has come for just a short while; he can't stay for long. These are bad times.'

'Yes, my son, the times are indeed bad. I don't let him leave the house for this reason; I let him set foot outside today because it was absolutely necessary.'

'But everyone is not idle like us. People have their business and jobs; they have to get out of their homes. Take our Jawad Miyan, for instance. No matter what happens, whether there is a hail of bullets or bombs going off, he has to reach his bank.'

'Yes, that is true,' Achchi Bi became thoughtful. 'My son, you must always remember to do something before you set out from your house. You must always recite the *Ayatul Kursi*. And when you reach the office, mark a circle around yourself.'[90]

'The things you say, Saadat's mother! Just because you remember the *Ayatul Kursi*, you assume that everyone would remember it. You should have said some smaller prayer. And sketching a circle is very

---

[90] *Ayatul Kursi* or the 'Throne Verse' is the 255th verse of the second chapter, Sura Al-Baqara of the Holy Quran. It is the most famous verse of the Quran and is widely memorized and displayed due to its emphatic description of God's power over the entire universe. The practice of *hisar khichna* or drawing a circle is practised in South Asia as a way to ward off evil and to keep the believer safe within that circle.

good. If you have drawn a circle then you can rest assured that the bank will be safe; then you don't need a guard or a watchman.'

'You know, there was only one day that I did not draw the circle. Whatever will be will be. That day I forgot to draw the circle and, on that very day, those black-faced rascals entered our house.'

'There is great benediction in Allah's words,' Mirza sahab said. 'Who is to blame if people have stopped reciting His words? Is it any wonder that there is no prosperity in this city?'

'Allah's curse is upon this city,' Achchi Bi tagged on.

'And it is no ordinary curse,' Mirza sahab continued. 'Such a curse has never been visited even upon the wrathful peoples.'[91] And he sighed. 'We are also not safe; we are a walking-talking bundle of sin. How can man be safe from sin if he lives amongst sinners? But what can we do? Where can we go?' he paused, then said, 'Miyan, the other day I was telling you about the mentally troubled man who kept saying that when he had come to the city, he was gold and that he had become silver, and the longer he were to stay in that city, who could say what he might turn into. Believe me, Jawad Miyan, when I had set foot in this land, I was like gold. Now, I am not even silver; I am copper and bronze. No, not even that; I am a pebble.'

With these words, he remained silent for a long time. Meanwhile, Achchi Bi appeared with the tea. I don't know when she had slipped away to make it. We drank our tea in silence.

At long last, Achhchi Bi broke the silence. She spoke in a sad voice, 'How were we to know that we would become pebbles?'

'No one ever knows. When the world is about to change, it transforms rapidly.'

'Indeed it transformed rapidly,' Achchi Bi spoke sorrowfully. 'We didn't know what was happening. Gold one day, pebble another day.'

---

[91] A verse in the Quran from the *Surah Fateha* which says: '*an'amta* (You bestowed reward and blessings) *alaihim* (upon them); *Ghair* (not) *al-maghzoob* (those having violent anger or wrath) *alaihim* (over them), *wa* (and) *la* (not) *az-zawllin* (the losers of the Path).'

'Allah alone knows what will happen in the future.'

'Yes, only Allah would know that,' Achchi Bi said. And then after a silence, she spoke in a worried tone, 'It must have been midnight when I woke up; a dog was crying copiously. My heart was beating wildly and I couldn't go back to sleep. I don't know who that wretched dog is who starts crying close to midnight every single night. And I wake up. I have chased away the wretched cat. She was crying one night. I said, "Go, you witch, go and eat your own flesh and blood." She disappeared that day and hasn't been seen since. But I still don't know what to do about this accursed dog.'

Mirza sahab spoke in a worried tone, 'It isn't a good thing when animals cry.'

'Especially when dogs cry,' Achchi Bi added.

'May Allah have mercy upon us,' Mirza sahab drew another long sigh and fell silent.

Achchi Bi was also quiet. I finally got to my feet. 'So, Mirza sahab, allow me to take your leave.'

'My dear, you have taken so much trouble for me.'

'What a thing to say, Mirza sahab! It was the greatest good fortune for me. In any case, I had to leave my office; I had some work at home so I wanted to leave early.'

'All right, we shan't keep you. One should get back safely home early; these days are not good days.'

'Mirza sahab, when were the days good?' Thoughtlessly, I tossed a remark.

'Yes, that is true. Our forefathers saw the good days. We did not have good days written in our fate. Anyhow, as Allah wills; who can go against His will?'

I left them and reached straight home. Majju Bhai wasn't back yet.

Nemat Khan said, 'The food is ready. Shall I lay it out?'

'What about Majju Bhai? He isn't here yet.'

'He had said as he was leaving that I should not wait for him for lunch.'

'All right, then, lay the food.'

Nemat Khan brought out the food instantly. I too ate quickly and was done with it. Suddenly a quiver ran through me and I thought: what a life I lead? I am stuck inside the bank all day. I get out only to be cooped inside my house. Now that I had got out of the bank early for a change, why not take advantage of my freedom? I resolved to set out on foot. I was about to dismiss Jamaluddin for the day when I remembered that Majju Bhai had to go somewhere in the evening. 'Jamaluddin, you may go home now; come back by six or six-thirty in the evening. All right?'

'All right, sir.'

*

I had set out on foot after an age. How enjoyable it was to walk! I began to realize that travelling by car was like being in a prison.

At least you don't feel caged in a *tonga* or *ekka*. A person has to be locked up in a car. He has no contact with the outside world. You can only savour whatever you can see swiftly passing by outside your glass window. Walking has its own joy. For one, you develop a direct bond with the earth when you are walking. Then, the world around you looks more spread out and more open. I was reminded of those days when, forget car, I did not even have a cycle. I either travelled in a bus or on my legs. How much I used to walk those days! I was like a measuring tape to measure distances! The distances I travelled in the heat and dust! My job at the bank had deprived me of the pleasures of walking. At first I had a scooter and then, as I rose up the ladder, I got a car and that too with a driver driving it, with me sitting in the back seat with my eyes closed and legs spread out. The living bond that my feet had kept up with the earth for a long time ended altogether.

The joy of walking is doubled during winter days when the sun is out. After a long time, I found a soft warm winter afternoon to walk in. I felt a strange sense of freedom. I could go where I wished, stop where I liked. When you are travelling in a car, you have to go on a predetermined way. And if you have to stop somewhere on the way, you have to make due arrangements. If nothing else, there is the issue of parking, whereas here I felt no such restriction. As I walked beside the park, the greenery spread out in the sunshine beckoned me and my feet instinctively turned in its direction. At first I sat on a bench, but soon I got tired of the seat and sat down on the grass. A young couple sat sunning themselves close by, but they were so engrossed in each other that they had no thought for the sun or for the stranger sitting a short distance away who was, perhaps, looking at them. But quite soon, I became disinterested in the couple. A group of adolescent boys had pitched their wickets in the middle of the lawn and begun to play cricket and my entire attention was focused on their game. Every now and then, the ball would roll over in my direction, and before one of the fielders could come over, I myself would throw the ball in their direction. And someone or the other would shout, 'Thank you, uncle.'

The repeated 'Thank you, uncle' began to create a strange intoxication in me. And I began to show a greater fervor in throwing the ball. In fact, if the ball landed at some distance from me, I would go over to fetch it and toss it towards the bowler. But my joy was short lived. A fight broke out over whether someone was 'out' or not. When the argument escalated, I thought I would adjudicate between the two parties, but before I could offer my services as an umpire, they were at each others' throats.

I left them fighting with each other and came out of the park. In any case, the sun was going down. The young couple too had got to their feet. As I was coming out of the gate, their scooter whizzed past me. The girl had her arm looped around the boy's waist and her hair was flying in the wind. My eyes kept following the scooter till it disappeared from sight.

Now I was passing by the teahouses. In fact, the entire stretch of footpath here was taken over by them: rows of tables stretched from here till there. There was not a single vacant table, or else I might have sat down. The joy of sitting down at a table set out on a footpath is matchless. One has to be very prim and proper to sit under a roof in a hotel or in a mezzanine hall and drink tea. Here, you wander up and plonk yourself down at any table. But there were so many tea-drinkers about at this hour that I could not see a single free table. Then I thought, 'It is all for the better; if I sit down, I will keep sitting here for ever and then I will be deprived of the delights of walking. So it is best to continue walking. We will see on the way back; perhaps some table will be free by then.' And so I walked on.

On the footpath, there were one set of people who were walking, another who were drinking tea, drinking soda, buying paan and cigarettes, and the third rush was of the traffic that was hurtling past. And this last one was the biggest. A little ahead was a row of wedding halls lit up with bright lights. Evening had fallen and the coloured lights laden on the wedding halls had come alive. I was a bit surprised to see this gaity; actually not a bit but quite surprised. I said to myself: where is the terrorism? Where is the firing? People like us sit in our offices and our homes and we are fearful for the state of the city and are losing our health worrying over it whereas life is going on here – in all its splendor and gaity!

At first I was surprised. Then I drew a sigh of relief and my feet began to move with greater confidence and speed. As I walked along, my ears pricked up. I could hear a noise coming from somewhere close by. Interspersed with the noise, I could hear slogans and cries of *Allah ho Akbar*. Dear God, what was this noise? Was a procession of protesters coming this way? But soon the mystery was revealed. I had barely gone a few steps forward when I saw a marquee packed with people. Some rally was going on. 'O Oblivious Musalmanon, Ghazi Ataullah asks you only one question: Why are your bosoms bereft of inner pain?' Oh, so Ghazi sahab was here! I was startled. I wanted to pass this spot as quickly as I could, but a wave rose within me, urging me to find out what Ghazi sahab said in a public rally. 'Musalmanon, just give me the answer to this one question. But who will answer me? Look at my foolishness, I am asking those people who are trapped in the deception of western ideas, those who have read western science and philosophy and are deprived of true insight. I am looking for light in the darkness. What is this if not my madness? Ataullah makes a full confession of his madness. This madman is in search of other men who are mad like him – mad men who will shatter the idols of modern thoughts and ideas, those who will clash with the Abu Jahls and Abu Lahabs of this day and knock down the Islam-hating mountains of the West ... Musalmanon, I only need 313 mad men. The day these 313 mad men appear at the sound of plaintive cries ...'

I had got a sample of his talk, so I hurriedly moved on. A new sight attracted my attention. The marriage halls looked more resplendent than before. Rows of cars were parked along the road. Ladies were getting out of the cars shimmering with pink and gold. How else can a city display its finery? And scores of legendary cities flashed before my imagination.

Hamara tumhara Khuda badshah
Kissi mulk mein tha koi badshah
(An emperor who is your God and mine
Such was a king in some kingdom)

And there was a prosperous public where the ordinary and the special folk alike were good and pious folk, and you could go where you wished wearing your gold – in jungles and bazaars – without fear of robbers and thieves. How content one felt!

I had walked quite a bit by now. I was tired. It may not have been a long walk by my old standards, but it was a long walk for me now. So I turned back and returned the same way I had come. By now I was really thirsty for tea. I thought of trying my luck at those teahouses which I had seen on my way here. Now that I had walked the lengths of these roads it was only appropriate that I should drink tea in one of these roadside places. Luck favoured me. There was quite a crowd, revellers were ordering kababs and tikkas and making loud demands for tea. I lurked beside the tables and, as soon as one lot got up, I made a beeline for the table.

I placed the order for tea and glanced at the watch strapped on my wrist; I suddenly realized that Majju Bhai must be sitting at home and cursing me. His programme would be about to start now. I placed my order for tea and asked the boy, 'Is there a telephone here?'

'Yes.'

I walked up to the counter and dialled my home number. Majju Bhai spoke; he was clearly angry. I tried telling him that I was sitting at home and getting bored; I had come out for a bit of fresh air and had got late. 'Jamaluddin would have reached by now; send him to pick me up. I am not far away; I will reach in a jiffy.' I called Jamaluddin to the phone and gave him directions to the teahouse.

I came back and found that another gentleman was sitting at my table. That's the way it is in these teahouses. You are in danger if you are alone; any stranger can walk up and share your table. What could I do? I remained quiet. But inside, I was feeling as though my free reign on this table had ended.

'What's the time by your watch?' he finally set the ball rolling.

I glanced once again at my watch and answered briefly, 'Half past six.'

While travelling in a train or drinking tea in a restaurant, when a stranger asks you the time, you can safely assume that it is the prologue to a lengthy conversation. And so I guessed that this man did not harbour good intentions. Metaphorically speaking, he had caught my finger and now he would make a grab for my collar. Surely he would attempt to embroil me in some chit-chat. But perhaps my dry and insipid response disappointed him. Instead of broaching the next subject, he picked up the evening paper lying on the table and began to read it with great concentration. I drew a sigh of relief. But it was strange that I had not bothered to glance at its headlines – let alone read the newspaper – when it was lying on the table. But the moment it went into another's hands, that two-page rag became an object of immense attraction for me. While sitting in my chair, I looked at that part of the newspaper which was facing me and tried to guess the contents of the articles from the headlines.

The man finished the newspaper after reading a bit and turning the pages. He put it down and muttered, 'May Allah have mercy on me.' He slid the paper in my direction and said, 'Do you want to read it?'

I felt as though he had guessed from my furtive glances that I was waiting for him to finish reading so that I could start. The thought made me a bit nervous and I immediately said, 'No, no, please carry on. I am not at all interested in these news reports.'

I didn't have the slightest idea that I would be trapped by my own statement. He started off in right earnest, 'You are right. Why would any decent person have any interest in such reports? Murder, abduction, rape, firing, bomb blast – it is as though there is nothing else happening in the city. At least the newspapers show that. God forbid that there should be any useful information! They simply want to fill their newspapers with terrifying incidents. Shouldn't there be some good news from somewhere? What do you think? After all, why don't these newspaper people ever give any good news? Or could it be that there is no good news to give? What do you think, sir?'

I was at my wits' end: what answer should I give? I couldn't even evade by humming and hawing because he had asked me a direct question. 'Your complaint is perfectly correct.' I gave a brief answer. 'But they can only print good news if there is one.'

'You are right. Truly that is so. What can the newspapers do if there is no good news; they can't produce it. The poor things are helpless. After all, they have to sell their newspapers. If they can't get good news, they have to publish bad news. What a strange time! Good news has disappeared. Whatever news we get is terrifying. I can't understand what is going on. What do you think? Tell me, what is going on.'

'First I should understand it myself,' once again I tried to get away by giving a brief answer. But that man was not one to be evaded.

'You are right; indeed it is so. No one can understand what is going on. But how long will this go on? What do you think? Surely there must be a cure. The government is deaf to everything that's happening. I am saying we can no longer sit idle and do nothing. We must give some thought to what is going on and what is the cure. So what do you think? What is the cure?'

'Cure?' I seemed to be getting deeper into trouble. 'I don't know; what do you think?'

'I have thought about it. I am convinced that there is only one cure for this affliction. And I am not suggesting a rhetorical measure. Verbal answers get swept away in the wind. I had once written a letter and explained in detail what our ailment is and what its cure is. I had sent that letter to several newspapers but no one printed it. These newspaper people are heartless; they have no sense of nationalism. They fill their newspapers with all sorts of useless news and have no place for things that are needed. Anyhow, I fulfilled my duty. In my letter, I told the people in no uncertain terms that this is our punishment for turning away from Islam. No cure will work. There is only one treatment: Islamic rule should be implemented with immediate effect. Tell me, what do you think?'

'And how will it be implemented?' the question slipped out of my mouth inadvertently.

'By use of force, how else? My dear sir, we need a Man of Iron who will beat us and straighten us out. We have tried out democracy. It is no cure for our disease. You can see with your own eyes what democracy has done to us.'

From the nearby table, an irate man, who had been eavesdropping on our conversation for quite some time, erupted, 'Arre sahab, why don't you ask what we have done to democracy?'

'What do you mean?' the man on my table asked angrily.

'The meaning is clear: will you call all that is going on democracy?'

The boy serving tea happened to pass by. I stopped him and asked, 'Miyan, how much longer will you take to bring the tea?'

Perhaps when I spoke up, my neighbour was reminded that he too was sitting here in anticipation of his tea. He reminded the boy in a wrathful tone, 'You twit, how much longer will you make us wait? Am I going to get the tea or not?'

'I am just bringing it.'

'Get it quickly.'

'Coming up right away!' The lad said this and ran away so swiftly as though he was indeed getting it right away.

By now my neighbour was quite unconcerned with me. So when he resumed the thread of the conversation, he did not feel the need to address me. His pronouncement was directed at the man sitting at the adjacent table, 'The West has given us two gifts: democracy and shamelessness.'

'May I ask: what is the conection between the two?'

'There is a huge connection. This new-fangled independence that you see among the youth is due to democracy. And girls have been completely ruined by it. Do you know the extent of shamelessness that is spreading all around us? Every girl watches TV through dish antenna. But our West-afflicted people do not consider it shamelessness; they call it emancipation of women. I ask you: What is meant by emancipation of women? What else but not giving the husband the respect that is due to him? And that is why I say we need a Man of Iron; we do not need democracy.'

'And what will he do?' the irate man asked angrily.

'First he will punish these politicians.[92] And rightly so! That should be the first course of action. He should line up all the politicians and ask them to squat and hold their ears. And then after punishing the politicians, he should ...'

'And then he will make the people squat and hold their ears,' the irate man cut him off mid-sentence.

'In my opinion, what he should do is shoot someone if they even let out a squeak! I tell you this nation will turn over a new leaf in a matter of a few days. And if it doesn't, I promise to crawl from under your legs.'

---

[92] The expression used in the original is '*murgha banana*' referring to a form of corporal punishment practised in schools across South Asia where errant school children are made to squat and hold their ears by looping their arms from under their bent knees. The position resembles a rooster or *murgha*.

The irate man's face flushed red. 'So you want martial law?'

'Mister, I want to be rid of this democracy. And I want Islam, understand?'

At that very moment, the sound of firing came from somewhere nearby. And with it an outcry, 'They've come!' A stampede broke out. Within a matter of seconds, the tables all around me emptied. I couldn't understand how people disappeared so quickly. I was still trying to understand when two taxis passed by. And close on the heels, came the sound of firing. And after that ... And after that, I lost consciousness. Swift as lightning ... I felt I was blown into smithereens.

Seventeen

I was dead. Or so it seemed at the time. As though I was no longer alive. That I was a corpse lying on the footpath. Yes, indeed. But a last gasp of life was still stuck somewhere inside me, or rather not a gasp of life but the trace of a sensation. Or you could say my entire being lay shattered. An atom fell away and lay quivering. Some voices came to my ears as though someone was speaking from miles away, or several people were speaking together. What happened … Has a bullet hit you … Okay … Yes … You can say that at the right time … The driver showed amazing presence of mind … Took him to the hospital immediately … What happened … They came suddenly and went away spraying … Blindly … They came and went in the blink of an eye … And the police … Show some fear of God … It's nothing new … May Allah have mercy … This is nothing short of a miracle … Yes, must be a miracle if his life is saved … If God wills … What are the doctors saying … The reports are still …

The sounds were coming as though one was asleep, or in a state where one was neither fully asleep nor fully awake. In that state of half sleep-half wakefulness, I could not understand fully who was being talked about. Who had been shot? When did it happen? Who was it? … Was it me? … No … All right … How surprised I was! That is, this atom that had fallen away from the dying self and was quivering. Whatever life remained was now in this atom and the atom now believed itself to be the entire being. It was thinking as though it was a complete self. It was surprised. When did it get hit by the bullet? … How? … And now … Am I still there or has someone … After all, I should know what … And somehow I, a quivering atom, collected myself … Not that there was much left to collect. Anyhow, as much as was there and as much as could be collected. I groaned, 'Khairul Bhai.'

'Yaar, how can Khairul Bhai come here? It is me … Majju Bhai.'

'Oh … so Khairul Bhai is not here. Where is he?'

'I am Majju Bhai.'

'And I?'

'You are Jawad.'

'Jawad? … Really?' How surprised I was!

'Do you recognize me?'

'Khairul Bhai, you …'

'Yaar, I am not Khairul Bhai … I am Majju Bhai and you are …'

'Me … where am I?'

'You are in the hospital.'

'In the hospital? … Really? … But why?'

'I think his memory is affected,' someone said.

'Do you remember anything, Jawad? How did you get hit by the bullet?'

'Bullet? … Did I get hit by a bullet? … But when?'

'Yes, try and remember. When did you get hit?'

'This is why I used to tell you to be careful. You can't afford to just walk off wherever you wish. I was scared of precisely such a day. Anyhow, Allah will show mercy …' I felt as though Majju Bhai was speaking from far away. And as though he was going on and on, and I did not have the strength to listen to so many words. How much capacity can there be in the hearing power of someone who has been reduced to a mere atom? How much can an atom hear? To hear even one word should be more than enough. But how was I able to hear? My entire being was lying in a heap there; only one atom was left quivering here, thinking itself to be an entire being as though it was whole and complete and full of all its strength. But its reality was soon revealed. The voice grew faint.

I was dead. Then what was going on inside me? I was surprised. So feelings remain even after death, as well as strength and hearing. The pulse of feeling was erratic and feeble; nevertheless, it was still beating. And not exactly beating but falling slowly and steadily. What if it were to sink altogether? It shouldn't sink anymore. Then I would drown completely. Once again I tried to collect myself. I had enough perception to know that I was completely scattered. How will I gather myself? Still, I found the courage to make another attempt to somehow collect myself. I collected myself and tried to remember what had happened. That is if I were to remember what had happened, I will enter myself. Was I really hit by a bullet? I began to struggle with my memory. I could remember a little but in such a strange way as though such an incident had happened a long, long time ago. The two taxis hurtling by, the stampede … Why were people running? Who were these people? No clear picture could emerge in my mind. The picture disintegrated before it could form properly as though my pulse was sinking yet again, as though the atoms of consciousness that I had gathered were scattering once again. Still, only one atom remained, a mere particle, no more than a speck … It is strange how one's entire being scatters and life ebbs away, but somewhere one atom remains, one speck saves itself and declares its self-sufficiency. So somewhere a speck remained. My entire being was now in that speck and my shattered self was trying to remember where was I when I was whole, when I had not been hit by the bullet. But when was I hit? Where did it come from? Where was I at that instant? Had I collapsed? Who had picked me up? Or not picked me up? If no one picked me does it mean that I am still lying there? It is strange when a grown-up man with a full-size body crumbles in an instant, and disintegrates. One's entire self disperses into scraps, and the shards and smithereens spread and scatter. There is another miracle in this strange phenomenon. Asserting its right to exert its own authority, one particle announces its self-sufficiency. It becomes a whole being in itself. And in that instant, I was entirely in that particle and fighting with my memory. I was trying to bring it under my control, but my memory had become rebellious; it was refusing to come under my control. It was playing strange tricks. I couldn't recall the things that I was trying to remember, and those that were not in my wildest imagination were coming back to me and that too as though they would sweep me away in their rush. It seemed as though everything that was there in my Niche of Forgetfulness had come rushing out, and the niche itself was either empty or destroyed. In any case, it had to end. If one's being is blown into atoms and particles how can the niche remain intact? It too must have got smashed. It was only now that I realized how important the Niche of Forgetfulness is for us; how many memories it contains; or else there would forever be a tumult of memories raging inside us – as was happening inside me at that instant. The Niche of Forgetfulness was broken. I was reduced to a speck, yet I was billowing and spreading with my endless memories – like the fish of Manu which was the size of a little finger, but when it grew and grew, it became so enormous that the river became small for it; it became so large that it swam into the sea. And I who had been reduced to a speck was now enlarging into a cosmos in the sea of my memories. A doomsday of memories had risen within me – as though someone had played a tune. Buried memories came to life – each intent upon settling its accounts but also shy of clearing debts. No memory was ready to fully settle old accounts. In the case of some memories, the beginning could not be found; in other cases, if the beginning could be found, the end was missing. Some memory would appear from the middle – with both its beginning and end missing. Then there were some memories that were mine, others that belonged to others but had come and mingled with mine – like a pigeon that belonged to someone else but would fly over and sit on our roof, see our pigeons pecking on their grain, get off the roof and mingle with them. So many memories from so many places, wandering, drifting and mingling with my own memories – what could I do to stop them? I was exhausted, almost in the last throes of life. I no longer had the strength nor the discernment to sift my memories and separate them from others. At the time, it seemed as though there was darkness all around, an intense darkness, which had countless fireflies flitting about in it. And memories seemed to be flickering like fireflies – burning bright one minute and dying out the next. And I was trying to catch them. I had collected so many fireflies in the hem of my kurta …

'Munnan! Come and see, Munnan … Look, it's a *beerbahuti*!'

Why was Maimuna calling out to me? Which 'me' was this? Is it the 'me' who was once Munnan and who is now 'he' for me? Is it he who used to go rushing after the *beerbahuti*, forgetting his butterflies? Maimuna is standing transfixed, her eyes filled with surprise and happiness, staring at that patch of land. So many *beerbahutis* are crawling among the damp green grass – like tiny red velvety knobs. How swiftly they are moving!

'Munnan, see there are so many of them,' Happiness is brimming out of Maimuna. Munnan goes to stand beside her.

Both are looking with such wonder and such joy at the tiny red *beerbahutis* crawling and scurrying in the green grass. Munnan can control himself no longer; he wants to touch one and see. He touches one *beerbahuti* with his finger. What was that? It stopped moving and became stationary.

'Munnan, what did you do?'

'What did I do? I did nothing; I just touched it a little,' Munnan said as though he has committed a terrible crime and he must give his defence.

'The *beerbahuti* is dead.'

'It is not dead; it is just cheating and has gone still.'

'You are lying! It is dead,' Maimuna is on the brink of tears.

'I am willing to bet it isn't dead.'

Munnan is holding his breath; his gaze is fixed at the still *beerbahuti*. What will happen if it is truly dead? May Allah will the *beerbahuti* to come back to life! 'Allah Miyan, please bring it back to life.' And Allah Miyan indeed hears his plea. There … it slowly unfurls its legs and begins to crawl.

'Aha, the *beerbahuti* has come back to life!' Maimuna is clapping her hands with joy.

'Didn't I say she isn't dead? The *beerbahuti* loves to cheat. You just have to touch it a little and she pretends as though she is dead.'

Then how does one catch them? They fall into a dilemma. Should they catch one, or should they not ...

'Maimuna!'

'Yes, what's it?'

'Hush, speak softly! There's a butterfly!'

'Where?' Mainuna asks in a whisper.

'There!' He shows by pointing his finger. It's perched on a leaf of one of the higher branches of the jasmine creeper; it has white and yellow spots on its shiny black wings. He moves quietly towards the jasmine; it flutters away and begins to circle the air ... And my dear when that princess would go to the garden, she would find the butterfly sitting on the same flower and she would be surprised as to why that butterfly always came and sat on that particular flower.

'Phuphi Amma, why did that butterfly always come and sit on that particular flower?'

'My dear, wait a while; wait and see what happens ahead. It wasn't a butterfly.'

'What was it if it wasn't a butterfly?'

'Be patient; listen to what happened next.'

'Shall I tell you what happened?' Maimuna interrupted.

'Why are you butting in? Let me listen to the story. Yes, Phuphi Amma, what happened then?'

'Then, my dear, what happened was that the princess ...'

'Jawad, open your eyes. Look who is here!' It was Majju Bhai's voice. The fireflies-filled darkness dissolved, and with great difficulty I wrenched myself out of that pleasurable darkness into the light and opened my eyes slightly. Arre, there was Syed Aqa Hasan and Basho Bhabhi!

'My dear sir, what have you done to yourself?'

'Ai hai, why didn't you say anything to those black-faced rascals? May they be racked by cholera! Who *were* they?'

'Bhabhi, it is best not to ask who they were. Whoever they were, they hadn't come from outside.'

'You are right, brother, we ourselves are bringing affliction on our lives. Anyhow, please tell us how he is. We hope all is well. What are the doctors saying?'

'The reports are satisfactory. There is no danger now.'

'Thank God!'

'Yes, his life has been spared. Bhabhi, actually the driver turned out to be a brave man; he showed great presence of mind. He drove the car out of there in a jiffy and went straight to the hospital. He received aid just in time.'

'Yes, because he was fated to live. Ai Majju Bhai, I was feeling quite ill last night. The wretched cat was crying so piteously that she woke me up. My heart beat so! I said, "Ya Allah, don't send me any bad news." I said and recited Ali's name three times and blew it; then I went to sleep. Believe me, it is because of the marvel of Ali's name that his life has been spared.'

'Yes, my dear, it is a miracle.'

'Bhai Majidul Hasan, this city is not worth living in anymore. One's honour is no longer safe here, nor one's life.'

'Yes, indeed it is no longer the place for decent people.'

'Imagine hitting a decent person such as Jawad sahab who has nothing to do with anybody. For heaven's sake, these are *your* political differences: you can smash each other's skulls if you like or cut each other's throat; we are not part of any of your issues. Why are you making our lives miserable then?' And suddenly Aqa Hasan sahab's tone changed. 'Arre, why have I started on this subject? We shouldn't upset the patient; let him rest.' And with these words, he got up. Actually, he had seen that my eyes were drooping and I was doing my best to keep them open.

'Yes, dear brother, you must rest; there is no need to talk too much. Just sleep,' Basho Bhabhi said as she left.

How could I sleep? The fireflies-filled darkness was returning once again but this time the fireflies were scattering. Now the fireflies were swarming around me. I couldn't understand which to hold and which ones to let fly away. But my memory was failing me. No, my memory must not perish. I must remember ... What should I remember ... Anything ... 'Pakistan has come!' A voice filled with happiness rang out in the darkness.

'Really? Has Pakistan come?' A wave of happiness coursed through the train compartment. Life ripples through the scared timorous people huddled there. Scrambling one on top of the other, each one is trying to peer out of the window to see what Pakistan looks like. But what could they see in the dark night? It is true that the night is waning and it is the last watch of the night and morning is about to break ... but it is still quite dark. The train has slowed down and is getting slower still.

'Thank God!'

'Pakistan has taken so long to come! My heart was jumping.'

'I have been praying all the way.'

'O sister, don't ask how I have spent the entire journey: my heart was leaping in my throat. Did you see at the Jallundhar station ... those ghostly figures standing there? One of those black-faced scoundrels held a gun with its barrel pointing straight at me. I was terrified that a bullet would whiz out and hit me. I began to recite the *Ayatul Kursi*. There is great blessing in Allah's words; the train began to move immediately. I said, "Thanks be to Allah!"'

'Don't talk about bullets now; we are in Pakistan. No one will point a gun at you.'

'Thank God we have come away from that land of fear,' a white-haired elderly man muttered and began to recite the *kalma*.

'Those were strange circumstances; neither honour nor life was safe.'

'Thank god we have been able to come away with our honour and life intact.'

'May Allah keep Pakistan safe and secure.'

'Amen.'

'Arre Miyan, my heart is still quaking.'

'But why is your heart still quaking? We have reached Pakistan now; what can trouble you here?'

'Badi Bi!' Someone said in a loud voice, 'Pakistan is the land of the faithful.'

Suddenly someone called out in a high-pitched voice, 'Pakistan!' and the entire compartments chorused 'Long Live!'

'What day is it?'

'Friday has begun.'

'It is a blessed day.'

'And which day according to the lunar calendar?'

'Today is the 9th day of the month of Zu-al Hajj. This year it is the Hajj-e Akbar.'[93]

'Even the date is blessed.'

And then a blank; I could recall nothing after that. On the 9th Zu-al Hajj, Friday, a little before dawn, a most auspicious entry into Pakistan. And after that? No matter how hard I try, I cannot remember anything. Days, months, years, a day, a moment, an occasion ... I could remember. Ya Allah, what is happening to my memory? A happy occasion, or a sad one, surely I should remember something? I can't remember anything. The slate of memory is clean. Ya Allah, what happened to all those days and nights I spent here? Where have they gone to hide? There were so many years ... in fact, an entire age. Was I really hit by a bullet or did the bullet eat up all those years? What sort of bullet was it that it gobbled up so many years, all those moments of joy and sadness, as though they had never existed? Can such a thing happen? I am suddenly reminded that something like this had happened to me once before. One entire period of my life had got lost once before. All those days and nights, those mornings and evenings, those long afternoons, all those seasons ... But then that entire caravan of days and nights did come back with all its intensity. Perhaps I would have been at peace if it had been lost. But all those days and nights

---

[93] The Zu-al Hajj is the twelfth and last month of the Islamic lunar calendar. The hajj pilgrimage is performed on the 8th, 9th, 10th day of this month. When the haj occurs on a Friday, it is generally considered to be Hajj-e Akbar or the 'greater Hajj'.

came back. They were alive as ever. In fact, they became more alive. It was a strange thing. I was hardly old enough then. Those days and nights were not too many, or too long. There were, after all, only a few afternoons, and some mornings and evenings. But they entered deep within me and acquired such a bright hue and grew so much that it began to seem as though they were an entire century of pearly mornings and smokey evenings. What worth do months and years have? A few well-spent hot afternoons, a few cool scented mornings and some poignant evenings can become an entire age. They contain so much within themselves that they cannot be confined to months and years; they keep growing and expanding. It is a miracle that one's entire being dies, but one particle breaks away in such a way that it acquires a greater life than the original being. And in this way, an entire era comes to an end, an age ends. But some of its afternoons, some of its mornings, a few pleasant or sad evenings stretch to become centuries. Look ... the fireflies can be seen fluttering about again, like birds that peck on grain and fly off at the slightest sound. It may seem as though they are gone and have flown far away, but they come back soon enough. And so my memories, too, are swarming back now. They are rushing to cover me. Yes, that memory I had forgotten in the middle ... what was that? I should remember it now, now that I am able to recall all sorts of long-lost memories. Yes, perhaps it is a memory from those days when, even after the last watch of the night, the story would remain unfinished. Phuphi Amma would postpone it for the next night and insist we go to sleep. The story would go on for several nights. And finally Phuphi Amma would manage to finish it one night. 'May the narrator prosper, and so may the listener. May he who didn't hear, and he who didn't narrate also prosper. May everyone prosper![94] Now, my son, go to sleep and Maimuna, you also go to sleep. It is very late. The jackals are howling.'

---

[94] In the convention of the *qissa-kahani* tradition, this is how most *qissas* usually ended.

'Phuphi Amma, is it the sound of jackals?' Is this Munnan's voice? Has he come back?

'Yes, my son, it is very late and the jackals are howling.'

The sound of the jackals coming from afar makes his heart beat faster. He is scared that they may come here. 'Phuphi Amma, where are the jackals?'

'Shall I tell you where they are?' Maimuna butts in. 'They are howling in the strip of wasteland.'

'You liar!'

'Why should I lie? That day when we had gone to the wasteland and spotted a den, that was the jackals' den.'

'But there were no jackals there at the time.'

'Son, the jackals come out at night.'

'Where do they hide in the day?'

'Shall I say?' Maimuna butts in once again.

'What would you know?'

'All right, don't fight; it is very late now. Go to sleep,' Phuphi Amma turned on her side and almost immediately began to snore. She could fall asleep as soon as she would finish a story. The sound of her snores ... The sound of the jackals howling in the distance.... And the sound of barking dogs coming from another direction ... He is scared. 'Maimuna! Hey Maimuna!' Maimuna too has gone to sleep. It seems there is no one else around and he is all alone in the middle of jackals and dogs who are barking and screaming in a circle around him. The circle is becoming narrower.

'Jawad, are you sleeping?'

'Hmmm ... No,' Munnan has disappeared. Now there is just me and Majju Bhai.

'Try and sleep.'

'But Majju Bhai, why are the jackals howling so much today?'

'Jackals? But there are no jackals here. Don't get into these hallucinations; try and sleep.'

How could I sleep? My mind was refusing to sleep. A wheel was turning constantly inside my head.

Hamara tumhara Khuda badshah
Kisi mulk mein thha koi badshah
(An emperor who is your God and mine
Such was a king in some kingdom)

'No, no, Phuphi Amma, tell us the story of the crow and the mynah.'

'Yaar Jawad, look ... Rafiq sahab has come.'

The fireflies scattered once again. With great difficulty, I opened my eyes. I could see two blurred faces. One was Majju Bhai's whom I had been recognizing all this while only through his voice; now I could see his face. And the other face? Yes, that's right ... it was Rafiq sahab's?

'How are you, Jawad sahab?'

I heard him, but I did not have the strength to respond. In any case, Rafiq sahab had asked as a courtesy; he also knew that I was in no condition to speak. So he turned immediately towards Majju Bhai who began telling him all about my condition. 'Yaar, in the beginning, he was completely confused; forget others, he could not even recognize me. I asked if he could recall how he got the bullet. He asked me in complete amazement, "Bullet? What bullet?" Anyhow, that phase is over now. He has begun to partly recognize people.'

'So that means his condition is improving.'

'Yes, it has improved a little but in the middle of a normal conversation, he introduces something completely irrelevant. There may be some connection in the first two sentences but the third statement is miles away from the topic.'

'What do the doctors say?'

'They can't comment on his mental state yet; they say the real situation will be clear only after the operation.'

'They are right; the bullet should come out first. Though every effort should be made to make him recall that incident.' And then the attention was diverted towards me. 'Jawad sahab!'

Once again, I tried my hardest to open my eyes.

'Jawad sahab!' Rafiq sahab was saying, 'I had left you sitting in the bank – you and Mirza sahab. When did you leave? When did this incident happen, and where?'

'When did this incident happen, and where,' I muttered to myself. But which incident? My eyes had closed again. And it seemed as though a strange brew was being concocted in my head. Which incident? Hearing about it repeatedly, I too had begun to think that surely something had happened to me. But what had happened … that I couldn't fathom. I began to struggle with my memory; I was in a wrestling bout. How much I had forced that stubborn thing to spit out every thing! And there was a great deal that I could now remember from long ago but each time, my memory would come and get stuck at one point. I could remember things from so many different times but I was not able to remember the incident that had recently taken place. Now what should I do? … I fell in deep thought. After all, how long … And now … I could understand only one thing. I decided that Rafiq sahab was right. I shouldn't try to directly remember that incident per se; instead, I should try and remember that time. If I could recall that time and along with it that place, I would automatically remember the incident. What time was it? …

'Who has lit this match? Put it out … put it out!' An angry voice said in the darkness. 'So you are very fond of smoking cigarettes, even if you lose your life in the process!'

'It won't be one life; these cigarette smokers are going to get us all killed.'

'Of course! This tiny fleck of light can be seen in the darkness. The bullet will come straight in its direction.'

'Hai Allah!' An old woman's terror-stricken voice came. 'Son, don't smoke a cigarette at this time; take the name of Allah at this time …' And then she muttered, 'Yours is the mercy, yours the wrath, remove the misfortune that has befallen us.'

'Why have these wretches stopped the train in the middle of the jungle? It's been so long; why isn't it moving?' Another feminine voice could be heard.

'Stay quiet, won't you? There must be some reason; that is why the train has stopped. Just pray.'

'Of course I am praying. I have read the entire *Ayatul Kursi*. Ai, brother, how far is Pakistan from here?'

'The last "special" was attacked at this very spot. The entire train was butchered. May Allah have mercy upon us!'

'Who has a watch? What is the time?'

'Twelve minutes past two o'clock.'

'Really? Is it just two o'clock? It is still a long time to go before daybreak.'

'This night has become a bit too long.'

So it was a quarter past two; morning was still far away. It was pitch black all around. A flicker of light would be seen on the tops of the trees in the distance like lightning.

'Brother, what is that light? May my mouth be filled with dust for speaking ill, but are the wretches about to attack us?'

'No, Amma, it is coming from the torchlights of the military guards; they are looking to see that all is well.'

There was a slight movement in the train. 'The train is moving,' exclaimed a satisfied voice.

'May Allah be praised,' came the relieved voice of the old woman.

I stopped myself with a start. Where had I set out? I soon realized I had wandered away. This incident is not from the present. There was a great deal of danger but there was no attack. The cigarette smokers had lit their matches and smoked their cigarettes not once but several times when the train had stopped in the middle of the jungle; still no bullet had come their way. So I thought: Surely this incident is not from that time. Then when did it happen? I was jousting with my memory and my imagination was going hither and thither …

'Liar!'

'No, truly … There … There, next to the bushes … I am scared.'

'I will hit it with a brick.'

'No, Munnan, no, it will bite you.'

Then? What happened next? ... What next? ... Where have I come? I was surprised but then I stopped myself soon enough. It is of those days when I was Munnan, and Maimuna ... Anyhow, Maimuna was still Maimuna though back then Phuphi Amma used to call her 'Mammo' sometimes. But Miyan Khan would reprimand her instantly, 'Sister, why do you distort my daughter's name? She has such a lovely name.' Be that as it may, I used to be Munnan then and how surprised I was to realize that he was completely different from me, as though he was someone else. Or, I thought to myself, that I was someone else, as though he was another body and I was another body now. And suddenly a doubt assailed me, a worrying niggling doubt. What if I too from a man had become ... 'Phuphi Amma, Jan-e-Alam was a man; how did he turn into a monkey?'

'Because his brain was addled and, when he regained his senses, he had turned into a monkey. And then he gave such fiery speeches that he surpassed any man. He pulled out such things from his memory and spoke in such an intelligent way that everyone was astounded.... The people were amazed, the rulers were perplexed. "So monkeys can also speak!" And the queen twisted the neck of her pet parrot and threw him out of the cage. The monkey lay in the lap of the merchant and flew into the body of the parrot. The parrot fluttered, the queen was pleased; she pulled him inside the cage. Everyone spoke in unison, "The monkey was an illusion; he was waiting to depart on the eternal journey. When his murder was proved, he died of fright and left the imprint of his memory on the pages of our heart ..." And then Malka Mehr Nigar said to the Minister's son, "Bring me a pretty little goat's kid; I shall nurture him and try and forget my sorrow." The children were pleased to hear this.... The queen lifted the kid and placed it in her lap; then she squeezed it so tightly that it died. As soon as it died, she set up a lament. He sat on the bed and made his spirit enter the body of the goat's kid ... Meanwhile Prince Jan-e-Alam sat in his cage and watched the entire spectacle. The body was empty; immediately he brought his spirit into his body. He said "Ya Allah" and stood up …" And then … Then … I couldn't remember what happened next. This act of not remembering had helped me get out of this rut. The body goes off on its own path. This is a story, I thought and I was trying to remember the incident or the time when that incident took place, whatever that incident may have been …

Anyhow, I was surprised to remember some story that I had read or heard some time long ago. I must have read it much later; I had heard it first. I had heard the story of Prince Jan-e Alam from Phuphi Amma. A monkey rides atop an elephant and gives a speech, a speech where people laugh when he laughs, and cry when he cries. So many people, a huge crowd of them are virtually dancing to the monkey's tune. I began to think who was to know which monkey would ride atop an elephant and start giving a speech and people would be completely taken in. A monkey should, I thought, stay in his own place and man should remain in his own robe, or rather in his own skin. When a monkey sits atop an elephant and a man does not stay inside his skin and changes his form, then … But Jan-e Alam had paid the price for not staying in his own skin and learnt his lesson and returned to his own body. But everyone does not return. How would he have felt when he returned to his own body after such a long time? Like a traveller who returns after a long journey, through hill and dale, after enduring many a hardship to come back to his own land? How happy he must feel upon his return. But who could tell if he remembered his monkey body? Perhaps he remembered with fondness those days spent jumping freely on the trees, and swinging from the branches. Or perhaps sometimes he might remember the parrot's body. What a pretty body it was … green with a bright band on the neck, a bright red beak! And days spent singing without a worry, pecking grain and being happy. Parrot nostalgia! And even greater than that was monkey nostalgia! I am reminded of those transient days of joy when I was a monkey, I was inside my skin but when … But I managed to control myself. I somehow managed to bring my wandering mind under control. Why did I get entangled in this story? I stopped myself. I was trying to remember when that incident happened to me, whatever that incident might have been … And this story? How did I enter this story? Anyhow let me not speak of 'me', I thought. Sometimes 'me' is hidden behind 'he'. After all, Munnan who is 'he' for me now was once 'me'. When a man is about to change, he changes so much that he cannot be recognized. Like Nal had changed and become an altogether different person. Damyanti, who loved him utterly, also failed to recognize him.[95] The poor woman kept thinking that Nal was so good looking; this ugly creature could not be him? Who was he then and where was he? Munnan too was so good looking – as though that was another birth and another body.

That is the other thing about births. The 'me' becomes a 'he' in such a way that it disappears altogether. Who could remember that 'I' was 'he' once? If one could remember would one not become Mahatma Budhha?

'O monks, a monkey came dripping wet in the rain and sat down on this branch. A mynah poked her neck out of her nest and spoke in a kindly voice, "O Monkey, if only you had built a home for yourself when the weather was good, you wouldn't have been getting wet in the rain." The monkey thought the mynah was taunting him for being homeless. Peeved, he pulled the mynah's nest down in a fit of pique. The mynah regretted trying to make the senseless monkey see sense. Soon, she and her mate flew away in the rain.'

Tathagat fell silent. Then he said, 'O monks, I was that mynah.'

The monks expressed surprise. 'You, O Tathagat? It was you who bore anguish at the hands of that unbelieving monkey?'

'Yes, it was me, and at that very instant, I let go of life. Then I was reborn in the form of a parrot. O monks, I shall tell you of those days when I was not this I; I was a parrot. Those days there

---

[95] The story of Nal and Damyanti is told in the *Mahabharata*. Damayanti was the princess of Vidharba who married King Nala of Nishadha. Married to each other in their previous birth too, they are symbolic of eternal mates who will triumph over the cycle of birth and rebirth, trial and separation

was a dense jungle beyond Taxila. There, this parrot built its nest in the hollow of a tree trunk. But it so happened that a snake too appeared and began to live in another hollow of the same tree. The parrot saw this and said to his mate, "O my wife, a poisonous snake has come and settled down in our neighbourhood. It has destroyed our peace. Our safety lies in our going away from this tree and making our home on the branch or hollow of some other nice tree somewhere." The she-parrot heard this and wept and said, "O Master, we had collected one twig after another and made this nest. And now when I was about to lay my eggs and this nest was about to come to life, this wretched snake has come and started living here. Now you are saying that we should leave this tree and go and make our nest somewhere else. O Master, just stop to think how many afflictions I faced while making this nest. How can I leave the nest that I had made with so much care?" The parrot heard this and sighed, "Dear wife, with these round eyes of mine, I have seen so many nests being formed and abandoned. And you are talking of your one nest? Open your eyes and look around at the other nests and homes around you. There is a fire raging around you. All of creation is on fire. Nests, homes, trees, forests, hamlets, towns, neighbourhoods, palaces, mansions – everything is caught in the flames."' And the monks were saddened to know that Tathagat did not know happiness even in the life of a parrot and was made homeless yet again. And Buddha-ji said, 'O monks, there is no peace in any birth and no settlement remains settled forever, and every home that is set up is set up to be abandoned. Centuries ago when I had taken the form of a bull and was yoked in the chariot of the prince of Varanasi....' And yet another story of another birth started. The Mahatma could tell the story of birth and rebirth with utter simplicity and speed, like good children reciting arithmetic tables. But Queen Nageshwari began to tremble with fright. She went to the King and said, 'O Master, today is not a good day. I don't know what happened but, all of a sudden, I remembered my previous birth.' King Dharamdutt was worried; he said, 'O Queen, the same thing happened to me. I too suddenly remembered my previous birth.' Queen Nageshwari heard this and wept; she said, 'O King, this is an ill omen.'

'Why is it an ill omen?'

'O King, if you remember your previous birth, you must talk about it and if you do, you die. And I cannot stop myself from talking about my previous birth. So you hear what I have to say, but do not speak about your own previous birth.'

'This is a grave situation; what shall we do?'

'Whatever will be, will be! Now we have both remembered our previous birth. We must narrate it to each other and be prepared for the consequences.'

Queen Nageshwari remained quiet for a long time; then she said, 'O King, in our previous birth, we were a pair of swans; you were the king of swans and I was your mate.'

'O Queen, but do think awhile … how did we become a pair of swans. We were something else in the previous birth. I was the Minister and you were the Minister's wife.'

'O Master, have you remembered the birth before the last one? That is very bad.'

'O my Queen, now whatever must happen, will happen. So, yes, you and I were husband and wife even in that birth. When I was fed up with the affairs of the state, I decided to go on a pilgrimage. But we were on our way when we were waylaid by scoundrels. We decided that before they lay their dirty hands on our honour, we must set ourselves on fire. So we collected some wood in the jungle, lit a fire and walked into it. But at that very moment a pair of swans was flying in the skies. How beautiful they were, with wings like sheets of silver, claws like gold, and beaks like coral! We forgot the fire and gazed at the flying swans. We were entranced by them and it so happened that one minute our spirits left our bodies and the very next minute we took the form of the swan and his mate. We flew far and wide; we brought news from distant parts of the skies and flew upon lakes of sweet water. But one day it so happened that we were flying in the skies when a storm came and strong winds blew. Swirls of dust rose from the earth till the skies and we got separated from each other. When the storm passed and the dust settled down, I was surprised to find my mate missing. I searched high and low, among lakes and ponds but I couldn't find you. Then I undertook a long journey and reached Lake Mansarovar. And you were present there! You were gliding contentedly in the pearly-white waters of the lake.'

And Queen Nageshwari was lost in thoughts of Mansarovar. She sighed deeply and said, 'Master, how fine were those days when we glided over Lake Mansarovar. You were the King of swans and I was your mate. How immersed in beauty was that life! O Master, we have endured this human life long enough; come, let us go back to that life. Let us abandon these matters of state and free ourselves from this life of trickery and deceit. Let there be Lake Mansarovar glistening like a pearl, sweet cold water lapping in gentle waves, cool breeze, an earth filled with love, a beautiful sky and us!' And with these words, her eyes began to close and kept drooping – hers as well as King Dharamdutt's.... So, this story is from the time when Queen Nageshwari recalled her previous life and death began to hover around her head. And this too is a strange matter that if you remember your previous life, there is no getting away without recounting it and if you do narrate it, there is no escape from death.

'Maimuna, do you remember that *sadhu* who used to say he remembered his previous life? But where did he go? We never saw him again afterwards.'

'O Master, when did this happen?'

'This happened when I used to live in Dwarka.'

'Dwarka?'

'Yes, Dwarka.' And Tathagat immediately launched into his story. 'This was centuries ago, when wealth rained down upon that city. Peace, happiness, joy!'

But Ganesh was not happy even there. Everyone was happy, except him. Those who cannot forget can never be happy. He was not able to forget the city of Mathura. And when the bad times came to Dwarka, he began to remember the city he had left behind more than ever. But it is of those days I speak when the river of joy was in full spate, men and women were happy and a river of love ran through their settlement. Limitless music echoed from the earth till the skies, yet the sorrow of being separated from his Mathura gnawed away at Ganesh. The alleys and cattle of that city danced before his eyes all the time. Every single day, he had the same thought: As though he was setting out at the crack of dawn from his alley with his cows as well as the cows belonging to others. And now dusk is falling and Mohan's flute can be heard in the gloam. It makes the Gopis restless; they rush to stand at their doorsteps. The sound of the flute, he remembers, draws them like a magnet. For a long time, the sound of the bells tied around the cows' necks tinkled in his ears. The white rivulets of milk gushing out of pink udders keep appearing before his eyes. How much milk came out of them! All the pitchers in the house would be full and every day they would make *kheer*. Sometimes, he would remember all this as though it had happened in a previous life, and sometimes as though it had happened yesterday. And, sometimes as though he is in a dream, and sometimes as though he is still roaming around in the streets and alleys of that city. Sometimes the years of separation seemed as though centuries had passed, and sometimes it seemed as though he had only just left Mathura. In the early days, others who had come from Mathura also remembered the city they had left behind. But the joys of Dwarka gradually made them forget the unhappiness of Mathura. It was almost as though gradually they were learning patience, and accepting the fact that they, that is the Yadavs, had to henceforth live in Dwarka. They were reminded of Mathura like one remembers a long-lost dream. But there was such hustle and bustle in the streets and markets of Dwarka and so much happiness all around that even the dream that they occasionally remembered faded away. Soon the dream was entirely lost from memory. All those who had come from Mathura soon became lost in the delights of the new city. Ganesh was the only one who still remembered Mathura.

But now the times have changed. Now the city of Dwarka is in peril; now its cows have begun to give birth to donkeys. One day

Prakash came with a most surprising report, 'Ganesh Bhaiyya, have you heard?'

'What?'

'It is so surprising that a goat has turned into a bitch.'

'Prakash! Have you gone mad? A goat turning into a bitch! That's a tall tale.'

'I am telling the truth, Bhaiyya. It so happened that a herd of goats were crossing the big bazaar. Suddenly, one goat broke free from the herd and ran away bleeting all the while. And as it was bleating it suddenly began to bark!'

Ganesh's eyes widened with disbelief. 'Prakash, this is most uncanny.'

'Yes, it is uncanny. That is why everyone is in a state of astonishment. And not just astonishment; they are also scared.'

And strange things kept happening. A large, black, well-built bald man appeared from nowhere. People saw him running; in an instant, he had circled the entire city. The warriors aimed their arrows at him. Some arrows hit him, but none of them wounded him. Then he entered an alley and disappeared and then it so happened that the howls of jackals could be heard from inside the big temple in the city. And the priests saw that a large pig was sitting in the sanctum. Whoever heard it fell in a state of shock. *Hey Ram*, what was happening here? And then a nymph was spotted who was saying in a loud voice, 'O People of Dwarka, go on a pilgrimage.' The people of Dwarka took the nymph's voice to be a divine message from the skies and immediately set out on a pilgrimage. But that voice became an invitation from Death. Was it a pilgrimage or a journey towards Death? The pilgrims spotted fresh green grass at one place along the way and set up camp. They ate and drank and consumed liquor to their heart's content. The intoxication came over them in such a strange way that they began to challenge each other. Those brave warriors had fought against each other at Kurukshetra and they were reminded of that war. They took up arms against each other and, in a matter of minutes, they were thirsting for each others' blood. They fell upon each other with a vengeance. They wanted to cut each other's throat. The green grass turned red with blood.

During those days, Ganesh's childhood friend, Narendra, travelled from Mathura and, encountering many difficulties along the way, came to Dwarka. Ganesh hugged him, remembered Mathura and cried.

'Ganesh,' Narendra said, 'your hair has turned white since you came here.'

'Friend, don't you see how much time has passed since I came here,' Ganesh sighed. The mention of time made the days long past dance before his eyes … The streets and alleys of Mathura, the cows and the dust raised by their hooves at sunset, and the Gopis. 'Friend, so how is Mathura?'

'Ganesh,' Narendra spoke in a sorrowful tone, 'Don't ask me about Mathura … that city has been widowed. Those who made her special left her and went away. Now there is neither the sound of Mohan's flute nor the echo of the sounds of love and nor do the hearts of the Gopis race wildly. Dust fills the streets, the Gopis are sad, and the cows have dried up. Those who left, took the city's beauty with them. That city is now deserted.'

Ganesh heard this and wept. Narendra too was extremely sad after narrating the city's woes. Then he said, 'You didn't do us a good turn by leaving Mathura. You set up a new city. You live in happiness and comfort in your new city, whereas we are left to wander like fools and endure all manner of hardships out there.'

'Friend,' Ganesh spoke sadly, 'Who told you that we live in happiness and comfort here? Yes, we did once, but not anymore. The good days have passed; now we are in danger. Darkness is spreading over Dwarka. All sorts of strange men walk about its streets and bazaars, goats bark, cows crawl and the sounds of howling jackals can be heard from temples and, in the sacred spaces of the sanctums, pigs are found sitting and mice crawling all about.'

'What are you saying, Ganesh? I can't believe my ears. Sitting far away, we have always believed that piety rains upon Dwarka and there is peace, love, happiness and joy here.'

'It was so once, but not now. Warriors from here went to fight in the war at Kurukshetra. There, they were divided and ended up fighting against each other. When they returned, they were burning in the fires of fury. They were thirsty for blood and eventually had their way. They turned this city of peace and love into Kurukshetra. Narendra, Dwarka is laid waste.'

'But, friend, that is strange indeed. No one appreciated the sacrifice. Mathura was destroyed and so was Dwarka. No one is happy.' Narendra paused and then spoke hesitantly, 'Ganesh, can I ask you something?'

'Yes, please do.'

'Shri Krishan Bhagwan is wise and all-knowing. Why did he leave Mathura?'

'Narendra, you have put your finger on my deepest worry. This question has kept me up many nights.'

'Perhaps,' Narendra paused and then said, 'Perhaps in leaving his birthplace, he ... perhaps ...'

'Why don't you say clearly that he didn't do well?'

'But what does he say now? What does he think?'

'What does he say now?' Ganesh laughed bitterly. 'What will he say now? He doesn't say anything. But I feel he is not happy; he had left his flute behind in Mathura. Since coming here, even the chariot and *chakra* have been taken away from him.'[96]

'What did you say?' Narendra jumped in surprise. 'The chariot and *chakra* have been taken from him? What are you saying? Is there such a one born who can take Krishan's chariot and *chakra* from him?'

'No brave warrior took it from him; it came from the skies and went back to the skies. Do you know what happened? Bhagwan's

---

[96] The *Mausala Parva*, the 16th of the 18 books of the *Mahabharata*, describes the death of Krishan in the 36th year after the end of the Kurukshetra War. Initially the kingdom of Dwarka is prosperous and peaceful, but soon the Yadavas become frivolous and hedonistic. Several ill omens afflict the city including the disappearance of Krishan's fabled *Sudarshan Chakra* as well as his conch and chariot. The incidents described in the above passages are from the *Mausala Parva*.

chariot was racing along with all its pomp and majesty when three heavenly nymphs appeared from up above. They took down the flag from the chariot. They were still doing it when the *chakra* flew off from Maharaj's hand and disappeared in the skies.'

Narendra was shocked into silence. He didn't know what to say. Finally, Ganesh spoke up in a scared voice, 'These are not good omens, Narendra. It appears that something is about to happen.'

'So much has already happened; what more will happen?'

'It seems that a lot more still has to happen.'

'What will happen?'

'Only a wise man can tell you that. So many times I thought of going to Guru Shambhu Maharaj and asking him about what is happening and what will happen.'

'Guru Shambhu Maharaj!' Narendra was startled. 'He is our Guru. He must be quite old now.'

'He is nothing but a string of bones. His hair is white as jute and his eyelashes look as though his eyelids are rimmed with snow.'

'Come, Ganesh, let us go and meet the Guru.'

Both went to meet the Guru; they touched his feet and Ganesh said, 'Guru-ji, one of your disciples has come all the way from Mathura.'

'From Mathura?' Guru Maharaj opened his white eyelashes. 'Who is it?'

'Maharaj, this is Narendra; your old disciple.'

'Narendra!' Guru-ji tried to remember. 'Yes, yes, I remember now ... Narendra! How is Mathura?'

'I am fine, Maharaj, but Mathura is not fine; we are the dwellers of a desolate land.'

'*Om tat sat*.'[97]

---

[97] This is a Sanskrit phrase that was used by Krishan when he was teaching the meaning of the universe to Arjuna and as a means of self-awakening. '*Om Tat Sat*' has no physical component. It is purely spiritual and beyond. It starts from the most primordial spiritual form Om and leads to the ultimate Impersonal God, the Formless One (Nirakar Brahm), Tat and the Non-dualistic Existence, Sat.

'Guru Maharaj,' Ganesh spoke hesitantly. 'Even Dwarka is not in a good state, and Narendra here has asked me a most incredible question. He wants to know what were our elders thinking when they decided to leave Mathura.'

'Sons,' Shambhu Maharaj said, 'Everything is the handiwork of Time; we are helpless before it. We sleep but Time is forever awake. Then it is Time that shakes us awake and when we rub our eyes and look around ourselves, we find that everything has changed. *Om tat sat*.'

'*Om tat sat*!' Ganesh muttered and said, 'O Guru-ji, but Shri Krishan Bhagwan is himself an incarnation of Time; he was awake.'

Guru Shambhu Maharaj sighed and then said, 'When all five of Draupadi's sons were killed, she went crying to Gandhari. Mother Gandhari saw her and said, "O Draupadi, five of your sons have been killed and you are lamenting. Look at me, for I am still quiet despite having lost a hundred sons." Then she looked at Krishan Maharaj and spoke wrathfully, "O you Divine Born, you are the root cause of all evil. You have destroyed my womb. So you wait and see, son, the sons of Yadavas will also be destroyed." Bhagwan Krishan answered sombrely, "O Mother, no one else can destroy the Yadavas; only I can do it. You have made my task easier with your curse."' Guru Maharaj paused then continued, 'Sons, Krishan Bhagwan is an incarnation of Time, but after all how long can that moment be postponed of which Mother Gandhari had warned?' And then Guru Maharaj closed his eyes and began to mumble, '*Om tat sat. Om tat sat. Om tat sat*.'

Oh, so this story is from that time … that time when … Though every city has the same fate. It is as though cities are settled simply in order to be laid waste … Then Abdullah spoke thus, 'My dear fellow, you are right in crying for your ancestral city of Seville. It takes a long while for a city to be settled but when it is time for it to be devastated, it can be laid waste within a few moments – like the city of my ancestors, Cordoba, was devastated. I read in the memoirs of my great-grandfather that was written during the upheaval of decline, though, of course, during that time one could only read at night. So I read in my great-grandfather's memoir about that blessed city which my ancestor remembered by the the title of 'The Bride of Andalusia'. It had countless markets and squares, with a bath-house at every corner and a mosque at every square. And among all the mosques was the Grand Mosque that was like an ornament on the forehead of Cordoba. The crowds who thronged it were unmatched compared to all other mosques around it. Further away, at the Madina Azahara,[98] the drums would be beaten morning and evening. But when this fragrant city was about to be laid waste, nothing could save it – not the crowds or the drums, not the calls to the faithful to prayer, nor the voices of the proclaimers of faith. Only Allah's name remains. There is no Victor except Allah.'[99] And Abdullah drew a long sigh and fell silent. Then, after some hesitation, he resumed, 'My dear friend, I want to say one more thing but I am scared that it may hurt your fragile heart.'

'My friend, this heart is no longer fragile; it has become used to enduring the most terrible of misfortunes. So tell me freely whatever you wish to say.'

'My friend, my great-grandfather remembered his city very dearly. He went about with the picture of the scented gardens and squares of Cordoba in his eyes, and cried constantly. So much so that he died one day. His son, that is my ancestor's ancestor, was a man of good sense. He drew a lesson from his father's sorry

---

[98] Literally meaning 'the shining city', the Madina Azahara is a vast, fortified medieval palace-city built by Abdur Rahman III (912–961), the Umayyad Caliph of Cordoba.

[99] Muhammad al-Ghalib laid the foundations of the Alhambra while further construction was made by his son, Muhammad II. Inside and around the Alhambra are inscriptions in Arabic such as 'The Kingdom is for Allah' and '*Wa la Ghalib illa Allah*' which means, 'There is no Conqueror (Victor) except Allah.' King Abu Abdullah (Boabdil) was known as 'Al-Ghalib' (The Conqueror). Yet, when recognizing his imminent defeat, he exclaimed otherwise proclaiming that none other than God was the Greatest. Hence, 'There is no Conqueror except God,' became the motto of his descendants.

state; one day he called his son and grandson and said, "My son and my son's son, you saw what sorrow for Cordoba did to your grandfather and how he left this world in a sorry state. Understand this: the sorrow of being separated from your city is deadlier than the sorrow of being separated from a woman. Whoever is afflicted by this sorrow, you can rest assured he is for all practical purposes dead and gone. And so my sons, surely we belong to the soil of Cordoba, but what is gone is gone. So bid farewell to that city or else its memory will eat you up like termites. Now, Granada is our Cordoba." And so, my friend, I will say to you what my ancestor said to his son and to his son's son.'

Ibn-e Habib heard these words and wept, 'My friend and counselor, the memory of Seville is leaving me on its own. What shall I tell you about the new incident that has befallen me? I knew the way to my ancestral house in Seville but God knows what has happened to me that I have forgotten the way now.'

Abdullah was surprised, 'What are you saying, my friend? When did you go to Seville that you would remember any of the ways in that land?'

Ibn-e Habib laughed a feeble laugh and said, 'Believe me, my friend. In my dreams, I have walked so often in that deserted place that I remember each and every pathway, but last night I had a strange dream. In my dream, I have gone to Seville and I am lost in a maze of streets. I am surprised: Ya Allah, which is that street where, the moment I enter, I see that tall and stately date palm and my feet would swiftly move in the direction of that house? The cat would spot me from a distance and run towards me. Dear Lord, where did that date palm disappear, what happened to the cat, and where did the house go? I am walking along, lost and wandering, when I see that up ahead the road is closed. Ya Allah, where should I go now? I had never ever thought that there would be a blind alley in the maze of alleys in Seville. I was wondering what to do and where to go when I woke up.' Ibn-e- Habib fell silent and then after a moment's hesitation, continued, 'I couldn't sleep thereafter. Perhaps it was the last watch of the night, for soon I heard the sound of the *azaan*. I got up and performed the ablutions, offered my prayer and then raised my hands, wept and cried a hundred times, 'Keep me safe from that day when I go to Seville and my land hesitates to recognize me and my streets decline to show me the way.' I cried so much that I went into a frenzy.' Ibn-e Habib fell silent. His eyes were moist and his voice choked.

Abdullah, who had been listening quietly all this while, spoke after careful consideration, 'O Ibn-e Habib, I understand your pain. In a way, I consider you fortunate because you are rich with the wealth of the pain of separation. I am the unfortunate one who has forgotten Cordoba and is happily sitting in Granada and there are so many homeless ones like me who have made their way to this city. Granada gave them refuge, honour, wealth but regrettably, it took away the wealth of pain from them. So, Ibn-e Habib, compared to them you are fortunate because Granada gave you refuge but did not snatch the wealth of pain from you.' After a pause, Abdullah continued, 'But it is the way of the world and such is the Constitution of Life. And it is out of respect for this Constitution that my forefather told his son and his son's son to stay away from the behaviour of my ancestor. The son took heed of the father's advice and began to think of Granada as Cordoba and kept getting mingled with its soil and air. My friend, this is the interpretation of your dream. Whether this is a sign from the Unseen or your mind has told you so, it is best that you understand this sign and recognize the demands of life.'

Ibn-e Habib heard this and ducked his head; for a long time, he remained engrossed in his thoughts. Then he raised his head and said, 'O my friend and sharer of my sorrow, your advice is sound. But you have not told me what I should do with the wealth of my memories, a wealth that is my sole heritage. If only there was a grave where I could bury them! O Abdullah, it is strange that when I had first entered this city of yours I was scattered and so were my memories. How well I remember that evening when I sat beside your warm oven and ate hot bread for the first time since entering this city! I don't know what sort of grain that bread was made from, for its taste is still alive on my tongue. I am grateful to that roof under which I sat and the oven from where I drew warmth and gathered my scattered being as well as my scattered memories. And the strange thing is that the more I began to feel settled in this city, the stronger these memories became, so much so that an entire country of memories was formed, a country that lives in my imagination and is attached to Granada. And right in the middle of this country stands a palm tree laden with bunches of dates, and under it sits a black cat. Now these are twin cities but ...' Ibn-e Habib paused and then said, 'The one thing I cannot understand is ...' And Ibn-e Habib fell silent.

'O Ibn-e Habib, why have you stopped? Tell me, what is worrying you?'

Ibn-e Habib hesitated, then said, 'O Abdullah, the very thought makes me worried that this city of yours was a very kind city. I swear upon Him who nurtured me, I found it more large-hearted than the ocean; so, why has it now begun to scare me?'

Abdullah gaped at Ibn-e Habib. Then he spoke in an anxious tone, 'My friend, after all, what did you see that has so scared you?'

'My friend, it is precisely this that is troubling me most: in real terms, I have seen nothing clearly, yet there is a fear swirling inside me and outside. Sometimes I get terribly scared. I don't know if this is a mere doubt on my part or ...

'Or ... what? Whatever your doubts may be, my friend, tell me without hesitation.'

'My dear, I would tell you if it were clear to me. Something like a suspicion is growing inside me. Sometimes it seems to me, as dusk falls or late at night when a bird flutters close beside me or rushes past me with a rustle of its wings, that rustle seems ill-omened and a ripple of fear courses through me.'

The door opens with a bang. A stretcher appears and Majju Bhai is issuing urgent instructions to the attendants as well as the nurses and others who have entered the room with him. The instructions seem to be about showing utmost care for me. And I seem as though I have scattered into bits; I couldn't care less. Let Majju Bhai take care of what he knows best, I thought to myself. Once again, I began to collect myself. So, it is about those days, those times when the heydays of Granada had passed and …

'Careful, my dear fellow!' Majju Bhai was saying. 'Which floor is the operation theatre on?' Now this subject, now another … Majju Bhai was going on talking whereas possibly the attendants were in a hurry to pick me up, take me away and reach me to the operation theatre. I was anxious – not because I was in any physical discomfort, but because my train of thought had scattered. Naturally, this caused me no small measure of agitation. I was angry because I was stopped just as I was about to reach the real issue; I was a mere hair's breadth away. Since I had remembered so much, if only I could have recalled the little that was left then I would have known … What would I have known? I fell in doubt. What was the issue? Why was I scraping my mind? If I remembered that incident would the rest of the things also … Rafiq sahab had also said something to this effect. Actually, at that point, I couldn't focus my thoughts; I was lying on the stretcher. I felt as though I was sitting on a bullock-cart and the bullocks were speeding along. When will we reach the operation theatre, how far is it, which floor is it on? I felt I was entering a tunnel, as though the bullock-cart was going through a blind tunnel and the tunnel is showing no signs of coming to an end. 'Why is this train crawling?' a voice asks in the darkness. 'Thank your stars at least it is moving,' says another voice. 'The last special was slaughtered right here; if only we could get away from here …' 'Then they should move the train very fast from here; why is it crawling like an ant?' Indeed, the train is crawling and it feels as though I am lying on a stretcher …

Eighteen

So I am alive! I feel surprise and such disbelief! From somewhere far away that sweet sound kept coming. It kept making constant assaults on my disbelief. The sound of a koel is like a magical spell. While the koel herself is a bird like any other bird, and not an especially beautiful bird either; as black as the crow, its voice is all there is to it. But where is this voice coming from? For a long time, I failed to understand that somewhere close or far, there must be a tree and the koel must be sitting hidden among its branches. It seemed as though the sound was coming from some land of dreams. That is why I couldn't fully believe that this was me – complete with my living self as well as my full senses and hearing power. I was nearly half-asleep when it seemed as though somewhere very close, almost at my headstand, a bird was singing loudly. I opened my eyes immediately, turned on my side and looked towards the head of my bed. For the first time, I realized that a lush green tree stood on the other side of the glass window. The bird was calling out from somewhere within it. It was joined by the chirping of scores of other birds. So it is morning. And I am alive or have come to life. A wave of happiness rippled through me with the speed of lightning. With happiness mingled with amazement, I craned to look at that tree as far as I could as I lay on my bed and peered through the window. My anxious eyes were searching for that bird among the branches, which had pulled me out of my half-sleeping half-waking state and announced the good news of my being alive. But I couldn't see it. Though, after a minute or two, I heard the sound of fluttering wings and the chirruping stopped. Perhaps it didn't care for my curiosity. Anyhow, it had done its duty and now it had no further chore here; so it flew away.

The door opened and a fair face appeared; the fair face came with a white gown. Light spread in the room for, indeed, it was morning. The thermometer clasped between those fingers looked so good. With a flick of the wrist, it was inserted in my mouth. Then, after a few minutes, it was pulled out and examined, the findings were jotted down in the chart kept at my headboard and she left the room as silently as she had entered. Anyhow, the atmosphere in the room had certainly changed by now as though a wave of freshness had coursed through it and so much light had spread all around. The haziness had dissolved and the morning looked brighter. Till yesterday, I did not know whether it was night or day, morning or evening. I had been breathing intermittently in a half-dark, pain-filled space. At some point, I went through the operation but that had been a time of unconsciousness. It was only now that I had regained consciousness. So this morning had come after a long night. And what a morning it was! Such a luminous morning had dawned for me after a very long time, and it was so fresh and peaceful too! Instinctively, I remembered the mornings from those days when I was still Munnan. One saw such luminous mornings only during those days. Every morning it seemed as though the earth had been born just then and the sky was freshly manifested. How pure the air felt and how invigorated the trees looked! And the birds ... best not to ask about them for they chirruped all day long and sometimes set up a real din. Why did they do that? Possibly just for fun! But in the mornings they became so volatile, it seemed as though someone had given them a dose of mercury. The tail of the shama thrush wagged up and down furiously. And the cooing of the wild pigeons filled the air with a soft, low echo. And the parrots were known to create a racket but when they descended on the neem in our *haveli*, they became quiet; no one coud ever tell that the parrots were perched on the top-most boughs and amongst the green foliage. It was only when they flew away in a swirl that one realized that the neem looked so dense and so green because of the parrots. The branches began to look so bare as soon as the parrots flew away and also so much less verdant. Who knows what made an entire flock of parrots swoop down on the tree and what made them fly away equally suddenly to trace a long green higgledy-piggledy line in the sky. It seems as though the mornings were created only for the parrots, mynahs, sparrows and crows; men were content to benefit from whatever was left of the morning. They are the ones who got up first, they are the ones who used it first, they are the ones who were unhesitatingly exuberant and whatever was left came into the use of those human beings who woke up in the mornings. And it wasn't just the mornings; both mornings and evenings were special times for the birds. It was as though evenings came especially for them and morning dawned only for them. As soon as the sun began to set, a tumult broke out among the birds – the crows became restless and the roller birds began to strut, anxiously craning their blue necks and looking hither and thither and calling out in their fear-filled voices.

I had wandered off in those mornings of long ago. Those mornings had disappeared. Yet I was feeling that this morning was a morning from that same caravan of mornings, one that had wandered off and come here today by mistake. In fact, the next morning seemed to be from the same sequence, except for the fact that the first morning was in the hospital and the next in my own home. Once assured that my life had been saved, Majju Bhai was not in favour of keeping me in the hospital for very long. The operation was over and the doctors had expressed satisfaction over my condition. There was no reason to leave me in the hospital now. He spent the entire day running around, meeting doctors, collecting reports and by the evening, he had taken me out of the hospital and brought me home. I too breathed a sigh of relief on reaching home. No matter how well attended one is in the hospital, a home is after all a home.

Majju Bhai too breathed a sigh of relief upon reaching home. He constantly looked tense and worried in the hospital. Even when the doctors announced that my condition was now satisfactory, there was only a nominal decrease in his anxiety. But the moment he set foot inside the house, it was as though all his worries were left on the other side of the threshold. He suddenly looked so much at ease as though he was finally assured that I was well and truly safe.

'Jawad Miyan, believe me you have come back from Allah Miyan's house.'

'Hmm,' I spoke softly in an assenting tone and stayed quiet.

'It was a very doubtful situation. The doctors were not too optimistic. I tried asking everyone but no doctor gave a clear answer. They kept saying they would know after the operation. It was a tricky operation. The bullet went and hit such a spot! Do you know what I was thinking?'

'What?'

'That I would be left all alone, yaar.'

'Alone,' I smiled. 'There are rows upon rows of your friends, acquaintances and admirers.'

'Yes, that is true. But yaar … anyhow you won't understand it.'

I could well understand this for myself. For, after all, Majju Bhai was all I had. And the other good people from respectable families that I knew were also thanks to Majju Bhai. But was I equally indispensible for Majju Bhai? I could never have imagined this before. I always thought I was one among a horde of his friends, the only difference being that we lived together.

'Anyhow, God has been merciful. Allah Miyan decided to have pity on me. I think Allah Miyan has been kind to me for the first time in my life.' Majju Bhai said this and laughed. And then suddenly his mood changed. '*Lahoulwillaquwwat* … The doctor had given stern instructions that you must rest as much as possible, and that you mustn't speak too much. And others mustn't speak too much either so that the patient may rest. So we can talk about all this later; you must rest now.' And he called out for Nemat Khan. 'O Miyan Nemat Khan!'

Nemat Khan came rushing out of the kitchen, 'Coming, sahab.'

'Yaar, couldn't you have cleaned the room a little? Shouldn't you have dusted and cleared his bed at least?'

'I have done everything; just get him to lie down on the bed.'

'All right, I'll do that. But keep a table beside his bed. And don't we have a flower vase? I should have thought of buying some flowers on the way home. And, look here, make some khichdi for Jawad Miyan.'

And he said several such things in one breath, and went on speaking. Soon, he supported me and made me lie down; then he cast one glance at the room and set about cleaning it up. In no time, Nemat Khan appeared with the khichdi; I ate it under Majju Bhai's supervision. Immediately thereafter Majju Bhai made me eat and drink several medicines. Then he instructed me, 'Now go to sleep.'

Perhaps there was a sleeping pill in those medicines, for I went to sleep so quickly. Or perhaps it was because tonight I was sleeping in my own house. It felt as though I had returned home, broken and bruised, after an age. My room, its doors and windows, my bed – how contented I felt! Soon my eyes began to droop. No matter how much one spends one's life in the comfort of silk and velvet, soft and warm beds outside one's home, nothing can match the satisfaction of sleeping in one's own bed. So I slept soon enough and that too such a deep sleep that I woke up only the next morning. Though, yes, I did get up rather early. The *muezzin* had just about cleared his throat on the loud speaker when I woke up, and woke up with such a start that I could not go back to sleep. For a long time, I lay there with my eyes closed hoping that sleep may return. After all, what could I do so early? It was still very dark. There wasn't a glimmer of light. Anyhow, I didn't have to wait for very long. The dense blackness kept dissipating. And the birds too began to speak up. That day I realized there were so many birds around our house. It seemed as though there were hordes of birds somewhere nearby that had woken up suddenly and begun to clamour simultaneously. And, yes, the sound of the koel too could be heard from somewhere far away. It was faint, but it could be heard. I was happy to know that it could be heard in our house, and that in this city, this sound was not limited to a season. Out there, it was only heard in the summer months. The moment the last of the rains were over, the koel's sound disappeared. Phuphi Amma used to say that the koel had gone back to the mountains. According to her, the koel was a native of the mountains; it came down to our groves when the mango flowers bloomed and there she cooed from the beginning of summer till the end of the rains. She would bid farewell to the rains with a last coo and go back to the mountains. But in this city, one felt that the koel did not come from anywhere, nor did it go away anywhere. And so its cooing could be heard in any season.

I slowly turned from my right to left side and then from the left to right side. But nothing brought relief. I had completed my cycle of sleep and now it was tiresome to lie in bed. I sat up and glanced towards Majju Bhai's bed; he was sleeping dead to the world. I finally gathered my courage and slowly got out of bed. Walking cautiously, I went to stand in the balcony. I couldn't tell in the room, but here I saw there was enough light. A hazy whiteness had spread in all directions. At the crossroad in the distance, I couldn't see anyone about – neither people nor transport. Though I did see a dog flirting with a bitch, and the bitch too was being coquettish. But soon enough, the sweepers appeared on the scene and interrupted their little romance. And then another dog appeared from somewhere ... yet another obstacle! Soon the dog and the bitch gave up and went away.

The street light that was planted in the middle of the platform on the crossroad was switched off now. The shops were still closed, though the tea shop that was clearly visible from our balcony had opened. A fire had been lit though no customers had shown up yet; the shopkeeper could be seen pottering around.

Suddenly a car appeared from one direction and, with its horn blaring, disappeared at the other end. And that was enough to make me realize that scores of rickshaws, taxis, buses and cars must have appeared on the distant roads and must be racing about noisily.

Nemat Khan came with a chair. 'Sahab, you will get tired standing; you shouldn't tire yourself out. Please sit down on this chair.'

I sat down. My eyes were still trained on the crossroad in the distance. The crossroad was no longer quiet and empty; I could see people moving around. A short while ago, a bus had come to a halt at the bus station on the right side of the street light, picked up the passenger who had come to stand there a short while ago, and sped away. Several people could be seen standing at that stop now. A rickshaw came from somewhere and stopped; a man jumped and sat down in it. The rickshaw started with a loud noise and went off raucously in the direction of the main road.

School-going children, college-going girls, men going to offices – all kinds of people were coming out of the streets and alleys. Some were standing at the bus stand waiting for a bus, others in search of a rickshaw and, yes, the boys and girls going to school and the young women going to college were waiting for their vans; all of them were looking fresh and radiant in their school and college uniforms.

So now the morning was at its peak. And I was both surprised and happy that a morning could be so pleasant and so fresh even in these bad times, as though nothing had happened to the city and it was still the same living city of those good old days with the same lively mornings. So this meant that the mornings of this city were still alive and well and that they were dawning and ending like all other mornings till now. This is a good sign, I thought. Birds still break out into song at the crack of dawn in this city, girls in sparkling white uniforms still go to their colleges crammed into their vans and children with their satchels slung around their necks can still be seen going to their schools. And so many others can be seen on foot or crammed into buses, wagons and rickshaws. Surely one can then expect this city to regain its health. Or perhaps like I had survived a prolonged struggle between life and death and endured much pain to stand here happily, this city too had endured its torment and made a full recovery. Anyhow, even if it wasn't so, I thought at least there was no threat to the purity of its mornings. The other parts of the day and night may be in any state, one must save the mornings. A pleasant morning is the last saving grace of a drowning city. When even the mornings have drowned, then ...

'Yaar, what are you doing sitting here?' Majju Bhai came and stood right beside me. 'I thought you were in the bathroom. I was surprised and worried that you were taking so long in the bathroom. What happened? Come on ... get up, wash up and eat your breakfast; we can't be late with the medicines.'

I had had my fill of the morning's entertainment; I got up, went to the bathroom, and washed myself slowly and carefully. Refreshed, I came to the breakfast table where Majju Bhai was already seated, waiting for me. How refreshed I felt after my encounter with the morning. By my own reckoning, I was healed. And with me, so was the city.

Majju Bhai looked at me and seemed satisfied. He asked, 'So how do you feel now?'

'I was restored by the morning. I am perfectly all right now, Majju Bhai. You can consider yourself free.'

'When was I restricted?'

'Why, your feet were bound with chains because of me!'

'Who says so?'

'I do. Have you ever stayed put in one place for so long? You had to cancel so many of your programmes and meetings.'

'What programmes and meetings do I have? If I had made a programme and lived my life according to it, I would have led my life in a totally different way.'

'I meant all those philanthropic tasks that you have taken upon yourself. Aqa Hasan's problem is far more important than mine; after all, it is about a daughter's marriage.'

Majju Bhai sighed. 'Jawad Miyan, don't even ask how I have been humiliated on that front. Though it had its silver lining!'

'What was that?'

'I have come to know the true worth of both Lucknow and Meerut. And these Meerut-walas of yours turned out to be not just Meeruti but also Kamboh, like the bitter gourd that grows on the neem tree! Hats off to them!'

'What did I tell you? Anyhow, tell me: what are they saying now?'

'The brother and sister duo are impossible to talk to and Baji Akhtari ... that woman is getting harder and tougher by the day.'

'And the Lucknow-walas?'

'First ask me how I am coping with them. At first, they were finding faults with the Meerut-walas and I was forever trying to draw a curtain over things. Now I am the one picking out these faults and they are drawing a curtain over everything. The more I bring the subject around to highlighting the fact that these people are actually Kamboh and truly they used to be knife-sharpeners, Basho Bhabhi hears me and out it goes from her other ear. Now even Aqqan sahab can see nothing but fine qualities in Tausif.'

'What will happen now?'

'What will happen is that one of these days, I am going to tell them clearly that we had laid the bait but the bird pecked at the grain and flew away.'

Meanwhile, Nemat Khan showed up. He laid out the breakfast quickly and then stood on one side. Majju Bhai looked at him closely and said, 'What is it, Nemat Khan?'

'Majju sahab-ji, I have two requests.'

'Not one but two ... All right, tell me what are the two requests.'

'The first one is that please have a small netted window opened in this door of ours.'

Majju Bhai looked meaningfully at Nemat Khan and asked, 'Fine, we'll have it made, but what good good will it do?'

'We won't be caught unawares, then. At least we will know who is coming in.'

'What does that mean?'

'Sahab-ji, you know how bad these times are. These attackers have come up with a new modus operandi. They come and ring the door bell. When you open the door, they barge in, round up everyone in the house at gunpoint and tie them up, collect everything in the house, shoot a few bullets and off they go. So, at least we will be able to see who is at the door before we open up.'

'Nemat Khan, where do you hear all this nonsense?'

'It isn't nonsense, sahab-ji. You know the Haji sahab who lived in the next alley? They came into his house like this.'

'Haji sahab is a wealthy man. Robbers had to come to his house someday through some means or the other. Nemat Khan, robbers are not fools; they know our worth. Why will they come here and waste their time?'

'Majju sahab, there is no knowing with these robbers. It isn't always necessary that they come to rob a house. Sometimes they don't rob. Sometimes they come, make the victim recite the *kalma*, shoot and go off. That has happened several times too ... And I have a second request too.'

'What is it?'

'Please correct my *kalma*.'

'So you think that if you recite the *kalma* correctly, they will spare you. Bravo, Nemat Khan, well said!'

'Let them not spare me. In any case, life and death is in the hands of Allah. But a man's *kalma* should be correct. We all must go, but at least we should go with the correct *kalma* on our lips.'

'Nemat Khan, talk sense. People come and tell you all kinds of nonsense and you believe everything.'

'No, sir, that isn't true. You have been in the hospital for the past several nights. Ask me: I was all alone and several times I felt that someone was at the door; in fact, someone even rang the doorbell. But I am not a fool. I lay quietly; I didn't so much as breathe, let alone open the door.'

Nemat Khan was prattling on and I was looking at his face. How scared he looked. My own beaming freshness was also gone. How pleasantly the morning had dawned – both outside and inside me. And how quickly it was sinking.

Nineteen

'Majju Bhai,' I hesitated, but then finally I asked, 'did the bullet actually come out?'

'What do you mean?' Majju Bhai stared at me. 'Do you think the bullet is still sitting somewhere inside you? That's a really stupid thing to say!'

'I was only asking for my own reassurance.'

'My dear fellow, what was the operation for? It was to take it out.'

'Okay; all right.'

'What do you mean by "all right"? It seems that you are still not convinced. Shall I write it on a piece of paper and give it to you? Or shall I get it written by the doctors?'

'No, Majju Bhai, I didn't mean that.'

'What did you mean, then?'

'I was thinking that if the bullet has come out, what is it that is constantly throbbing inside me?'

'You will have that sensation for some time; after all, it was a bullet and not a seed of sesame. You must rest. You will be fine. In a few days, you won't even realize that you were hit … provided you rest! That too, complete rest! The doctor has given strict instructions that you must not go to the office or go out.'

'I am resting; it isn't as though I am fond of going out. You are the one who used to take me around. As far as office is concerned, I have taken leave from there.'

'Yes, just rest.'

'That is the strange part: I *am* resting, yet there is something that is throbbing inside me, as though the bullet penetrated deep inside me.'

'Do you know what is throbbing?'

'What?'

'Your brain.'

'Brain?'

'Yes, it is your brain that is throbbing away. My dear fellow, even the brain needs rest. If you don't let it rest, it will keep troubling you. Rather, it *is* troubling you. At least in your present state, you should have abstained from thinking. But even when you were lying unconscious, you were not desisting from this bad habit.'

'Majju Bhai, was I in any condition to think then? My brain was as helpless as my body. Idle thoughts and memories had made an assault on my poor brain.'

'Do you know what you were mumbling in your unconscious state? It was as though all the deserted cities of the world had entered your mind and were creating a ruckus.'

'Really? What was I muttering? I don't rememember anything.'

'Yes, you don't remember it now; at that time, you remembered a lot; in fact, all sorts of things from long ago. Yes, I remember now. In the course of your rambling, you said, "Yes, Majju Bhai, I now remember the thing that I had forgotten from the middle. That thing was ..." But the doctor's instructions were that you mustn't be allowed to talk too much and so I stopped you. I told you to sleep and say it some other time.' Majju Bhai laughed, 'So tell me now, what was that thing?'

'Is that what I said?' I fell into deep thought. I was also a bit worried in case I had said something inappropriate again. Majju Bhai tends to latch on to certain things. I tried my best to remember but I couldn't think of what it was that I had remembered and wanted to tell Majju Bhai. "Majju Bhai, at that time I could remember all sorts of things but now ...'

'That's all right; you can recall it some other time and tell me. Don't put any sort of burden on your mind now,' Majju Bhai said and called out to Nemat Khan. Nemat Khan came running.

'Look here, Nemat Khan, I am going out for a while. You take care of Jawad Miyan; give him some broth after some time. And for lunch, give him only gravy and the top half of a roti.' Then he addressed me, 'Yaar, this Ghazi sahab is well and truly stuck to me. I had said a few perfunctory words of praise, simply as a courtesy, and he seems to think I have also become a disciple like Baji Akhtari and Tausif. He is about to deliver an important sermon and he is very insistent that I go and hear him.'

Startled, I looked at Majju Bhai, 'You are going to hear Ghazi sahab?'

'What can I do? He is so insistent. One has to do these things for the sake of civility. I am going to ask Rafiq sahab to be with me in my difficult time. If I will go with him it will be easy to come back early; he is adept at making quick getaways. I simply have to mark my presence; I will peep in and rush back.'

'Go, then; May Allah have mercy upon you.'

And Majju Bhai left with a few more words of apology. The fact was that Majju Bhai was fond of being out and about. My condition had chained him for a bit; all during my hospital stay, he had remained by my side. And now that I had been freed from the hospital, he too had, in a way, been liberated. So he had to leave the house for one reason or another. He couldn't be expected to sit with me in the house as though he was imprisoned. After all, Nemat Khan was there to look after me. He had no reason to worry. And I too sighed with relief after he left. He was constantly in the way of this new series that had begun: of meeting myself. These meetings demanded solitude, and solitude was something I wasn't getting. In fact, a new thought occurred to me. I had emerged unscathed from the tussle between life and defeat. My life was obviously stuck somewhere, for it refused to leave my body despite all odds. I was fine now. But that pleasant feeling that I had regained full health went away after only two mornings.

I had got up feeling fresh and happy on the second morning since coming back home. I felt as though I was as healthy as before, or perhaps healthier. But the feeling vanished with the morning. I couldn't understand why this feeling perished. Earlier, I couldn't understand why I was feeling cured so quickly. Perhaps Nemat Khan had a role to play in the decline of that pleasant state of mind that had arisen from the sense of physical well being. At the first opportunity and – as always – behind Majju Bhai's back, he had narrated all the recent alarming news and gossip. With the decline of that bright morning, I began to sense the decline of the morning inside me. As though my old state of mind was returning, as though I was flowing along the same track as before. But soon I became alert. I thought I mustn't let myself flow along in the same way, on that same path as before, lest I am swept away completely. Gather yourself, get a grip on yourself, find the strength to defend yourself, and build a dam to keep out scattered, distracted thoughts and vagrant memories. So solitude was truly a necessity right now. Majju Bhai had tossed a new ember; he thought he had done his duty by telling me not to burden my mind, and that I should tell him about that incident when I remembered it. But I was steeped in anxiety. Had I really given away something to Majju Bhai when I was in that state? Or had I given him the impression that I was about to spit out something, but didn't? I checked myself: What did I have to give away? Perhaps this was some ploy of Majju Bhai's. Be that as it may, I had to search myself to make sure if I had, indeed, remembered something when I was in that state and had I really said so in front of Majju Bhai. And so solitude was essential to do all this and search myself. But I wasn't fated to get it. Majju Bhai had barely left when Mirza sahab showed up.

'Arre Bhai, why have you gotten yourself in this state?'

'Come, Mirza sahab,' I tried to sit up in bed.

'No, no, you must lie down. I had just peeped in to check on you. I had met Rafiq sahab; he told me. I was stunned. I went home and told my wife and she too was shocked. She has been after me all morning to come and see how you are. So tell me: how are you?'

'I am fine now.'

'Thank God for that. You life has been saved. You must rest

now. Insha Allah, you will be fully recovered in a few days. But how did this happen?'

By now I had remembered everything, that is, I had come out of that stage when I could remember all sorts of other things but not this recent occurrence, and even when I could recall this incident, it was as though it had happened centuries ago. But now I could narrate the incident in every detail. But my health was still not permitting me to speak for very long. Then there was also the feeling that why go over that incident again and again? Anyhow, Mirza sahab had only made a token enquiry. And after some customary small talk, he launched upon his own lament: 'This city has no place for people like us. How do we find the courage to see what is happening around us? Miyan, I want to die now. No one believes me; they seem to think I have lost it in my old age. No, Miyan, no … I am saying this in my full senses. I am ready to go in any case; I have lived to a full old age. How much longer do I need to live? I have seen enough of the world. Given the present state of the world, I no longer have the strength to see anymore. So, Miyan, I truly want to die now.'

'What a thing to say, Mirza sahab!' I remarked casually.

'So, you don't believe me either. No, Miyan, really; I am telling the truth. But death is not in my control. There was one such person who saw that the world was not meant for living in any longer and he announced that he was going; and he went away. He put his head on the pillow and closed his eyes. His disciples thought he was sleeping; they didn't know that he was sleeping the eternal sleep. Subhan Allah, what a willing death! And look at me! I live in the street of death, yet I do not die. Believe me, these sinning eyes of mine see a couple of people die every single day, but no bullet comes my way. What happens is that the moment I step out of my house, my neighbours tell me that the firing has stopped a moment ago, and when I go out and return home, I hear that the firing has resumed. Now hear what happened yesterday: I usually go to the mosque to offer my prayers. Yesterday, I happened to miss my *maghrib* prayer, and yesterday itself a bomb went off in that mosque. Look at my deprivation; had I gone to the mosque, I would have gained the death of a martyr. But how could I have gained it? It was not acceptable to Nature. I don't know how my death is foretold. O You who sustain, take me away with dignity.'

I listened in silence. I didn't at all feel like speaking. Still, in an attempt to keep up his spirits, I said, 'But Mirza sahab, why are you so disenchanted with life?'

'Yes, Miyan, you are right; life is a God-given gift. Live what has been granted to you with patience and gratitude. You have to live it – whether you are happy or unhappy. But Miyan, where should I take my thoughts and fears? After all, why is Nature keeping me alive? What else is left to show me?' And then after a pause, he continued, 'My Delhi is called 'the Threshold of 22 Sufis', yet it has been devastated seven times and resettled seven times. Our ancestors had witnessed the sixth devastation and I witnessed the seventh one. Yes, we saw it and suffered it. I had heard from my mother's mother that at the time of the Revolt, you couldn't see a lit lamp in Delhi till as far away as 12 *kos*, and Delhi was a city without lamps. You just saw cats and dogs on the streets, not a human face in sight! I used to hear this and be surprised; in 1947, I saw it with my own eyes. I had left my mohalla perfectly intact and stepped out till Chandni Chowk. I passed the Jama Masjid; the market around it was full of people. Its stairs were crowded as always though there was a slight tumult. I paid no heed to it at the time. I had barely set foot in Chandni Chowk when a stampede broke out. I asked people around me what was happening, but no one told me anything. Anyhow, I retraced my steps back home. As I went past the Jama Masjid, Miyan, believe me, it was completedly deserted – with neither shopkeepers nor buyers, neither *imam* nor those offering the *namaz*. Though, yes, on the topmost step, a cage had got left behind; in the cage was a partridge that was flapping wildly and creating a din. I felt sorry for it but under those circumstances, it was foolhardy to stop and release it. I moved on. But I couldn't help myself. I returned, leapt up the stairs and opened the window of the cage. The partridge rushed out and flew away.

Quickly I came down and hurried home. I had barely set foot in my neighbourhood when I realized that it was in tumult. People were running out of their homes. I tried asking each one of them but who had the time to answer? A good neighbour said as he ran, "Mirza sahab, there is going to be an attack. Just leave this place." I somehow reached my house and told my family, "Come, let us go; it is time for us to leave Delhi. We can't live here anymore." My wife said, "After all, which calamity has struck? We have been living here for generations. We are not vagrants that we can get up, dust our clothes off and get ready to leave." I said, "Of course, calamity is upon us and within a matter of minutes, the water has risen above our heads." And my wife dug her heels in while I kept shouting and asking her to hurry up.' Mirza sahab paused and then said, 'So, Miyan, I have seen that day; may God never show such a day even to one's worst enemy. But we saw it and we suffered.'

'You are absolutely right; it was just such a time.'

And do you know the first complaint my wife made when she came to Karachi? She said, "Ai hai, there is no Jamuna river here!" And I said, "My dear, there is the sea here." She replied, "This wretched sea fills my heart with terror."' And after a pause he continued, 'But you know, gradually we learnt to live in this city beside the sea. You must be thinking that I am digging up old corpses, and you would be absolutely right. Why, we had buried the corpse and thrown tonnes of dirt over it. We had forgotten everything and settled down here. But, God knows why, those things are coming back as though they had happened just the other day.'

Mirza sahab fell silent. For a long time, he sat silently. I too remained quiet. Then he spoke in a sad tone, 'Jawad Miyan, this isn't only about the present times. The Muslims have never done good to themselves. When the hurt becomes unbearable, I tell myself: "Mirza Dilawar Baig, what are you complaining about? Just think of all that has been happening in your history. The fact is, Jawad Miyan, we have been stung by our own history. We are not scared of anyone; we are only scared of our own history.' He was quiet for a moment and then he began to mutter, 'We had our Maulana Hali.[100] May Allah have mercy on him! What a *Mussadas* he wrote. My father used to read it and weep … "Go and see the ruins of Cordoba …" And at that point, he would begin to cry uncontrollably. And he would say, "Why go there to see the ruins? Is there any shortage of things here to learn a lesson from? If only someone were to see. These wretched people are blind to the world around them."' He stopped then said, 'Not that I am saying don't see there; of course, you must look there as well. That too is our history. And what an awe-inspiring history it is with its admonitions and lessons!' And after a long deep sigh, 'Jawad Miyan, if only someone were to derive a lesson. I tell you the Andalusians were a very unfortunate people. What an edifice they constructed and, with their own hands, they brought it down!'

Mirza sahab was in full flow and I was reminded of those years when I used to be his sole and constant audience. Gods knows what he saw in me for, from his entire staff, he had chosen me. He knew that page of history by heart. The sorrow of leaving Delhi was still fresh. He would describe the past glory of Delhi with such ardour and such exquisite anguish. And one way or another, the references to Cordoba and Granada would also come in and, with those references, he would inevitably jump and reach Andalusia. However, when that pain lessened, the references too gradually disappeared. Or perhaps they still appeared; it was just that I didn't meet him as often. Since leaving that office, I met him only infrequently. And suddenly it occurred to me that perhaps I was influenced by him. It was odd! At least, Majju Bhai should have noticed it. No, I instantly put a stop to my misgivings. It is true

---

[100] Altaf Husain Hali (1837–1914), inspired largely by the reformist ideals of his mentor, Sir Syed Ahmad Khan, wrote an epic poem called *Musaddas: Madd-o-Jazr-e Islam* (The Ebb and Flow of Islam). See Shackle and Majeed (Eds), *Hali's Musaddas: the Ebb and Flow of Islam*, Oxford University Press, New Delhi, 1997. Making explicit the hortatory character of his poem, Hali wrote in the introduction to his *Musaddas*: 'This poem has not … been composed in order to be enjoyed or with the aim of eliciting applause, but in order to make my friends and fellows feel a sense of outrage and shame.'

that I would give a patient hearing to his lyrical musings but I was in no way influenced by any of it. I used to hear him as I heard my grandfather. But then I always heard my grandfather's ramblings with great interest …

'Dear Brother Bande Ali, I am saddened to read about the history of Andalusia. It holds so many admonitions and lessons.'

'You are absolutely right.'

'But Brother Bande Ali, that age had a lot of miracles but the unfortunate still did not come to their senses. One incident in particular was truly remarkable.'

Bande Ali drew a long puff of the huqqah and looked closely at Dada Miyan. 'What was that?'

'It is said that when the books of the Muslims were being burnt …'

'Books were also burnt? But what was their fault?'

'Was it not enough that they were written by Muslims? Ten lakh books were piled at the Bab-ur Mila and set on fire. It is said that a copy of the Holy Quran was also among them.'

'The Holy Quran was also burnt?' Bande Ali's eyes opened wide with disbelief. A quiver ran through his body.

'Listen, Brother, when all the books were burnt, people were surprised to see one book shining brightly among the pile of ash. It didn't have so much as a mark on it. When they opened it, they saw it was the Quran.'

'Subhan Allah! Subhan Allah!' Tears rained down from Bande Ali's eyes.

And I was reminded that if Mirza sahab had lived during my grandfather's time, they would have got along very well. He too would have been seen sitting beside Bande Ali and reciting 'Subhan Allah! Subhan Allah!' Anyhow, after an age, I had seen the same reference in his conversation. After an age, too, I had seen him speaking in his typically emotionally-charged way. He was alone for a change today. He was hardly able to hold his own in front of Achchi Bi. Today that Achchi Bi was not around, the field was clear for him. Moreover, Majju Bhai wasn't there either; only I was there. He must have found such a quiet listener after an eternity. He was showing no signs of getting up. In fact, he had just about reached his real topic. The ancient history of the Muslims – that was his favourite topic. He knew so many pages of this history by heart. My fear was that any minute now he would begin to recite the *Mussadas*. I remember the last time when the subject of the *Mussadas* was raised and how he had gone on. He remembered so many paragraphs by heart. Anyhow, it so happened that every now and then, my eyes would droop. This probably made him realize that I was not listening attentively to him, or perhaps he realized that he had put too heavy a burden on a patient. Who can tell? Anyhow it was his decency and civility that after such a realization – whatever that realization may have been – he got up immediately. 'Well, my dear, I have wasted far too much of your time. You rest now; I will take your leave.'

'Oh no, Mirza sahab won't you stay? You have come after such a long time.'

'No, no, my dear. I had only come to enquire after your well being. She was nagging me to go and find out and I was also worried; so I came. One shouldn't trouble the patient too much. You need rest. Allah is the one who gives health. And Masha Allah, you are looking healthier now.' He hesitated and then said, 'There is one thing, though. Majju Bhai is like cat on a hot tin roof; he can't sit still. He can't rest in peace till he has gone and peeped into four different houses. But is this the time to be gadding about? This is the time to hide one's face and sit at home. So my dear, whether you like it or not, my advice to you is to be a bit more careful. You must rest. And when you have recovered – and God willing you shall recover very soon – you must refrain from going out. Let the world go to blazes. God has shown great mercy: your life has been saved. Those wretches had left little to chance. For them, a Kalashnikov is any pistol; it makes no difference to them. Arre, we didn't use our sling guns with such blithe disregard! Our pellets were not just stones and pebbles; it took some time and effort to prepare our pellets. It wasn't as though the moment we saw a mynah or any bird, we would aim our slingshots. One had to think before one took a shot. Not like these people for whom human beings are like birds and parrots and their bullets are like pebbles and stones. It seems they have an itch in their hands. The moment they spot a human being, they don't stop to think. A man's life has never been so cheap. May God keep us safe from the evil hour!' And with these words, he got up.

'Arre Mirza sahab, are you really leaving?'

'Yes, my dear, you need to rest. And as far as I am concerned, if I am even a little late coming back, my wife gets very agitated. And I don't blame her. The world is such. Listen to what happened to a neighbour of ours. He comes from Lucknow, from a good Syed family. He had to go to Sadar.[101] I told him to take me along too as I needed to go to the bank. He reached a little later than the designated time. He apologized and said he got late in having the Imam Zamin[102] tied. Surprised, I asked him if he was planning to go on a long journey. He said, "No, I only have to drop you off at the bank and I have an errand in Sadar." I asked him why he needed an Imam Zamin. He replied, "Ever since the situation has deteriorated in the city, my mother insists on tying the Imam Zamin before I set foot outside my doorway and makes me walk under the Holy Quran." And I say she does well, for the world we live in is a very bad one.' Mirza sahab paused on his way out and said, 'Miyan, remember one thing, for I am older than you and I have seen more of the world than you have. The signs of our times are not good. These wretched Muslims, may Allah give them sense,

---

[101] Sadar is the central business district in Karachi.

[102] A cultural practice among some Muslims in South Asia where coins are wrapped in a piece of cloth and tied around the arm for safety and good luck during travel. Upon the successful completion of the journey, sweets would be bought and distributed as thanksgiving. There could also be embellished armbands with holy verses embroidered in zari on velvet. Both versions are called Imam Zamin. However, the Imam Zamin is usually tied before a long and perilous journey and not an outing in the city.

are bent upon repeating their history.' And with these words, he left the room hurriedly.

For a long time after Mirza sahab left, I kept lying there with my eyes closed, dead to the world. Perhaps I got tired listening to Mirza sahab's long monologue. Nemat Khan brought me some broth. I drank it and felt some warmth and energy course through my body. But I could not get out of the mood Mirza sahab had created with his words. In fact, I was feeling as though once again I was being swept away. There I was thinking that at long last I had got my much-needed solitude; now I would gather myself and build a dam on my many scattered selves that were flowing in many different directions. But Mirza sahab had created such an ambience with his words and that too not just any ambience! And even though he had made only a passing reference to the devastation of Delhi, such is the skill of master artists that they can paint an entire picture with just a few brush strokes and recreate an entire history in just a few pithy sentences. We are attracted towards what we fear the most. Miyan, we are not scared of anything; we are only scared of our history. It is strange: Achchi Bi is scared of the sea and Mirza Dilawar Baig is scared of history. Go and see the ruins of Cordoba. And what about our own ruins? The echoing Jama Masjid and its deserted stairs, empty except for that one cage lying on the top-most stair and in that cage a fluttering partridge. And for 12 *kos* all around not a human being nor the flicker of a lamp. The lampless city of Shahjahanabad. The lamp was still flickering in Granada, and Abdullah's oven was still hot, for fresh bread was still being baked in it and its moist sweet smell was spreading in the warm air. But it had not the slightest effect on Ibn-e Habib – neither the moist sweet smell nor the warmth. He sat morose. Abdullah looked closely at him and said, 'My dear friend, I can see that you are listless today. Even the bread that I have made – which makes the people of Granada lick their lips – you have eaten today as though it is stale. What should I make of your mood, my friend? Tell me why you are so distracted today?'

Ibn-e Habib hesitated and then said, 'Every day I see something in this city that makes me feel more scattered and distracted than ever and a hundred different doubts assail me. I look at the twists and turns of the world around me and I am amazed that this city of yours was once like a mother's embrace for me; now it is a sea of fear. Listen to what happened today: I was passing by the al-Qaisar when my gaze fell upon a mendicant who had appeared from somewhere and seemed not in full possession of his senses as he was reciting "There is no Conqueror except Allah" in a loud voice. He stood in the middle of the avenue, looked up at the sky and spoke as though he was making an announcement: "*Wata izzu man tashao wata zillo man tashao*".[103] And then after a moment's hesitation, he called out again, "Alas! Alas! Alas!" Hearing this, the agents and shopkeepers, shoppers and buyers, pedestrians and passengers stopped in their tracks and became motionless. An elderly man found the courage to ask, "O Ye Who Knows the Truth, why do you lament?" The mendicant looked closely at the elderly man and said, "I do not have the permission to speak anymore." And with these words, he moved on. I followed him quickly but he dived into a narrow alley and disappeared into thin air. I combed through all the alleys and streets in the neighbourhood but I couldn't find him.'

Ibn-e Habib seemed lost in thought. Then he spoke in a sorrowful voice, 'I had set out in search of one thing and I ended up searching for something else.'

Abdullah looked at Ibn-e Habib with curious eyes, 'What a strange thing to say! What had you set out in search of?'

'That which my eyes are for ever searching for.'

Abdullah's curiosity increased with this remark. 'What are your eyes forever searching for?'

Ibn-e Habib hesitated and then said, 'My dear friend, I don't want to hide things from you. I will now show you the one wound

---

[103] A verse from the Surah al-Imran of the Quran, it is often quoted by the faithful; it means Allah honours those He is pleased with and disgraces those He is not happy with.

I have hidden from the world. That moon-faced beauty, whose name is Kulsum, is enshrined in the hidden chamber of my heart. These yearning eyes of mine are forever searching for her.'

'Kulsum? Which Kulsum? Tell me in which street of this beautiful city does she live? Tell me her whereabouts so I may help you in your quest.'

Ibn-e Habib drew a long sigh and said, 'If only she were in this city! That moon had risen from the soil of Malaqah. I was deeply, passionately in love with her. Yearning for one glimpse of her, I would spend the entire day roaming around her alley. And when I did see her, for days I would remain intoxicated with the sight of her. What a beauty she was! Heavy-hipped, big-bosomed, with hair as dark as rain-heavy clouds and a face as fair as a full moon on a cloudy night. When the harassed populace began to leave Malaqah, I lost sight of her in that tumult. In the last few days, I have felt as though she is somewhere here, in this very city. And ever since then I have been roaming around restlessly, searching for her in every street and alley.'

Abdullah heard this and said, 'No wonder I was suspicious that my friend is heart-sick and hiding something from me!'

'As always, I was going around from street to street looking for her when I saw that mendicant and followed him. From al-Qaisar, I came out into the Zina Qata al-Vari and turned towards Bab Almeria and there I stood stock-still.'

'Why?'

'I don't know but whenever I pass Bab Almeria I don't know what happens to me and I stop. Anyhow, I came out of Bab Almeria and walked till I could see the domes and parapets of the Madinat-ul Hamra. And at that very moment, I heard the rustling of a bird's wings from somewhere close beside me. And a fear came over me and I turned back.'

Ibn-e Habib fell silent. Abdullah, who had been listening quietly, remained quiet and still. After a long time, he said, 'O Ibn-e Habib, may the Almighty have mercy upon you. Listening to your fears, my own fears – which I had buried for so long –

are beginning to resurface. Listening to you, I am reminded of a legend I had heard from the people of Baghdad.'

'What was that legend?'

'My friend, legend has it that one day at the time when day and night meet, a black bird with crooked claws and bent beak appeared in the skies above Baghdad like a dense black cloud. It descended on the Caliph's palace and sat down on the top-most parapet from where it called out in a human voice, "O people of Baghdad! O people of Baghdad!" It called out thrice in this manner as though it was forewarning. And then it flew away God knows where. Its call was heard all over Baghdad. No one could understand what sort of bird this was and what its call meant. But everyone was terrified. And then what happened to Baghdad thereafter, how it was ruined – you know that well enough.'

Abdullah sighed and fell silent. For a long time, both sat silently and kept looking at the sparks flying out of the oven. For a long time, they sat lost in their thoughts till ash began to settle on the embers in the oven and the fire gradually went cold. Finally, Abdullah and Ibn-e Habib noticed this and got to their feet.

Abdullah and Ibn-e Habib had got up because the furnace had gone cold but what about the fire that was raging inside them? Its heat made them restless and they walked on and on. The night was getting drenched with dew. The streets of al-Qaisar were silent and the lights in the Grand Square were being dimmed, and so was the hustle and bustle. Abdullah and Ibn-e Habib moved on in the direction of Bab Almeria. Then passing through the Rabta al-Tuut, they moved towards Bab al-Nabuud. Ahead lay the Mosque al-Jauza. They skirted it and went past the Jauza Baths and on towards the Bab al-Vari. It seemed as though that night they would traverse the entire city of Granada. When they got tired of walking, they sat down beside the Fakh al-Vaza. 'My friend, my legs are giving way,' Abdullah said and sat down on a white alabaster bench beside a water tank as though he would collapse.

Ibn-e Habib too sat down nearby and said, 'You are right; we have taken a long walk today. My legs are numb but oddly enough, my heart is as restless as ever and sleep is miles away from my eyes.'

'Who knows which hour of the night this is, though it seems to be one of the last watches of the night,' and Abdullah cast his eyes towards the sky where the brightly-twinkling stars were spangled from here to there. 'It seems as though there are only two people awake – and restless – in Granada; all other living things are engrossed in dreams.'

'My dear Abdullah,' Ibn-e Habib spoke thoughtfully. 'Sometimes I think there is a great deal you know and understand, but for whatever reason, you have sealed your lips. Or perhaps you do not consider me worthy of your confidence.'

Upon this, Abdullah said, 'My dear friend, you have made the wrong supposition. I have nothing to tell. If there is anything I know, it is that there is a time to row your boats and there is a time to make your boats. That time is long gone when our forefathers got off at the shore, turned their backs to the sea and burnt all their boats. Now the angry sea is not behind us but ahead of us, and we have made no boats.'

Ibn-e Habib heard this and cried. 'My dear friend, I had guessed right, for indeed you know more than me. And if only I had not tried to find out what you know. The fact is that I am petrified whenever you speak up. O Abdullah, understand that I am a terrified soul. Your words have made me even more scared. Now I feel that, that bird is flying somewhere close beside us and at any moment …'

'Sahab-ji, shall I bring the food?'

'What?' I was startled as I looked at Nemat Khan.

Actually, I did not even come to know when Nemat Khan came into the room. Even earlier, he had the habit of entering a room silently; now he had become even more careful since he didn't wish to disturb me as I rested. He tiptoed into my room as though walking on eggshells. So I don't know when he entered my room and came to stand beside my bed.

'Food … Oh, so it is ready … Yes, bring it.' I had to come back from far away to answer Nemat Khan's question. But possibly I had not quite come back fully. I was eating my food but in an entirely mechanical manner where the morsel would enter my mouth and my jaws would begin to move. And once the jaws began to move, a kind of wheel began to turn inside me. The mouth was doing its job and my wandering imagination was doing its job. You could say that the carder sitting inside me was at work. It was carding away at the cotton. I was surprised because there was very little cotton but the carding had turned it into a mountain. The thing is that the same practice was continuing: all sorts of memories from all over had come and mingled with my memories. Of course, then I had been far too exhausted; I didn't have the strength to stop other memories from getting mixed up with mine. But now I was not so weak. I was much better now. I was on a liquid diet; I was eating roti with gravy.

'Sahab, you have eaten very little,' Nemat Khan looked dissatisfied with my diet.

'The fact is, sahab, your appetite has gone down. You will recover your strength only if you eat well.'

'All right, get me some water.'

Nemat Khan quickly handed me a glass of water. I drank the water and immediately slid down to lie on the bed. My eyes began to droop almost immediately. I felt sleepy and it seemed that soon I would sleep. But the carding inside me did not let me sleep. A mound of cotton was forming.

But, yes, as I was saying that at that time I could see my memories mingling with memories and incidents from the world over, yet I was far too weak to stop it. Now I was not so weak, yet the same thing was still happening. Perhaps now I was not even aware of it. Incidents from all over, anecdotes from here and there …

'My precious one, how many times are you going to hear that story?'

'Once more, Phuphi Amma!'

'All right, then, listen. Once there was a mynah. Her neighbour was a crow. The mynah had a nest but the wretched crow was homeless. The mynah would dive into her nest every day as evening fell and spend the night peacefully asleep. The poor crow would get back tired and settle down on the branch next to the mynah's nest and spend the night somehow on his perch. One day, the mynah taunted, "O Brother Crow, how long will you be homeless and roofless like this?" The crow was stung by the mynah's words. He thought, I must build a nest too, that too a nest that will make the mynah turn green with envy. And so the crow identified a grocer's shop; he would fly in repeatedly and fly out with a bit of rock salt in his beak. In this way, he collected a lot of salt and with that salt, he built a nest for himself.'

'Phuphi Amma, a nest made of salt?' How surprised Munnan was!

'Yes, my son, a nest made of salt. In summer afternoons, it would glisten as though it was made of glass and not salt. But soon the rainy season came and it poured cats and dogs. And lo and behold, that nest dissolved in the water and disappeared. Again the mynah taunted, "O Brother, you made a nest and that too with salt of all the things. Did you not know that the weather never remains the same? The rains had to come after the summer. Your nest was made of salt; of course, it had to melt." The mynah's words pierced the crow like darts. He decided to build a home with material that would not be affected by the rain and, with this in mind, he collected a lot of wax and began to build a nest. His home was washed clean in the rain and looked as though it was made of marble. Winter came after the rains and the crow spent the entire season in great comfort. But soon after came the summer and, my dear, when the sun shone brightly, all the wax melted. Once again the crow's nest collapsed, or rather melted in a puddle. The crow felt very sad. He sighed deeply and said, 'There is no nest in the fate of a crow.' And once again he began to live on a branch.

My attention wandered once again towards Queen Nageshwari. She was right; it was tragic to remember one's previous life.

Security and well-being lie in memory, going round and round in its designated gyre. Memory has it own *Lakshman rekha*. The moment you step over it, you land into trouble. Ahead lies nothing but a jungle and that too a dense, endless jungle. And a jungle full of ogres. So Queen Nageshwari was right when she cried, and indeed she cried rather a lot because her husband the King also remembered his previous life. Trouble was added to trouble. Is one life not enough to be disgraced and dishonoured? Then why a second life? And not just a second birth, for there is no end to the cycle of birth and rebirth; it is an endless series of disgrace and dishonour. Queen Nageshwari thought that when she and the King were the Swan King and his mate and lived peacefully on Lake Mansarovar, then they were happy. But how long did that happiness last? Once again, a storm had come upon them. Once again, they had been separated from each other. It took Queen Nageshwari some time to remember this. And once again she became unhappy. And look at Maimuna … she just couldn't remember when Phuphi Amma had told this story. And when she remembered she became sad. But she still couldn't remember that they had met again after being separated in the storm. 'When did they meet again? They didn't.'

'They met again,' I said and prodded her memory with several other details from the story that followed. She remembered with great difficulty. 'All right, so they may have met again,' she said as though she couldn't fully believe that they had indeed met again. Then she stayed quiet for a long time, looking extremely sad.

'The poor she-swan's plight has made you sad,' I teased her thinking she might respond.

'That's just a story,' she said, 'Actually, I was reminded of Amma.'

Now it was my turn to feel sad. I remembered Phuphi Amma all the time when I lived there, but Maimuna mentioned her in such a way that I felt her absence far more acutely at that moment. This happened before Badi Bhabhi had jumped into the picture. In fact, after that fiasco, I realized with painful certainty that had Phuphi Amma been alive that situation would never have risen. Had she been alive would Maimuna have spoken to me in that rough manner? Anyhow, this subject came up in the middle of nowhere. The topic here was the sheer number of stories Phuphi Amma had told me and especially the ones about a pair of swans. The swan and its mate would meet and separate, meet and separate yet again as though this epic of union and separation was a dastaan of eternity and successors.[104] And which country did they come from and which lake would they descend upon or the parapet of which palace would they alight upon in such a way that the princess sitting inside the palace would see them and be instantly enamoured. And sometimes they would be seen flying high in the skies – unconcerned with lakes and ponds, indifferent to settlements and forests, disinterested in palaces and mansions – as though they were swimming serenely in a clean and pure lake. And within a matter of seconds, they would disappear from sight and, after aeons, one would come to know that they were actually the king and queen of some distant land, or a prince and princess who had become a pair of swans in this life, but in the next one, they would once again have to become king and queen. At the time, I couldn't understand why all these stories about the swan and his mate were bobbing up in my memory, why I was trying my best to make Maimuna also remember these stories and why, upon every narration of the union and separation of the swan and his mate, she would become quiet and sorrowful – as though she too in a previous birth … And the thought troubling me was that I had a previous life and I … Anyhow, no wonder then that I was constantly reminded of that *sadhu* who used to say that he remembered his previous life. So many times I felt that I should look

---

[104] The original has the word '*abdali*' referring to the concept of '*abdaal*' or 'the substitutes or lieutenants' or certain righteous persons of whom the world is never destitute, and by whom God rules the earth. The substitutes and successors of the prophets shall always remain. Intizar Husain uses the iconic image of the *hans-hansni*, the swan and his mate, which have been popular in folklore as well as the *qissa-kahani* tradition, to reinforce the idea of an eternal presence of goodness and happiness, which may be threatened by 'storms' and may be separated but is destined to be reunited.

for him. Where was he? Was he alive, or dead? When did he die? After he narrated his previous life? ... He was born in a good time. Wealth showered down upon Dwarka during those days. But towns and hamlets never have the same fortune for too long. Who can tell when the shower of wealth will end and calamity will be let loose?

'O Narendra, when I looked at the sea, I saw there was nothing but serpents in the sea as though it wasn't the sea but a sea of snakes. Immediately, I turned away and moved on. I saw Baldev-ji[105] sitting in a meditative pose under a tree; his eyes were closed, but his mouth was gaping wide open like a pit. And, O friend, I saw that Baldev-ji, who was like an ox among warriors and brave men, had shrunk and become tiny. He was nothing but a handful of bones. And between those bones was his gaping mouth like a snake-hole and from that hole emerged a snake – a snake white as the ash that is rubbed on the bodies of ascetics.'

Narendra was looking at Ganesh with surprise. Then he said, 'O Ganesh, then this city is surely in peril. Only a wise man can tell us the meaning of this play. All I know is that we should go to Guru Shambhu Maharaj and ask him the meaning of all this.'

Both got to their feet instantly and reached the Guru. They touched his feet, prostrated before him and sat down with folded hands. Guru Maharaj opened his eyes after a very long time, looked at them from behind his overgrown white eyelashes and asked them why they had come.

'O Guru Maharaj, I have seen such an unlikely thing that my heart trembles in narrating it.'

'O disciple, you have seen nothing yet.'

'O Guru, if this is nothing then I have seen a great deal. I have seen the mouth of Baldev-ji turn into a snake-hole and a snake emerge from it.'

---

[105] Baldev, also known as Balram, was the elder brother of Krishan and is regarded as an incarnation of Shesha, or the King of Serpents.

Guru Maharaj closed his eyes. He opened his eyes and mumbled '*Om tat sat. Om tat sat*'. Then he looked hard at Narendra, 'O ye who live in Mathura, what are you doing here? Why don't you go?'

'Guru Maharaj, this city does not let me leave.'

'What are you saying?'

'Every morning, at the crack of dawn, I tuck my bundle under my arm and set out but as soon as I set foot outside the city limits, a roller bird sitting on the top-most branches of a peepal tree flutters its wings, flies down and crosses my path. I immediately turn back.'

Guru Maharaj was quiet. Then he said, 'O Fool, was there any shortage of sorrows in Mathura that you came all the way here to endure hardships? Go back to your hell and endure your sorrow. And let us remain in our hell and endure our hardships.'

'But Maharaj, what about that roller bird?'

'Roller bird? But where is it now? The snake has swallowed all the birds.'

'And Guru Maharaj, what about us? ... Will the snake ...' Ganesh trembled as he spoke and fell silent.

Guru Maharaj closed his eyes in response and began to mumble, '*Om tat sat. Om tat sat. Om tat sat* ...'

Trring. Trring Trring. The telephone rang. 'Hello. Oh, Rafiq sahab ... Yes.... Majju Bhai? He was supposed to go to your house first. That's what he said when he was leaving, that he would take you and then go to Ghazi sahab's rally.'

'Yes, yes, indeed he had come here. But I haven't gone mad that I would want to go and listen to Ghazi sahab's sermon. Majju Bhai is the only one with so much time to spare. Actually, I wanted to find out if he has reached home or not, because if he hasn't reached home yet, I will go and look for him. You know there is no place for respectable people in these modern-day rallies. Who knows what has happened there?'

Rafiq sahab's worried tone betrayed the fact that something had gone amiss at the rally.

'Why, has something gone wrong there?'

'Is it possible that we have a rally in our neighborhood and something does not go wrong? Something must have happened. I will go and find out.'

'Rafiq sahab,' I was worried by now. 'You have alarmed me.'

'No, no, there is nothing to worry about. This is an everyday occurrence. Something small happens and these people from our neighbourhood exaggerate it.'

'Yes, but it is still worrisome.'

'It is worrisome no matter what! Anyhow, don't get too worked up. I am going; I will come back and call you immediately. Or, better still, I will bring Majju Bhai and come straight to your place.'

'Come quickly.'

'Yes, I will be quick.'

The phone went dead. I put the receiver down and looked up to find Nemat Khan standing before me. He looked ashen. I said to myself: What's wrong with this fellow?

He asked, 'What was Rafiq sahab saying?'

'He was saying that something happened during Ghazi sahab's rally.'

'Jawad sahab, a bomb has gone off there. Many people have lost their lives. May Allah have mercy upon us!'

The ground slid from beneath my feet. I could now understand why Rafiq sahab was sounding so anxious.

'Who did you hear it from? People are prone to gossip.'

'No, ji, it isn't a rumour; the whole neighbourhood is agog with the news.'

'Really?' I could say no more. My heart was sinking.

'Why had Majju sahab gone there?'

'One doesn't know when these things will happen.'

'May Allah have mercy and may Majju sahab come home safely.'

'Dont worry; Allah will have mercy. Rafiq sahab has gone to get him; he will come here.'

'So when will he come?'

'Soon.'

Nemat Khan stood about looking worried, as though he didn't know what to say next and what to ask. Then, silently, he went away. I couldn't quite understand what to do. That state of being lost in my thoughts was gone now. My mind that was, at the slightest provocation, prone to wander off, forgot its ramblings; it seemed numb now. I sat like a statue. I was startled when Nemat Khan brought the food and quietly placed it before me. It was the same bland food. He asked me to eat and I began to eat. I can't say what I ate. I sat there lost in my thoughts. After a long time, Nemat Khan peeped into my room again.

'It is quite late now; hasn't sahab-ji come yet?'

'Yes, he should have been here by now.' I tried my best not to show any trace of anxiety.

'May Allah keep us safe,' Nemat Khan said quietly and went away.

But a lot of time hadn't passed when Nemat Khan entered the room again. He came close and asked, 'Has there been no phone call either?'

'No,' I answered in a dry tone.

'Then why is it taking so long?'

For a long time now, I had been trying to make myself believe that there was no reason for worry. But Nemat Khan would repeatedly come into the room, say a sentence or two and ruin all my attempts at reassuring myself. Now he sat down on the floor beside me with his head resting against the side of my bed – which was good because at such times it is better to have company. Having someone to talk to diverts your mind and keeps your thoughts at bay. But my silence had such an effect on him that he too seemed to have sealed his lips.

'Sahab-ji,' he finally unlocked his tongue. 'You go to sleep. In any case, the doctor has told you to rest. So you sleep; I will stay up. If there is a telephone call, I will get it.'

'All right, I will sleep if I am sleepy.'

'It is difficult to sleep when one is worried,' he said quietly and became silent. After some time, he said, 'Please call Rafiq sahab's house and find out. Let us find out if ...'

This suggestion indeed forced me to think. For some time, I was doubtful, but soon I made up my mind. I thought Rafiq sahab's wife would be needlessly worried. I tried to reassure Nemat Khan by telling him that it wasn't appropriate to worry Rafiq sahab's family by calling them so late at night.

'Yes, that is true,' he mumbled and became quiet.

'Sahab-ji,' he unlocked his tongue after a long time. 'I am planning to stay awake though one can never tell with sleep; it comes unbidden when a man is on the scaffold. So, in case I happen to fall asleep and the doorbell rings, please don't open the door.'

'Why? What do you mean?' I was perplexed.

'Sahab-ji, you can't tell with anybody these days. People latch their doors during the day; this is, after all, night time. In any case, I have suffered.'

'You have suffered? What have you suffered?' I was curious.

'As I was once telling Majju sahab but never got around to completing the story. You were both in the hospital when one night – possibly the middle of the night – when the doorbell rang, I said to myself, "Nemat Khan, this can't be good; who is likely to come at this hour?" So I stayed quiet. The bell rang again. And again I stayed quiet. When the bell rang for the third time, I pretended as though I wasn't there. I didn't even breathe. The bell didn't ring again and it sounded as though someone was going down the stairs. I said to myself, "Nemat Khan, you have been saved." Jawad sahab-ji, there is no knowing these days. In any case, this is a bad time.'

I listened to him quietly and gave no answer. Perhaps this account had no particular effect on me. Still, my ears were peeled to the door as though any moment now the doorbell would ring. I may not open the door, but I would still ask who was there. But should one not even ask that? Or maybe, they may not ring the bell. I strained my ears to listen to the sound of footsteps. But there was no such sound.

'Actually, I am reminded of something my father once said.'

Taking advantage of my silence, Nemat Khan continued. 'Ours was a very small settlement; it was surrounded by a forest on all four sides. I had to go to the city for work and it would be evening by the time I returned. Sometimes, it used to get very late in the night. I would carry a stout stick but still my heart used to beat furiously. My father used to say, "At night, or in the middle of the afternoon, if someone calls you and you can't see that person, don't ever turn around to answer." Once it so happened that I was returning from the city and was right in the middle of the forest when night fell. I walked along, banging my stick on the ground and clearing my throat, when I suddenly heard someone calling my name. I craned to hear; indeed, someone was calling out, "Nemat Khan! Nemat Khan!" I pretended that I had cottonwool stuffed in my ears. I didn't so much as grunt in response but kept reciting the *Qul* under my breath. Soon the voice stopped. At the time, I remembered the entire *Qul*; I used to recite it every day. I haven't recited it recently and now that I don't recite it every day, I have forgotten it. Can you please help me remember the entire *Qul*?' he stopped, then said, 'At that time, whenever night fell and I was in the forest, it was the *Qul* that saved my life. Once it so happened that I became really very scared. It was late at night and I was in the middle of the forest. The trees looked like ghosts. I was walking along when a bird, hidden in the branches of a tree, fluttered suddenly and let out a loud noise. My heart thudded and I began to recite the *Qul* immediately.' Nemat Khan quivered and fell silent.

The bird couldn't be seen; only the flutter of its wings could be heard in the silence of the night and its long loud cry was enough to instill fear. But Ibn-e Habib had never heard its voice nor heard the flutter of its wing; only the rustle of strong feathers as though a large bird had flown quickly overhead. It had caused an unknown fear to ripple through him. So many doubts were growing in him. It seemed as though the city would devour him.

'O Abdullah, this city of yours is strange; for the intensity with which it attracts, it scares me in the same way. Filled with mosques, baths, gardens, it has cast a spell over me and seeped inside me. So many times, I have felt as though the heavy-hipped moon-faced beloved of mine is somewhere here. How much I have scoured this city in search of her! But in these happy streets and alleys, past these scented baths, walking under the cool shade of the mulberry trees, I have sometimes had the strangest sensation – as though I am wandering about in a wasteland. And O Abdullah, the Seville that I had almost forgotten, has come back to me in my dreams.' Ibn-e Habib fell silent. He hesitated, then said in a sorrowful tone, 'But last night, I had a strange dream – as though I have gone there and am wandering about happy as a lark, as though it is the same house, the house that belonged to our ancestors. I am happy. Then I am startled. I ask: "What happened to the date palm that used to stand here?" But no one answers me. I am worried. What do I then see? A cat sitting on a wall is staring at me. I am scared. I am thinking that the elderly cat we used to have …'

'Sahab-ji, the phone is ringing.'

Startled, I turned towards the silent phone. 'No, it isn't ringing.'

Nemat Khan yawned. Then he said thoughtfully, 'Oh, but it seemed as though it was. I had nearly nodded off. It seemed as though the phone was ringing and I woke up.' He yawned and spoke in a sleep-filled voice, 'Now it seems as though it is the last watch of the night; it must be close to dawn.'

His words made me realize that we had indeed spent the entire night sitting up in vigil. And almost immediately, I was overcome with sleep. I slid down from my sitting position. I had barely put my head on the pillow that I fell asleep instantly. I did not even come to know when the birds chirped and when the cock crowed and when the *muezzin* called out to the faithful. The sound of the telephone finally woke me. I got up with a start. I was about to pick up the receiver when the call ended. It had been ringing for a long time and had finally stopped. Nemat Khan was not in the room. Perhaps he had gone to sleep in his quarter. He too must have fallen asleep at some point; he was right when he said that sleep is such a wretched thing that it comes even when a man is on the scaffold. So the phone had stopped ringing and I was feeling angry at myself. I had stayed awake all night; did I have to fall asleep now? And even if I had fallen asleep, why did I have to sleep so soundly that the phone kept ringing right beside my bed and

I did not wake up. I had been waiting for this very call all night long and had fallen asleep when it came. Anyhow, the phone rang again. This time I leapt to pick up the receiver. 'Hello. Who is it? Rafiq sahab? Yes, tell me quickly … Is all well? … Yes, yes, please come … But Majju Bhai … Why?…. So you will come alone? … But Majju Bhai … All right, I will wait for you.'

Rafiq sahab did not tell me anything clearly; he just kept saying that he would come soon and that I should wait for him. Still, a lot was clear. But despite a lot being clear, I was still suspended between hope and despair. I was on tenterhooks. If only Rafiq sahab were to come quickly. If only I were to be freed of this uncertainty.

I don't know when Nemat Khan entered the room. When I raised my eyes, he was standing there looking at me quietly. In an effort to reassure him, I told him, 'Rafiq sahab is coming. He will be here soon. Make some tea.'

'Okay, ji. What is he saying?'

'He will be here soon. Make the tea.'

Nemat Khan was far from reassured; if anything, he was more worried than ever. He didn't know whether he should ask more questions, or go away. He wanted to say something but then he stopped and went out.

Rafiq sahab didn't take very long. But by the time he came, I had passed the threshold of hope and despair and was free of all my anxieties. So when he came, I was in no fear of what he might say.

'Last night was so chaotic,' Rafiq sahab said as he sat down, 'that it was hard to say what was happening to whom and who was with whom and in what state. There have been many casualties but more wounded than dead. So, anyhow, we hope that … There was a crowd of relatives and well-wishers both inside and outside the hospital and so it was hard to find out anything. How could one find out anything so quickly? The hospital staff is right in their own way.' Rafiq sahab's tone betrayed that he was trying to keep our spirits up and was not giving an entirely truthful account. He was speaking and I was watching his face silently. I had no question to ask, nor any anxiety to betray. Rafiq sahab looked at me as he spoke and he too fell silent.

Nemat Khan came with the tea. He poured it for us and slid a cup each in our direction. Then he went out quietly with his head down. The tea was indeed very hot. A slight steam rose from both the cups. Soon it settled. The tea kept getting cool. We sat morosely. We didn't speak, nor did we touch our cups.

The tea kept getting cooler till it became ice cold. And we kept sitting glumly and so still that we made not the slightest movement. We were motionless like two lumps of clay and between us were two cups brimming with cold tea.

After a long time, Rafiq sahab stirred. He got up. 'So, I will go now. Are you all right? Is there any pain?'

'No.'

'All right, then. But don't move about too much. The wound will take some time to heal.' Then as he was leaving, he said hesitantly, 'Actually, I haven't yet given up hope. I am going back there now; who knows …'

I stayed quiet.

Rafiq sahab was leaving the room. Nemat Khan came in silently and spoke in a dead voice, 'Rafiq sahab-ji, what will happen now?'

'Nemat Khan, have faith in Allah.'

'Yes, ji, who else can we trust?'

'So hold on to your faith. I am going there now.'

Rafiq sahab left. Nemat Khan too left the room. He must have gone to see him off till the door. But he did not come back. He must be somewhere in the house. But it seemed as though he too had gone. I was alone now, completely alone as though night had fallen and I was walking all alone in the forest … But was I walking? I was rooted in the same spot. It seemed as though I would never move from this spot. This place where I was seated had held me tight. I kept sitting there as though I was bound. I don't know for how long. Had I any sense of time left, I might have known for how long I sat there stock-still.

After a long time, a quiver ran through me. 'How long will you sit here like a stone?' I admonished myself. A friend is out looking for him. Truly, who knows if … Life has become cheap but it is also sturdy. And then miracles are also known to happen in this very life. So why have I assumed the worst so soon? I too should go out in search. Again, a quiver ran through me; it coursed through my body like an electric current. I immediately got to my feet.

I had just about set foot across the threshold when I paused. Which city is this? The same city. Then I am not the same person. I had suddenly become a stranger in this known and familiar city. I stood stock-still. A forest lay in front of me and night had fallen. Then? How long could I stand in doubt like this? I gathered my courage. I tried to gain control over my uncertainty. These feet have wandered through the dust-filled streets and alleys of this city. They will find the way on their own.

I walked for a long time. Not me but my feet kept finding the way, they kept walking. Mosques, baths, trees of mulberry, olives and dates. I know these streets. This is the Bath of Jauza and this is the Rabta al-Tuut and this is the Zina Qata al-Vari. If I go down this way I will come out at the Madinatul al-Humra. I turned towards the al-Qaisar and the avenue of the Grand Mosque. And the Grand Mosque is so quiet. Where have all the *namazi* gone? I then passed the Jamia-ut Tabaeen. It too is silent. Then as I passed the Bab-ul Nabud towards the Masjid-ul Qatanin and, as I passed Abdullah's inn, I was surprised. The oven was cold and Abdullah … ? Where was he? Surprised and worried, I walked towards the Bab-ul Ziyad. I walked on and paused suddenly. Where had I come? This is the Bab Armelia but why is the Bab Armelia so deserted. Day and night were coming together and separating. Why were the lamps not lit then? The fire had gone cold. The crowds that had thronged here had dispersed. Bab Armelia was still and silent. Ash was flying about. A half-burnt page of some poetry collection, a book, the manuscript of a philosopher, a *malfuzat* of a sufi fluttered occasionally. The rest was all stillness. A cat sat in the middle of the road staring at me with its glassy eyes.

Glossary

Adaab	a more secular greeting or salutation in comparison to *Assalam alekum* which means May God's blessings be upon you; its full form is '*Adaab arz hai*'
Aji/Ai/Arre/Ai wah	exclamations to denote a range of feelings such as surprise, remorse or incredulity. Often, sentences begin with such an exclamation, eg. 'Ai Majju Bhai'; they are particularly favoured by older women.
Alam	pennant or standard, a replica of the one carried by Husain (the younger son of Ali and the grandson of Prophet Muhammad) and his army in the Battle of Karbala; it is carried at the head of the Muharram procession
Ama	also an exclamation, but used exclusively among men; a bit like 'mate'
Aqiqa	the Islamic practice of sacrificing an animal at the time of the ritual shaving of hair from a baby's head shortly after birth; it is also the occasion to name a child
Arbi	colocasia; its root is cooked as a vegetable and its leaves are fried in a batter of ground gram flour and eaten as a snack during the rainy season. However, the leaves are considered hard to digest and are not advised for those with a weak stomach.
Asr	the third of the five daily prayers, it is offered in the early evening
Atthanni	short for eight *annas* or fifty *paise*, a coin of eight *annas* was called *athhani*

Aza — mourning; so *azadari* is the ritualistic remembrance and mourning in memory of the incidents of Karbala during Muharram; *azakhana* is a hall or room where *alams* are stored and where the *majlis* is held during Muharram

Azaan — the Muslim call to prayer given five times a day

Beerbahuti — a tiny insect that comes out during the rains, it is also called rain bug or red velvet mite

Bhabhi — a term for sister-in-law, brother's wife, or brother-in-law's wife; *Badi Bhabhi* means elder sister-in-law

Bhai/Bhaiyya — a form of address for brother; also used for one who is not really a brother but like a brother or where the relationship is such that one does not want to use 'sahab'

Bhadon — the month of rains

Bhatiyare — those who run an oven or a roadside inn; belong to a low caste

Bibi — a form of address for a young(er) woman, especially an unmarried one

Boriyat — a coinage used as a slang by Urdu speakers to mean boredom, tedium, ennui and weariness

Bua — form of address for an older woman; could be a family retainer or distant relative; roughly equivalent to 'aunt'. Though not to be mistaken for the Hindi 'Bua' meaning paternal aunt

Burqa — an all-encompassing outer covering, usually black, worn by women over their everyday clothes when going out in public

Chacha/Chachi — term for father's younger brother and his wife

Chaliswan — also called *chehlum*, it is the ceremony on the fortieth day after someone's death; it marks the end of mourning

Chaprasi — the peon or office boy; a colonial relic that continues to be found in most offices today

Chavvanni — a four *anna* or twenty-five paisa coin

Chillum — a clay pipe used to smoke tobacco

Dada/Dada Miyan — form of address for father's father

Dastaan — story, fable, tale

Dharamshala — a lodge for Hindu travellers

Doli — a small covered palanquin for a single lady passenger, usually no more than a box hoisted on long poles that would be carried on the shoulders of two or more men

Dulhan — literally meaning bride, but often daughters-in-law would be addressed as *Dulhan* for years, even decades, after their wedding; as a result, they often acquired monikers such as *Dulhan Chachi* or *Dulhan Khala* by nephews and nieces.

Ekka — a horse-drawn carriage similar to a *tanga*

Gazak — a brittle made of *gur* and sesame or peanuts; like other *gur*-based sweets these are considered unsophisticated and rough when compared to milk-based preparations. While *gazak* is usually cut in long flat slabs, *rewri* comes in bite-sized pellets that can be popped several at a time

Ghasiyare — those who cut grass; a caste

Gopi — the maidens of Mathura who flocked around Lord Krishan

Gujia — a sweet comprising a pastry casing stuffed with dried fruit and condensed milk that is fried, dipped in syrup and dusted with powdered sugar and grated coconut

Gur — jaggery, a natural product of sugarcane and an unrefined version of sugar

Hadith — narration of sayings or actions of the Prophet Muhammad; many such narrations have been compiled

Haveli — a large house or mansion built in the old style;

	different, for instance, from the bungalow which was a colonial construct
Huqqa	a pipe for smoking tobacco through water
Imam Bara	a place where the *taaziya* is kept and where Shia Muslims congregate for *majlis* during the month of *Muharram*
Insha Allah	meaning 'If Allah so wills'
Jihad	literal meaning in Arabic is 'to strive' or 'to endeavour'; it is used to mean any 'just' war for a 'just' cause in the name of Allah
Jinn/jinnat	also a creation of Allah, a spirit-like creature; *jinnat* is plural for *jinn*
Jogi	mendicant, travelling ascetic
Kabab-paratha/parathe	a combination of minced meat roasted on skewers, eaten with a form of unleavened bread that is fried on a skillet
Kalma	the Muslim profession of faith *La illaha illala Muhammad-ur Rasool Allah*, meaning 'There is no God save Allah and Muhammad is His Prophet'
Khamira	a form of medicine in the Unani system; it has a fermented base and is in a conserve or syrupy form
Khala	term for aunt, mother's sister: Khalu is Khala's husband
Khand	the powdery stage of the process in which sugar is made from jaggery
Khandoi	steamed dumplings made from *besan* (chick-pea flour) and put in a *salan* or curry
Khatna	the practice of male circumcision
Kheer	a sweet dish made from milk, pound rice and sugar
Kos	a measure of distance, equal to approximately two English miles
Kotha	a prostitute or courtesan's place; it can be an elegantly appointed salon with musicians, etc. or dingy quarters in a red light district

Kothi	large, well-appointed mansion
Kutcha	crude or unformed, for roads it refers to dirt tracks without paving or tarmac; the opposite of *kutcha* for roads or houses would be *pucca*
Laddu	an immensely popular round ball of a sweet, it comes in a variety of ingredients: condensed milk, pound lentils (*besan*), nuts, jaggery, besan among others
Lakshman rekha	refers to the line Lakshman drew for Sita when Ram, Sita and Lakshman were living in the forest; it is used to mean a line beyond which one is not safe
Maash	a sort of lentil with small black grain
Malai	the thick layer of cream that forms on milk that has been boiled; its correct pronunciation is *balai*, meaning 'topmost'
Malfuzat	dialogue, discourses and sayings of sufis, compiled by the disciples
Marsiya	elegiac poem describing the events and main characters associated with the Battle of Karbala
Mashak	skin of goats fashioned into a sack to carry water
Mem	used initially for anglicized non-native women, including native Christian women; now used for any westernized woman and not only an Englishwoman
Misri	crystallized sugar lumps
Miyan	tagged on to a name, as in Jawad Miyan, as a form of address for a younger man
Mondha	a somewhat rustic chair or stool fashioned out of reeds and twine
Muhajir	an Arabic word for immigrant; the Islamic calendar Hijra starts when Muhammad and his companions left Mecca for Medina. They were called *muhajirun*. The Arabic root word for immigration and emigration is *hijrat*. In Pakistan, the immigrants from India were called *muhajir*.

Muharram — the first month of the Islamic lunar calendar; the tenth day of Muharram is the day of Ashura when the decisive events of the Battle of Karbala, 10 October 680 AD, reached their tragic culmination. The battle was between a small group of supporters and relatives of Muhammad's grandson Husain ibn Ali, and a much larger military detachment from the forces of Yazid I, the Umayyad caliph, to whom Husain had refused to give an oath of allegiance. Husain and all his supporters were killed, including Husain's six-month-old infant son, Ali Asghar with the women and children taken as prisoners. The dead are regarded as martyrs by both Sunni and Shia Muslims, and the battle has a central place in Shia history and tradition, and has frequently been recounted in Shia Islamic literature.

Muezzin — person appointed in a mosque to recite the call to prayer, the *azaan*, to announce the time for prayer

Mushaira — a literary soiree where poets assemble to recite their poetry to an invited audience

Musla — pejorative word for a Muslim

Naan — a form of leavened bread that is made in an oven instead of a skillet

Nikah — marriage ceremony

Paandan — a container to keep all the ingredients of assembling a *paan*, such as catechu and lime paste, betel nuts, etc.

Pakwan — spicy crisp-fried savouries; usually eaten as a tea-time snack, especially during the rains

Peda — a disc-shaped sweet made from sweetened milk that has been cooked on slow fire and flavoured with cardamom

Peepal — a species of the fig tree native to the Indian subcontinent

Pehelwan — one who practises Indian free-style wrestling

Phulka — a smaller, lighter version of the roti

Phulki	a fried dumpling made of ground chick-peas, a smaller version of the *pakoda*
Phuphi/Phuphi Amma	a form of address for father's sister
Purdah	literally meaning curtain or screen, refers to the form of gender segregation as well as the practice of wearing a burqa or *chadar* or some outer garment that covers a woman
Qasba	an administrative unit in the Awadh region, smaller than a town
Qibla	since a *qibla* is an object of veneration or reverence, this is a form of address for a king, a father or a senior or older man
Qul	literally meaning total or whole, the four *qul* or four verses of the Quran constitute four important prayers
Rabrhi	a street food made from sweetened milk
Rakaat	consists of the prescribed movements and words followed by Muslims while offering *namaz*; the five *namaz* have different number of *rakaat* or 'unit' of prayer
Rishi	Hindu sage or saint; and a *sadhu* is an ascetic or holy man who need not be versed in the Vedas as a *rishi* would be
Saiyad	those claiming descent from the Prophet
Sawan	fifth month of the Hindu lunar calendar, it coincides with July-August of the Gregorian calendar; it is traditionally the month of the rains, as is *Bhadon*, the next month
Sawani	songs sung during the rains
Shurfa	plural of *sharif*, the respectable well-born folk
Subhan Allah	literally meaning 'All praise is for Allah' or 'Glorious is God' but is used also to express admiration or assent, as in 'Bravo'
Surah Yaseen	one of the most recited verses, called the 'heart

	of the Quran, it is the 36th chapter of the Quran comprising 83 verses
Tamboli	those who sell *paan*; a caste
Takht	a rectangular, low settee or diwan, usually covered by a white cloth and edged with sausage-shaped bolster cushions called *gau takhiya*
Tehmad	a rectangular piece of cloth, much shorter than a sari, which is tied around the waist and worn by men; unlike the sari which is wrapped around a petticoat, the *tehmad* is wrapped loosely once and secured with a knot and remains open from the side
Tehsildar	an administrative officer in charge of an administrative unit called a tehsil whose job was primarily to collect tax
Teli	those who press oil; a caste
Tesu	In an Indian version of Halloween, on a day between the festivals of Dusshera and Diwali, children buy dolls; the 'boy' doll is called Tesu and the 'girl' doll is called Jhanji. Children would often collect money to arrange for a wedding between Tesu and Jhanji. While Tesu looks like a human face on a stick with large eyes and a prominent moustache, Jhanji is a decorated clay pot with perforations; when a lit *diya* (lamp) is placed inside the Jhanji, which can also twirl like a top, the light coming out of it makes a beautiful dancing pattern
Til bugga	a cruder and less refined version of *gazak*, it is a mixture of sesame seeds (*til*) and *gur*
Tanga	horse-drawn carriage used as public transport
Ustad	a colloquial form of address, a bit like 'Boss'; literally, it means master or teacher
Wazifa	prayers
Yaar	rough colloquial equivalent of 'mate' or 'friend'
Zuhr	the second of the five daily prayers; this begins only after noon